Readers can't resist Cathy Bramley's charming, feel-good stories:

'**A perfect blend of the two greatest pleasures in life** – love and gardening!'
Fern Britton

'Beautifully drawn characters, with **love and humour across four seasons**. I fell in love with this book'
Rachael Lucas

'Like a warm rug to wrap acound yourself in winter and picnic on in the summer . . . **A delicious warmth, optimism and sheer lust for life**'
Sue Watson

'**A perfect cup of sunshine** on a cold and dreary day . . . a beautiful way to escape from the world'
Josephine Moon

'**Wonderfully witty** . . . I couldn't put it down'
Jenny Hole

'A fantastic read filled with **laugh-out-loud funny** moments. A **lovely, heart-warming** story – highly recommended'
Compelling Reads

'Filled with **friendship, humour and genuinely loveable characters** of all ages, shapes and sizes'
One More Page

'Such a **charming, feel-good** story'
Carole's Books

'**Satisfying, dreamy and delicious** – leaves yo~~u wanting just a little bit more~~'

'This was one **of the funniest stories I have
ever read** . . . I loved every word'
On My Book Shelf

'I loved every single character! Full of
warmth and belonging'
Jeras Jamboree

'I adored this **gem of a book** . . . *Ivy Lane* has **everything
I love about a novel** – wonderful characters, a gorgeous
setting and twists ready to be unveiled at any opportunity'
Reviewed the Book

'This is a **perfect book** to take with you to your garden
on a sunny summer day'
Dreaming With Open Eyes Reviews

'I loved it! Cathy Bramley is the most effortless of
storytellers, she has a total knack of drawing you in.
I could read her books every day, forever'
Donna's Room for Reading

'A **sweet, lovely story** that will leave you wanting more'
Laura's Little Book Blog

'**Captivating** . . . A wonderful quick read!'
The Love of a Good Book

Cathy would love to hear from you! Find her on:

f Facebook.com/CathyBramleyAuthor

t @CathyBramley

w www.CathyBramley.co.uk

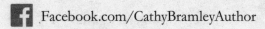
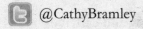

Appleby Farm

Cathy Bramley

CORGI BOOKS

Coventry City Council	
FML	
3 8002 02233 073 4	
Askews & Holts	Aug-2015
	£6.99

TRANSWORLD PUBLISHERS
61–63 Uxbridge Road, London W5 5SA
www.transworldbooks.co.uk

Transworld is part of the Penguin Random House group of companies whose
addresses can be found at global.penguinrandomhouse.com

Penguin
Random House
UK

First published in Great Britain as four separate ebooks
in 2015 by Transworld Digital
an imprint of Transworld Publishers
First published as one edition in 2015 by Corgi Books
an imprint of Transworld Publishers

A CIP catalogue record for this book
is available from the British Library.

ISBN
9780552171595

Typeset in 11½/13pt Garamond by Kestrel Data, Exeter, Devon.
Printed and bound by CPI Group (UK) Ltd, Croydon CR0 4YY.

Penguin Random House is committed to a sustainable future for our business, our readers
and our planet. This book is made from Forest Stewardship Council® certified paper.

1 3 5 7 9 10 8 6 4 2

For my nanna, Mary –
three hand squeezes

A Blessing in Disguise

Chapter 1

The door opened with a ding of the bell, letting in a welcome blast of fresh air as a group of teenage girls left the café.

'Adios, amigos!' I called. 'Ciao, bellas!'

It was the Thursday before the Easter weekend, children were off school and the spring sunshine had brought us a steady stream of customers all day long. Now, at four o'clock, we were having a quiet spell, which was just as well, because the service side of the counter, where I stood, looked like a scene out of *Titanic*.

I had spent the last hour training Amy, our new recruit, in the art of making espressos, cappuccinos and lattes. The work area was awash with her efforts; we were marooned in a sea of brown liquid, puddles of spilt milk and numerous abandoned mugs, spoons and jugs. The pair of us were looking a bit worse for the experience, too: my red hair had turned to frizz after repeated exposure to random gusts of steam and Amy had a streak of coffee across her forehead like a third eyebrow.

On the plus side, despite the steamy atmosphere, there was a heavenly aroma of fresh coffee and I'd felt enormous satisfaction from seeing Amy get the hang of the equipment

– eventually. I watched over her shoulder, a bit close, actually, seeing as her short ponytail was tickling my nose, as she poured steamed milk from a stainless-steel jug into a tall glass.

'Yay! Perfect,' I cheered. 'That's it; nice and slow so you don't spoil the foamy bit on top.' Phew! I thought she was never going to get there.

Amy placed the jug on the counter with a shaky hand and exhaled. We both examined her first latte.

'What do you think?' She pulled her bottom lip between her teeth and wrinkled her smeared brow.

'I think you've cracked it,' I said, and grinned.

Just in time, because I was hanging up my apron any second, leaving early and then she would be on her own behind the counter. I flung an arm around her shoulders and gave the sixteen-year-old a squeeze. 'But now you've got to pass the boss's taste test.'

I nodded towards the far corner of the café. Shirley, head down over a pile of invoices, sat at a small table with one foot raised on the chair beside her. Her ankle was completely better now; it was simply a habit she'd fallen into after being told to keep it raised when she broke it last autumn.

That foot was the reason I was here. Shirley's daughter, Anna, is a friend of mine and when Shirley had her accident, Anna begged me to come and help out in the café for a few months until her mum was back on her feet. At the time I was working in promotions, handing out free samples and money-off coupons in supermarkets around Manchester – a job that had lost its sparkle early on. So I moved to Kingsfield, a small town on the outskirts of Derbyshire, and into Anna's spare room, and I'd been working at the café ever since.

I watched Amy creep towards Shirley, the tall glass rattling in its saucer as she placed one foot cautiously in front of the other. I held my breath; it was like witnessing a tight-rope walker crossing Niagara Falls.

'Delicious. Well done, both of you,' Shirley declared, lifting the latte in approval. 'Amy, you're now officially allowed to use the coffee machine and, FYI, I like three sugars in mine.'

'Go Amy, go Amy,' I hollered, waving my fist in the air as my student smiled bashfully, dipped her head and twisted one foot behind her other leg, looking far younger than sixteen all of a sudden.

I also dropped into a curtsey, holding out an imaginary skirt with my fingertips. 'And my work here is done.'

Shirley chuckled, shook her head and went back to her paperwork.

Is it?

As soon as the words were out of my mouth a fluttering sensation worked its way from my head to my heart. *Was* my work here actually done? Was it time to move on? Again? Eek! I stared at the top of Shirley's bowed head until it dawned on me that Amy was looking at me rather oddly.

I gave myself a shake, pointed Amy in the direction of the floor mop and, leaving her to soak up the spillages, went to clear the table vacated by the teenagers.

Yikes. My face felt scarlet now after that unbidden thought, which, seeing as I almost qualified for official albino status in the pale skin department, was pretty hard to hide.

Freya Moorcroft, you are up to your old tricks. Can't you stick at a job for more than five minutes? And anyway, what about you-know-who? Aren't you in L.O.V.E.?

I puffed out my cheeks and began to stack plates loudly to crowd out my snarky inner thoughts.

Shirley's café was booming. And without being big-headed about it, the boom had something to do with me. When I arrived six months ago the coffee had been instant, the menu consisted almost entirely of jacket potatoes and barely any customers bothered coming to the café after two o'clock.

Now we had a fancy chrome coffee machine hissing like a contemptuous goose on the counter, a panini grill permanently making posh toasties and we did a roaring trade in afternoon tea. The free WiFi, which I'd suggested we install, had also proved a hit, especially with teenagers. The café was heaving with youthful hormones for an hour after school, earning us the reputation of being *the* place to hang out and doubling our sales of hot chocolate and smoothies. A win-win, as far as I was concerned.

It had been a whirlwind few months, which was exactly how I liked my life to be. The whirlier the better, in fact. Shirley had pretty much let me have free rein once I'd convinced her to pimp the place up a bit and I'd had a ball. And, outside of work, my life was good too. I loved living with Anna, I'd made loads of new friends and, most importantly, I'd met Charlie, my boyfriend of four months.

Charlie.

You know those ads for yogurt where the actors go all dreamy when the spoon goes into their mouths? Well, that's what happens to me just thinking about him. Tall, fit, amazing blue eyes, the cheekiest smile in the universe and, to top it all, he's a fireman. I mean, hello?

So yep, my life in Kingsfield's pretty good.

But now . . . I paused from swiping cake crumbs into my hand and glanced out of the window at the row of shops, the pub on the corner, the parked cars, the total lack of greenery. It was the same view I'd been looking at since October. I could do the job standing on my head. Blindfolded. One hand tied behind my back.

Unlike Amy, I noticed out of the corner of my eye, who was making hard work of clearing up the kitchen.

I took the dirty crockery over to the counter and handed it to her. 'So how has your first day been?' I asked. 'Can you see yourself as a waitress? Or have I scared you off with caffeine-options overload?'

'It's OK,' she replied, nodding earnestly. 'As a part-time job. Till I go to uni.'

'Great.' I suppressed a smile but I must have raised my eyebrows higher than I'd intended because Amy blushed. There's nothing like being told by a teenager that your career choice is merely their stepping stone to greater things.

'Sorry,' she muttered, plunging her arms into the sink. 'That came out wrong. Not that there's anything wrong . . . Oh God.' She bent low over the sink so I couldn't see her face.

'Hey, no worries,' I laughed. 'Good on you for knowing what you want to do with your life. I got the grades at A level to go to uni, but I had no idea what to study.' I shrugged. 'So I opted for a gap year instead.'

Ten gap years, as it turned out . . .

Auntie Sue referred to my decision to go travelling after sixth form as studying at the university of life. My mother called it a waste of a private education.

Amy glanced over her shoulder at Shirley and then looked back at me. 'I can only work here until I leave sixth form. I'm going to study architecture and it takes seven years to qualify, and then I want to move to London, so I really need to save up.'

13

'Right. Well, good luck!' I swallowed, smiled and shuffled off.

Flippin' heck. Sixteen and she'd got a ten-year plan. I thought I was being organized when I had a ten-*day* plan.

A career butterfly, that was me. I couldn't seem to help it. I'd start a job full of enthusiasm, throw myself into it, loving the whole 'new challenge' thing. Then, as soon as I'd mastered it and put my own spin on the role, for some reason I sprouted wings and an urge to fly off somewhere new.

Uncle Arthur reckoned that one day I'd find my niche and my career would take off. My father, on the other hand, put my transient tendencies down to lack of ambition and commitment. I hoped Uncle Arthur was right because I couldn't bear it if Dad was.

The edited highlights of my career included: apple picker in New Zealand, stablehand in Dubai, chalet girl in Austria, barmaid in Cornwall (eighteen months – a personal record for me, largely down to a lifeguard called Ivan), a short-lived stint as a tour guide at a pencil museum and now here, waitress in the Shenton Road Café in Kingsfield.

I was sure all the random experience I'd gained was preparing me for something; I just wished I knew what that something was. I dropped down into the empty chair opposite my boss and pondered whether to tell her that it might be time for me to move on. Or should I, for once, keep my ponderings to myself?

'You're wasted here; you know that, don't you?' Shirley said without looking up. Which was just as well because my face was now as red as my hair.

I shifted in my seat. Shirley Maxwell should never, ever, be underestimated. She had an uncanny knack for reading minds. Not that I'd been thinking that I was wasted, just a bit . . . unchallenged.

'Meaning?' I asked, playing for time. I pulled the sugar bowl towards me and started mashing the crystals against the side of the bowl.

Shirley dropped her pen on the table, looked at me and exhaled in a 'what are we going to do with you?' sort of way. She moved the sugar bowl out of my reach and I folded my arms.

'Bright girl like you. You could be running your own business like my Anna. Or managing your own branch of Starbucks or . . .'

'Trying to get rid of me, are you?' I said, giving her my fake haughty eyebrow raise.

'Oh, Freya.' She swiped a hand at me. 'You've revamped the menu, you've organized the dreaded paperwork and now you're even training new staff. I'm so grateful for all your hard work at my café.'

She pronounced it caff, which always made me smile. She leaned forward and mouthed with exaggerated facial expressions, 'But I can't pay you what you're worth and that upsets me.' She pressed a hand to her bosom. 'You might want to buy a house, settle down—'

'I'm not money-orientated, Shirley,' I said. 'I know people who are. People who put pursuit of wealth before happiness and, believe me, I have no desire to go down that route.' I shuddered. My parents, for instance. 'No, as the saying goes, "all you need is love", as far as I'm concerned.' I grinned at her as she rolled her eyes.

'And as the other saying goes, "every little helps",' she retorted and we both laughed.

'You're a case, Freya Moorcroft, you really are.' Shirley sighed.

I reached out and squeezed her hand, the one that wasn't nestled on her cleavage. 'Thank you. It's nice to be appreciated.'

'Be honest with yourself, Freya. Waitressing isn't your future.'

The doorbell dinged and we both turned to see who it was. A familiar pink velour-clad bottom backed into the café, pulling a complicated-looking pushchair.

Saved by the bell before I talked myself out of a job.

'Gemma!' I cried, breathing an inward sigh of relief. I jumped up to help my friend and one of our regulars negotiate the door and the step.

'Nightmare dot com,' grunted Gemma, as she attempted a three-point turn with the pushchair. 'You need a blooming HGV licence to drive this thing.'

'Oh dear. Let me make you something healthy, herbal and foul-smelling in a mug.' I heard Shirley huff at my alternative approach to hospitality as I kissed Gemma's cheek. I stood back to let her manoeuvre herself and the baby past me and peered in at him. Parker was wide awake (hurray, I could have a cuddle!) and aiming a determined swipe at the toys suspended across his pushchair.

'Actually, sorry to take liberties,' said Gemma, making a beeline for the loos, 'but I only came in to use the facilities. His Lordship's nappy is beyond bearable and I say that as a mother with a very high threshold to bad smells.'

'TMI, love, thank you very much,' said Shirley with a wince. By comparison, Shirley had a low threshold to many things: smells, pain, loud music, most yellow foods . . . I once saw her nearly faint at the sight of mashed banana. Even a jacket potato gave her the shivers if it dared to err on the yellowy side.

'Not even a quick herbal brew?' I offered. I was due to

16

meet Charlie at his allotment in half an hour and then I had the whole of the Easter weekend off, but I hadn't seen Gemma since the baby's christening and I wanted to hear her news. And get my mitts on Parker, obviously.

Gemma paused and then flapped a beautifully manicured hand, which made me tuck my own scruffy nails into my jeans pockets. 'Go on then. Camomile if you've got it, please.'

Five minutes later I was sitting down with a freshly changed baby boy on my knee, watching Gemma squashing and swirling her tea bag round in her white mug.

I couldn't abide those mugs.

Shirley and I had only clashed on a couple of things since I'd been here. I was Team vintage china, she was Team cheap-practical-and-dishwasher-proof. I'd suggested pretty mismatched cups and saucers, stacked on shelves in pastel shades of pink, yellow and blue. But Shirley had gone pale at the thought of crockery not matching and had put her foot down.

Parker was concentrating on scrunching up a fabric toy between his fingers, which made a rustling noise when it moved. Gemma and I exchanged smiles as he babbled away quietly to himself.

'There's one scone left, do you fancy sharing it?' I said.

I made the café's scones using my Auntie Sue's recipe. The secret is in the mixing; over mix and you've got yourself a batch of primitive weapons. Mine, though I say so myself, are sultana-stuffed clouds of deliciousness.

Gemma shook her blonde curls and patted her stomach, which, given that Parker was only about four months old, was in pretty good shape. 'I shouldn't really . . . unless . . . does it come with clotted cream?'

I shook my head. 'Whipped cream,' I said, adding more

loudly, 'See, Shirley, someone else thinks it should be clotted cream.'

This, believe it or not, was the other thing we had disagreed on.

'No. Not having clotted cream in my café. That yellow crusty bit . . . urgh.' Shirley shuddered.

'I'll leave it then, thanks. Probably for the best,' Gemma said, wrinkling her nose. 'Anyway, what are you up to for Easter?'

The café would be closed on Good Friday, plus it was my weekend off, double-plus I'd tagged on an extra couple of days next week – my first proper break since working here.

'Nothing much.' I shrugged, wishing I'd bothered to organize an adventure or two. 'Just chilling out with Charlie, hopefully.'

'Bliss.' Gemma sighed, her blue eyes going all dreamy for a second. 'What I'd give to chill out. But with a fifteen-year-old daughter hell bent on making us suffer because *she's* got exams and a husband who's decided to dismantle a lawnmower in our back garden, I doubt very much that I'll be doing much of that this weekend.'

I tightened my grip around Parker's tummy with one hand and tucked a wayward strand of hair behind my ear with the other. 'Just give me a shout if you want a babysitter for a few hours.'

Her face softened as she leaned forward to hand Parker back the toy he had just dropped.

'Aww, thanks, Freya. Are you getting broody, by any chance?'

I thought about it for a moment.

'Yes and no,' I replied honestly. 'I'm not ready to do the whole settling-down thing yet. But at some point, yes. I can see myself with a couple of munchkins, cottage in the country, a horse and a dog . . . But at the moment, I'm happy to borrow Parker every now and then.'

No idea why I'd suddenly blurted all that out. I felt my face redden. I'd never been conscious of this plan before. I did want to be a mother at some point, though. And at the risk of sounding a bit 1950s, I wanted to be the sort of mother who was there when my children got in from school, with a kiss and a cake straight out of the oven. Like my Auntie Sue. I'd have to work on the cakes bit; my repertoire consisted of one thing – scones.

'Does Charlie know how you feel?' Gemma asked, gazing at me wide-eyed.

The only problem with Kingsfield is that everyone else has been here for donkey's years. I might only have met Charlie a few months ago, but Gemma's known him for ages from Ivy Lane allotments. Unlikely as it seemed looking at those nails, Gemma had her own allotment plot until Parker came along.

'Whoa! Steady on, Gem, we've only been together five minutes!' I bent to brush my lips against Parker's head to hide my hot cheeks. 'I'm sure we'll broach the subject when the time comes.'

'It's just that . . . oh, nothing,' mumbled Gemma. She lifted the mug to her lips and sipped at her tea.

My stomach lurched. Just that what? But before I had chance to ask, Gemma squealed and reached into her bag.

'I nearly forgot to show you this!' She handed me a postcard with a picture of a tortoise on a deserted beach on it. 'Came this morning, from Tilly and Aidan. Sounds like they're having an amazing time in the Galloping-wotsit Islands. Aww,' she sighed, lifting Parker from me and arranging him back in his pushchair, 'they are such a perfect match, those two.'

19

My friend, the lovely Tilly Parker, the baby's namesake, was another of the Ivy Lane allotment posse. She was the girl I credited with getting me and Charlie together and she met *her* fella, Aidan, when he came to Kingsfield last year as part of a film crew making a documentary about the allotment. He was filming something else now, in the Galápagos Islands, and Tilly had joined him for a holiday.

A perfect match. The words ran rhythmically through my head while I read Tilly's postcard and Gemma prepared to depart.

I waved her and Parker off with a smile. I didn't feel overly smiley on the inside; I felt a bit churned up. Gemma hadn't uttered the exact words and I might have been putting two and two together and making a fuss about nothing, but it felt as though she thought that in some way Charlie and I *weren't* a perfect match. And as Shirley had pointed out only a few minutes ago, Shenton Road Café wasn't my future.

My stomach flipped queasily. When I woke up this morning my life had seemed quite straightforward, but now . . . well, I wasn't sure of anything.

Chapter 2

By the time I'd finished up at the café, scurried along Shenton Road, into All Saints Road, down Ivy Lane and made it as far as the allotment gate I was back to my normal happy-go-lucky self and smiling at my own daft thoughts. What had all that self-doubt malarkey been about?

I pushed open the heavy gate and closed it behind me.

It wasn't like me to over-analyse things; life's far too short to agonize over my career choice or to worry about the state of my relationship. Or anything else, for that matter. Far better just to go with the flow. I loved my life and anyway, no one really has the perfect job and the perfect partner. Charlie and I were fine. No, better than fine – we were great, we made each other happy and we had a laugh together. And that was what made us so well-suited.

I half-walked, half-ran along the road towards Charlie's plot and waved to Peter, the allotment committee chairman, as he appeared at the pavilion door, fastening the buttons of his anorak.

'Afternoon, Freya. It's a cool breeze, isn't it? I think we might be in for a light frost tonight.' He pulled a tweed flat cap out of his pocket and settled it on his balding head.

'Hi, Pete. Yes, it is a bit chilly.' I smiled and supressed a giggle. I'd yet to meet one member of the allotment community who wasn't totally obsessed with the weather.

'Changed your mind about joining the waiting list for your own plot yet?' he called.

I laughed and shook my head. 'No time, these days. I'm too busy being Charlie's assistant gardener.'

Peter gave me a disappointed smile and touched his cap in a cute old-fashioned gesture, and I carried on my way.

He asked me the same question every time I saw him, hoping to change my mind. I'd toyed with the idea of having my own plot last year and he had shown me round. But I was glad I didn't go for it in the end; helping Charlie on his plot was a much better solution. I got to spend time outdoors, which I loved; I got to spend time with Charlie-boy, which I also loved; and I only had to do the nice bits (planting seeds and picking stuff) and not the grotty bits (spreading muck and digging up weeds).

My stomach flipped as I spotted my gorgeous man further ahead in his greenhouse and I jogged the last few metres to join him. He was lifting huge bags of something or other onto shelves and didn't spot me at first.

The air in the greenhouse was warm and tinged with the fragrance of tomato plants. I leaned on the open door frame and watched him for a couple of seconds while he arranged growbags in rows with his back to me. He was wearing his old gardening jumper with holes in the sleeves, a woolly hat, jeans and an old pair of boots.

'Hey.'

Charlie turned around and grinned. 'Hello, beautiful!'

I squealed as he scooped me up and spun me round, knocking over a watering can and several plant pots in the process.

'Put me down this instant and kiss me,' I giggled breathlessly.

'I love it when you're bossy,' he murmured, his blue eyes crinkling with humour as he did as he was told and lowered me to the ground.

He unzipped my jacket and threaded his arms around my waist, pulling me close. I lifted my face to meet his and felt my body sigh as we kissed. His face was rough with stubble but his lips were full and soft. He smelled of earth and wood smoke and something sweeter . . . vanilla, maybe? Whatever it was, I approved. His kiss deepened and I stopped wondering about anything and reached up on my tiptoes to wrap my arms around his neck. When it was just us, him and me, close like this, it felt as if nothing could ever come between us, like we were the only two people in the universe who mattered.

'What's on the job list today, then?' I asked, pulling back and smiling up at him. I snuggled my head against his chest and wriggled my fingers into the back pockets of his jeans while he rested his chin on my head.

'Tomatoes,' he said, easing us apart and dropping a kiss on my nose. 'I thought you'd never come and help me plant them. I've got about twenty good ones to get in this afternoon. If you do a good job I'll buy you a pint at The Feathers after.'

'Payment in cider?' I laughed, striking a pose and resting my hands on my hips. 'What sort of girl do you think I am?'

Charlie winked at me. 'The best sort. Come on, Green Eyes, here's a trowel.'

He showed me the trays of seedlings and demonstrated how to lift them without damaging the soft stems and how to transplant them into the waiting growbags.

'Is it me, or are there two different types here?' I asked, looking from one tray to the other.

'Clever girl,' said Charlie, placing a soft kiss on the side of my neck, which gave me a warm feeling in the pit of my stomach. 'These are Sungold, they're sweet little cherry tomatoes. I'm hoping to get Ollie to try them. He reckons he doesn't like tomatoes, but I might convert him with one of these.'

The warm feeling grew a bit bigger. Yet another reason to adore him. 'The world's greatest dad, you,' I said, nudging him playfully. 'What are these other bigger ones?'

Charlie cleared his throat. 'Um, they're Outdoor Girl. I saw the packet and thought of you.'

'Me?' I gasped. I threw my arms around his neck and kissed his cheek.

He shrugged and turned his face away but I could tell he'd gone a bit pink.

OK, so growing a variety of outdoor tomatoes in someone's honour might not be everyone's idea of a romantic gesture, but I knew how Charlie's mind worked and my heart bounced all over the place. He worshipped his six-year-old son Ollie, who was quite literally at the centre of Charlie's universe. So if he'd been thinking about both of us when he'd made his tomato choices, that must mean that I was special too, mustn't it?

More than that, I loved the fact that he knew me so well. My favourite jobs have been those where I could spend time outside. My idea of absolute hell is being desk-bound like my housemate, Anna, who is a web designer and barely moves more than five metres in an entire day.

'Can I plant them outside, then?' I said, dragging my eyes back to the seedlings. 'I quite fancy a bit of fresh air.'

Charlie rolled his eyes and chuckled. 'I don't know why

you work in a café when you're so mad keen on the great outdoors. You should be a park ranger or a policewoman or something. But no, sorry, they're not hardened off yet. Here, stick these in instead.'

'Peas! Oh, I love these!' I said as he handed me a tray of sturdy pea plants. A picture of me hiding in Auntie Sue's veggie patch floated into my head, sitting in the sunshine, popping fat peapods with my thumbs and eating the contents like sweets.

Charlie chuckled indulgently. He dispatched me towards a wigwam of bamboo canes and we both settled into our tasks. I knelt down in a patch of low sun and began to dig a small hole. I sprinkled a bit of fairy dust into it and then placed a tiny pea plant into its new home. I knew it wasn't fairy dust. Obviously. It was just far nicer to think of that than what it actually was, which might have been very nutritious for plants but absolutely stank.

Policewoman. I started to laugh.

'It's the handcuffs, isn't it?' I shouted over my shoulder.

'What is?'

'That's why you imagined me as a policewoman. So that you can play with the handcuffs. I know your game, mister.'

'Er, excuse me, Miss Moorcroft,' Charlie laughed indignantly, 'it wasn't my idea to stay in bed all last Sunday and look at pictures of you naked. That was entirely your doing.'

The patch of sunlight that had been warming my back suddenly disappeared and I heard a discreet cough. A prickle of embarrassment ran along my spine as I turned around to see Christine, the allotment secretary and coincidentally Gemma's mum, standing at the end of Charlie's plot. My eyes made their way from her wellingtons to her quilted jacket and up to her bobble hat. I scanned her face, holding my breath in case there was a sliver of hope that she hadn't overheard.

'Lovely looking beetroot, so it is,' said Christine in her broad Irish accent, smirking away to herself.

'Oh, yes,' I said, unsure whether Charlie grew beetroot or whether it was simply a blunt observation about the state of my face. 'It was my baby album,' I spluttered. 'That's why I was naked. And not in all of them, obviously . . .' I trailed off as Christine's shoulders began to shake with laughter.

'Ah, you youngsters. It's a long time since my husband Roy and I spent the day doing that.'

I gulped and laughed nervously. TMI, as Shirley would say.

'Hello, Christine,' said Charlie, joining us both, totally oblivious to my discomfort. 'Everything OK?'

'Grand, so it is.' She nodded. 'Just came by to remind you about Sunday. The Easter egg hunt. Great fun for the kiddies. Gemma will be here. Come if you can, won't you? Ollie would love it.'

Charlie and I made the right noises and Christine bustled off in the direction of the pavilion.

'You've got the weekend off, haven't you?' I said, a picture forming in my head of him and me under a huge blue sky with no buildings or people for miles.

'I have.' He nodded, his expression knotted in concentration as he took a piece of string from his pocket and gently tied my newly bedded pea plant to its cane. 'Four days off. Can't wait.'

'Remember that deal we made, when I came cycling with you even though I didn't want to and in return you promised to come horse riding with me?'

'Ye-s,' Charlie replied, not meeting my eye as he straightened up. I abandoned my planting, hooked my fingers through the belt loops of his jeans and stepped towards him, closing the gap between us until I could feel his warm breath on my cheek.

'Well, we could do that, this weekend. I found some stables just outside Kingsfield that said I could go and ride their horses. What do you think?'

I stared up at him and held my breath. I knew what he thought. He thought horses were all teeth and nostrils, but a deal was a deal and there was nothing – nothing – I'd rather do over the Easter weekend than canter through fields with the wind in my hair and Charlie by my side.

He pressed his lips to my forehead and shook his head. 'No can do, I'm afraid. I'm having Ollie over for a few days. In fact, I might bring him here to the Easter egg hunt. What do you reckon?'

My happy bubble burst and I felt my shoulders sag.

But you had him last weekend.

Eek! I very nearly said that out loud! Luckily my one diplomatic brain cell jumped in first and stopped me from making a huge mistake. Charlie would always choose Ollie over me. Quite rightly. I wished my own dad had shown even a tenth of the enthusiasm Charlie had for spending time with his son. So I wasn't complaining – well, maybe a bit.

'He'd love it.' I nodded. 'Perhaps we could all . . . ?' I swallowed and waited for Charlie to pick up on my thoughts and dive in with a suggestion that the three of us spend Easter Sunday together.

Charlie was a fab dad. I'd have loved a dad like him. Reading between the lines, I don't think he'd always been such a good father, but he certainly was now. And Ollie was a delight. He had big blue eyes just like his dad, was cute, well-mannered and had an inquisitive streak that made me laugh and kept Charlie constantly on his toes.

I have met Ollie twice. Both times when Charlie brought him into the café for something to eat.

I wasn't introduced. Well, strictly speaking, I suppose I was. Although 'Say thank you to the nice lady, Ollie' wasn't exactly what I'd had in mind when I'd envisaged meeting my potential stepson for the first time.

Charlie blinked at me, pulled off his woolly hat and scratched his head, dislodging my hands from his waist as he did so.

'Why don't you go horse riding on your own?' he asked gently. 'I'll come another time, I promise. But I think Ollie and me will just have a quiet one this weekend. It's too soon . . .' His voice petered out and he shrugged awkwardly.

That was a no, then.

I struggled to get my feelings under control, but there were no two ways about it. Charlie didn't want to tell Ollie about me and that stung. Was I an embarrassment or something?

Bright smile, Freya.

'Honey, you and I have been together four months. Haven't I earned my girlfriend badge yet?'

'Oh, come here.' He wrapped me in his arms and I burrowed my face into his jumper. 'I know it's tough. Believe me, I'd love to spend time with the three of us all together. But I want to be the best dad I can be. I've only been in Ollie's life properly myself for a few months and it's still early days for you and me. I don't want to confuse him by bringing a girlfriend into the equation.'

Four months was longer than some of my relationships, but I didn't think that admitting that would be particularly helpful to my cause.

I bit my lip. 'Yeah, but Tilly and Aidan have only been

together a couple of weeks longer than us and they're already halfway across the world together.'

And they're a perfect match.

Charlie puffed out his cheeks and a frown wrinkled his brow. 'That's different.'

I flushed, wishing I hadn't said that.

Tilly's first husband had died in a car crash a couple of years ago. I could totally see why she was ready to get serious with Aidan so quickly; she had settled down once and she wanted to do it again. On the other hand, Charlie had had his fingers badly burned by his wife and I could understand why he was treading cautiously; apart from having a crush on Tilly last year, I was the first woman that Charlie had let into his life since splitting up with his ex. I just wondered how long I'd have to wait until he let me into Ollie's life too.

I let out a long sigh. Charlie tilted my chin up to meet his gaze and I managed a weak smile.

'Hey, cheer up! We have fun, don't we?' he said, breaking into a cheeky grin.

A wave of disappointment washed away my smile. 'Is that what I am to you, Charlie? A bit of fun?'

My heart was pounding all of a sudden. How had the conversation got so heavy? Only two minutes ago we were talking handcuffs and nude photos.

We stared at each other as a weird sort of tension crackled between us. His expression faltered and I scanned his face, willing him to say that I was more than that. I could see him battling to find the right words but before a suitable reply occurred to him my mobile phone rang.

I loved the lyrics to Pharrell Williams's song 'Happy'. Hence choosing it as my ring tone. Normally I indulge in a full thirty seconds of clapping along as per Pharrell's instructions before accepting the call.

This time I fumbled in my jacket pocket and stabbed at the green button sharpish.

'Hello?'

'Freya, is that you?' The voice was higher than usual and a bit tremulous, but I recognized Auntie Sue instantly. My heart, already beating at top speed after the uncomfortable conversation with Charlie, thudded louder.

'Yes, it is. Is everything all right?'

'No, lass. It's Uncle Arthur, he's had an accident.'

'Oh no,' I gasped, turning to Charlie. He frowned with concern and reached a hand out to my arm. 'Is he OK?'

'He's out of hospital but he's a bit worse for wear and he's mithering something chronic. I hate to bother you and I know it's short notice, but do you think you could come up and help out for a few days?'

Charlie was still looking at me anxiously but I didn't make eye contact. I had a few days off and as Ollie was around it looked like I wouldn't be 'having fun' with Charlie. I glanced at my watch. Five o'clock. The train journey would take a couple of hours at least, plus I'd need to pack a bag . . .

'I'll be on the next train,' I promised, crossing my fingers that there would be a train at some point tonight.

I ended the call, telling her that I'd let her know what time the train would be in as soon as I was on board.

Finally, I looked Charlie in the eye. 'I've got to go home.'

'To Paris?'

My parents lived in Paris. Before that they'd lived in Brussels. Before that Johannesburg, Singapore, Sydney, Kuala Lumpur and Washington, DC . . . From memory they'd moved house seventeen times. But I'd only ever called one place my home.

I shook my head. 'Appleby Farm.'

Chapter 3

The train hissed to a standstill at Oxenholme station shortly after ten o'clock. Only a handful of passengers disembarked and by the time I'd faffed about stuffing my belongings into my rucksack and left the carriage, the platform at the little station was eerily deserted. I searched up and down for a familiar face – or any face, come to that – but couldn't see another soul. There was, however, a long metal sign displaying the message 'Welcome to The Lakes', and despite the circumstances of my impromptu visit, my heart skipped with happiness as I inhaled my first lungful of the fresh night air.

I was in the Lake District. My favourite place on earth.

I walked towards the exit with an eager bounce in my step, out of the station and towards the tiny taxi rank where, hopefully, the lift that Auntie Sue had arranged for me would be waiting. The journey to the farm took about half an hour and I couldn't wait to see her and Uncle Arthur. I had a quick scan around but the car park and taxi rank were completely devoid of cars so I plonked my rucksack on the floor against a stone wall and sat on it while I waited.

The last few hours had whizzed by. After Auntie Sue's call for help, Charlie and I had hugged each other for the longest time and then I'd dashed back to Anna's house to pack while she booked me a ticket online. Anna, being the ace friend that she was, made me a cheese and pickle sandwich, reminded me to pack my wellies and drove me to the station. I didn't breathe a word to her about the whole 'bit of fun' convo with Charlie because . . . well, because she'd probably think I was making a fuss about nothing and also because, after me, Anna was Charlie's number-one fan and she may well have sided with him.

The way things had been left between Charlie and me bothered me a lot. But during the train journey, I'd tucked my worries aside and decided to concentrate on what had been going on at Appleby Farm. I'd called Auntie Sue from the train. Apparently, Uncle Arthur had had an accident in his tractor this morning. The tractor had overturned and he'd broken his wrist, split his head open and bruised several ribs. He was OK now, a bit shaken-up, but nothing too serious. Poor old sausage.

There was still no sign of my lift and I strained to listen for an approaching car. Nothing. I was just contemplating calling for a taxi when my mobile rang. My heart fluttered when I saw Charlie's name flash up on the screen. Thank goodness.

I slid the phone under my hair to my ear and smiled as I answered his call. 'Hey.'

'Are you there yet?'

'I'm off the train. Just waiting for a taxi.'

'On your own? In the dark? You be careful.'

My smile grew bigger at the concern in his voice. He did care about me, of course he did.

'This is Oxenholme village, Charlie,' I giggled. 'The most dangerous thing I'm likely to encounter is a lost sheep.'

'Even so . . . Freya?'

There was something about the tone of his voice – softer, lower – that made my insides quiver. I gripped the phone tighter and swallowed. 'Yes?'

There was a pause down the line and I heard the creaking of leather, which probably meant he was on the sofa in his flat. 'I just wanted you to know that you make me very happy.'

'Ditto,' I said, smiling down the line at my big softie of a boyfriend.

'And you are a lot more to me than a bit of fun.'

His words flooded through me like warm honey. I leaned back against the cold stone wall and cradled the phone to my cheek. 'Well, that's all right, then,' I said softly. 'You mean a lot to me, too.'

A car with a rasping engine and rattling exhaust pipe came into view and flashed its headlights at me.

'Maybe when you're home . . .'

Home. My heart thumped at that. After six months, Kingsfield still didn't feel like home.

'. . . we can all go out for the day: me, you and Ollie?'

'I'd love that!' I jumped to my feet and performed a five-second tap dance.

The car, which I could see now was actually a tatty red van, came to a halt in front of me with a ratchety yank on the handbrake.

'My lift's here, Charlie. I've got to go.'

I blew him a kiss down the phone, said goodnight and slipped the phone back in my pocket, grinning like a loon. I felt so much better after talking to him. Shame he wasn't here with me now; I'd have loved to show him off to my family. Maybe next time.

The driver's door of the van opened with a creak and out stepped Eddy Hopkins, my uncle's right-hand man – quite literally at the moment, given his injuries – and the man who taught me to milk a cow when I was eight.

'Eddy! Gosh, what a lovely surprise!'

I sprang over to him, threw my arms around his neck and kissed his surprisingly smooth cheek.

'You're here, then.' He stepped back, holding me at arm's length, and squinted at me. I'd forgotten he wasn't one for physical contact. He had a piece of rolled-up tissue protruding from one nostril and his aftershave was eye-wateringly strong.

'Looking well, Eddy.' I beamed at him and waited for some sort of reciprocal compliment.

'You've filled out a bit,' he said, a shadow of a smile lifting one side of his face.

'Cheers.' I rolled my eyes, but couldn't help grinning. Ever the charmer, our Eddy.

He strode to the rear of the van and opened one of the doors.

'Thanks for fetching me,' I said, swallowing a chuckle at the worn-out elbows of his tweed jacket and the elastic bands around the soles of his boots, presumably to stop them flapping. Eddy was in his late fifties, he'd never been married, had a minimalist approach to anything vaguely domestic and was what you might call frugal when it came to clothing.

'I swear you were wearing those boots last time I came,' I said, shaking my head.

'Nowt wrong with these.' He inspected his footwear and shrugged. 'And I've put new elastic bands on 'em specially for you.'

He hefted my heavy rucksack onto his shoulder effortlessly and slid the bag inside.

'Get yourself in't van. Your aunt and uncle will be waiting

up for you,' he said, nodding towards the passenger side. He pulled the tissue out of his nostril, inspected it with a grunt and shoved it in his pocket.

I yanked the handle several times before the door swung open. 'What happened to your nose?'

'Cut myself shaving, trying to rush so I wouldn't be late picking you up.'

I pressed my lips together to smother a giggle. I remembered now. He was always stubbly by noon because he shaved before going to bed instead of in the morning to save himself time when he got up.

'Well, I appreciate it. Thank you.'

The passenger seat was missing most of its upholstery and was currently occupied by a small, wiry black terrier, who turned excitedly on the spot several times with its tongue hanging out.

'Out the road, Buddy,' growled Eddy, hooking his finger through the dog's collar and pulling him out of my way.

I sat down, shut the door and did up my seatbelt. Buddy sat down too, on my lap, his face inches from mine. Eddy started up the engine – foregoing his seatbelt, I noticed – and seconds later we were on our way.

We trundled along dark country lanes towards Lovedale village and Appleby Farm for several minutes before Eddy spoke.

'Glad you're here.'

I turned to face him and tried not to inhale Buddy's hot meaty breath. There were no street lamps on this stretch of the road and only a faint glow from the dashboard to light Eddy's features, but I could see his furrowed brow.

'Uncle Arthur's OK, isn't he? I mean, apart from a few cuts and bruises, and the broken wrist?'

Eddy sucked in air through his teeth and shook his head. 'I'm probably speaking out of turn but I dunno.' He shrugged. 'Hitting a ditch and overturning the tractor? It's not like Arthur. He knows them fields like I know me own face.'

The face you sliced into earlier with a razor? I snorted softly to myself.

'Better, probably,' he said, shooting me a flinty look.

'Do you think there's more to this accident than meets the eye, Eddy?'

The van rounded a sharp bend, Buddy dug his claws into my jeans to keep his balance and I gasped in pain. Eddy, seemingly oblivious to his passenger's anguish, sighed. 'I hope not, lass. For his sake, and your auntie's. Farming's a tough business. Arthur's got me to help him, but even so, there's a lot to do.'

I nodded. My memories of holidays spent at the farm when I was growing up were happy ones. In fact, I'd spent the happiest days of my life there, but my aunt and uncle were on the go all day long. The farm spanned 150 acres of land, mostly given over to sloping grassland where the cows grazed, with some crops grown on the flatter bits to keep the cattle going during winter when the grass didn't grow. Eddy was their only employee and for the first time since leaving Kingsfield it dawned on me that I was going to have to roll up my sleeves and muck in.

The farming calendar was pretty full on, day in, day out, seven days a week. Time off was scarce, money was in short supply and every day brought new challenges, from bad weather to sick animals. And yet Auntie Sue and Uncle Arthur were the most content people I knew and devoted to each other, even after goodness knows how many years of marriage.

'How can I help?' I asked, as much to myself as to Eddy. It had been years since I'd milked a cow and even then I had only been playing at it. I could probably drive a tractor at a push, but I didn't fancy doing anything complicated like spraying crops. My heart sank as reality hit home: I wasn't much use to them at all, really.

Eddy chuckled. 'Oh, Sue will keep you busy. She's got a dodgy knee now, so she'll probably get you to look after the hens.'

'Right. I can do that.' One of my jobs growing up had been to collect the eggs. That would be a piece of cake.

'Veg patch probably needs looking at, too.'

'OK.' At least my experience on Charlie's allotment would come in handy.

'And the office is a bit of a state.'

I shuddered. 'Not my forte, offices, but I'll do my best.'

The next section of road was lined with street lamps as we entered the tiny village of Lovedale. Eddy indicated right just after the White Lion pub and thankfully slowed down as we turned on to a bumpy track.

The farm gate was pushed back as far as it would go against the hedge and I could just make out the Appleby Farm sign attached to the top bar.

Ahead, at the top of the track behind the cowsheds, stood the stables, and to the side of the barns sat the farmhouse. It was a moonless sky and the building itself was barely visible amongst the shadows of the night, but lights twinkled in every one of the nine windows in its front façade. I don't think I'd ever seen a building look so inviting and welcoming in my entire life.

'I'd forgotten how lovely it is,' I gasped, clutching a surprised Buddy to my chest as tears pricked at my eyes.

Eddy stopped the van in the yard. I jumped out and

dragged my rucksack out of the back before he even had a chance to get out.

The noise of the van had woken up the cows. One or two began to moo and I could hear the swishing of straw and snorting and sniffing coming from the cowsheds as the animals protested at having their evening disturbed.

Eddy opened his window instead and I reached in and hugged him tight before he could lean away.

'Thanks for the lift, Eddy. Goodnight. See you tomorrow, I expect.'

'Damn,' he grumbled, ferreting in his pocket until he found another piece of tissue, or possibly the same piece as before. 'You've set the bleeding off again.'

I waved him off and opened the wrought-iron gate in front of the farmhouse, my fingers fumbling with the latch in my haste. A wide shaft of light suddenly illuminated the path and Auntie Sue emerged, her face beaming as she wiped her hands on her apron.

'Welcome home, lass.'

She opened her arms and I raced into them.

Chapter 4

Auntie Sue's hug sent me straight back to my childhood. She pressed me to her bosom and I breathed her in – fresh bread and Nivea face cream – exactly as I remembered. I sighed contentedly.

'I've missed you so much, Auntie Sue,' I said, feeling ridiculously emotional all of a sudden.

She leaned back against my arms and peered at me. Two fat tears escaped from the corners of her eyes. 'Well. This *is* a blessing in disguise. I think you've grown even more beautiful in the three years since you were last here.'

'Three?' I gasped. 'It can't be, surely.'

My aunt nodded sagely. She was in her seventies, had a cloud of fine white hair, the figure of a woman who enjoyed both baking and eating, and the brightest blue eyes I'd ever seen.

A pang of guilt stabbed at me as I did a mental calculation. The last time I was here must have been the summer before my parents moved to Paris. I'd come back for a few days before starting a new job. I racked my brains to remember which job it had been . . . the pub in Cornwall, that was it. The following Christmas I'd spent two days at my parents' elegant Parisian apartment and ever since then,

I'd worked over the Christmas period – which gave me an excuse not to join them again. And my summer holidays were usually spent somewhere hot, with friends.

I'd neglected the two members of my family whom I loved the most and the fact that it had taken Uncle Arthur to be mangled underneath a tractor to get me to visit them made me feel awful.

'I'm a terrible niece,' I muttered.

'Pshh. Rubbish,' she replied briskly, dabbing at her face with the hem of her apron. Auntie Sue had shrunk, I realized. We used to be the same height, but now she had to look up at me.

'You're here now and I can't tell you how grateful we are. It'll do your uncle the world of good seeing you about the place. He's so stressed with his accident and everything. I hope we haven't put you out?'

I shook my head. 'There's nowhere I'd rather be and as luck would have it I've got the whole of the Easter weekend off anyway.'

'Is that young Freya?' Uncle Arthur's gruff voice travelled through the open door and we both laughed.

'Sure is!' I replied, breaking our hug. I planted a kiss on my aunt's soft cheek and carried my rucksack inside.

The front door led straight into the farmhouse kitchen. The room was warm and cosy, and smelled of wood smoke and baking. On one side of the room, a gleaming black Aga was tucked into an inglenook fireplace next to which two cats were curled up in a basket, soaking up the range's warmth. A huge scrubbed-pine table with benches running along its sides and a chair at each end dominated the centre of the room, and at the far side an assortment of comfy armchairs were arranged around a blazing log fire.

Wisps of dark grey hair were just visible over the back

of the middle chair. Uncle Arthur was in prime position in front of the fire, his feet propped up on a footrest and Madge, the black and tan mongrel dog who had to be at least fifteen by now, was stretched out under his legs. I dropped a kiss on his cheek and squeezed my bottom on to his footrest so that I could see him properly. Madge nudged my leg with her nose and I scratched the top of her head.

'Blimey, look at you! Looks like you've done ten rounds in a boxing ring,' I exclaimed.

His hair had been jet black when he was younger, but it was still thick and he had bushy eyebrows to match, although one was now covered with a bandage. His left arm was in plaster and his chin was cut and bruised, but his dark eyes were still twinkly behind his glasses.

'Looks worse than it is.' He grinned. 'I'll be fine in a couple of days.'

'Are you in much pain?'

'Nooo,' he said, rather too quickly for my liking. 'I'm drugged up to the eyeballs for starters. Don't tell her indoors, though,' he chuckled and then winced, laying his plastered arm across his ribs, 'I quite like being waited on hand and foot.'

Auntie Sue tutted affectionately, bustled over to the Aga and slid the kettle on to the hotplate.

'Tea, love?' she called.

'Um . . .' I was ready for a drink, but I was shattered, too. And I knew that the pair of them would usually be in bed by now. Uncle Arthur was already in his dressing gown and pyjamas.

'Or hot milk?' she asked, selecting two mugs from an overloaded pine dresser.

'Oh, yes, please.' My eyes roamed the shelves of the dresser, stacked with crockery: pretty milk jugs hung from a row of hooks, Auntie Sue's 'everyday' mugs filled one shelf, cups and saucers another, and the top was lined with her collection of teapots of every shape, colour and size, from novelty cats to vintage china. I'd spent hours playing with them when I was a little girl.

'Sweet dreams special?'

'Oh, Auntie Sue, that would be perfect,' I sighed.

I looked across to see her smiling to herself. My favourite bedtime supper ever, which she used to say would guarantee me a good night's sleep, consisted of real butter on toasted homemade bread and hot milk with a sprinkling of nutmeg and a bit of sugar.

The cats stirred from their slumber and wrapped themselves around my aunt's legs as she retrieved a jug of milk from the fridge.

'All right, Benny and Björn, just a drop.'

I shook my head and chuckled, catching Uncle Arthur's eye; Auntie Sue had always had a soft spot for ABBA. 'Which is which?'

'Björn has two white socks,' said Auntie Sue. 'And Benny has three.'

'And plays piano,' Uncle Arthur hissed. We both laughed and Auntie Sue tutted.

He squeezed my hand gently and I held it up to my cheek. I caught the faint scent of cows on his skin – not as unpleasant as you might think – sweet and grassy and precisely as he had always smelled.

'Thanks for coming,' he whispered. 'It's not that we can't manage, but she needs a bit of female company. You'll cheer her up no end.'

'I hope so,' I said, biting my lip.

It looked as if they were both keen to have me for the other person's sake. I couldn't escape the feeling that there was more going on here than just a few cuts and bruises. OK, so Uncle Arthur wouldn't be driving a tractor any time soon, but surely Eddy could handle that side of things, or they could hire in some extra labour for a few weeks?

I opened my mouth to voice my thoughts but Uncle Arthur cut me off with a gigantic yawn. Poor thing, he looked exhausted after his traumatic day.

Auntie Sue was quick to act. 'Right then, Artie. Bedtime for you after all the excitement you've had today,' she said, brandishing a butter knife in his direction from her position at the kitchen table.

'I was only allowed to stay up until you arrived,' he said, with a wink. 'Ouch.' His hand flew to his bandaged brow. 'Must remember not to keep doing that.'

He swung his feet off the stool and I helped him to his feet. 'I haven't even heard any of your news,' he moaned and lifted up my left hand to inspect. 'But no ring yet, I see.'

'We'll catch up in the morning. Promise.' I kissed his cheek, taking care not to touch his ribs. 'Anything special you need me to do tomorrow?'

'Plenty of time for all that,' he said, batting my offer of help away with his hand. 'See you in the morning.'

I watched him go out into the hallway and towards the stairs before I dived into a plate of thickly buttered toast at the table.

'Ooh, thank you,' I breathed, taking a piping-hot mug of fragrant milk from my aunt.

'Now, then,' Auntie Sue's eyes sparkled as she tipped a generous measure of brandy into our mugs of milk and sat down at the table beside me, 'tell your Auntie Sue everything, and I mean everything.'

*

Maybe it was the brandy or the heavy woollen blankets (Auntie Sue didn't do duvets) or perhaps it was simply that the air here was stuffed with extra oxygen. Whatever it was I slept like a log and it was nine o'clock when I climbed out of my single bed the next morning and pulled the curtain aside.

I'd like to say that a soft blue sky gave me a perfect view all the way down the valley to Lake Windermere from my bedroom window. Sadly, that was not the case. The rain had begun hammering it down by the time Auntie Sue and I had gone to bed after our catch-up, and although it had stopped now, the sky was bulging with fat low clouds that seemed to hover over the landscape, barely skimming the tops of trees and distant scattered rooftops.

Ten minutes later, I'd showered, dressed, scooped my hair up into a ponytail and was helping myself to tea from a blue-glazed teapot I'd found sitting on the Aga. There was no one about, so I slipped into my coat and wellies and took my mug outside.

I meandered down the mossy path at the front of the farmhouse, through the little cottage garden blooming with spring flowers and out through the gate.

Phwoar! I grinned to myself. What a pong! How had that unmistakeable farmyard aroma sneaked past me last night? I sipped at my tea, crossed the cobbled yard pitted with puddles and took a good, long look around me to remind myself of the farm's layout. Most of the buildings faced on to the yard: the old three-storey farmhouse, a stout sort of building made from weathered dove-grey stone, was at the heart of the farm. A couple of barns stood on one side of the house and Auntie Sue's veggie patch and orchard on the other. The cowsheds, the milking parlour and the old dairy opposite were built of the same stone as the farmhouse and I walked slowly past them, noticing the holes in the slate roofs. Yet despite the farm buildings' slightly tumbledown appearance, there was an irresistible charm to the old place and it warmed my heart to be back.

I paused next to the old dog kennel that had been in the yard for as long as I could remember and peered into the small field beyond, which was fenced off for the chickens. Thirty or so plump brown hens wandered around, pecking purposefully at the grass. A scruffy wooden mobile hen-house complete with windows, a ramp and pitched roof stood in the centre and behind it, a pair of wellington-clad feet were just visible between its wheels.

'Hello, Auntie Sue! How's Uncle Arthur today?'

'Morning, love!' Auntie Sue's head popped out from behind the nesting boxes. 'He's sulking in his office because I wouldn't let him come outside.'

'Oh dear.' I pulled a face. The ground floor of the farmhouse had a dining room that no one ever used and a small office where Uncle Arthur liked to spend as little time as possible. But then he didn't like being inside much, full stop.

My aunt held out a wicker basket. 'Guess what's for breakfast?'

'Fresh eggs! Yum. Would you like me to cook? I can boil them, but my poaching needs work.'

And then some. I was actually a terrible cook. My scones regularly lulled people into thinking I was a whizz in the kitchen. The truth was sadly quite different. But what I lacked in skill, I made up for in enthusiasm, which had to count for something.

'Not today,' Auntie Sue replied diplomatically. 'Anyway, we had ours hours ago.'

45

So much for me coming to help; I was more like a lazy guest. That would have to change.

'You should have woken me,' I said, feeling rather sheepish. 'Never mind, I'll get straight on with some chores.'

She flapped a hand at me and looked down at her watch. 'Has that dog turned up yet?'

I turned to see Madge ambling slowly towards me.

'She's here now,' I replied.

'Watch this,' Auntie Sue chuckled.

The old dog flopped down in front of the kennel and, as if she'd rehearsed it, an escaped hen waddled past Madge and into the kennel, clucked noisily and reappeared almost straight away. The dog, with sudden stealth, sprang to her paws, stuck her head in the kennel and retrieved an egg, which she gobbled down in two seconds flat. She wagged her tail at me triumphantly and sauntered back off to the farmhouse.

Now that was what you called a fresh egg.

'Wow. Does that happen often?' I asked, shaking my head.

'Every day. Nine thirty sharp,' said Auntie Sue. 'You can set your clock by those two. Right, I'll make you some breakfast while you go on round to the stables, there's someone I think you'd like to meet.'

I raised an eyebrow, intrigued, but Auntie Sue just jerked her head in the direction of the stables and strode off, limping slightly. *Dodgy knee*, I suddenly remembered Eddy telling me last night, as I walked down towards the stables.

I used to have my own pony called Bailey years ago but I outgrew her and my uncle sold her. I'd cried myself to sleep for a week. But once I'd left school I'd only been back to the farm for a few days at a time and it hadn't been worth getting another. I know it was a childish sort of ambition to hold, but one day I'd have my own horse. Fact.

The stable block was further along the yard, set at a right angle to the cowsheds. I rounded the corner and came to an abrupt stop. A girl roughly my age was leading a skewbald horse out of the end stall by its head collar.

I made a whinnying noise of unbridled joy, not unhorse-like itself, and the girl looked around and beamed.

'I think I'm in love,' I squealed, virtually galloping over.

The girl scratched the horse's neck and laughed. 'Hurray, you can muck out then. This one's a right messy mare.'

She tied the horse to a wooden post and picked up a fork. Even in her waterproof jacket and scruffy jogging bottoms I could see she was gorgeous. She had one of those to-die-for complexions that looked as if she was wearing make-up even though she wasn't: olive skin that probably tanned even on a grey day in Cumbria, and naturally peach-tinted cheeks.

Jealousy is not an attractive trait, I told myself, trying to forget that I'd once spent an entire summer in Greece and had still looked like a peeled prawn at the end of it. And her hair: long, shiny and straight except for a top section that she'd gathered up in a quiff. It was probably really silky too, whereas mine . . . I reached a hand up to stroke the horse's mane. Yup, my hair was as wiry as that.

I surreptitiously tucked the end of my ponytail into the back of my jacket and hoped I'd remembered to pack my Frizz Ease. 'I would love to help, seriously – mucking out, grooming, anything. I'm Freya, by the way.'

I could barely keep my cheeks under control, my smile was so massive. A person my age *and* a horse. At Appleby Farm! I was so glad to be here. Although, of course, Uncle

Arthur had had an accident, which was bad. Mustn't forget that.

'I know. Your aunt almost fell over herself racing round here to tell me about you. I'm Lizzie Moon. This is Skye.'

I rubbed the horse's nose and she nudged at my shoulder. 'Hello, Skye, pleased to meet you. You too, Lizzie.'

'Don't say it – I know. Moon and Skye. Utterly ridiculous. My sister's pony is called Star. It's my dad's idea of humour. He's hilare. Not.' Lizzie rolled her eyes dramatically. 'I'm running late, actually, so if you really don't mind helping, you could brush her while I do her bed. Brushes are in there.' She pointed towards the tack room.

'Yeah, I know.' I pressed my lips into a small smile and went in search of a curry comb. I'd spent most of my spare time as a child down here, grooming Bailey.

'Ooh, God, sorry, course you do.' Lizzie disappeared into Skye's stall and began lifting poo and tossing straw.

I started brushing the horse's neck in small circles, working my way down to her chest. 'So how long have you kept Skye here?'

'I only started work at the White Lion a few weeks ago as a live-in barmaid.' She stuck her head out of the stable and arched an eyebrow. 'For barmaid read slave. Anyhow, it said in the job advert that I could bring a pet.' She pulled a face. 'Apparently Bill the landlord meant a hamster or something. Not a horse. Luckily, your uncle came into the pub and I told him my probs and, bless him, he sorted out DIY livery for me here. Twenty-five quid a week for stable and grazing. Plus there's usually a cup of tea and a slice of cake going too. Bargain.'

It was a bargain. And with the White Lion being the nearest building to the farm, it was ideal for her. And me.

I sighed enviously. 'You must get to ride loads.'

Lizzie straightened up, swept a stray piece of straw off her face with her forearm and leaned on her fork. 'Ha. Slave, remember? Take today, for instance. What does three-quarters of the population of the civilized world do at Easter? Hmm? They come to the Lake District, clog up the roads and demand food and drink every five seconds.'

'Yeah, of course, the pub will be busy, won't it?' I kept forgetting that today was Good Friday. Was it only yesterday that I was showing Amy how to use the coffee machine? It felt like a lifetime ago.

'I know.' Lizzie tutted. 'Cray-cray. I'll be lucky if I get five minutes to have a wee this weekend, let alone take Skye out for a hack.'

'I could ride her, if you like . . .' My voice faded as I remembered I was supposed to be here to help out.

'Would you? Brillo pads. Can you groom her afterwards and then stick her in the field? Eddy will show you which one I use.'

'Sure.' I swallowed guiltily. I would just have to work really hard later to make up for it.

'Right, I might even have time for a shower before starting work if I hurry.' Lizzie threw her arms round Skye's neck and kissed her noisily. 'Sure you don't mind looking after my baby? I owe you one.'

'Are you kidding me? You've made my bloomin' day, week even. I owe *you*!'

'Fill your boots, Freya.' Lizzie laughed and began to walk away. She stopped suddenly and turned back. 'Ooh, are you single?'

'No.' I smiled quizzically at her.

'Good. Don't want some flame-haired beauty pinching the meagre supply of eligible men from under my nose. See you in the White Lion soon, yeah?'

Flame-haired beauty? Yup. Definitely friend material. I grinned. 'Sure.'

I waved her off and fetched a saddle for Skye. A quick ride. Half an hour, tops, and then I would definitely do something useful.

Chapter 5

My ride on Lizzie's horse had put me in an excellent mood. By the time I'd groomed her and moved her to a field for a spot of grazing, most of the morning had gone.

In my defence I did use the time to do a bit of a recce while I was out and about and remind myself where everything was on the farm. One hundred and fifty acres was big. Huge! It was a lot of farm for poor old Eddy to manage on his own.

Eddy's comments last night were playing on my mind so I made some coffee and took a mug through to Uncle Arthur in his office. I could tell he was still in there by the whistling. Uncle Arthur had always been a whistler. I took it as a good sign. You have to be fairly relaxed to whistle. You don't see people on the top of buildings threatening to throw themselves off whistling away to themselves, do you? So maybe Eddy was imagining the worst.

Uncle Arthur was sitting at his desk. He looked up as I entered, stopped whistling, dropped a pile of papers into a drawer and slammed it shut.

'Ah. My favourite niece. Come into my room of doom.' He spread his arms wide and then made a space on the desk in front of him for the coffee I held out.

'Your only niece.' I grinned at him.

I'd never liked this office either. It was dusty and dark, and made chaotic by piles of invoices, fertilizer catalogues and tractor manuals weighted down with half-drunk mugs of cold tea. It also smelled of egg which, given the fact that I'd seen a hen lay an egg in a dog house this morning, didn't surprise me as much as it should have. I glanced round for any speckled, brown egg-shaped offerings.

'Tell me about this accident of yours, then. What was that all about?'

Uncle Arthur's shoulders sagged and he scowled as if he'd been dragged through this a million times. 'Blooming two-way radio crackled at me, I looked down and lost concentration for one second. An' that is all. Why, what's anyone been saying?'

Honesty is the best policy, that's what I always say. I took a deep breath. 'Eddy's worried about you, about the farm. Should he be?'

Uncle Arthur folded his arms and leaned back in his chair. 'No. He hates making decisions, that's his problem. I swear he'd phone me in the morning to ask which socks he should wear if I'd answer him. Tell him I've broken my wrist, not my brainbox.'

'I will.' I sidled up to him and hugged him gingerly. Avoiding his arm, ribs and forehead was actually quite tricky. 'We just love you, that's all.'

We stayed silent for a few moments and I felt him sigh against me. It broke my heart. I wished I could do something useful for him.

He sniffed and straightened up, drawing the topic of conversation to a close. 'Anyway. Having a good time?' He was wearing a flat cap even though he was indoors and looked like a tweedy pirate with his bandaged eyebrow and bruised face.

I tutted. 'That's not what I'm here for, is it? To have a good time.'

Nonetheless, I was having a great time. Even on a grey day, the Lake District was heavenly. The landscape here seemed to have its brightness settings stuck on maximum. And the lovely fresh air! It smelled heavenly too. Well, except in the office.

'Where's Auntie Sue? I'll take her a drink.'

'She's in the new dairy.'

I left him whistling something cheerful yet unrecognizable and went off in search of my aunt.

The new dairy was the most recent addition to the farm, built after one hot summer before I was born when Auntie Sue had been on an ice-cream making course and Uncle Arthur had built her a new-fangled hygienic room that was all stainless steel and hi-tech freezers.

Of course they'd still had a dairy herd in those days. Last night on the drive to the farm, Eddy had told me that they only farmed beef now, although Auntie Sue still kept two Jersey cows called Gloria and Gaynor, one of whom had just calved and the other was due any day.

She was dressed in white overalls and clogs, and her hair was tucked into a sort of shower cap. She was loading plastic tubs into the freezer when I poked my head in. Without gowning up, I wouldn't be allowed into her sterilized environment.

'Sticky toffee ice cream.' She beamed at me proudly. 'My newest flavour. This lot is for the White Lion.'

'I'll drop it off later, if you like? You were right, by the way; I liked Lizzie a lot.'

She slammed the freezer shut. 'Thought you might. Right, that's done.'

Her eyes glazed over for a few seconds and she stood stock still, hands on hips before she seemed to remember where she was, then lifted her shoulders and clapped a hand over her mouth.

'Freya, love, you never got your breakfast!'

Ten minutes later I was tucking into a plate of buttery scrambled eggs.

'OK, lady.' I pointed to the bench on the opposite side of the kitchen table. 'Truth time. Sit and talk.'

Auntie Sue chuckled but did as she was told. She steepled her fingers together and watched me blow on a forkful of fluffy egg before she began to speak.

'I want him to retire,' she said, glancing over her shoulder to check no one was in earshot.

'Is there any chance of that?' I picked up a pottery chicken and sprinkled a cloud of pepper on my eggs. It was the white dusty sort rather than black pepper. It flew up my nose and made me do that hovering sneeze thing that never actually turns into a sneeze but makes you look ridiculous. And burns your nasal passage.

She shrugged. 'He's not got the strength for the job any more.' Her blue eyes blinked sadly at me. I laid my knife down and reached for her hand.

Uncle Arthur must be seventy-five at least. Did farmers actually retire, or did they just plod on until . . . I sniffed to dislodge the pepper. No point going down that road. If only they'd had children, things would have been much easier for them. I'd always presumed they couldn't have them, although nothing had ever been said.

'And I don't think he's safe to drive. Take that accident

yesterday. He got off lightly, really. Thank heavens he had his walkie-talkie; at least he could call for help. But imagine if it had been more serious. He could have been lying there injured for hours before anyone spotted him.'

I abandoned my brunch, moved to Auntie Sue's side of the table and gave her a hug.

'Would more staff help?' I meant proper farm staff who called animals by their proper names, not like me who called everything a cow regardless of its sex, age or reproductive capabilities.

Auntie Sue rubbed her thumb and fingers together. 'Money, Freya, that's the problem. We've enough trouble paying—' The kitchen door opened and she jumped up with a yelp, nearly flinging me off the bench. 'Eddy! Ready for your lunch?'

Eddy nodded to me. 'It's pouring with rain and looks like it's set for the day.'

'Is it?' I murmured, not really paying attention. I was miles away. Auntie Sue was right: Uncle Arthur should be able to retire if he wanted – or needed – to. And in the meantime, an extra pair of capable hands was needed. This problem was way too big for me to solve on my own.

While Auntie Sue clattered about the kitchen heating soup, buttering bread and slicing cheese, I nodded to Eddy to join me at the far end of the room near the fire.

'Auntie Sue wants him to rest. She's persuaded him to stay in his office today but you know what he's like.'

Eddy and I grinned at each other knowingly.

I had a plan of sorts forming but I needed his help. 'Can you do me a list of jobs that will need doing in the next couple of weeks?'

He nodded. 'I can, but with respect I don't think you could—'

I shook my head. 'I know, we need reinforcements. I'm going to make a call. On my mobile, so Uncle Arthur can't hear me.'

There was only one phone in the house, in the office. And I didn't want to be overheard.

'Oxtail soup, Eddy,' Auntie Sue called. 'Your favourite.'

Eddy's eyes rolled back in his head in a distinctly un-favourite-like manner. 'You'll have to go up the bridle path between us and Willow Farm to get a signal. Right to the top of Knots Hill.'

Willow Farm. Now there was a blast from the past! 'Thanks for tip, Eddy, I'll go now.'

It was the sort of rain that drenched your body in seconds. Relentless big splodges of it. My thighs were soaked and cold, and the ground was really slippery as we climbed the bridle path up Knots Hill. I'd decided to take Skye and I was glad I had; the path had long grass on one side and wet hedgerow on the other and I would have been even more miserable climbing uphill on foot. Skye, on the other hand, didn't seem to mind the mud, which was just as well because it would be even worse on our descent.

By the time I emerged into open ground and approached the spot Eddy had directed me to, I was feeling pretty fed up. And to my annoyance there was already a man on horseback sitting at the top of the hill, hogging all the signal and shouting into his phone in a bid to compete with the pounding rain. I couldn't see his face or catch what he was saying but I heard him laughing. He was wearing a wide-brimmed waterproof hat and one of those long wax jackets with a cape thing around the shoulders. I was wearing my jacket with a fur trim around the hood. A bit daft really, but in my haste to catch the train yesterday, it was the first thing that had come to hand. Now the fur had gone all soggy and forlorn, and water had started to drip down my face and neck.

I rarely lose my temper but as the seconds ticked by, my sense of humour began to desert me. Skye was getting fidgety too. I checked my phone for signal: one bar, no – no bars, ooh one bar and . . . damn, gone again. There was no point trying to make a call yet, I would just have to wait my turn for the top spot.

What was this chap even talking about for so long? And why did he seem so cheerful about it? And why hadn't I waited for the rain to stop . . . ?

For goodness' sake. 'Oi, there is a queue, you know!' I shouted.

I felt guilty as soon as I'd said it. How rude. Couldn't help myself, though. I was wet, shivery and absolutely dreading making this call.

The man turned briefly towards me, raised a hand, then jerked on his reins and rode off in the opposite direction, still apparently talking.

OK, then. Deep breaths. I nudged Skye with my heels to walk on, picked up a measly two bars on my phone and called Julian.

'Freya, I'm at work. Whatever it is, it had better be important.'

My brother and I had never been close. He is fifteen years older than me. We share a set of parents, a surname and for three years after I was born until he'd gone to university we had shared the same address. But that was it. We were as different as two siblings could be. Julian wasn't married. He had a partner, not that I'd ever met her. Apparently he'd looked into marriage but – and I quote – it didn't stack up financially. Oh, the old romantic.

'Hi, Julian, I'm at Appleby Farm.'

'And?'

I knew better than to indulge in small talk with my brother. He liked to get straight to the point; beating about the bush was strictly prohibited. I launched straight into the problem.

'Uncle Arthur's had an accident and he needs extra help. Auntie Sue wants him to retire. I wondered if you could advise him. You know, financially? Maybe come up for a few days and lend a hand?'

There was a snort from the other end of the line. My heart sank. Why, why, why had I thought he might be inclined to help me out? Without some financial incentive, that is. Julian was some sort of business angel, which I think meant that he sorts out finances for businesses. Which in turn should imply that he was in a better position than I was to help Auntie Sue and Uncle Arthur. In my heart of hearts I hadn't really thought he would come up from London and roll up his sleeves, but it was worth a shot.

'Yes, Freya, here's some advice for him. Sell up. He should have got out of farming years ago. And there's no way I'm coming to help. You're the one without a career; you stay and sort it out. The old duffer has always preferred you anyway.'

'I just thought—' I moved the phone from my ear and stared at the screen. He'd gone.

I looked down to Appleby Farm, at the farmhouse surrounded by fields, bordered with century-old drystone walls, the green squares of grassland dotted with cattle, and the fields with their spring growth of barley bending under the force of the April showers. My heart squeezed at the sight of it.

It looked like I was in this one alone.

Chapter 6

It took me until seven thirty that evening to cheer up and thaw out. I had Auntie Sue's cottage pie to thank for that. It was like a big hug. Right there on the plate. There should be a law, I decided as I scraped up the last delicious morsel, a cottage pie law. Everyone should be made to eat it at least once a week. It would solve a lot of the world's problems. Although come to think of it, as comforting as my dinner was, the how-to-run-Appleby-Farm-without-Uncle-Arthur dilemma remained.

Eddy had pressed a to-do list into my hand earlier this afternoon, as requested. There were some big jobs in the fields – like fertilizing and spraying – plus the daily maintenance of the herd: feeding, bedding and clearing the yard and cowsheds, moving them round from field to field and bringing them in at night. And the vet would be making his routine monthly visit in a few days.

I wasn't particularly well up on my animal husbandry, but I was pretty sure that you needed two good arms for most of it. It was all very well saying that Uncle Arthur needed to rest, but unless I could come up with a solution that he both approved of and could afford, I couldn't see how Auntie Sue and I were going to keep him from going wandering off round the farm in the morning.

I slid along the bench and collected everyone's plates from the table, while Auntie Sue delved into the Aga for pudding. Pudding! Yet another reason why I loved being at the farm. Madge jumped up optimistically and followed me to the sink.

'Sorry, dog.' I ruffled the short fur behind her ears. 'No leftovers, I'm afraid. That was a-ma-zing, Auntie Sue, thank you. If it's OK with you, after I've washed up I was going to pop over to the White Lion. Fancy joining me for a pint, Uncle Arthur?'

'A pint.' He sighed, untucking his napkin from his shirt collar and rubbing a blob of gravy off his chin. The look of longing on his face was a picture. 'Don't mind if I do.'

Auntie Sue stopped spooning apple crumble into bowls. Her eyes flicked back and forth between us like she was watching a mini tennis match.

'The lane will be treacherous and it'll be dark soon.' She pressed her lips together. 'And I don't think you should drink, Artie.'

'But I'm delivering the ice cream, remember?' I added. 'And I don't fancy walking in on my own.' Besides, I wanted to get him to open up a bit more and I reckoned a pint in his hand and a change of scene might do the trick.

Auntie Sue gave him her stern look. 'One, Arthur Moor-croft. Just one pint.'

Half an hour later we were on our way. Recalling Lizzie's 'flame-haired beauty' comment from this morning, I'd taken a bit more care with my appearance than an ice-cream delivery should truly warrant. I'd changed into a long yellow and black stripy jumper, donned some black leggings and a pair of boots, zhuzhed up my hair to make it look tousled and flicked a mascara brush over my lashes. Uncle Arthur had changed his flat cap.

Auntie Sue was right: the track was über-treacherous. The rain had stopped but it was very blustery. However, Uncle Arthur was practically running along in his eagerness, waving the torch in front of us while I staggered under the weight of the cool box. It was one of those large plastic ones with a complicated locking handle and Auntie Sue had topped the three cartons of ice cream with about six industrial-sized ice packs and issued strict instructions to remind Bill, the landlord, to stow it straight in the freezer. Despite the bracing wind, a line of sweat beads had popped up on my forehead.

'Can you manage, lass?' my uncle shouted over his shoulder.

'Sure,' I panted, swapping the cool box to the other arm. The ground suddenly fell from under me.

'Arrghhhh!' I screamed, dropping to my knees and splashing into a deep puddle. I immediately lifted my arms to save the ice cream, fell forward and bashed my lips on the cool box. 'Owwwch.'

I could taste blood. My knees stung and my mouth throbbed.

'There's a pothole there,' said Arthur, shining the torch in my face.

The best that could have been said about my arrival at the White Lion with sodden muddy knees, wild hair, a fat lip and mascara tracks left by a couple of escaped tears was that at least I made an entrance.

The pub was heaving with people, all available space was filled with jostling bodies, and there was a line of customers at the bar.

'Emergency!' I cried, pushing my way to the front of the queue with my cool box. I could see Lizzie pulling two pints at a time behind the bar.

'Brandy for shock, please, Bill!' shouted Uncle Arthur, pressing his good hand into the small of my back to propel me forward. 'Coming through!' he added with too much enjoyment at all the drama for my liking.

'Arthur!' called a squat bald man in a polo-neck jumper, wearing one black and one green wellington. 'Heard you had a brush with death yesterday. Let me get you a pint.'

The hand fell away from my back and my uncle was gone.

'Bleedin' Nora.' Lizzie relieved me of the cool box and handed me a bar towel to wipe my face and dab at my knees. A brandy appeared on the bar. I smiled my thanks at Bill, the landlord, a balding man in a very snazzy waistcoat, and swigged at the glass. I squeezed my eyes shut as the fiery liquid burned the back of my throat. My lips felt bee-stung and not in a good way. I swiped at a bit of dribble.

That was better, sort of. I took a deep breath and a second mouthful.

'Oi, there is a queue, you know,' a voice chuckled in my ear, mimicking my stroppy outburst from the bridle path earlier this afternoon.

I swallowed the brandy and whirled round to locate the source of the jibe. A man, elbowing a path away from the bar while balancing three pint glasses in his hands, turned back and winked at me. I gasped for air and a hand flew to my mouth. Was that . . . ? It must be. It was. Harry from Willow Farm. And it must have been him on the phone shouting away at the top of the hill.

Wow! I almost didn't recognize him. He hadn't changed a bit. That didn't make sense. He was bigger. Obviously.

And older. Duh! My heart was thumping. What was it – ten years? It must be. Ten years since I'd seen him. Blimey, where had the time gone? Same cheeky smile, though. Fancy that.

I watched him until his broad shoulders became swallowed up by a noisy crowd of men.

Harry Graythwaite. My neighbour, my mate, my partner in crime – through my tomboy phase, through my teenage years, every school holiday I spent on the farm. Until I was eighteen and we'd gone our separate ways.

Bloody hell, it was good to see him. He looked . . . well . . . great. I should go and say hello properly. Apologize for my manners earlier . . .

I set my brandy glass down on the bar and surveyed the wet patches on my knees. Maybe not tonight. I might not be the most preeniest of girls, but I did have some standards.

'Er, hello!' Lizzie was grinning at me, arms folded, head cocked to one side. 'I thought you said you were spoken for.'

I turned back to the bar and giggled. 'Sorry, Lizzie. Had a bit of a shock.'

Understatement. I didn't know which was worse, falling over on the way to the pub or bumping into Harry again looking like a bedraggled wasp.

'I can see that. Now, do you want a proper drink?'

'Yes. Cider, please.'

I pulled my phone out of my handbag while I waited for her to come back with my drink. No signal here, either. How did people cope, I wondered, not being able to talk to their other halves? My stomach flipped.

Like Charlie.

I hadn't spoken to him since arriving at the train

63

station last night. I should have phoned him from Knots Hill earlier. He'd be thinking about me. I hoped. I'd been thinking about him, too, in between everything else that had gone on today. I made a mental note to call him from the farm's landline and slipped my phone away.

'Get your chops round that.' Lizzie placed a pint of cider in front of me. I sidled round to where it was quieter at the glass collection end of the bar and Lizzie followed me down. 'So, tell me about this fella of yours, then.'

Tonight she was wearing a cropped cotton top decorated with white and yellow daisies, her hair was arranged in loose curls and her lips shone with a soft pink gloss. She looked like the Goddess of Spring. I was surprised she'd even consort with me, looking as dishevelled as I did. But I was glad of her company and began to tell her about Charlie – how we met and my job and his allotment. I chatted away for some minutes but couldn't help noticing that she kept glancing over my shoulder. Finally, I could take it no more and turned round to see what was catching her eye.

'Don't look,' she hissed.

'What at?'

'I'll be back in a sec,' she replied, nodding at a woman who was waving an empty wine glass at her.

Just as she returned, Uncle Arthur appeared at my shoulder, holding a full pint.

I frowned at him. 'What are you drinking, Uncle Arthur?' That wasn't his first pint. He was swaying and his eyes were slightly crossed.

'Not for me, lass, thank you.' He lifted his pint to toast Lizzie and me, and took a long slurp.

'So what brings you to Lovedale, Lizzie? Ha,' he chortled into his glass, 'Lovedale Lizzie. Sounds like a boat.' He raised his glass again. 'God bless Lovedale Lizzie and all who sail in her!'

Lizzie and I exchanged amused looks. Actually, mine was more worried than amused. I was going to be in so much trouble with Auntie Sue if I brought the invalid home roaring drunk.

Lizzie started pouring a pint of Guinness, ripped a bag of peanuts off the card strip next to the optics and popped the lids off two bottles of beer pretty much all at the same time before answering.

'I'm from Ambleside. Split up with my boyfriend just after Christmas. Irreconcilable differences.' She smiled a sad smile. 'Three pounds fifty, please,' she added to a youth who didn't look old enough to be drinking lager.

'What do you mean?' I took a sip of my cider and pressed Uncle Arthur's arm back down to the bar as he tried to gulp at his pint. 'Slow down! I had enough trouble negotiating the lane on the way here without having to carry you back up it.'

He shrugged me off and took a deliberately long drink.

'I couldn't take it any more,' said Lizzie. She held her little finger in front of our faces and waggled it. Uncle Arthur choked on his pint.

'Oh!' I said, not knowing quite how to respond to that. I banged my uncle on his back.

'Pinky ring. To start with. I let that one go. Then it got worse. Choker chains, dog tags . . . A man shouldn't wear more jewellery than his girlfriend, should he?'

Uncle Arthur's mouth fell open. I shook my head.

'When he bought a bracelet with snake heads on it, enough was enough. So I dumped him and moved to Lovedale where I intend to marry a farmer and ride my horse all day long. Farmers don't wear jewellery.' She folded her arms and I caught her darting a glance at Uncle Arthur's hands and neck. Unsurprisingly, he was not bejewelled.

'Oh my God, oh my God, he's coming.' Lizzie tossed her hair over her right shoulder and then again over her left. 'Act natural.'

I began to turn round but Lizzie shook her head frantically. 'Don't look,' she hissed.

'I'm off to join the lads,' said Uncle Arthur, spotting a gap in the conversation.

'Hi, Ross, what can I get you? Same again?' purred Lizzie.

Ross nodded. He was tall and slim with sandy hair, long pale eyelashes and high cheekbones. He held out his glass to Lizzie: rough hands, dirt ingrained into scrubbed fingernails. No jewellery. Not beefy enough for my tastes, but he had a friendly face and Lizzie was clearly besotted.

'Are you a farmer, Ross?' I asked after introductions had been made. Lizzie simpered over the Windermere Pale Ale pump and batted her eyelashes at him.

'Not yet, but that's the plan.' Ross flashed a shy smile at me. 'I'm studying for a degree in agriculture at the moment. And then I'm hoping to invest in my own farm. I'm a mature student, before you ask, but I've had to take a year out after a family bereavement. I'm the only one left now . . .'

Lizzie arrived back with his pint and pressed a hand to her chest. 'Poor lamb.'

Ross flushed and quickly dipped his face into his glass.

He was such a sweetie; I could see why Lizzie was smitten. And how awful to lose his parents so young.

'I'm so sorry to hear that. You must have had a lot to deal with,' I said softly, pretending not to notice his blushes.

He nodded. 'Thanks. I've had to sort out my mum's will

66

and stuff. The university has kept my place open so I can start again in September to do my final year. Most of the house clearing and legal stuff is done now, though, so I'm spending far too much time in the pub these days.'

'Lucky us,' said Lizzie, tossing her hair again.

Ross cleared his throat. 'I'll be honest, my mates, this pub, that's what's got me through the last few months. But now I'm ready to do something. Get some practical farm experience.'

'So . . .' I glanced over my shoulder to where Uncle Arthur was sitting in the middle of a group of men, slapping his thigh appreciatively and guffawing at some joke or other. 'You could say you're at a loose end for a while?'

Ross nodded and slurped his ale. My brain was whirring like billy-o. It could work. It could be absolutely amazing. I pulled Eddy's list out of my handbag and handed it to Ross. 'Do you know how to do this lot?'

Ross put down his glass and scanned the list, frowning with concentration. Lizzie was darting me curious what's-going-on looks and I tipped her a teeny wink.

'Shouldn't be a problem,' said Ross. 'Although I might need a bit of guidance on some of it. Why?'

Out of the corner of my eye, I saw Uncle Arthur stagger to his feet. Offering guidance to a young would-be farmer was right up my uncle's street. It would keep him occupied and out of mischief at the same time. There was just one potential sticking point . . .

I took a deep breath. If you don't ask you don't get, right? 'What would you say to some unpaid work experience at Appleby Farm until you go back to uni?'

Ross opened his eyes wide, Lizzie squealed and clapped her hands, and Uncle Arthur stumbled up to the bar, squeezed himself in between me and Ross and burped.

'Pardon me.' He stared up at Ross, bleary-eyed. 'Who's this, then?'

'I'm your new apprentice, sir,' said Ross, extending a hand to Uncle Arthur. 'If you'll have me.'

Chapter 7

The following Monday was a bank holiday. Unfortunately cows don't appreciate the rare opportunity for a day off so it was business as usual at Appleby Farm. It was also Ross's first day. After a hearty breakfast of sausage sandwiches cooked by me (a bit black on the outside but nothing that a dollop of brown sauce couldn't cover up) it was smiley faces all round as the farm's vast staff assembled in Uncle Arthur's tiny office to receive orders. I say 'vast staff' because everything is relative and with the addition of Ross, me and Lizzie (it was her day off and apparently she had nothing to do except make huge doe-eyes behind Ross's back) to the workforce of one – i.e. Eddy – that was an increase of 300 per cent.

Auntie Sue had been so delighted about the news that Ross was joining the team that she forgot to be cross with her husband for drinking too much when I'd finally poured him back into the farmhouse after eleven o'clock on Friday night. And she was still smiling three days later.

At that moment Benny and Madge, as if wanting to be considered part of the team, trotted through the door. Benny immediately slalomed his body around everyone's legs and Madge, who was licking her lips suspiciously, slunk under the desk to lie on Uncle Arthur's feet.

'It's like old times, isn't it, Arthur?' Auntie Sue beamed from her position behind her husband's chair with her arm around his shoulders. 'With all these people in here.' I felt a wave of love for them. Such a great team, the pair of them. They didn't have much, but they had each other.

Like I had Charlie.

My face broke into a grin that I just couldn't wipe off.

I'd spoken to him last night. And after he'd told me about him and Ollie having a great time at the annual Ivy Lane Easter egg hunt and I'd told him about the cow that had had trouble calving on Saturday but was OK now and we'd declared that we missed each other, something marvellous happened. At the very same moment, just after a tiny pause in our news, we both said those magical three words. The words that change a relationship from being a bit of fun into something special.

I love you.

And I did. I loved him and even though the Cumbrian landscape and the nose-achingly fresh air and the fickle weather made my heart sing with exquisite pleasure, I couldn't wait – *could not wait* – to get home to my boy.

And in forty-eight hours I would do just that.

In the meantime, I had chores to do. I tuned back in to Uncle Arthur's rundown of the day and tried to keep my contented sigh to myself.

'Can you get on with fertilizing some of the grassland, seeing as we've had it dry for a day or two?' he asked Eddy.

Eddy nodded. He was swivelling round in the ancient office chair opposite the desk and slurping at the third mug of tea I'd seen him drink since breakfast. Probably trying to wash down the carbon-coated sausages.

'Want me to take the young-un out with me?' he asked.

Young-un was Ross. Eddy had admitted that he was pleased to have extra help, although I did catch him muttering that he wasn't going to play nursemaid to a wet-behind-the-ears student. But I took the fact that he was requesting the pleasure of Ross's company on the tractor as a good sign.

'Not till this afternoon,' replied Uncle Arthur. He was pretending not to be enjoying himself, having a bigger team to organize. But he wasn't fooling me. There was a spark back in his eyes and more energy in his movements. Having a young man about the place was better than any dose of medicine. 'First I want him to check on the calves with me. How do you fancy learning how to worm a herd of cows, lad?'

'Smashing.' Ross nodded, folding his arms across his chest. I smothered a giggle. If that wasn't proof of a serious intention to become a farmer, I didn't know what was. 'I'd love that. Tha—' He closed his mouth just in time.

Ross hadn't stopped thanking everyone this morning until Uncle Arthur had told him to 'put a sock in it'. And he looked every inch the farmer in his navy overalls and boots.

Lizzie looped her arm through mine and mouthed 'bless him' at me. Another one who couldn't wipe the glee from her face.

Ross could only stay until September when he was due back at university, so it wasn't a long-term solution, but for now, it gave the farm some much-needed breathing space. And I felt a huge sense of relief knowing that when I went back to Kingsfield, Uncle Arthur wouldn't be overdoing it all summer.

'I'm off to tackle that veggie patch near the orchard,' said Auntie Sue, pulling a pair of secateurs from her apron pocket. 'I haven't even cut my raspberry canes back yet. At this rate my home-grown raspberry-ripple ice cream won't be home-grown, it'll be via Sainsbury's.'

'And Lizzie and I are making an honesty box to put down on Lovedale Lane,' I said, zipping up my jacket. Auntie Sue had more eggs than she could sell on, so I'd come up with the idea of turning an old henhouse into a road-side help-yourself shop. Plenty of cars came past the farm entrance and this would be a chance to make a bit of extra cash and sell our surplus produce.

'Right, see you back at dinner.' Uncle Arthur slapped his hands on the desk and we all dispersed.

Lizzie and I grunted and heaved as we wheeled the disused henhouse out of the shed and into the yard. It was tiny compared to the one Auntie Sue used now and worked like a big wheelbarrow with two large rusty wheels underneath, a wooden strut to help it stand upright and double doors at the front, which would open up to make our little shop.

'Let's set up it at the edge of the orchard,' Lizzie suggested breathlessly, steering us along past the barn.

'But here is so much closer to the tap,' I panted. And the orchard was completely impractical to work in.

'Come on,' said Lizzie, putting her back into it with grim determination. 'It's got a lovely view and we get to smell the apple blossom while we work.'

At the edge of the orchard I flopped down on to the grass, exhausted. She was right; the white and pink apple blossom flowers had a lovely delicate scent. In front of us was Calf's Close, the field where Uncle Arthur was currently weaving in and out of his herd with an attentive Ross at his side.

'See,' giggled Lizzie, collapsing beside me. 'I told you the view was great.'

*

The first job was the worst: scraping off several years' worth of chicken poo. For the next half an hour we distracted ourselves with a game of 'would you rather . . .' in which we tested each other's preferences for random things. We found to our delight that we shared a love for Harry Potter and cinnamon on cappuccino but clashed over Brussels sprouts (I could eat them by the plateful).

'Sorry,' Lizzie declared finally. She held up a hand and made a choking noise. 'But I'm not choosing between gherkins and pickled onions. Neither should be fed to humans.' She screwed up her nose. 'Nor animals, come to that.'

'Ha!' I dropped my disinfectant spray on the floor and threw my arms round her neck. 'You passed my friend test, Lizzie, because that one was a red herring. I'm with you there one hundred per cent. Ooh, you're buzzing.'

I stood back to let her retrieve her phone from her bra. 'No pockets,' she giggled, followed by a grimace, eye-roll and stab at the phone.

'Victoria,' she said, her face losing its customary warmth. 'What do you want?' This last uttered in a flat, un-Lizzie-like tone.

I raised my eyebrows but she just frowned, so I left her to it and wandered back into the yard to wash my hands. Odd that she'd got mobile phone reception in the yard. Must remember that. I was just contemplating popping into the kitchen to stick the kettle on, when Eddy arrived in the yard on the tractor, pulling the fertilizing unit behind it.

'Dinner time already?' I called as Eddy got closer.

'No, your uncle's radioed me over,' Eddy shouted above the fut-fut-fut of the tractor engine. 'He's here, look.'

73

I turned to see Uncle Arthur and Ross, both of them with hands wedged in pockets, striding towards us.

'Crofters Field was looking a bit churned up,' said Eddy, jumping down off the tractor. 'So I've moved the cows to Oak Field. That OK, Arthur?'

'Ay.' Uncle Arthur pushed up his cap and scratched his forehead. The stitches were starting to pull and it was driving him crazy. 'Ground's heavy up there after last week's rain.'

'What's up, then?' said Eddy. 'I've only done half of one field.'

'Come and take a look at this calf.'

'Problem?' I said, traipsing behind the men as we headed back to Calf's Close.

'One of the calves isn't doing too well,' said Uncle Arthur. 'Her ears are back and judging by the mother's full udders, she's not feeding.'

'I spotted it,' added Ross proudly.

'Well, that has ruined my day,' Lizzie said with a scowl as she fell into step beside me. 'Ruined it. Where we going, by the way?'

'Calf's Close to see a poorly cow,' I said, linking my arm through hers. 'What has ruined your day and who's Victoria?'

'My older sister. She's only sodding-well moving back to The Lakes from Liverpool. I thought I'd got rid of her once she got a job on Liver FM. Honestly,' Lizzie huffed, 'she's got a mean streak longer than Lake Windermere, that one. If she was here now, she'd try to steal you off me.'

I felt a rush of warmth for my lovely new friend and her unexpected insecurity. 'She wouldn't, would she?'

She widened her eyes. 'Yep.' *And him*, she mouthed, nodding at Ross. 'Even if she didn't fancy him herself, she'd flirt with him just to scupper my chances.'

'Is this the one with a pony called Star?'

Lizzie's face softened. 'No, that's Poppy. She's only twelve. I love her to bits.'

I did a rough sum. Lizzie was twenty-five. Not quite as big an age gap as Julian and I but a completely different relationship by the sound of it. 'Twelve! I bet your mum was shocked when she found out she was pregnant again.' Mine certainly had been, by all accounts.

'Hardly,' said Lizzie, pulling an as-if face. 'She idolizes that child. Calls her her precious miracle.'

Precious miracle.

I too was an unplanned baby who had turned up late in my mum's life. How different would my life have been if my mother had cherished me like that? I wondered.

'But your dad,' I probed, determined to find a chink in their armour of perfect parenting, 'I guess he'd thought the days of nappies and no sleep were well behind him?'

She puffed out her cheeks. 'He didn't mind. All my dad says when somebody points that out is that nine months before Poppy's surprise arrival was "one bloody good weekend". Parents.' She tutted in disgust.

I thought her dad sounded fun. But perhaps other people's families always sound more fun than your own.

'Anyway,' Lizzie sighed, 'the point is that Victoria will be back in The Lakes in one month's time to start a new job as a radio presenter on Radio Lakeland and she'll try to muscle in on my life. Again.'

'I won't let her. Promise,' I said, giving her arm a squeeze.

Lizzie and I followed them as far as the gate. Ross closed the gate behind them and as soon as the older men were out of earshot, he blinked furiously at Lizzie and turned crimson. 'Don't suppose you fancy going for a drink tonight, do you?'

In a flash she jumped up on to the bottom bar of the gate, grabbed Ross's face and kissed him noisily on the lips.

'Is that a yes, then?' he gasped.

'Yes!' Lizzie squealed, making thirty Hereford cows and their calves leap into the air.

Day not entirely ruined then.

Almost before I knew it, my five days in Lovedale were up. It was weird, I thought, as I bumped my rucksack down the stairs on my last morning, I wanted to stay, but I was ready to leave, too. My stomach felt jittery and a lump kept rising in my throat. I felt as if I were homesick for both places at once: Kingsfield where Charlie and my job were, and the farm where I felt needed and so at home.

Lizzie and I had finished the honesty box and now it sat at the entrance to the farm with its hand-painted sign, proudly displaying Appleby Farm's wares. Only free-range eggs at the moment, but soon there would be fruit and vegetables from Auntie Sue's veggie patch and apples by the tonne in autumn. We had made ten pounds on the first day alone!

The last two days had flashed by in a busy blur as new life seemed to spring up from all quarters around the farm, from chicks hatching, now sunning themselves under a heat lamp in the barn, to the last and final calf being born to Auntie Sue's beloved Jersey cow, Gaynor. Lizzie and I had been tasked with naming both the Jersey calves and had come up with Kim and Kanye, which went over Auntie Sue's head but gave us hours of amusement. The barley was shooting up in Bottom Field, the grass was flourishing after a couple of days of unbroken sunshine and, of course – hot news – there was a new romance blooming between Ross and Lizzie.

As much as I was going to miss being part of the family

at Appleby Farm, seeing the two of them together had made me miss Charlie even more. He would be working an early shift when my train arrived back into Kingsfield, so I'd have to wait until the evening to show him exactly how much. And I planned to leave him in no doubt about my feelings on the matter.

'It'll be quiet without you, lass,' sighed Auntie Sue as I entered the kitchen. She was packing a cake, jam, a still-warm loaf, half a dozen eggs and some leftover hotpot into plastic tubs for me to take back with me. Uncle Arthur sat at the table reading *Farmer's Weekly* magazine.

I wrapped my arms around her waist and kissed her plump cheek. 'I'll come back very soon, I promise. With Charlie, hopefully.' I crossed my fingers.

'Make sure you do,' said Uncle Arthur. 'You've been a breath of fresh air for us, hasn't she, Sue?'

'I've loved it,' I said, swallowing that pesky lump that had returned to my throat. I walked over to him and peered over his shoulder. 'Is that calf all right now?'

The little calf who hadn't been feeding had needed a vet's visit. Lizzie and I had been hoping we'd have to bring her in and bottle feed her back to health, but the less intervention the better, Ross had informed us, and he seemed to know what he was talking about.

'Yes, love, she's brighter today and she's feeding now. The cow's a good mother, she'll be fine.'

'Good.' I was going to miss all this – the cows and the hens, these two lovely people, Lizzie . . .

I pressed my face against my uncle's bristly cheek. 'Take care of yourself,' I said, kissing him tenderly. 'And go easy on the beer, OK?'

There was a knock at the door and Madge and I fell over each other to answer it. Madge, because she had a vendetta against the postman for some reason and me, because I was expecting Eddy to arrive any second to take me to the station.

Madge won. I scooped her up with some difficulty and opened the door. The postman, a thin and unsurprisingly nervous man wearing shorts and a woolly hat, held out a letter. Out of the corner of my eye I saw Eddy's van pull into the yard. My heart bounced. Time to go.

'Recorded delivery,' said the postman. 'Needs signing for.'

'I'll sign!' Auntie Sue bustled over, tutting affectionately at the writhing dog I was doing my best to hold on to.

Both of us saw the official-looking red stamp on the envelope at the same time. Auntie Sue bundled the postman and his letter outside on to the step and I dropped the dog to the floor.

Ten seconds later, she came back in.

'Auntie Sue?'

She flashed me a silencing stare and darted off towards the office. 'Forget you saw that,' she said quietly over her shoulder.

FINAL NOTICE in large red letters wasn't that easy to forget. And the fact that she *wanted* me to forget hardly put my mind at rest. I frowned and opened my mouth to say something but the front door flew open again and Eddy's face appeared.

'Make haste, lass, or you'll miss this train!'

Chapter 8

Anna was waiting for me outside the station in Kingsfield as planned. She wrinkled up her nose as I climbed into the passenger seat of her Mini Cooper and gave her a hug.

'Poo! You stink,' she laughed, extracting herself from my arms and turning on the engine.

I scooped up the ends of my hair and sniffed it. 'Of what?'

'Well, not to put too fine a point on it, animal poop.' Anna put the car into reverse, pulled out of the parking spot and accelerated away rather quickly.

'Oops. Soz about that.' I looked down at my boots, which were pretty disgusting. And the little mats in her car were immaculate, or had been at any rate. 'That could be cow pat, chicken poo or horse manure.'

Anna grinned at me. 'It has been so boring without you.'

On the surface, Anna and I were unlikely mates. I was outgoing and she was not. She was neat and orderly and I was not. If she were one of my uncle's herd, she'd be the timid one, the one most likely to hang back and miss out on all the food, whereas I'd be the troublemaker, the one encouraging the rest of the herd to join me on the rampage, breaking for freedom at the earliest opportunity.

We met at a music festival a few years ago. The girl I had

gone with had had to go to the first-aid tent after only a few hours, suffering from sunstroke. Her parents had come to collect her, leaving me on my own. As luck would have it, Anna had pitched up next to my spot on the campsite, only to realize she'd left her tent poles at home. I'd offered her room in my little pop-up thing and we'd been friends ever since.

The Mini hurtled round a corner and I grabbed on to her shoulder as I was flung towards her.

'Sorry.' She grimaced. 'In a bit of a rush. I'm on a deadline and I've fallen behind.'

'Really? That's not like you.' I studied her out of the corner of my eye. Was it my imagination or did she look a bit shifty? 'What are you working on at the moment?'

'A new website for tickle my fancy dot com.'

I snorted with laughter. 'You're kidding, tell me more!'

I love hearing about Anna's business. She specializes in creating websites for the nichiest of niches in the online dating world and has come up with some corkers since I'd been living with her.

Anna flicked a grin at me and put her foot down to get across the traffic lights before they changed to red. 'It's for women who love men with facial hair.'

The two of us burst out laughing. I'd stopped being surprised by the weird and wonderful dating websites that Anna told me about. I mean, for example, who would have thought there would be a niche for those whose overriding criteria in finding a mate was a shared passion for the ukulele?

Anna is probably singlehandedly responsible for more romantic couplings than any other person on the planet. Ironic really, I mused, surveying her pretty face; she'd been single for two years.

'So when are you going to sort out a date for yourself?' I asked, quirking an eyebrow her way.

'I'm working on that next, as it happens,' she giggled.

'Seriously?' I turned my shoulders round to face her properly.

'Yep. Kingsfield curves dot com,' she smirked. 'For men looking for boring homebirds with big bums.'

'Anna!' I folded my arms and tutted. 'There's nothing wrong with loving where you live. And you are neither boring nor in possession of a big bum. I'd love to have curves like you.'

'Urghh, child-bearing hips, you mean.' She shuddered. 'Not that I intend to bear any children, suitable hips or not, ta very much.'

I rolled my eyes and patted her on the head. 'Sure,' I said, earning myself a frown from my housemate.

In my experience career girls always declared that. Until the right man came along and they changed their minds. Anna had a lovely figure, more curvaceous than mine. Not that she was a chubster, she was just soft and more feminine and had boobs that met in the middle. I, on the other hand, could be mistaken for a teenage boy from a distance.

She steered the car round a corner, more slowly this time, and brought her hands back to a perfect ten-to-two position on the steering wheel. Anna always sits completely straight-backed when she drives. Not that I'm a careless driver, but my own particular set of wheels is a sky-blue VW camper-van and when you drive it (or him, I should say: he's called Bobby) you just sort of naturally relax. Every journey in him has the potential for adventure, rather than being simply a means of getting from A to B. Anna's car was smart, reliable and efficient; Bobby couldn't boast any of those attributes, but he was a real head-turner and I adored him.

'Charlie came round last night, by the way.'

Anna's words roused me from my reverie. I blinked at her but she was staring ahead and concentrating on the road.

'Did he?' My voice came out a little sharper than I'd intended. 'Why?' I added, more gently.

Anna flicked her honey-coloured hair from her face. 'Wanted to check what time you'd be back, he said.'

He knew that. I'd phoned to let him know yesterday.

My silence must have worried Anna because she reached across and squeezed my arm.

'Hey, he was just lonely. He missed you, Freya. A lot. He talked about you non-stop and I think he felt bad about upsetting you before you left.'

I nodded. Of course that was the reason he'd been round and it was so sweet that he'd been pining for me. 'Thanks, Anna,' I said with a smile.

We pulled up into a space behind Bobby outside Anna's terraced house and she cut the engine.

'Home sweet home,' she said with a contented sigh.

After stashing all of Auntie Sue's goodies in the kitchen and unpacking my rucksack, I took a long, hot shower. Whilst I was amused by Anna greeting me with 'poo, you stink', I didn't want Charlie to do the same. Actually, I was quite attached to the aroma of the farmyard but nothing said passion killer quite like Eau de Cowpat and I didn't want anything to spoil our reunion.

Thirty minutes later, I was scrubbed, shampooed and shaved in all the right places and wrapped in a towel in front of my bedroom mirror.

I was tugging a super-sized comb through my tangled locks when Anna appeared in the doorway.

'Wow, your hair's grown long,' she whistled, folding her arms and leaning on the door frame. Her own hair was cut into soft layers framing her face and finished at her shoulders. Annoyingly she didn't even have to do anything fancy to it, like daily blow drying or straightening or curling. A brisk rub with the towel and it just seemed to behave itself.

'Do you remember those Play-Doh hair studios, where the hair sort of erupted out of the plastic heads like volcanoes?' said Anna, miming a hair eruption with her hands.

'Yes, a volcano!' I laughed as I fought to release my hair from the comb. 'That is exactly what this looks like!'

'A gorgeous fiery volcano, in your case,' she added, sighing wistfully. 'I don't think mine would grow that long if I wanted it to.'

'I've always had long hair,' I said with a shrug and inspected the ends for splits.

'Anyway. I'll leave you to it.' She wandered off into her own room.

I distinctly remember the moment I vowed to always have long hair. It was during a rare trip to see my parents at their house in Sydney, Australia. I was floating in the pool on an inflatable lilo. Julian was there too, on holiday from work.

'What would you like for your fourteenth birthday, Freya?' asked my mum, carrying a tray of drinks out to the poolside.

I knew my parents would spend a fortune on me if I wanted them to. But even at that age, I was unimpressed by wealth and the way they thought that they could flash their cash in my direction and I would forgive them for sending me to England and forgetting about me for ninety per cent of the time.

'A boyfriend,' I'd replied slyly. Partly because I knew it would provoke a reaction from my dad, who was sitting under a parasol working – always working – and partly because it was true. All the girls in my class had boyfriends – real or imagined, I wasn't sure. It was hard to tell at an all-girls boarding school.

My father had lowered his sunglasses briefly and looked at me over the top of them. 'Perhaps you'll have more luck next year,' he'd said, returning to his financial report, 'when you look less like a boy yourself.'

I'd slipped off the lilo and into the water to hide my burning face and when my lungs couldn't last any longer I came up for breath to find my mother holding a towel out for me.

Julian, despite being nearly thirty, still apparently felt the need to compound my humiliation.

'One–nil to Dad, I think, sis,' he chortled.

So that was it. Cue long hair, vest tops with hidden support and a pair of those flobbery bra-stuffers. I seem to remember Harry Graythwaite going red the next time I saw him. So at least somebody noticed.

Dropping the comb on my dressing table, I opened my single pine wardrobe and rummaged inside for something girly to wear. An outfit that said 'take me off', preferably. My lips tweaked into a smile. Could I ask Anna to disappear for an hour when Charlie arrived or was that too rude? Not to mention too obvious.

I was just pulling my arms into on an off-the-shoulder soft green jumper to go with my denim skirt when Anna called to me.

'Charlie's here.'

'Eek, I'm not dressed yet!' I squeaked.

I stuck my head through the neck of the jumper, dived to

the doorway but Anna rushed past me and clattered down the stairs.

'I'll open the door for him. Then I'm off to my mum's. See you later.'

'Thanks, Anna!'

She was a fab friend, I thought, as I dashed down the stairs a few seconds behind her. The front door was wide open, Anna had gone but Charlie hadn't yet appeared. And then suddenly there he was, with a bottle of wine in one hand and a bunch of pink tulips in the other.

I launched myself at him, jumping up and wrapping my legs around his waist, covering his face with kisses.

'Whoa!' he laughed, desperately trying to hold on to me, the flowers and the wine all at the same time.

'Charlie! I've missed you so much!'

'Me too. Welcome home, gorgeous girl.'

He carried me in and kicked the door shut behind us.

'Into the kitchen first,' I demanded with a giggle, 'for glasses and a vase for those lovely flowers.'

Charlie poured the wine while I arranged the tulips, though it took me longer than normal because I kept stealing glances at him; it was so lovely to see him. And when his eyes caught mine my heartbeat almost doubled.

He stepped close to me and handed me a glass.

'I know we haven't been together very long,' he said, tucking a strand of my still-damp hair behind my ear, 'but life's so much brighter when you're around. Does that sound really cheesy?'

I shook my head and swallowed the lump in my throat. We'd always had such a playful relationship and serious moments between us like this one were rare. Sometimes he almost felt like a big brother. A nice one, obviously, not like Julian.

'No, Charlie. It's not cheesy at all.'

'To us.' He touched the edge of my glass gently with his and we both sipped at our wine.

It was cold and delicious, and luckily gave me back the power of speech.

'On the phone, you said we could perhaps have a day out, you, me and Ollie. Did you mean it?'

Charlie grinned. 'If you think you can handle it. He's a bit full on.'

I nodded, a huge smile plastered across my face.

'How about Sunday?' he suggested.

'Perfect! We could go out in Bobby, have an adventure.' I started planning it in my head. We could have a picnic, go to a zoo, where was the nearest zoo . . . ?

'He'd love that.' Charlie smiled and reached for my glass. He set it down and pulled me close so that I could feel the warmth of his body through his shirt.

'Mmm,' he said, placing slow, soft kisses in the hollow above my collarbone, making me shiver. 'You smell divine.'

Mission accomplished in that department.

I pulled his face up to mine and traced his lips with my fingertip as I gazed into his eyes.

He was mine and I loved him.

'Exactly how much have you missed me?' he murmured.

I looped my arms around his neck.

'This much,' I said, covering my mouth with his.

Chapter 9

The day out with Charlie and Ollie dawned. Very early, in my case. I'd been awake since sunrise (six a.m. approximately) worrying about our interview, I mean our excursion, and I had been giving myself little pep-talks ever since. Like, for instance: *For goodness' sake, Freya, it's a day out with a small boy, not a grilling by Lord Sugar.*

But what do you even say to a six-year-old boy?

Although I'd moaned about it (privately) at the time, meeting Ollie at the café had actually been a good idea. Asking if he wanted a straw for his banana smoothie was an awful lot less complicated than . . . well, whatever I managed to conjure up today in the way of conversational gambits.

Sweets, the coward's way out, I thought, as I stuffed packets of popping candy into one of the campervan's narrow cupboards. If all else fails, we could bond over E-numbers.

But what if he's not allowed sweets? Or what if he goes home and tells his mum that I fed him junk food all day? My stomach lurched and I dashed back inside, grabbed a bag of apples and a tub of raisins, and stuffed them in behind the sweets.

OK. I was ready.

One last look in the rear-view mirror to check I didn't have toothpaste on my chin and I set off on the short journey across Kingsfield to pick up Charlie and Ollie. I hoped my outfit was OK. I'd plumped for jeans, my Converses and a hoody. And yes, I had looked like a teenage boy when I stood back to check out the ensemble in my mirror, so I'd added a push-up bra. Then took it off again as it seemed inappropriate. And put it back on again on the basis that Ollie was six and therefore more likely to be interested in the popping candy than my sideways profile.

Bloody hell, I was nervous. My hands kept slipping on the leather cover round the steering wheel.

Much as I loved my campervan, it was too long to park in a normal-sized space and the steering was heavy too, so by the time I pulled up outside Charlie's block of flats, diagonally to the kerb, I was perspiring with exertion as well as nerves.

The entrance door to the flats flew open and Charlie and Ollie appeared. My heart melted at the sight of them: the broad handsome daddy, holding hands with a small blond-haired boy, who was waving and bouncing on his toes as he came down the path towards me.

I waved back madly, a grin – albeit a slightly hysterical one – stretching from ear to ear.

This was it.

I exhaled and inhaled yoga-style as they approached. If Charlie really was The One, then today really mattered. Today I was being auditioned for the role of Stepmum. Charlie and Ollie came as a package and I was under no illusion: if I failed to pass muster with Ollie, it could well be curtains for the story of Freya and Charlie.

'Cool!' marvelled Ollie, with big wide eyes as I opened

up the pair of rear doors to let him see inside. He slipped into one of the little seats and rested his elbows on the table. 'Do you live in here?'

'No,' I laughed, kissing Charlie's cheek and feeling relieved that he didn't flinch under his son's watchful gaze. 'I live in a normal house. Very boring, sorry.'

Ollie jumped up and started opening cupboards. 'I'd live in it if it was mine. Is there a bathroom?' he asked, peering up to the far end.

I shook my head. He was adorable. 'No. Kitchen sink, yes, but bathroom, no.'

He stared at me from under long eyelashes. 'Then I definitely would.'

Charlie laughed, climbed in beside his son and ruffled his hair. 'A shower dodger, aren't you, mate?'

'Freya?' asked Ollie, bounding over to where I was leaning on Bobby's open door.

Eek. I wasn't sure I was prepared for an awkward question so early on in our day. I swallowed. 'Yes?'

'Would you like to wear my Lightning McQueen watch?' he asked solemnly, already unfastening the watch that was shaped like a red sports car.

I could have kissed him. 'I'd love to.'

'Here.' He handed it over ceremoniously. 'It's my most favourite thing.'

Charlie beamed and gave me a thumbs-up sign.

'Thank you,' I murmured, strapping the plastic watch to my wrist. 'Thank you, Ollie.'

'Shall we get going then?' said Charlie and I nodded.

'Can you play Skylanders?' Ollie piped up, to which I pulled a confused face and he rolled his eyes.

'This is a bit like an ice-cream van, isn't it, Freya?' he continued. 'Can we have an ice cream, Dad?'

Charlie's eyes met mine and we burst out laughing. By the time we were strapped into the three front seats I'd relaxed. Today was going to be fun and it looked like I needn't have worried about conversation, Ollie had enough for all of us.

Heaven. I tilted my face to the sunshine and grinned. It felt so good to be here, next to Charlie, his arm pressed against mine. I was not your helpless female type; I didn't need a man to validate my existence or to protect me. I was perfectly capable of looking after myself. I opened one eye and peered at him. But a partner, someone to share life's adventure with, well, I couldn't think of anyone more perfect.

'I thought you might not come back, you know.' Charlie leaned forward and wiped my cheek. 'Ice cream on your face,' he tutted, 'you're as bad as Ollie.'

We were sitting side by side at a picnic bench, watching Ollie tear around a play area made from hay bales with a couple of other boys his age. It had been a beautiful spring day: bright sunshine for the most part, although a few grumpy-looking clouds had begun to assemble now, I noticed. Still, it was almost time to head back.

We'd walked around a castle, rowed across a lake, eaten bacon sandwiches cooked on Bobby's diminutive hob (Ollie had been enthralled at the plastic crockery stowed into the little side cupboards) and demolished the last of Auntie Sue's cake. Now we'd stopped off at a children's playground and petting farm. And even though Charlie and I were still stuffed from lunch, Ollie had persuaded us to have an ice cream.

'When I talked to you on the phone, you sounded, I don't know, so full of the farm,' said Charlie softly. 'Telling me all about the calves, about that horse you'd been riding, that mate of yours, Lizzie . . . I was preparing myself for the worst. I was quite worried.'

'You big softie.' I nudged him in the ribs before biting into my cherry ice cream. 'How could I stay away from you for too long? Besides, I think Shirley would have had something to say if I hadn't turned up to work last week!'

Charlie popped the end of his ice-cream cone into his mouth and gave me a sheepish shrug. Bless him. 'Will they be all right now, your aunt and uncle?'

'Well, Ross has turned out to be a superhero,' I chuckled. Not least to Lizzie, who had texted me daily with the Lovedale news, including all three dates so far with Ross. 'But I worry about them. The farmhouse is lovely but it's a time warp. What if one of them becomes ill? There's no central heating upstairs, the only bathroom is on the middle floor and the stairs are really steep. What if one of them can't get upstairs?' I sighed and let my body slump against his. 'I don't know how to help them, really.'

'Hey,' Charlie pressed his lips to my temple, 'it's good that you care. It says a lot about you. But try not to worry today, OK. Today is about us. You and Ollie and me.'

'I know,' I said, leaning against him. He was right, I supposed. I was worrying about things that might never happen. Although that envelope with 'final notice' stamped across it was still niggling away at me.

'You do understand, don't you?' said Charlie suddenly. 'You understand why I've been cautious about doing this, the three of us? Anyone I bring into Ollie's life has to be special.'

Charlie's eyes searched mine and I found my vision sparkle as my eyes glittered with tears. *Special.* I nodded.

Right on cue, Ollie ran over to us with his arm

outstretched, a long object clutched tightly in his hand, excitement animating every fibre of his body.

'Dad! I think I've found a dinosaur bone.'

I gazed at the pair of them fondly as Charlie oohed and ahhed over Ollie's find. It was a sheep bone. A tibia, probably. I used to find things like that all the time on the farm. My granddad had been a sheep farmer before Uncle Arthur changed to beef when he took over. But I kept my lips sealed – finding a dinosaur bone was a million times more exciting.

'Ooh look, Ollie,' I said as one of the staff strode past with an armful of bottles of milk. 'I think they're about to feed the lambs!'

Ollie tore off to the lamb pen, dinosaur bone abandoned at our feet.

'Come on.' I pulled Charlie to his feet. 'Let's go and watch. If Ollie gets picked to hold a bottle, we can take a photo of him.'

I smiled to myself; that would be a lovely way to end the day.

We strolled towards the animal pens, hand in hand, me still finishing my ice cream.

The animal handler had climbed into the pen and the lambs were bleating and jumping up at his legs. 'Now, who would like to feed a lamb?' the young man asked the assembled group of kids, whose hands shot up instantly.

There weren't enough bottles to go round and the lad seemed to dither between Ollie and a little girl, unsure how to proceed without generating a fight or waterworks, or both.

'It's all right,' said Ollie bravely, 'this little girl can feed the lamb. I've already been on an adventure in Bobby and found a dinosaur bone.'

I couldn't look at Charlie. My eyes filled with tears. Talk about proud, and he wasn't even mine.

'I know I'm biased, but he's a great kid,' Charlie whispered gruffly.

'You're allowed to be biased, he's adorable,' I said, wiping my fingers on a napkin and sneakily dabbing my eyes. 'That ice cream was delicious but I don't think I'll need to eat again for a week.'

'Mmm,' said Charlie, pulling me in for a kiss, 'your lips are freezing, but yes, I agree, delicious.'

'Anyway,' I shot him a sideways glance, 'I'll be the same with my babies.'

He blinked at me and scratched his nose.

'Biased, that is,' I added, just to make sure he'd made the connection.

I swallowed and was suddenly aware of my breath rattling in my chest. I'd said it. Put it out there. Broaching the subject of kids hadn't been on my agenda, but standing here, watching Ollie and seeing Charlie's adoring face, gave me a sudden longing for my own family.

And as today seemed to be a tipping point in our relationship, testing his response suddenly seemed important.

I waited. Waited for his expression to change, to become more serious, to gaze at me and make some comment about *our* kids.

'Babies. *Plural,*' he chuckled, removing his arm from round my waist as Ollie came running back, shouting something about ducklings. 'One's quite enough for me. Whoa!' The little boy launched himself at his dad and the two of them collapsed in laughter.

The sun disappeared behind a cloud momentarily and I looked up at the sky.

People change. They do. They definitely change. Some

men even have the snip, they're so adamant that they're not up for fatherhood, only to have it reversed when Mrs Right walks into their life. Fact. I'd seen it on a documentary about childbirth.

I dropped my gaze to the dusty ground as first one fat raindrop, then another and another made dark spots on the dry earth.

'Time to call it a day, I think,' said Charlie. 'Come on, fella, let's get you back to Mummy's.'

The three of us walked back to the campervan, more weary now, as gathering clouds marked the end of our perfect day.

Chapter 10

Lunchtime at our little café was typically a noisy affair and today was no exception; there was only one tiny window table free and Shirley, Becky (the part-timer who did the lunchtime shift while her kids were at school) and I were frothing, chopping and microwaving like nobody's business. Our clientele, as usual, was a mix of mums chatting over lattes and paninis, their offspring banging spoons on highchair trays and catapulting food on passing waitresses (i.e. me), retired couples sharing a sandwich (I always added extra crisps when Shirley wasn't looking), assorted local residents and one or two people from the allotment.

'One leek and bacon jacket potato and a mug of tea.' I grinned at Dougie as I set his order in front of him. He was one of the allotment regulars, an elderly Jamaican with grizzled dreadlocks poking out from beneath a battered sailor's hat. I liked Dougie, who had a twinkle in his eye and a soft spot for Shirley, often bringing her gifts from his plot. She appreciated the vegetables but wasn't so keen on his wandering hands.

He tipped his face up and stared at me. 'You've got some colour in your cheeks today. You been on holiday?'

'My freckles have joined up, you mean?' I laughed,

holding my white arm up against his. 'I've been to my uncle and aunt's farm. I spent all my time outside. I think I'm weather-beaten rather than tanned. Plenty of fresh air, though.'

'Suits you,' said Dougie, turning his attention to his lunch.

'Thanks,' I said, moving away. Fresh air suits everyone, I reckoned.

I tucked my hands in the front pocket of my black apron and looked around me for a second. It was good to be back at the café and quite a relief to be busy. Taking orders, toasting paninis, making coffees . . . It took a surprising amount of skill and timing to keep customers happy. And while I was rushed off my feet, it stopped me thinking about my conversation with Charlie.

I sighed and turned my gaze to the street outside the window.

Surely it must have crossed his mind that I might one day want children, and that saying he categorically didn't want any more would have an on impact on our relationship? Or perhaps men didn't think that way. And perhaps I was over-analysing. I shook myself. I was at it again – thinking.

'Can I get you anything else?' I asked two mums whose latte glasses were empty.

'Actually, I ordered a croissant?' said the taller one with a head of wild, curly black hair.

'Freya!' shouted Shirley. 'Have you left something in the microwave? I can smell burning.'

'Eek! Sorry, yes!' I darted round the back of the counter and yanked open the door of the microwave and stared at the croissant. At least, it had been a croissant; it was now a wizened smoking lump, reminiscent of a piece of leftover bonfire toffee.

'I'll do you a fresh one,' I called to the mum, who smiled and nodded. Shirley planted herself next to me and my shoulders slumped under the weight of her stare.

'Sorry,' I mumbled. 'I'm a bit distracted for some reason.'

Today's big news: the Case of the Caramelized Croissant. It suddenly dawned on me what the problem with this job was: even the biggest dilemma I faced was minuscule in the grand scheme of things. Help, there's no skimmed milk! Oh no, I'm not sure if the coleslaw is gluten-free! Whoops, I've cremated a croissant!

Compare these benign four walls to the 150 acres that Uncle Arthur and Auntie Sue had to shepherd on a daily basis with all the issues that go with it: an unexpected storm damaging crops, a fox getting into the chicken pen and leaving five of Auntie Sue's hens dead and strewn across the grass (which sadly happened while I was there), a poorly calf . . . My job at the café suddenly seemed so trivial.

'TBH, love, you've been distracted since you got back after Easter.' Shirley bent forward to peer into my face.

I puffed out my cheeks. 'I know, I'll snap out of it, I promise.'

'This might cheer you up, look – your friend Tilly has just walked in. I'll do the croissant.'

I was over at Tilly's side in a flash and hugged her tight.

'Hey, you,' she giggled, as I nearly knocked her over with my exuberance. 'I always forget what a ball of energy you are.'

'Well, get you and your suntan!' I stood back and examined her at arm's length. What a transformation from the pale-faced, anxious girl I'd met last winter.

'You *have* to go the Galápagos Islands, that's an order,' said Tilly, sitting down at the only free table and scanning the menu. 'Hi, Dougie!' She waved to her fellow allotmenteer. 'Soup and a roll, please. Ooh and a pot of tea.'

I couldn't help but grin; her happiness was contagious. Whatever she was on, I'd like some, please. 'We don't usually see you in here during school time.'

'I know. But I haven't been food shopping since I got back and today's school dinner didn't appeal.'

I ladled the soup of the day into a bowl, added a brown roll to the plate, made her a pot of tea and set the whole lot in front of her.

'I'm glad to see you so perky, I must admit,' I said quietly. 'I thought you'd be really miserable. Haven't you left Aidan to finish his filming?'

Tilly nodded, her forehead furrowing in concentration as she buttered her roll.

'This is my brave face. I only got back at the weekend and I'm still riding high from our two weeks together. Quite frankly, I don't know how I'll cope without him for four days, let alone four weeks.'

I made a soothing noise and squeezed her shoulder. I felt the same about Charlie; I'd missed him even during my few days at the farm.

Then she beamed at me. 'But looking on the bright side, when he does come back we're moving in together. So I'm going to start looking at houses while he's away.'

'Wow. I mean, wow!' I stammered. 'That's amazing.'

'I know it's fast.' She shrugged, her cheeks turning pink. 'But we had plenty of time to talk when we were away. And when someone's right, you just know. No point hanging around.'

'Absolutely.' I swallowed.

'Freya!' Shirley shouted.

'Coming.' My heart plummeted; what had I incinerated this time?

'Your mobile phone is vibrating in your bag. Can you turn it off, please?' Shirley gave me her stern look.

'Sorry. Again.' I winced at my boss. At least it had been on silent. I rummaged in my handbag and glanced at the screen, intending to reject the call and turn the phone off completely. My heart thumped. I didn't recognize the number but the area code was familiar.

'It's a Lake District phone number.' I whirled and gave Shirley my best pleading look. 'Do you mind? It might be important.'

Shirley rolled her eyes and smiled. 'Go on then.'

I accepted the call. 'Hello?'

'Oh, lass . . . I'm . . . It's your Auntie Sue calling, from the hospital. Uncle Arthur's had a heart attack.'

For a second the café swam out of focus. My knees gave way and I sagged forward across the counter, knocking a stack of dirty plates as I did so. Goosebumps appeared all over my bare arms and along my spine, and a whooshing noise filled my ears.

'Oh my God.' I pressed my free hand to my forehead. Shirley frowned at me with concern. 'Is he . . . ? Will he be OK?'

'Now, I don't want you to panic,' Auntie Sue said and then promptly burst into tears.

Between the two of us both sobbing down the line I managed to establish that it had all happened this morning at breakfast time, thankfully, before he had had a chance to leave the farmhouse. He'd suddenly gone pale and clammy, sunk down on to a chair and pressed his hand to his chest. Despite him saying it was probably nothing, Auntie Sue had called an ambulance straight away. Paramedics had confirmed he was having a heart attack and now he was in hospital, hooked up to wires and monitors.

'I've never been more terrified in my life, Freya,' she sobbed.

'Oh, Auntie Sue, you poor thing. Please don't cry, you're making me cry.'

'What if they can't save him? I won't know what to do with myself.'

'You mustn't think like that. Give him my love and I promise, I'll come and visit as soon as I can.'

We ended the call arranging to speak as soon as the results of Uncle Arthur's tests came through.

'This was exactly what I was worried about,' I wept into Shirley's chest after she had bustled me into the tiny store room at the back of the café. Tilly had joined us and both of them were doing their best to console me. Shirley tightened her grip around my shoulders and was making soft shushing noises into my hair, while Tilly held my hand and was stroking my arm.

'I don't know how they're going to cope,' I said, taking a tissue from Shirley. 'Auntie Sue can't even drive.'

'At least he's alive,' Tilly pointed out, giving me a weak smile. 'And he's in the best place.'

'Yes, and now he's been diagnosed, he'll be put on the right drugs to keep it from happening again,' Shirley assured me.

'Buggeration!' Tilly looked at her watch. 'I've got to get back to school.'

I released myself from Shirley's clutches and gave her a hug. Tilly dashed off, leaving me with my boss. We looked at each other for a long moment.

Shirley sighed. 'How about I give you some time off, unpaid, while you go up there and see what's what?'

I could have kissed her. In fact, I did kiss her. 'Are you sure?' I sniffed. 'Thank you. I could tell Auntie Sue wanted me to come but I didn't like to ask as I've only just got back.'

'We can manage here between us. Anyway, you deserve it. You came to my rescue when I broke my ankle and I'll always be grateful for that. And it'll be peace of mind for your auntie. Go on, why don't you get yourself home?'

Anna was there on the doorstep waiting for me when I got back.

'Mum called me from the café,' she murmured, pulling me in for a hug.

'Bless her. Your mum is the best boss ever. Fact.' I swallowed down another sob.

'I'm so sorry. What can I do to help?' Anna asked. 'Shall I book a train ticket while you pack?'

I shook my head. 'Thanks, but I'm going to drive.'

Anna raised her eyebrows. Bobby's top speed was fifty miles an hour.

'I know, I know. It'll take me hours, but at least I won't have to rely on Eddy for lifts once I'm there. He'll be busy enough as it is.'

Besides, I mused, I didn't know how long I'd be gone. I followed her inside; she disappeared into the kitchen while I ran upstairs to start packing.

'Have you told Charlie?' Anna shouted up.

Charlie! My stomach flipped. I needed to let him know. I racked my brains to remember what shift he was on but my mind had gone blank. I pulled out my phone and sent him a quick text.

Hey. Bad news, Uncle Arthur is in hospital. Had a heart attack this morning, but doing OK, I think. Am driving up there now to help out. Call me when you get a minute. Love Freya xoxo

Fifteen minutes later I'd thrown most of my stuff into bags and was loading up the campervan. One of the major benefits of owning a home on wheels is that there's never any need to travel light.

'Wow.' I heard a familiar voice behind me and I spun round to find myself nose to chest with Charlie in his fire-fighter's uniform. My face lit up and I felt my body relax for the first time since Auntie Sue's call; I was so pleased to see him.

'Looks like you're off for good with all that stuff. I've just caught you in time, I see.'

'Yeah, it's a bit chaotic . . .' The laugh faded from my voice. Charlie didn't look in the least amused.

His eyes blazed at me. 'I can't believe you'd just bugger off after sending me a text, without even saying goodbye.'

'It isn't like that,' I exclaimed in horror, folding my arms.

He snorted in derision and looked away. 'No?'

What? I hadn't seen this side to Charlie before. And I can't say I was too keen on it either.

'Hey, Charlie, this isn't about me and you. This is about helping two people that I love, and I need to leave as soon as I can.'

He sighed and leaned against the side of the campervan. Neither of us spoke for a few seconds. The sound of my heart thumping was deafening.

'Yeah, sorry, you're right, and I'm sorry to hear that your uncle's ill,' he conceded. 'I'm being selfish. But you've only just got back and I miss you when you're gone.'

'I know; I miss you too. But you can't expect me to ignore what's happening at the farm. Uncle Arthur could have died today.'

And besides that, Charlie was behaving like a petulant child not an adult.

'Sorry,' he mumbled again and pulled me towards him. We squeezed each other tightly and he buried his face in my hair as we stood holding each other for a long time.

Charlie bent down to kiss me. 'You'll be back next weekend, though, to take Ollie swimming?'

I hesitated. I'd forgotten about that. Ollie wanted to go to the waterpark with the big slides and Charlie had promised him we'd take him. At the time I'd been flattered – it was proof that our date on Sunday had been a success – but I didn't want to promise I'd be back in time. Just in case I wasn't.

Charlie's eyes hardened. 'Great.'

What? I blinked up at him, gobsmacked. All couples have rows. It's normal. I just wasn't expecting it. And certainly not about this.

I took a step back to give him a good glare. 'Can I just get this right? Uncle Arthur's in hospital and you're sulking because I won't come swimming with you?'

He shook his head in disgust. 'Freya, this is exactly what I was trying to avoid. Want to know the first thing that Ollie said to me on the phone last night? "When are we seeing Freya again?" Now what shall I tell him? Hmm? "I don't know, son, maybe never?"'

My eyes filled with tears. First the news of my uncle's heart attack and now the two of us fighting. My own heart would be in tatters soon. I grabbed hold of his hands and squeezed them.

'Come with me,' I begged. 'Take some time off, bring

Ollie. He'd love the farm. He can be in charge of collecting the eggs; I used to do that . . .'

Charlie shook his head slowly. 'My life's in Kingsfield, near my son. And so is yours. Freya, I don't want you dashing off up the motorway. Your uncle is OK, you said so yourself. They'll be fine. He'll come out of hospital and he'll just have to take it easy for a while. Think about it, what can you actually do to help?'

He exhaled sharply and looked at me, his eyes stony, jaw set rigid. 'You need to make a choice, Freya.' He stabbed a finger into the space between us. 'I won't have my son messed about.'

'Charlie!' I cried, grabbing on to his arm. 'You're behaving like a bully. In fact, right now you remind me of my brother Julian and that is not a compliment.'

He flicked me off as if I was a minor irritant and strode away.

I pressed my shaking hands to my face. I was a bewildered, tearful wreck and, frankly, lost for words. Anna materialized at my side, looped an arm around my waist and the two of us watched him disappear into the distance.

'Are you all right?' she asked.

'Not really. I don't know what to do,' I said, silent tears still streaming down my face.

'Follow your heart; that's what you'd tell me to do,' Anna said decisively.

You need to make a choice, Freya. My life's in Kingsfield . . . and so is yours.

'Oh my goodness, you're right,' I gasped, turning to Anna. My pulse started to gallop. What was I even doing still standing here? I stood tall, swiped the tears roughly from my face and ran round to the driver's side. 'I've got to go, Anna.'

I slammed Bobby's door behind me and blew a kiss to my housemate through the window. 'Wish me luck.'

I started the engine, my heart beating wildly as I began my next adventure.

A Family Affair

Chapter 11

A chink of sunlight found its way through the gap in the curtains and directly on to my face, waking me up instantly with its golden glow. I turned away and stretched, reaching my toes down to the cold bit at the bottom of the bed where the blankets had become untucked.

Blankets? Of course! I was at Appleby Farm. I blinked rapidly, shot up to a sitting position and bumped my head on the sloping ceiling in the process. I rubbed my skull, wincing from the pain, my heart knocking against my ribcage as the dramas of yesterday came flooding back.

The phone call from Auntie Sue, the row with Charlie, the endless journey up the motorway and then the grim reality of the cardiac unit at the hospital, where Uncle Arthur lay, anxious and dwarfed amidst the monitors, wires and machinery.

It was the stuff of nightmares, but at least Uncle Arthur appeared to be out of immediate danger. Now I was here, I was going to do my utmost to see that it didn't happen again. My eyes gradually focused on my surroundings and for a few seconds I let the comfort and joy of being back at the farm work its magic.

My bedroom was on the top floor of the farmhouse,

tucked under the eaves – hence the thud to the head. It was a large room with a lovely old sash window overlooking the valley. The window sill was deep enough to sit on and had been the perfect spot to snuggle up and read my beloved *Horse and Pony* magazines as a child. My single bed was ancient. It had a high iron bedstead but the most comfortable deep mattress I'd ever slept on, and I always felt like the princess from 'The Princess and the Pea', minus the pea, when I stayed here.

Too comfortable, I mused, glancing at my watch; so much for my plans to get up early and get cracking. It was eight o'clock and Eddy and Ross would already be here somewhere. I jumped out of bed and strained my ears for any sounds but the house was silent except for a couple of creaking floorboards underneath my feet. I pulled back the curtains and, sure enough, there was the Land Rover, making its way up to where the cattle were grazing in one of the fields furthest from the farmhouse. It would have a name, that field, as did each and every field on the farm. I only really knew Calf's Close, the one nearest to the cowsheds, but Eddy, my uncle and aunt, and probably Ross by now, knew all of them off by heart.

The early May sky was the palest blue with cotton-wool clouds bobbing along merrily and the sun was just visible over the treetops to the east. Simply looking at that sky made me feel better. And then I felt guilty for feeling happy . . . Oh, I was so confused.

Right, Freya Moorcroft, I told myself, glancing at my sleep-creased reflection in the mirror, *a cup of tea and then the chickens*. My hair was rather bird's-nesty, but I was sure the chickens wouldn't judge.

I pulled a jumper on over my pyjamas and tiptoed down the stairs. A low rumbling noise was coming from Auntie

Sue's room, like a hibernating bear echoing in its wintery cave, and I had to clap a hand over my mouth to stifle a giggle; for such a delightfully dainty old lady, my aunt's snores could wake the dead. I was glad she was still sleeping, though; it had been after midnight when we'd got in from the hospital and the poor thing had been on her knees with exhaustion. I don't think I'd ever known her have a lie-in in her life, so this one was long overdue.

The hens still had to be let out, though, and I'd volunteered to do that.

So after being on the receiving end of an exuberant greeting from Madge and a more restrained one from the cats, I made myself a mug of tea, slipped on my wellies and skipped my way across the yard through the early morning sunshine.

The air smelled wonderful: straw, wood smoke and an underlying aroma of cows, although that was fainter now that the cattle were out on the grassland for the next few months. Despite the trauma of yesterday, I felt a bubble of happiness rise in my chest at being back at the farm.

'Morning, ladies!' I cooed as I unbolted the henhouse door.

The hens waddled down the ramp from their rather pongy sleeping quarters, clucking noisily, and instantly began looking for breakfast. Feeding the hens was easy – I chucked a few handfuls of pellets on to the ground, hopped back to keep my wellingtons from getting pecked and went to check the water feeders.

Little Ollie would love to do this. And to collect the eggs, I thought automatically, before a surge of panic rose from the pit of my stomach to my chest.

Charlie.

The thought of him and our row made my throat ache with sadness.

You need to make a choice, Freya: that had been Charlie's ultimatum.

And here I was, at the farm. When push came to shove, I'd chosen Cumbria over Kingsfield, my family over Charlie. But really, what choice did I have? I couldn't possibly leave Auntie Sue to manage on her own and it was wrong of Charlie to ask me to do so. The way he had reacted – well, that wasn't love, it was possession. I totally understood why he was so protective of letting a girlfriend into Ollie's life, and I was terribly sorry to let the little boy down, but right now my heart was telling me that Appleby Farm was where I needed to be.

At my feet, the cockerel was puffing out his chest in an attempt to show one of his fluffy ladies who was boss. He was a handsome chap: glossy dark feathers on his body with amber ones around his head like a lion's mane. The hen was pecking at her breakfast unperturbed, completely ignoring his display of manliness.

I'm with you, missus, I thought with a sigh.

I hadn't had the chance to phone Charlie since I'd arrived in Cumbria, and I planned to put it off as long as possible. I had a sinking feeling that our relationship might be over.

It didn't look like Ollie would ever get the chance to visit Appleby Farm.

I brushed a flurry of tears from my eyes and went to the back of the henhouse to check the nesting boxes. There were around fifteen newly laid eggs nestled into the straw; some almost white, others a deep brown and some with a speckled shell, all shapes and sizes. I selected the biggest and cradled it in my hand. It was huge! Poor hen, that would have taken some laying.

I'd forgotten to pick up the egg basket, so I put the egg

back with the others for the moment, left the hens behind and headed back towards the farmhouse to get myself dressed. I only made it halfway across the yard when the Land Rover rounded the corner, came to a stop by the shed, and Ross and Eddy climbed out.

Great.

'Hi,' I called, tugging my jumper down over my pyjamas as the pair strode towards me.

'How's our Arthur?' grunted Eddy from under knotted eyebrows. He was wearing a pair of brown trousers, a checked brown shirt and a belt on top of which perched a large belly. His sleeves were rolled up and there was mud all the way up his arm. At least, I think it was mud. Returning from a cattle inspection, Eddy could be covered in something far worse.

I took a step back and tried not to inhale.

Ross was looking on the scruffy side too, I noticed, which made me feel slightly better about my own outfit. He was dressed in his navy overalls as usual, but was covered from head to toe in a fine golden dust, like he'd had a tussle with a hay bale and lost.

I looked back at Eddy. 'He's going to be OK. It'll take a few days to get his medication sorted out, but luckily there wasn't too much long-term damage to the heart. Auntie Sue knows more, of course. As soon as she's up I'm taking her back to the hospital.'

'Good, good.' Eddy nodded. 'You want to go and get the weed sprayer ready, lad? Bottom Field first.'

'Sure.' Ross turned to go. 'Oh, Freya, you missed Lizzie earlier. She says to pop into the pub if you get chance.'

I pushed my bed-head hair behind my ears and smiled at him. 'I will, definitely.' Without Anna nearby I had no one to confide in about Charlie. And I'd have to talk about the whole disaster with someone, or I'd go barmy.

Eddy coughed, breaking into my thoughts. 'So?' he said expectantly.

I dragged my eyes away from Ross's retreating lanky form and met Eddy's frown.

'You're wondering whether this heart attack is connected to his accident, aren't you?' I sighed.

''Tis a coincidence,' he said gruffly, scuffing the toe of his boot against the cobbles.

I glanced up to see movements in the kitchen; Auntie Sue must be up.

'Come on.' I jerked my head towards the orchard. 'Let's walk and talk.'

I marched off at speed before Auntie Sue caught sight of us, with Eddy bringing up the rear and grumbling about not even getting a cup of tea.

'We'll know more today; he wasn't in a fit state to talk much last night,' I said, taking a seat on a rather splintery-looking bench at the edge of the orchard. 'But I do know he won't be allowed to do anything much around the farm for up to six months, and certainly no driving for a while.'

In front of us were two small fields. Lizzie's horse, Skye, was grazing at the far side in one of them and the two Jersey cows with their calves were in the other. The newest calf was suckling and neither he nor his mother, Gaynor, were interested in our arrival, but the other cow, Gloria, ambled over, her calf bumping along beside her.

Gloria stuck her nose over the stone wall and stared at us with her gentle brown eyes. I lost sight of the calf – she was too small to reach the top of the wall.

I patted the space beside me and Eddy sat down with a groan.

'Buggered then, aren't we?' he tutted. 'Me and Ross'll never manage the farm between us.'

'Really?' My heart sank. Naively, I'd thought that as we'd got Ross here for the summer, the farm would be OK.

'Don't get me wrong,' said Eddy, 'he'll make a good farmer one day. But we'll be starting making silage next month and there's over a hundred acres of grass – that's a lot to cover for an old duffer like me and one apprentice.'

Silage was the huge mountain of chopped-up grass that was held under plastic in an area called the clamp and weighted down with old tyres. It was used to feed the cattle when the grass stopped growing over winter.

I nodded, wishing I knew what the answer was.

Gloria snorted for some attention and we both got up to see her. My brain was whirring: could I help out, learn to drive a tractor and . . . everything else? Or would that just mean extra work for Eddy? If not me, then who? And where would the money come from to pay for extra labour?

'Lovely beasts, the Jerseys,' said Eddy, rubbing Gloria's broad nose affectionately. 'Good natured, docile . . . a bit like young Ross, I suppose.' He chuckled.

I smiled. At least he approved of his apprentice; that was something.

The calf edged a bit closer. I held out my hand but she was too timid. She was a lighter shade of brown than Gloria, although they both shared the same gorgeous brown eyes.

'Those lovely eyelashes are wasted on you,' I said. A thought occurred to me and I gasped in horror. 'Oh gosh, they haven't been milked today. Poor cows, they must be desperate!'

Eddy shot me a sideways glance and shook his head. 'No

rush when they've got calves feeding. Your aunt will milk the extra off later.'

I flushed. 'Of course.'

Charlie was right. His words from yesterday rang in my ears: *Think about it, what can you actually do to help?*

'By the way . . .' Eddy pulled at his collar and looked awkward all of a sudden. 'I saw our vet in't village yesterday and he asked about his bill. Overdue, he reckons.'

'Right.' I nodded, pulling myself up tall. 'I'll have a look in the office and see if I can find it.'

Now tidying the office *was* something I could tackle, I thought, with a welcome spurt of optimism. Not that I wanted to be indoors especially, I was more of an outdoor person, but I was quite good at organization, plus I could try to sneak a peek at that 'final notice' letter I'd seen the last time I was here. If there was an issue with money at the farm, now might be a good time to get to grips with it, before Uncle Arthur came home.

'Want my opinion?' asked Eddy as we began to make our way back to the yard.

I nodded. Any opinion would be welcome at this point in time.

'Get a contractor in to manage the grassland for the summer and make the silage ready for winter.'

'Will that be expensive?' I asked, not sure I wanted to know the answer.

Eddy grunted. 'Cheaper than buying feed for the winter.'

'Of course,' I said, chewing my lip. Without enough silage the feed bill would be enormous and that was a cost we could definitely do without.

'Who's this now?' he tutted, glancing over to the road.

I followed his gaze to see a small van turn into the farm track and begin the bumpy journey towards us.

'Me and Ross can manage the herd between us and look after the crops. But it would take the pressure off if someone else could handle the silage.'

I squeezed his arm. 'Leave it with me, Eddy; I'll add it to my list.'

Eddy nodded. 'Give Arthur my best. Tell him I'll be in later.'

As I left him to check up on Ross, a smart white van with *Lakeland Flowers* written on the side of it bounced across the yard at speed and came to a halt in front of me at the farm-house gate.

A short wiry man with a thatch of silver hair jumped out, darted to the rear of the van and retrieved a huge bunch of lilies.

'Delivery for Freya Moorcroft?' he called, scanning me up and down with a hint of a grin.

I cringed. I was never feeding the chickens in my pyjamas again. On the other hand, there was a man here bearing flowers with my name on them. Yay!

'That's me!' I cried, bouncing on the spot.

'Here you go then, miss.'

'Thank you!'

He handed me the bouquet and I tried not to snatch it out of his hands. Hardly daring to breathe, I pulled out the card that was tucked into the top and opened it with one hand.

There was quite a long message but the word I most wanted to see was there in black and white: *Charlie.*

I squealed, grabbed the man round the neck and hugged him. 'Thank you!'

'They're not actually from me,' came the muffled voice from my jumper.

'I know,' I laughed, 'it's a bit like shooting the messenger, only I like the message, so no shooting required.'

'Thank heavens for that,' said the delivery man, extracting himself from my arms.

'They're from my boyfriend,' I said in a wobbly voice. 'He must still love me. After last night I wasn't sure.'

'All right, miss, there's no need to explain. Sign here, please.'

He handed me an electronic pad and a plastic pen. I scrawled my signature – quite tricky with an armful of flowers – and gave it back to him.

The man tapped away at his little screen and frowned. 'Don't happen to know the time, do you?'

The kitchen door opened and Madge came trotting out, padded across the yard to the dog kennel and lay in wait for her morning egg.

'Time for an egg, I'd guess,' I giggled.

The man shook his head, straightened his tie and, looking rather relieved, jumped back into the van.

He tooted his horn and I waved him off, hugging the flowers to my chest.

Charlie still loved me. And as long as we had love, the rest would work itself out, wouldn't it?

Chapter 12

Auntie Sue was putting the kettle on when I practically danced my way into the kitchen.

'Look! From Charlie!' I tickled her nose with flowers as I waltzed past and told a white lie. 'They're for both of us. To cheer us up.'

Björn wound his slinky body around my legs and I scooped him up, dropped the flowers on the table and kissed my aunt's cheek in one happy circuit of the room.

'Ooh, what a kind man; how lovely! Here, let me find a vase.'

'Thank you.' I sat at the table, cuddling the cat's silky body to me while I read Charlie's note.

And cried.

Gorgeous girl, I am a total pillock and don't blame you if you've written me off. It is just like you to dash off at a moment's notice to come to your aunt and uncle's rescue and the fact that you're so caring is one of the things I love about you. I know you need to be at the farm right now. I hope your uncle is doing OK and I can't wait to see you.

Your apologetic, grumpy, childish and loving Charlie xxx

OK, I forgive him.

*

When we arrived at the hospital later, a black nurse with eye-wateringly tight hair braids was making notes on a clipboard at the end of Uncle Arthur's bed. His face lit up when he spotted us. His skin was still pale, except for the remnants of the scab over his eyebrow, but he looked a lot more with it than last night. He was propped up on at least three pillows, wires protruding from a gap in his pyjama jacket, a clip on the end of his forefinger and, of course, he still had his wrist in plaster.

'You two are a vision of loveliness to an old codger,' he wheezed.

The nurse coughed.

'Er, you *three*, I meant,' he added. The nurse let out a huge lilting laugh that shook her bosom and Uncle Arthur rolled his eyes comically. I kissed him and arranged two chairs, one each side of the bed, while Auntie Sue hugged him until he groaned.

'Gave me such a shock, you did,' she said and sniffed. She poured him a glass of water from a jug and held it up to his mouth.

Uncle Arthur sipped at it and smacked his lips. 'Sorry, love. I'm a flippin' nuisance, aren't I?' He patted her hand gently. 'But don't worry, I'll—'

The nurse cleared her throat. 'Now, Arthur,' she said sternly, 'you've got some talking to do. Or I'll do it for you, you hear me?'

Uncle Arthur's eyes darted from the nurse to me and then finally to his wife, and he swallowed. 'Loud and clear, nurse.'

The nurse hooked the clipboard back over the metal bar at the end of the bed, wagged an ominous finger at the patient and moved to the next bed, swaying her hips as she went.

Auntie Sue stared at her husband expectantly. 'Well?'

Uncle Arthur turned a lighter shade of grey. 'You know that accident I had . . .'

Eddy had been spot on, thinking that there was more to the tractor accident than his boss was letting on. It hadn't been a crackly radio that had caused Uncle Arthur to hit a ditch, it had been a painful squeezing sensation in his heart, but because it only lasted a few seconds and because he doesn't like making a fuss he'd decided it was nothing.

But it hadn't been nothing; it had been heart attack number one.

'The consultant was quite snooty about it,' said Uncle Arthur, raising his bushy eyebrows indignantly.

'I'm not surprised.' Auntie Sue tutted. She looked torn; poised at the edge of her seat as if she couldn't decide whether to box his ears or fold him into her chest and never let him out of her sight.

The ECG he'd had done the day before had picked up the previous damage to his heart straight away. Now he would have to have a stent fitted, followed by a few more days in hospital to sort out his medication, which would hopefully make sure this would never, ever happen again.

'Look, you two,' I said, reaching across the pale-blue standard-issue blanket for both of their hands, 'for the next few weeks, I just want you to concentrate on Uncle Arthur's recovery. Let me handle the farm. Eddy and I can sort out any problems between us. OK?'

Awkward silence. Worried looks flashed back and forth.

'What?' I felt my cheeks colour. 'Don't you think I can do it?'

121

I swallowed back a lump in my throat. I would expect that sort of reaction from my parents, but not from these two. My role in the family had always been the free-spirited girl, never sticking at anything, no direction, no long-term plan. And it had never bothered me before; well, why would it? It was true. It bothered me now, though.

'Of course,' said Auntie Sue. 'It's just that . . .'

'It's all right, love,' said Uncle Arthur, squeezing his wife's hand. 'I can't think of anyone I'd trust more than our Freya, can you?'

I let out a long breath. I would do this and I would do it well. My stomach bubbled nervously, but I fooled him with my breezy smile.

'Fab,' I said, kissing his forehead and giving him a gentle hug. 'Anything specific you want doing today?'

My uncle drummed his fingers on his stubbly cheek. 'There's a passport application to fill in for Gaynor's calf.'

I opened my mouth and shut it just in time. That could have been embarrassing. It wasn't because Gaynor was planning a little trip abroad with her newborn calf; all cattle had to have their own passports. I knew that, I'd just temporarily forgotten.

'OK. Anything else?' I said, trying to look confident.

'I spotted a dead badger in Crofters Field by Colton Woods . . .'

I racked my brains – which field was that?

'I'll show you the map of the fields,' said Auntie Sue.

I flashed her a grateful smile.

'And we're low on nitrogen phosphate and pot ash.' He pressed himself back into his pillows. 'Which is fertilizer,' he added, noticing my bemused expression.

'Yep, I knew that,' I laughed. Not. 'Oh and apparently there's a vet's bill to pay?'

'Um. Right.' He frowned and whistled through his teeth. 'Bottom drawer in my desk, bring it in next time you visit and I'll write him a cheque.'

'Right then, I'd better get back to work.' I beamed at them. 'I'll make a brilliant farmer. You wait and see. It's in my genes.'

The office was even more dark and gloomy without Uncle Arthur's cheery presence in it. And the usual whiff of egg was joined by the doggy smell of Madge, who was pining for him in his chair.

'Come on, Madge,' I said with a grunt, pulling the solid little dog on to my lap. 'Uncle Arthur will be home soon and in the meantime you can help me with the jobs. I bet you could find the dead badger without a map, for starters.'

She licked my face, which I took as a 'yes'.

The farm's phone was on the desk and my fingers itched to phone Charlie. But first I had the vet's bill to find and a passport form to fill in for the Jersey calf. The passport sounded complicated so I'd work my way up to it. Uncle Arthur's battered mahogany desk had three drawers in it. I pulled out the bottom one and gasped. Sitting on the top of a heap of papers was that envelope with FINAL NOTICE stamped across it in large red letters.

Chest pounding, I lowered Madge to the floor – the licking was getting a bit much – and glanced at the door. I could hear Auntie Sue banging about in the kitchen.

Was it really bad to pry?

I lifted the envelope out and turned it over in my hands. Uncle Arthur had told me to look in here for that vet's bill. In fact, he probably wanted me to find this letter. Perhaps it was his way of asking for help.

It had already been opened and I slipped the contents out. I'd only just had caught sight of the word 'bailiff', when—

'I'm glad you've found the bill, to be truthful,' said Auntie Sue.

'Blimey!' I yelled, clutching my throat and throwing the letter up in the air.

I stared at my aunt, my chest heaving with panicky breaths, Madge cowering under my feet. Auntie Sue sank into the chair next to me and I sat back, my eyes wide and GUILT almost definitely written across my face in huge letters.

'I was looking for the invoice from the vet . . .' My voice faded. Auntie Sue's bottom lip was starting to wobble and her blue eyes sparkled with tears.

For a second I was stunned. My aunt was such a cheerful soul, such a no-nonsense, let's-make-the-best-of-it person, and sometimes I forgot that she was, in fact, quite an old lady. An old lady whose beloved husband could have died yesterday. But now she looked almost . . . defeated.

'There's more where that came from,' she said, dabbing her eyes with the corner of her apron. She pointed to the drawer. 'They keep coming: from the bank, the tractor company and now the vet. We're behind with the tax man and the seed supplier, too. We're in debt up to our necks. This is why we can't retire; we can't afford to. We have to keep going or else we'll lose the farm.'

'Things can't be that bad.' I swallowed. 'Can they?'

Sitting beside my aunt on the wooden bench at the kitchen table, over a pot of tea, I heard the whole story of how one unfortunate event followed another: the finance deal for the new tractor, the bull who had had to be put down, the calves lost to pneumonia last winter, the wet summer that had ruined the barley and the silage yield, and the subsequent big fodder bill. Each thing was relatively small in itself, but added together they had had a devastating effect on the farm's cash flow.

Auntie Sue sighed. 'And now the loan company has put up the interest rate and we can't keep on top of the payments. We should never have bought that tractor, even if it was only second hand. I keep telling him to sell up, leave the farm.'

'That does sound sensible,' I said tentatively. *Although incredibly sad.*

I looked round the kitchen. The two cats were in their spot in front of the Aga and Madge had relocated herself to her master's armchair. This place had been home to three generations of Moorcroft farmers and it was unthinkable that Appleby Farm would have to be sold, especially under such circumstances.

She shook her head and pressed her lips together. 'Your uncle says he won't be forced off his own land by banks. He says while he still has breath left in his body he'll fight to keep his farm.'

And yesterday he could so easily have taken his last breath. I felt tears prick at the back of my eyes and quickly blinked them away.

Auntie Sue pulled her handbag towards her and took out a handful of leaflets.

'They've given me all these booklets to read.' She flicked through them, dropping them one by one on the table. '"Healthy Diet, Heathy Heart", "Living with Heart Disease", "Avoiding Stress". And how can he do that with all this pressure hanging over his head? Tell me that, eh? It was probably the stress of our money situation that landed him in the hospital in the first place. And I can't see this problem going away.'

We looked at each other and neither of us spoke. It felt like there was a ping-pong ball stuck in my windpipe and my heart was breaking for the pair of them; they worked so hard and it just didn't seem fair. Auntie Sue and I leaned together until our heads touched and I wrapped my arm around her shoulders.

Suddenly the ping-pong ball sensation vanished. I sat up straight and grabbed Auntie Sue by the top of her plump arms.

'I'll save the farm,' I blurted. No idea how. Well, not yet anyway, but I was sure something would come to me.

'Oh, Freya.' She gave me a sad smile and blinked, causing two tears to roll slowly down her face.

I wiped them away with my thumbs. 'I mean it. I love challenges. Thrive on them. In fact, this is just what I need. The waitressing job was beginning to feel a bit easy; I'm ready for something new.'

'But you're a young woman, love.' She tutted. 'You don't want to be stuck out here with us old folks.'

'I love you old folks.' I grinned.

'Having to go out in all weathers.'

'I like all weathers and I love the outdoors. Even you've got to admit that.'

She cocked her head to one side and raised her eyebrows. 'And there's no money in it, you know that?'

'Ha,' I scoffed, 'since when has that bothered me?'

Auntie Sue shook her head anxiously. 'What about Charlie?'

Good point. I hesitated for a second. 'Charlie will understand. And I only need to stay until things are settled. Think of me as one of those interim managers that go in to businesses to keep things ticking over until the real boss comes back.'

For the first time in ages, I felt a whoosh of exhilaration. The farm needed a solution and I was good at solutions. I started pacing around the table, following the well-worn grooves in the quarry tiles. Made by the footsteps of the Moorcroft family.

Wow. A shiver sent tingles up my spine. Generations of Moorcroft farmers had paced these floors and now I suddenly felt part of it.

I stopped circling and smiled brightly. 'Uncle Arthur said one day I'd find my niche.' I held my arms out and spun round on the spot. 'Perhaps this is it! Maybe my forte has been under my nose all this time at Appleby Farm!'

Chapter 13

I pushed open the door to the White Lion and Lizzie waved at me immediately.

'Hey, Lizzie, bet you didn't expect to see me so soon?' I said, leaning over the bar to give her a hug.

'It is *ace* to have you back in Lovedale. But I'm so sorry that your cute little uncle is poorly. Is he going to be OK? How long are you stopping this time? Or are you staying for ever? Your coat smells horsey, by the way.'

I sniffed my arm. 'Oh, it does!' I sniffed it again. 'I love that smell. I took Skye out for a quick mosey up to Crofters Field this afternoon. You don't mind, do you?'

I missed out the bit about finding the dead badger and disposing of it in Colton Woods. I didn't want to relive the moment myself, to be honest.

'Course not!' she cried, swiping at my arm. 'We'll share her. We can share everything if you want. Like sisters.' She pulled a face. 'Maybe not like sisters. My sister Victoria has never been keen on sharing. Except if it was mine in the first place. Well, anyway,' she said dismissively, 'forget her. How are you?'

I busied myself finding a bar stool so that I could avoid her eyes. I'd been putting a brave face on for the last twenty-four hours since receiving that call from Auntie Sue, keeping my own feelings hidden in order to support her. But now, having discovered the scale of the farm's debts coupled with the seriousness of Uncle Arthur's health situation, I was feeling a bit wobbly.

'Sad, worried,' I murmured shakily. 'Oh, I think you're wanted.'

Bill, the landlord, was clearing his throat repeatedly and Lizzie, taking the hint, served a couple of waiting customers before returning to me with a frown.

'If you don't mind me saying, Freya, you look a bit tired. You OK?'

'Oh my word, Lizzie. I've got *so* much to tell you.' I sighed, tapping the cider pump. 'But first, half a pint and one for yourself. How's Ross? By which I mean, how are *you* and Ross? Obvs.'

'Oh fine, fine, fine.' She flicked a hand. 'But let's talk about Freya and her amazing return to the farm.'

'Aww, thanks. I must admit, I am glad to be back, except for the circumstances.'

Lizzie nodded.

'Ooh, before I forget, that really nice farmer was asking about you earlier.'

'Who, that mate of Uncle Arthur's with the bald head and odd wellingtons?'

'No!' Lizzie giggled. 'The good-looking one who's always drumming his fingers on the bar and whistling. In fact . . .' She scanned the pub. 'No, looks like you've missed him.' She pulled a disappointed face. 'Harry. Don't know his surname. Next farm to you.'

I knew exactly who that was: the boy who'd wanted to be a drummer when he grew up. I clapped a hand over my mouth.

'Harry Graythwaite.' I felt a flush of guilt. 'What must he think of me not going to see him? We were inseparable as teenagers.'

'I bet. You lucky thing.' She arched an eyebrow suggestively.

'Shame I missed him,' I said, blatantly ignoring Lizzie's innuendos.

'Mmm, I used to have a bit of a soft spot for him myself. Until I saw Ross's face. And then it was, like, swoon!' She pretended to stagger, presumably under the effect of Ross's good looks. 'I swear that boy could have been a model.' She sighed dreamily, propping her chin up on her palm.

'What did Harry want, anyway?' I asked, taking some money out of my pocket.

'Um,' Lizzie gazed up at the ceiling. 'Asked if you were back for good. I said probably not because you had a boyfriend at home. Which is right, isn't it?'

'Of course.' I waved a five-pound note at her. 'I'm sooo thirsty.'

'Oops, sorry,' she said. 'My head is in the clouds at the moment. You know what it's like when you first get together with someone. It won't last.'

'No . . .' I agreed, tongue in cheek.

'Won't it?' She looked at me aghast.

I giggled. 'I'm joking, you two seem great together. By the way, how come you got mobile phone service at the farm? I have to virtually climb Mount Everest for mine to work.'

Lizzie tapped her nose. 'There's a new phone mast gone up the other side of Colton Woods. I've changed network and now my phone works. Simple. You get money for having a phone mast, you know. You should get one on the farm.'

'Funny you should say that . . .' I leaned across the bar and lowered my voice. 'I need to raise some money – quickly, without going to a loan shark.'

Lizzie's eyebrows shot skywards and her jaw dropped. She poured my half pint in silence and placed it in front of me, opening a bottle of orange juice for herself.

'I've got to pay off some . . . well, quite a lot actually . . .' My words caught in my throat and I pressed my lips together.

If it was just about me, I'd have no qualms about confiding in Lizzie, but it wasn't and I didn't think Auntie Sue and Uncle Arthur would take too kindly to me broadcasting to the entire pub that Appleby Farm was up to its eyeballs in debt.

Lizzie slurped her drink, checked to see where Bill was and added a shot of vodka.

'Aww, credit cards?' She wrinkled her nose in sympathy. 'Know the feeling. It's tempting, isn't it? I once went on a shopping spree with mine and bought a new saddle for Skye and a leather jacket for me. Two grand, I spent. Mind you, we both looked gorgeous. Still paying it off, actually.' She gave me a cheeky grin and lifted one shoulder.

'Something like that,' I said, sipping my cider. Not terribly ladylike, I know, but I've never been a fan of wine; it's those spindly little glasses that worry me – so easy to knock over with clumsy hands like mine.

I sighed. Two thousand pounds. If only the farm's debts were so small. Add a nought, double it, then add some more . . .

'Ah well, it's only money.' She giggled. 'But to answer your question. I suppose I'd go to the Bank of Mum and Dad.'

'Oh no.' I shuddered. 'I can't do that.' Even the thought of asking my parents for money made my scalp prickle.

'Yeah, it is a bit embarrassing. But at the end of the day, they are family. My parents would be devastated if I had money troubles and I didn't go to them about it. Although that's unlikely to happen – my mum knows everything about my life cos I speak to her every day. Oh my God!' She paled and clapped a hand over her mouth. 'That was tactless, Freya. I'm so sorry, honey.'

I choked on my cider. 'What was tactless?'

Lizzie blinked at me. She'd gone quite heavy on the eye-liner today and had an air of 'mournful bushbaby' about her. 'Well, me saying "Bank of Mum and Dad", "talk to her every day".' She wagged her head from side to side mimicking herself. 'And there's you – an orphan. Sometimes my mouth goes galloping off before my brain has even grasped the reins. Please forgive me.'

'I'm not an orphan,' I gasped. 'I'm just not close to my parents. Literally. They've lived abroad all my life and I was sent to boarding school when I was seven. I spent most of my school holidays on the farm.'

'Sent away!' She shook her head incredulously. 'I assumed Sue and Arthur brought you up because they had to.'

I shook my head. 'Sometimes I stayed at the farm be-cause the flight to where Mum and Dad were living was too long for me to do on my own. Other times I chose to stay because I preferred it here.'

I stared into my glass. What I didn't say was that my aunt and uncle brought me up because a child would have stood in the way of my parents' busy lives. Consequently they felt like distant relatives and my aunt and uncle were my close family. And on the odd occasion I did spend a school holi-day with my parents, they knew so little about my interests, my friends and my life that they didn't know what to do with me or say to me. I couldn't pretend it didn't bother me, but I was twenty-seven and old enough to move on. Anyway, would I really have wanted to miss out on all the adventures I'd had at Appleby Farm?

No. Not for all the lakes in Cumbria. But sometimes, as Lizzie so eloquently put it, I felt a bit . . . orphan-like.

'So.' She held her hands out with a cheeky smile as if presenting me with my answer. 'Bank of Mum and Dad!'

I swallowed the last of my cider and pushed my empty glass towards her. 'Maybe. As an absolute last resort. Listen, I'll have to go. Eddy's taking Auntie Sue to the hospital tonight and I want to pick her brains before she goes.'

I stopped off at the henhouse honesty box on the way back to the farm. This afternoon Auntie Sue and I had picked bunches of herbs, tied them with raffia and arranged them in a vase next to the eggs. Fresh thyme, chives, mint and rosemary at one pound a bunch. Only one slightly weary-looking bunch of chives and half a dozen eggs remained and there were fifteen pounds in the old toffee tin we used as a cash box.

I removed the chives and pocketed the money to give to Auntie Sue. It was a nice little extra cash but the merest drop in the ocean compared to the size of Uncle Arthur's tractor loan. And it wasn't just the loan that was worrying me. There were bills to pay right now and I still had to find out how much it would cost to subcontract the silage job to help Eddy out.

I traipsed up the farm track, racking my brains for bright ideas. What the farm needed was a way of earning more money without making extra work for Auntie Sue and Uncle Arthur. A source of income that someone else could manage for them.

The obvious answer, of course, was to sell the farm.

I paused and leaned on the wooden fence that bordered the track. The sun was low in the sky and glinted off the top of the slate roof of the farmhouse. Some of the cattle and their calves were grazing in Calf's Close, heads down, tails swishing as they ambled along looking for the sweetest grass. In the orchard the apple trees were in full leaf and several fat brown hens were pecking amongst them. I spotted neat lines of some sort of root crop – swedes or turnips, I could never tell the difference – in one of the flatter fields and fronds of green barley beyond. The whole farm was so perfect, so much a part of me, of my family, that my chest heaved with panic at the thought of letting it go.

Selling all this . . . I swallowed the lump in my throat and carried on walking . . . No, not an option at all.

As I walked across the yard, my head still buzzing, I heard a faint mewing noise. I stopped and strained my ears.

'Mia-a-a-ow.'

One of the cats must be trapped somewhere, poor thing. I walked over to the shed and opened the door, expecting Benny or Björn to run out. But there was no one in there. I froze and listened again.

This time the little voice appeared to be coming from further away, so I headed for the barns at the side of the house, pausing every few seconds to listen for sounds.

There were two barns: one was open and used to store hay, straw and cattle feed. The other was a more substantial building with huge double doors, some small windows high up in the stone walls and a slate roof. At one end was a flight of stairs leading up to a pretty wooden gallery and at the far side was a primitive little loo, presumably providing the original facilities for the farmhouse before the days of indoor plumbing.

The plaintive feline sound was getting louder. With some difficulty I wrenched open the heavy wooden doors and out scrambled a very grateful cat, accompanied by a cloud of hay-dust.

'Hello, sausage,' I said, bending to stroke his head as he wended through my legs affectionately. I counted the white socks: three. 'How did you get in there, Benny?'

With one final miaow, the cat trotted off in the direction of the farmhouse and probably his supper, leaving me to explore the barn. I stepped inside the cool building and looked around slowly.

It was vast and empty except for a pile of stuff shrouded in dust sheets, which lurked in one corner. Disused farm machinery, I guessed. Huge old oak beams spanned the width of the barn and bright rays of sunshine from the windows sliced through the dim light and bounced on the warm stone floors. At one end was a sort of wooden platform; I wandered over and perched on the edge, my brain whirring. The barn had been used for parties in the past but I hadn't been in here for years. Auntie Sue and Uncle Arthur's golden wedding anniversary had been a really lovely do and several of my birthdays had been celebrated in here, too.

This could be it. This could be the source of income that I was looking for. The barn was just too good a space not to use. I hugged my knees to my chest.

Think, Freya. How can the barn make us money?

I closed my eyes and tried to imagine the space full of people. What were they doing? Working? Playing? Dancing?

And whatever it was, how could I raise the funds to transform it into something special?

I opened my eyes again and walked back out into the

135

yard. Whichever way I looked at it, everything came down to money. Having money had simply never mattered to me before and now I couldn't stop thinking about it.

When I hadn't followed some high-flying career path, Dad was quite clear on his position: 'Don't expect me to bail you out,' he had warned. 'You'll have to live on what you earn, so choose wisely.'

And I had. Lived on what I earned, that is. Some of my choices cannot truthfully be classed as 'wise'.

But, technically speaking, I didn't need money for myself, so . . .

The Bank of Mum and Dad. I couldn't. Could I?

I found Auntie Sue in her bedroom, sifting through a pile of pyjamas on Uncle Arthur's half of the bed.

She looked up and gave me a twinkly smile. 'I'll have to pop into Marks and Spencer in Kendal if he stays in hospital much longer. He'll be done for indecent exposure with most of this lot.'

We both chuckled and I picked up her perfume bottle from the dressing table. It was one of those old-fashioned ones with a satin tassel and the squeezy bit that puffed out scented air.

'I found that dead badger,' I said, spraying my neck with a lovely floral scent.

'Filthy things.' She grimaced. 'And you still fancy yourself as a farmer after that?'

'I do, as it happens.' I grinned, throwing myself on to her bed and landing on my side.

I resisted the urge to bounce – just. I'd always loved bouncing on this bed with its satisfyingly creaky springs. Once I'd brought Harry up here to have a go and between us we'd bounced so hard that the bed had suddenly disappeared from under us. One of its legs had cracked the floorboards and poked through the kitchen ceiling, sending a shower of plaster dust onto my aunt below. We had both apologized through a fit of giggles and Harry had scuttled home still snorting with laughter.

Auntie Sue had kept her lips pressed together for the entire afternoon, muttering, 'Wait till your uncle gets home.'

But when he'd seen the leg sticking through the ceiling, Uncle Arthur had laughed until he couldn't breathe. And so had Auntie Sue. It turned out she'd been trying to keep a straight face for hours. Happy times.

'In fact, next time you milk Gloria and Gaynor, can you show me how to do it?' I rolled on to my stomach and smiled. 'That'll be another job off your list.'

Auntie Sue stopped folding pyjamas and clasped them to her chest. 'Oh, Freya. You are an angel, you really are. You've been like a daughter to me and you've brought so much happiness into mine and Artie's lives.'

'I'm glad I'm like a daughter to someone,' I muttered. I rolled off the bed and moved to the window, running my fingers over the faded flowery curtains.

'Oh now, shush,' tutted Auntie Sue. 'We'll have less of that. Your mother loves you very much and it pains me to hear you talk about Margo like that.'

The window sill was as deep as the one in my room. I sat down on it to face her and folded my arms.

'Really? She has a funny way of showing it,' I grunted. 'She didn't even want me around. Boarding school at seven years old? You've been a better mum to me than she ever has.'

Auntie Sue stopped what she was doing and took a deep breath. 'Oh, Freya, that's a wonderful thing to say, lass, and I'm glad you feel that way. But things aren't always as cut and dried as you think. For all her money and fancy houses, your mother hasn't always been happy. She did what she thought was best at the time but she has always felt guilty about sending you away.' She turned her back on me and started stuffing the discarded pyjamas back into the drawer messily.

'What do you mean?'

She stared at me for a long, steady moment. 'Follow me,' she said finally.

My heart was in my mouth as the two of us climbed the stairs, Auntie Sue hobbling and me pressing closely behind her impatiently.

'Oh, give me a bungalow any day of the week,' she panted, rubbing her knee when we reached the top floor. 'All these stairs play havoc with my arthritis.'

There was no loft in the farmhouse as the roof space was taken up with my bedroom and one other: a room opposite mine that I always remembered being locked. Over the years, I'd just accepted I wasn't allowed in.

Now she pointed to the top of the door frame. 'There should be a key up there.'

I reached up on my tiptoes and felt along the edge of the frame through the dust until my fingertips met with something metal. I handed her the key and stood back.

Auntie Sue unlocked the door and gestured for me to go in. 'Go on,' she chuckled, sensing my discomfort. 'It's only the nursery, not Miss Havisham's boudoir.'

The nursery.

I swallowed my nerves and stepped inside. The room was a study in 1970s décor. The pale-yellow walls had a frieze of little people and animals painted around the edge and as I got closer I saw they were all taken from nursery rhymes:

Little Miss Muffet, Baa Baa Black Sheep, Jack and Jill, Mary Mary Quite Contrary . . .

'These are beautiful,' I murmured, tracing the figures with my fingertip. 'Did . . . did you paint these?'

'All my own work,' she said hoarsely. I shot her a look; her eyes were glittering.

All this time I'd been sleeping in the room next door and I'd had no idea . . .

The room was completely empty except for a stack of brown luggage trunks and a white wooden cot with a gorgeous scene of three gambolling rabbits painted on each end. I looked from the cot to my aunt.

'Who was this for?' I asked.

'For the baby who never lived,' whispered Auntie Sue, pleating her apron between her fingers. The sadness on her face broke my heart.

'Oh, Auntie Sue.'

I opened my arms and she stepped into them. I tried dismally to hold back the tears while she sobbed into my neck.

'Listen to me, silly old fool,' she sniffled. 'I'm doing nothing but cry at the moment.'

'Not at all, crying is perfectly understandable,' I murmured, pressing my cheek into her soft white hair. 'Do you know, I'd always wondered why you didn't have children. I think I must have guessed that it wasn't through choice.'

'I couldn't carry a baby full-term, Freya. Nobody knew why, it was just one of those things. I used to spend hours in here, painting and sewing and imagining what it would be like to hold a baby in my arms and put him down to sleep in this cot.'

'Oh, Auntie Sue, I'm so sorry. You would have made a fantastic mum and you're the best auntie a girl could have.'

'Thank you, love. I would have given everything to have a baby. Everything.' She pulled away and dabbed at her eyes with her apron. 'It didn't matter as much to your uncle, but to me the house felt so empty and quiet without a child.'

She looked up at me with a watery smile. 'Until you arrived.'

My heart seemed too big for my body all of a sudden.

'So Mum sent me to England for you? So you could have a child to look after?'

I swallowed the lump in my throat. The intention was well meant but I couldn't help feeling a bit like a library book, lent out to a good home.

Auntie Sue took hold of my face with her hands and pinched my cheeks. 'Oh, love, there was more to it than that. Your mum had her reasons. But that's something you need to talk to her about.'

Talking to Mum had never been easy. I was resentful of being sent away and the times we did spend together were usually awkward and strained. But maybe it was time to do something about that.

I took a deep breath and nodded. 'Do you know what? I think you're right.'

Chapter 14

It had only taken me a few days to sort out a visit and I couldn't quite believe I was in Paris. It was Sunday morning just before ten and the streets were still quiet.

The Parisians had obviously not finished their *petit déjeuner*. Lucky devils, I thought, glancing upwards at the elegant pale yellow edifice of apartments, the louvred window shutters – many still closed – and the wrought-iron balconies perched imperiously above rather tacky souvenir shops at ground level.

My stomach rumbled loudly as I turned into Rue de Rivoli. A metal shutter rattled as the bureau de change on the corner opened up for business and the smell of warm croissants wafted out from the bakery next door. My mouth watered and I very nearly succumbed; I'd fallen asleep on the plane and missed out on the chance of breakfast, although I was betting the airline's pre-packaged croissants weren't quite as delicious as the ones in the *boulangerie* window.

I pressed my hand to my tummy and scurried past. Mum would have baked something sophisticated – she always did. It was one of the main benefits of having a mum who was a born hostess. Besides which, I'd only managed to scrabble together a handful of euros from my bedside drawer last night and I would need my change for the métro ticket back to the airport later. Or – if things went really badly and I found myself back out on the street within the hour – I might have to buy myself some lunch and hitchhike back to the airport.

I swallowed.

Think positive, Freya. Dad might have mellowed with age.

I was starting to perspire and I forced myself to stop walking so fast.

The last few days had been stupidly manic. Once I'd made the decision to scrounge off my dad – sorry, I knew it was for a good cause, but I'd spent all my adult life trying to stand on my own two feet and it really, really galled me to cave in now, but needs must and all that – I'd had to catch a train back to Kingsfield to fetch my passport. Charlie had been there to meet me at the station and we had stood on the platform kissing like something out of a film, me tearful with happiness and him, well, getting a bit horny, actually, and we'd had to scarper back to his flat sharpish.

I smiled at the memory. And went pink. A man in a tight leather jacket and dark glasses, walking a white poodle, inclined his head as he minced past.

'*Bonjour.*'

I bonjoured back in my best French accent and hoped he couldn't read my mind.

I was nearly there now, thank goodness – my legs were beginning to ache from the walk from the station.

Anna had helped me book a flight. That was something I needed to do at the farm as soon as possible – sort out an internet connection. It was literally like having your arms chopped off not being able to get online, and I couldn't believe it was still possible to run a business without a computer. Applying for a passport for the calf had taken me an age, what with filling in three million forms and then finding the right sort of postage stamp – I can't remember the last time I'd used a stamp! *Do it online and hit send*: that was my motto.

The absolute best news, though, was that Uncle Arthur had had his surgery to have a stent fitted and was doing really well. The cardiac consultant reckoned that he'd be home soon, all being well.

I stopped to catch my breath next to an ornate street lamp and stared at an unassuming glass door set back from the pavement underneath stone arches: *Honoré Appartements*.

Technically, this was my family home.

So why did my legs turn to jelly as I began the ascent up the staircase to the fifth floor?

The door flew open before I had a chance to knock, frightening the life out of me.

'Darling! Welcome home! You should have let me collect you, you must be exhausted!'

I staggered backwards with shock as Margo Moorcroft, my mum, with hands fluttering at her neck and a jittery sort of smile, hopped from one foot to the other in the doorway.

Mum *had* offered to pick me up from the airport, but I'd declined. Having lived in so many countries over the years, Mum is a bit blasé about road etiquette and seems to drive by the mantra 'he [or in her case she] who dares wins', and while I admired her attitude, I hadn't fancied a white-knuckle ride so early in the morning. Besides, I'd planned on using the train journey to work out what to say to my parents. Unfortunately, after a night in Charlie's bed, I'd dropped off to sleep instead.

'Hi, Mum,' I laughed shakily. 'Were you listening at the door?'

She shook her head and held out her arms. I stepped into them. It was a crisp sort of hug and neither of us relaxed into it. She pulled away to scan my face with darting green eyes.

'Watching the street, actually. Have been for twenty minutes.'

My mother was eternally immaculate. She had picked her style icons in her twenties and stuck rigidly with them through the decades. Now in her sixties she still looked amazing. I swallowed a familiar groan. Today her hair hung in bouncy, chocolatey waves and even though it was a Sunday, she looked elegant in a tailored shift dress. Beside her I morphed into a gangly teenager: a scruffy one whose limbs are too long for her body.

She gave her shoulders a little shimmy. 'This is such a treat, Freya. I've been looking forward to your visit ever since your call. Although your father and I were surprised to hear from you.'

I smiled, wanting to say something equally warm, but the words seemed to get stuck. I cleared my throat instead and managed to mumble a thank-you.

Her smile faltered for a second and then she sighed happily.

'Anyway. Come in, come in.' She ushered me into the narrow mirrored hallway. 'Your dad is in his study.'

Quelle surprise.

It had been Mum's idea to come on a Sunday. 'Not even your father works then, as a rule,' she'd said, sounding a bit weary down the phone when I'd called her from the farmhouse.

'He's only reading the newspaper,' she said defensively, catching sight of my arched eyebrow.

144

'Rusty?' she called. 'Freya's here.'

'I'm on the phone,' came the curt response.

'Right.' I exhaled, rolled my shoulders back and took a step towards the study.

'No.' Mum grabbed at my arm, making me jump for the second time. 'Let's go into the kitchen. We can chat while I make the coffee.' And she led me away.

The kitchen was probably the smallest room in the apartment, which was a shame because my mother liked to entertain. I leaned over the sink to peer out of the window while she spooned coffee into the percolator.

Wow. I whistled, impressed as ever by the view. My parents' apartment was in the most perfect spot in Paris. Fact.

Directly opposite was the Jardin des Tuileries with its wide paths, octagonal pond and smart outdoor cafés. In the distance, on the other side of the river Seine, the Eiffel Tower dominated the landscape. To the left I could just make out the glass pyramid in front of the Louvre and to the far right the obelisk that marked the centre of the Place de la Concorde.

I had to admit it was an incredible place to live.

'How's poor Arthur?'

Having switched on the coffee machine, Mum turned her attention to a wire cooling rack and a batch of finger-shaped biscuits with their ends dipped in chocolate.

My stomach rumbled appreciatively. I was sure we used to make those together years ago . . . I shook myself. Whatever.

'Coming home soon, hopefully,' I said. 'Auntie Sue has been so worried about him and . . .' I hesitated and twirled a frond of my hair around my fingers. Should I launch

145

straight into their money worries or wait until I'd got Dad in the audience too?

Mum selected a serving plate from the cupboard and sighed. 'I feel terrible that we haven't been over to see them.'

I felt the familiar rise of tension and fought to keep my voice level.

'So why haven't you?' I knew my teenage stroppy self was on the verge of making an appearance, but I couldn't help it.

Mum broke off from my gaze and concentrated on the biscuits. Viennese biscuits, I remembered suddenly. With delicate movements she arranged them into a neat star shape on the plate. If that had been me, they'd look like a collapsed game of Jenga by now.

'It's a difficult time for your father. The bank is restructuring and it's a faces game, you know . . .' she said vaguely.

Dad is a banker. Foreign investments, that sort of thing. He spots booming markets, sinks money into them, waits for them to explode and takes the money out to reinvest into something else. Weird stuff that no normal person would ever think of. The Chinese wine industry, for example. It sky-rocketed last year. They can't get enough cabernet sauvignon in China, apparently. Who knew? Apart from my dad, obviously.

'Not really, no.' I stared at her, unblinking.

She circled a biscuit in the air. 'You know, you need to be seen at all the right parties.'

'Oh *well*, if it's about *parties*,' I said sourly.

Mum is a banker's wife. It's a tough job. It involves agreeing with everything the banker says, handing him a Scotch and ginger when the bottom falls out of the Taiwan

146

tin market and serving toast soldiers dunked in caviar to his boring banker friends at drinks parties.

Meanwhile Uncle Arthur is gasping for breath in a Lake District hospital and I'm looking after a whole massive farm.

And breathe, Freya . . .

Mum looked at me and two pink spots appeared high up on her cheeks. The biscuit in her hands snapped in half.

'Go on through to the living room,' she said, her voice little louder than a whisper. 'I'll call your father in.'

I did as I was told, sat down on one of the stiff Louis-the-something-or-other armchairs and squeezed my eyes. What was I doing here? Why could I never manage to have a civil conversation with Mum? And why was it that I would much rather be in Auntie Sue's kitchen, sitting on one of her baggy old armchairs with the stuffing hanging out of them and claw marks on the legs where Benny and Björn have used them for a scratching post, than spend five more minutes in this elegant high-ceilinged room with its artfully draped gold brocade curtains, ornate cornices and to-die-for fireplace? It was all just so . . . opulent.

'Ah, the wanderer returns!'

Tall, upright, stiff upper lip . . . actually, I couldn't see his lip under his bristly moustache but I knew it was there all the same. *Dad should have been in the army*, I thought as I stood to give him a hug.

'Hi, Dad, good to see you.' *Even though you make me sound like a gypsy*, I added mentally.

'Your mum says Arthur is out of danger. Excellent, ex-cellent.'

He stroked his head absentmindedly, as if expecting to find a full head of hair there. My dad was follicly challenged these days. Ironic really, that his nickname is Rusty after the ginger hair he no longer has. His real name is Michael but no one ever calls him that.

Mum had set out a tray of coffee and biscuits on the glass table in front of us. And by the time we were all seated, each of us on our respective rock-hard armchairs, she had magically poured us all coffees in exquisite gold-edged china cups.

'I bet everywhere is looking lovely in Cumbria,' Mum sighed. 'Green and bursting with life. People say you should visit Paris in spring but you can't beat England for natural beauty.'

'What's the farmhouse like these days, Freya? Still got the Aga?' asked Dad.

I nodded. 'The kitchen hasn't changed a bit. And the beds still have blankets.'

I caught the tail end of an exchange of glances between my parents and frowned. It was not like them to be nostalgic for the farm. Anyway. I straightened my shoulders. That wasn't why I was here.

'So . . .' I took a sip of coffee, crunched my way through a buttery, melt-in-the-mouth biscuit and went for it. 'Uncle Arthur is out of danger, but the farm isn't.'

'Meaning?' said Dad sharply. He sat up in his chair and frowned.

Oh God. My empty stomach was churning like Auntie Sue's butter machine.

'Meaning that they've got into a bit of debt and I've offered to help them out. Well, I say, *I*. I was rather hoping you might help them out. I'm looking at ways to reinvigorate turnover, but—'

Dad swallowed his mouthful of coffee with a splutter.

'Farming!' His face had turned an uncomfortable shade

of red. 'I will not invest in farming. Plough, sow, harvest; plough, sow, harvest; breed cattle, sell cattle . . . You start the year with nothing and finish the year with nothing. Except, perhaps, more debt. British farming is a money pit. Oh, no, thank you very much.'

'And your industry is so different, is it?' I retorted, ears burning with frustration.

'For goodness' sake, Freya, it is *completely* different,' he groaned, rolling his eyes like I was a complete imbecile, which, funnily enough, was how I was beginning to feel. 'The financial markets are never the same two days running. The farming landscape never changes.'

I sprang up from my seat, eyes stinging with tears. 'Well, it will soon. If I can't find a way to raise some money, Appleby Farm will be out of the Moorcroft family and gone for ever. Is that change enough?'

'Good God,' muttered Dad.

Mum reached out a hand and touched my fingers but I shook her off.

'How much do you need, love?' she asked.

'Fifty thousand pounds.'

I actually heard Mum gulp. I sat down. I had to before my legs gave way totally.

'Good grief! FIFTY—' grunted Dad.

'Actually,' I broke in, holding up my palm. My pulse began to race. I cannot *believe* I hadn't thought of this before. Why, oh why, hadn't I put some more thought into this? I could probably even have saved myself the trip and the humiliation, not to mention the fact that I'd given my dad ammunition to criticize not only my life choices but Uncle Arthur's too.

'Actually, I've just remembered. I only need half of that. I can use twenty-five thousand pounds of my own.' I said

149

this to myself as much as to anyone else. Dad clearly wasn't going to help me.

'How does a waitress amass that sort of money?' Dad frowned.

'It's my inheritance from Grandpa,' I said airily. Only I could be as clueless as to forget I'd got twenty-five grand in savings somewhere.

My dad's jaw fell open and Mum muttered something about the apple not falling far from the tree.

One—nil to me. Not that it would do me any good but I'd shocked him into silence. That was a first.

Julian and I had both inherited twenty thousand pounds on our eighteenth birthdays from Mum's side of the family. My brother had blown his on a BMW. I hadn't needed mine so I'd stashed it in some sort of bond in the bank. I'd been gobsmacked last time I'd seen the statement.

'Gracious! Sounds like you made quite a good investment with your money, Freya.' Dad pulled at his moustache.

'Suppose.' I lifted one shoulder in a rather Gallic fashion, I thought.

'Even so, borrowing that sort of money is a serious step to take.'

Mum jumped out of her seat, rattling her cup and saucer as she placed it on the tray and excused herself.

I felt drained all of a sudden. I'd failed in my mission and now all I wanted to do was get back to the farm, crawl into my 'Princess and the Pea' bed and sleep. Maybe tomorrow I'd come up with some other cunning plan to turn Appleby Farm into a gold mine. But this one had failed dismally. I wanted to go home. To my proper home.

I set my cup down slowly and deliberately, and wearily got to my feet.

I met my dad's critical gaze and we stared at each other for a few seconds. I didn't think I'd ever felt so dejected in my life. Finally he sighed.

'I've lived all over the world, Freya, but Appleby Farm takes some beating, so I do understand why you want to come to your aunt and uncle's rescue. Your intentions are admirable, and I can't say I'm not impressed. But I really can't invest in farming. I might as well set fire to a pile of notes.'

'That's not true!' I gasped.

He shook his head. 'Arthur is an old man. He's ten years older than me and he should seriously think of retiring. Focus on his health, not on the endless problems that farming brings.'

I exhaled sadly. It was always about the money with Dad. Where was his compassion?

'Dad, I'm not asking for investment. This is family. Your brother needs your help. I need your help. If I can only get Appleby Farm into profit, then who knows, maybe next year—'

'Next year,' Dad interrupted, getting to his feet, 'there'll be another crisis, and another. I don't want to see you get sucked into farming.'

He held out his hands, expecting me to hold them. But I turned to the door so that he didn't see my tears.

'Then don't watch,' I said and stormed out of the door.

I was halfway down the stairs when I heard Mum shouting. 'Freya, Freya, wait!'

She had left the room quickly enough when the going had got a bit tough, I noticed. I rubbed my tears away with my sleeve while I waited in the stairwell for her to catch up.

'You're leaving already?' she gasped, pressing a hand to her bosom. 'Gosh, I'm so unfit.'

I nodded. 'I don't think there's anything left to say.'

'Oh, Freya, there's plenty to say.'

Her face drooped and tears began to trickle down her cheeks. I wanted to reach out and hug her, but I couldn't. I wanted to ask why I could be so loving to everyone else in my life and yet I struggled even to touch my own mother.

She looked at me and her gaze seemed to carry a message that I couldn't read. I stared back and held my breath, hoping that she had the answers to at least some of my questions.

Finally she nodded and held out her hand to me. I looked down and saw a wad of notes and a small padded envelope. 'Some money for a taxi,' she whispered.

Money. Her answer to everything. I watched her turn away and jog back up the stairs.

I sighed, a great shuddering breath.

Well, that went well.

Chapter 15

Back out on the Rue de Rivoli there were more people milling about and quite a bit of traffic. Taxis were few and far between, though, and it took me some time to flag one down.

I instructed the driver to take me to Charles de Gaulle airport and turned my attention to the little envelope. It had my name written in Mum's graceful writing on the front. I squeezed it: a bit lumpy and not very thick. Not stuffed with twenty-five grand, then.

I slid my finger under the flap. Out fell a note and a familiar item that I hadn't set eyes on in years. It was a keyring with a tiny little book attached to it. The rubbery cover had the words 'The World According to Freya' embossed on the front.

I laughed softly to myself, intrigued. I remembered the keyring really clearly; it had been one of my prize possessions for years.

The letter was written on an ordinary sheet of paper, torn from a notepad as if done in haste, which, judging by the way Mum had left the living room so suddenly, it probably was.

Even before I got to the end of the first line my eyes were blurred with tears and my throat was throbbing. Everything I thought I knew about her shifted.

To my darling daughter,

*From the moment you made your entrance
into my world with your fiery red hair, huge
curious eyes and - it has to be said - gloriously
strong lungs, you captured my heart. Seeing
you today has given me such a deep joy, which
I seem unable to communicate face to face. So
maybe I'll do better on paper.*

*Do you remember this keyring? I've had it
all these years in a keepsake box along with
your first pair of shoes, a baby tooth and a
lock of your hair. You adored it and used to
make me read it to you every day at breakfast.
That was our special time of day, just you and
me, and I treasure those memories of the two
of us. You were such a bright and bubbly little
girl, a whirlwind of energy bringing light and
laughter into my life.*

*I chose the name Freya for you. I fell in
love with the meaning of the name and
I suppose I wanted you to be everything I
wasn't. Look at the first page and you'll see
what I mean . . .*

I tore my eyes away from the letter, rubbed the tears from
my cheeks and lifted the plastic cover of the keyring to
reveal several tiny pages. I read the words on the front page.

Freya
You are a natural leader, headstrong and stubborn,
efficient and determined. You have a wealth of
creative ideas, you are proud and need to feel
appreciated.

My skin tingled with goosebumps. Was that how she saw me? I'd had no idea. I was just Freya, the girl with no life plan, no career. I closed my fingers around the keyring and turned back to Mum's letter.

Sound familiar?!

Sending you away to school in England and making Appleby Farm your home out of term time was the hardest thing I have ever done in my life.

And since that day I have applauded and regretted the decision in equal measure. But I've always known that you resent me for it and that you will probably never forgive me.

I hope one day we can talk about this properly and that you'll let me explain the circumstances, but you need to know this: you were, and still are, the most precious thing in my life. I was determined to give you a warm and loving home, even though that meant letting you go.

Now, seeing you stand up to your father, putting your pride aside to ask for his help, has filled me with such a sense of achievement and I know with absolute certainty that I did the right thing. You live up to every single bit of your name and I couldn't be more proud of the woman you have become. I only wish I had an ounce of your courage.

With all my love
Mum xxx

She was proud of me? I'd never known any of this; I'd no idea that she felt this way. Tears streamed down my face and I lunged forward and banged on the glass screen separating me from the taxi driver.

'Monsieur, turn around! Rue de Rivoli, *s'il vous plait*!'

Five minutes later I was back outside the *Honoré Appartements*, handing a twenty-euro note to a bemused taxi driver, not least because the fare had only cost eight euros. I was still trying to persuade him with my limited vocabulary to keep the change, when the glass door to the apartments swung open. A familiar elegant woman with glossy hair, wearing a camel-coloured trench coat stepped out into the street and strode away purposefully.

'*Zut alors, au revoir!*' I cried, not sure what else I could say to get him to unlock the door. Finally, the door-release light came on and I leaped out of the car.

'Mum!'

She stopped in her tracks and turned towards me. Seconds later we were in each other's arms. This time our hug was real. She held on to me so tightly that I couldn't breathe and I cried big fat tears and left mascara tracks on the lapels of her smart coat. But I don't think either of us minded. Because for the first time in nearly twenty years we had shown each other what was really in our hearts.

'I can't believe you came back.' She pressed a hand over her mouth, her eyes glistening with tears.

'I read your note, I . . .' I swallowed. My heart was racing and suddenly I wanted to talk and to listen and to really get to know my mum. 'It was so beautiful. I had to come back. I wanted to hear more.' I shrugged self-consciously and we both smiled.

'Let's go into the park,' said Mum, tucking her hand through my arm.

*

We headed for Café Renard, just off the Allée Centrale within the Jardin des Tuileries, and chose a table underneath the red awning, surrounded by sycamore trees. My head was in a whirl. I was arm in arm with my mum – something I wasn't sure we'd done for twenty years – the sun was shining and I was in Paris. Even the air smelled French: an exciting mix of fresh coffee, strong cigarettes and delicious pastries. Even though I was dying to have the proper talk that Mum had mentioned in her letter, for the moment I was happy just to soak everything in.

A rather aloof French waiter presented us with huge cappuccinos and for a few moments we sat quietly, simply watching the world go by, both of us content in each other's presence for the first time I could remember in so long.

I watched a young couple with a pram, arms entwined around each other's waist, both unable to drag their eyes away from their baby, and my heart twisted as an image of the unused cot at the farmhouse flashed into my head.

'Auntie Sue took me up to the nursery at Appleby Farm,' I began, peering over the rim of my cup. 'It must have been heartbreaking for them not to have children if that was what they wanted.'

Mum sipped her cappuccino and pressed a napkin to her lips. 'She lost the babies very late on in the pregnancy each time, I think. Before your father and I even got married. But in those days you just got on with it. Such a shame. In some ways I think it made them stronger; they've always been such a loving couple.'

My face softened. 'And they spoilt me rotten!'

Our eyes met and Mum placed her cup down gently in its saucer.

'You were happy with them, weren't you?'

It was a question, but at the same time it wasn't. She was

157

justifying her actions and as much as I was enjoying this new intimacy, I needed to get to the truth.

'Yes, Mum, I was eventually. But I'd been happy with you before you sent me away.'

She winced and gave her head a tiny shake as if she wasn't sure where to begin.

'When you were seven several things happened. Your father was offered a new post in Kuala Lumpur. It was a fabulous opportunity for him but when we arrived we found out that the nearest school to the house was fifteen miles away. And on top of that, it didn't have the best reputation.'

I remembered that house. It had been a sprawling, single-storey thing, surrounded by masses of tall trees with rubbery leaves. The maid had spotted a huge snake slithering across the road once, screamed her head off and the gardener had leaped out and sliced through its body with a machete.

My pulse raced and I stared down at the dusty ground. 'Closer than England, though.'

'True.' Mum nodded. She reached for my hand and squeezed it. 'Your father was very focused on his career; he's never been what you might call a "people person".'

We exchanged knowing glances at that. Understatement of the year!

'But back then,' she continued, 'he was even more single-minded. If it wasn't about making money, Dad wasn't interested. And I had my role, too: holding the best dinner parties, making connections with the managers' wives, organizing our social calendar to ensure we were seen in the right places. Status became everything.'

'And there was no room in this social whirl for a little girl?' I asked, working really hard to keep the resentment out of my voice.

She sighed and patted my hand. 'Of course there was, but I already felt that I'd failed your brother . . .'

Mum began to explain how Julian had been overlooked by his father, the man he idolized, until he finally unlocked the key to gaining Dad's attention: money. My brother had started to become more and more interested in making a profit, even asking Dad to invest his pocket money in the stock market so that he could have his own little share portfolio.

'By the time Julian came back from university that summer, aged twenty-one, he'd turned into a younger and even more extreme version of your father. Only interested in what he could get out of others, judging people's value by how much they were worth in monetary terms. I blame myself, of course, and your father. We were caught up with the lifestyle and it rubbed off on him. He was obsessed with status and possessions, and he treated our staff so badly that our maid left. I was at my wits' end. Our social circle revolved around the bank, we mixed with wealthy, money-orientated people. I felt as if it was inevitable that you would turn out the same way.'

I shook my head. 'But I've never been like that. I mean, look at me . . .' I plucked at my skinny jeans and T-shirt. 'Hardly the look for someone besotted with finery, is it?'

Her lips twitched at that. 'You're beautiful, darling, and that smile is worth a million dollars, believe me. Sue and Arthur have very little and yet they radiate happiness, and that was the sort of environment I wanted for you. When I suggested to your father that we send you to boarding school in England and ask your aunt and uncle to look after you in the holidays, I half expected him to say no. But Kuala Lumpur wasn't the safest of places back then and we both agreed you would be better off in their care. On the day Julian accompanied you to Heathrow on that flight, my heart broke into a million tiny pieces. From that day on I felt like I'd lost my little girl for good.'

I tried to lift my cup but my hands were trembling. I remembered that day so clearly: I had been terrified at the airport and convinced that I must have done something terrible to warrant being sent away from my mum.

'Why did you never tell me any of this?' I asked shakily.

Her eyes met mine. 'Because I've been a terrible mother. I made very selfish choices. Because I felt guilty and sad. I still do.'

'Oh, Mum.'

I leaned forward and hugged her, inhaling her delicate scent of fresh laundry, shampoo and vanilla.

She pulled away after a few moments, clasped her hands in her lap and slipped her diamond ring on and off her finger.

'If I'd been a better person, I could have kept you with me and made sure my influence was the strongest one in your life. But I was caught up with the luxury of the ex-pat lifestyle. I liked having maids and dressing up and going to parties. I've led a very shallow life and I apologize for that. And I've paid the price: your father and I have made friends all over the world but my own children are virtually strangers to me. You don't know how lonely that makes me feel.'

My heart ached with sadness for her as she lowered her head so that I couldn't see her eyes.

'Don't cry, Mum, please. I'm glad I know the truth and, for what it's worth, I think you probably did the right thing. Auntie Sue and Uncle Arthur looked after me as if I was their own. And . . .' I hesitated and took a deep breath. 'I love you.'

'Oh, Freya. You don't know what it means to hear that. Can we start again? Can I be a part of your life?'

I couldn't speak so I nodded instead.

'And if I ever get the chance, I promise I'll make a better job of being a grandmother than I made of being a mother.'

We hugged again for ages until the French waiter cleared his throat and collected our empty cups noisily. We pulled apart and smiled at each other shyly. We still had a lot of catching up to do and we would have to work at getting to know each other again. But it felt like we'd recaptured something special today.

I rummaged in my bag for the euros I'd managed to scrape together last night and dropped them on the table.

'Come on, Mum.' I grinned, pulling her to her feet. 'I've still got a few hours until my flight. By the time I leave Paris, you'll know every last detail about me. Promise.'

As I headed back to the airport to catch my evening flight I could not wipe the big daft grin off my face. The day had been a huge success. OK, I didn't get the money I needed, but I had something better: I had my mum.

Chapter 16

My boomerang brain kept me awake with its constant to-ing and fro-ing from scheme to scheme for the whole flight home from Paris, which was amazingly short, and even the train journey up to the Lake District, which was tediously long. Just as well because while I was availing of the train's free WiFi to google 'making money from farms', an email from Dad popped up.

'What have I done this time, Dad?' I muttered, steeling myself for another dressing-down as I clicked 'open message'.

I scanned the email and whilst I only had a vague idea about part of it and one word seemed a bit rude, I got the gist of it and the gist was abso-bloody-lutely marvellous.

Dear Freya,
After you left – rather abruptly, if I might add – I did a bit of digging into that investment of yours. An ROI of 25 per cent in today's flaccid market isn't remarkable [*thanks, Dad*] but it's not to be sneezed at, either. Therefore I've decided to loan you the full amount that you need for a fixed term to be agreed. Please note, Freya, that this is a loan and I expect it

to be repaid. Your mother assures me that you will do so and I hope she's right. Good luck.

Best

Dad

PS I'm charging you interest at half a per cent over base, which I'm sure you'll agree is more than generous.

If you say so, Dad, whatever 'base' is.

Sometimes I found it next to impossible to put Uncle Arthur and my dad together as siblings. Were there any two men in the universe less alike? Anyway, putting family differences aside for a second . . . HURRAH!

I was so amazed and delighted that I squealed and drummed my feet on the floor, waking up the only other occupant of the carriage: a rumpled-looking vicar who'd been dribbling in his sleep all the way from Manchester.

'Sorry!' I trilled to the startled clergyman, holding up my phone. 'Good news!'

'I thought it was a fire alarm,' he stuttered. He looked a bit odd now he was awake – his chin had been digging into his dog collar during his nap and it had left him with a sad-looking crease under his mouth. 'Thank you, anyway. I think this is my stop.'

I was still full of the joys of Parisian spring when Ross collected me from the station. His car was much nicer than Eddy's skanky old van and had the added benefit of no Buddy, the black terrier with halitosis. It was, however, one of those souped-up hatchbacks with an exhaust that sounded like it had whooping cough and such low-profile tyres that when we went over a humpback bridge I feared mightily for the skin on my backside.

'I'm not much of a one for words,' Ross shouted over the hum of his turbo-diesel engine. I sneaked a peek at his fine-featured profile – amazing eyelashes. 'But thanks for fixing me up with work at the farm. I've learned more in the last couple of weeks than in two years at uni.'

'Ha,' I yelled back. 'You're a godsend: free labour and Eddy hasn't got a bad word to say about you. I should be thanking you.'

Ross went pink and stared out of the windscreen.

'How much do you think it'll cost to get a subcontractor in to do the grassland for the summer?' I asked.

He sucked in air thoughtfully. 'A hundred-odd acres of grassland . . . now then, um . . .'

I waited patiently.

'Mow, forage and transport by trailer to the clamp?'

I nodded, pleased that I understood all the jargon. Foraging meant chopping the grass up into tiny bits. Thank you, Google.

'Well . . .' He scratched his head and gave me an apologetic grin. 'No idea, sorry. Fancy a drink at the White Lion before I drop you back at the farm?'

I rolled my eyes and giggled. I suppose it was a bit too much to expect from a student farmer. And actually a quick drink at the pub and a chat with Lizzie would be nice. But before I had a chance to answer, my mobile rang.

'Hello, Auntie Sue!'

'Uncle Arthur is definitely coming home tomorrow, love!' cried Auntie Sue. 'Isn't that great?'

'That's fantastic,' I agreed. 'Just popping to the pub before I come home. That OK?'

'Of course, you enjoy yourself. I'll put your dinner in the Aga to keep warm.'

'Oh yum, thank you. Oh – Auntie Sue? I've had the best

day ever at Mum and Dad's, and everything is going to be fine. Really.'

We said our goodbyes and I sat back in my seat, gripping the door handle as we raced towards Lovedale, with a massive smile on my face and a fizzy feeling in my stomach. The future of Appleby Farm felt like it was back on track and I had never been so excited in my life.

The White Lion was its usual busy Sunday-night self. Consequently, Ross and I didn't spot Lizzie straight away as we made our way to the bar and elbowed our way in between a group of hikers, who were hogging most of the bar even though they'd all been served. But then I heard her shouting 'excuse me' on the far side of the pub as she collected empty glasses rather bravely, I thought, in the direct path of the darts board.

She looked across, spotted us and marched in our direction. Her thunderous expression startled me; she was flouncing, flaring her nostrils and tossing her hair vigorously. I'd never seen this side to Lizzie and judging by the way Ross tucked himself behind me, neither had he. She had eight empty beer glasses pinched between her fingers and if I didn't know better, I'd have thought she was spoiling for a fight.

'She doesn't look very pleased to see us, does she?' muttered Ross.

'What's up, matey?' I joked, in an attempt to raise a smile.

She came to halt in front of us and dumped the glasses down on the bar forcefully. Her pretty face was all screwed up and there was a peachy-pink flush to her cheeks.

'Ross kept his hands on the steering wheel at all times. Scouts' honour,' I said, doing a three-fingered salute.

Lizzie's face sagged. 'Oh, I know, sorry.' She tilted up her face to Ross and I turned away discreetly while the pair of them smooched their hellos.

'I've missed you,' murmured Lizzie, curling her arm round his neck.

Ross went red. 'I'm nipping to the Gents,' he said, sliding out of her grasp and disappearing round the bar towards the loos.

'You look stressed, Lizzie,' I said, giving her a quick hug.

She rolled her eyes and sighed. 'I know I should ask about Paris, Freya. But seriously. What a chuffin' day. You'll never guess . . .'

She glanced over my shoulder to the other side of the bar, watching Ross, I guessed, and then huffed. 'Look at her! What the bobbins is she up to now?'

I followed her glare to where a petite twenty-something with dark hair, fake eyelashes and far too much lipstick for a country pub was picking bits of fluff of Ross's jumper.

'That's it,' Lizzie muttered grimly, picking up a bar towel and wrapping it round her hand like a boxing glove. 'I'm going to lamp her. Ross hasn't been here five minutes and she's moving in on him already.'

The penny dropped, as did my jaw. 'Is that—' I gasped.

'Victoria, yes.'

Luckily, just as Lizzie looked like she was about to float like a butterfly and quite possibly sting like a bee in her sister's direction, Ross managed to dislodge Victoria and flee to the Gents.

'Where's she staying, when did she arrive and what else has she done to get you so riled up?' I asked, unable to drag my eyes away from the creature who seemed capable of pushing all of Lizzie's buttons at once.

'With me, here, temporarily. She arrived today, even

166

though she wasn't due for another week. And you name it
. . . shoving her new job presenting the lunchtime slot on
Radio Lakeland up my nose every two seconds, sneering at
my career choice and generally behaving like a diva.'

At that moment, Victoria took a sip from her cup, held
the liquid in her mouth, swallowed and then made a great
show of pulling a face as if she'd swallowed sour milk.

'This tea is rank! When was it brewed, Christmas?' she
shrieked in disgust. 'Where do I have to go to get a decent
cup of tea around here?' I had to admit, Victoria did have
a point, even if she had put it across a bit crudely. The tea
at the White Lion was foul. The coffee was just as bad.
Nothing like the frothy delights I used to concoct at the
Shenton Road Café . . .

'Bloody hell, Lizzie,' I hissed.

'Told you!' She shook her head, her full lips pressed into
an unusually thin line. 'She thinks she's better than everyone, she—'

'She's a genius!' I gasped. My pulse started to race, adrenalin pumping through me like I'd been mainlining caffeine.
'That's it! That's actually it!'

I emitted a peculiar laugh-cum-gasp, gave the astonished
Lizzie a smacker of a kiss, yelled goodbye and ran from the
pub all the way back to Appleby Farm.

I stuck my head in through the farmhouse door, shouted
hello to Auntie Sue, grabbed a torch and then dashed back
down the path and along the yard to the empty barn. The
evening light had faded but the moon had crowned all the
old stone farm buildings with a glorious silvery halo.

Sometimes the beauty of this place makes me want to cry, I
thought, pushing open the barn doors.

Once inside, I paused to catch my breath and turned

in a slow circle, casting the beam of the torch around me. The oak, the stone, the potential of this building filled my heart with joy. Could it work? Could I turn this barn into Appleby Farm Tea Rooms? I wandered round the space, picturing it: the kitchen at that end, tables and chairs along one side, maybe an ice-cream counter too . . . We'd have to extend the water and power supplies from the house but . . . it had potential.

I'd worked in pubs, cafés and hotels but I'd never set one up from scratch before and I'd certainly never managed one. On the other hand, Shirley was always telling me I should run my own business. Could I do it? Could I turn the barn into the only place around here to get a decent cup of tea?

I shrugged my shoulders and took one last look around before heading back to the farmhouse.

This was either the most brilliant or the most ridiculous idea I'd ever had.

After catching up with each other's news over a late supper of cockle-warming chicken casserole, Auntie Sue took herself up to bed, while I settled myself in the office to use the phone. Björn jumped up on to my lap as soon as I sat down and I smoothed my palm along the length of his silky spine.

'Oh, thank you for joining me,' I murmured as I dialled the first Kingsfield number. 'I might need a bit of moral support.'

'Shirley? It's Freya. Do you mind if I pick your brains about something . . . ?'

When I came off the phone ten minutes later, my 'flabber' was well and truly 'gasted'.

Shirley Maxwell had completely bowled me over with her enthusiasm for the tea rooms idea and had even suggested adding 'vintage' into the mix. Genius!

She'd informed me in no uncertain terms that if I *didn't* give the tea rooms a go she would never forgive me. Not only that, but she'd almost made me cry by extoling virtues that I didn't even know I had – tenacity, determination and charm, to name but three. She'd ended by saying that she was one hundred per cent behind me, that she'd send me a list of suppliers to get me started and promised that even though I wouldn't need it, I could have my old job back whenever I wanted.

One down, one to go. I was too young for hot flushes, surely, I wittered, fanning my face with one hand and looking up Charlie's number on my mobile with the other.

The thing is, Charlie, I'm going to set up a business at the farm, working all hours, and I might not come back to Kingsfield for weeks, months even.

That's fine, Freya, take as long as you need . . .

Yeah, right.

I was mid-gulp when he answered the call.

'Freya! I've been thinking about you all day! It's very lonely in my bed tonight without you in it.' He chuckled.

It was a deep, sexy laugh and my body pinged like a tight bra strap as I recalled last night in his flat. It felt as if it had been years ago already, so much had happened since I left Kingsfield this morning.

'Glad to hear it,' I laughed softly, cradling the phone to my face and wishing it was his hand on my skin.

'Early shift tomorrow. Ha, a fire-fighter's day is as unsociable as a farmer's, isn't it, getting up early to milk the cows and plough the fields?'

I grinned. 'Just like it.'

A grain of hope swelled in my imagination as I envisaged Charlie and I working on the farm together . . .

'Not that I'd ever want to live on a farm. Give me a city skyline with taxi ranks, Indian takeaways and a bit of good old-fashioned pollution any day of the week,' he added.

The hope dissipated and a sigh escaped before I could rein it in.

'Hey, Green Eyes, less of the sighing,' Charlie said soothingly. 'You're doing great. I've had a lot of time to think over the past few weeks. You up there, me down here. This separation isn't easy for either of us, but you know what? I'm very proud of you. How many other women would sacrifice their nice cosy lives to help out family?'

'Really?' I could feel a sob pressing at my throat and I bit down on my bottom lip.

'Yeah, really. So, how did it go in Paris?'

I told him about my heart-to-heart with Mum and the loan from Dad and about my madcap scheme to turn the barn into tea rooms and that it might take ages but that if I couldn't make the farm profitable then Auntie Sue and Uncle Arthur wouldn't be able to retire. All the time I was thinking that every word was a nail in the coffin of our relationship. Finally I ran out of things to say and I fell silent, breathless and anxious.

Charlie was quiet for a few moments. I could hear his breathing and I tried to match my breaths to his, as if somehow that would close the gap between us.

'Babe, you do what you need to do,' he said softly. 'I'll support you as much as I can from this end. And we'll get together as often as possible. It doesn't have to be the end, does it? Unless that's . . . is that what you want?'

I shook my head. Tears were streaming down my face; I was a lucky girl to have Charlie in my life. 'No,' I managed to blurt out.

'Don't cry. Listen, if it's not too much for your aunt and uncle, why don't I move my shifts around, get a few days off and come up to stay?'

'I'd love that,' I croaked. 'It's a good job this isn't a video call, I'm a complete mess!'

'I doubt that,' he said gently.

Suddenly a massive wave of doubt reared up in front of me. What was I doing, thinking about staying in the Lake District away from my lovely man? Perhaps I should just bail my aunt and uncle out of their debts, sort out extra labour for the summer and leave them to worry about the farm's future. Oh God, I was so confused.

'You're doing the right thing, Freya, and I'm proud of you.'

He couldn't have said anything more perfect if he'd tried. My heart throbbed with relief. I closed my eyes and imagined his strong, comforting arms around me.

'Thanks, Charlie, I needed that,' I sighed.

Fifteen minutes after our call ended I climbed into bed and zonked out as soon as my head touched the pillow. Hardly surprising after the all the travelling I'd done in the last forty-eight hours, not to mention the monumental journey my emotions had been on.

The next morning I woke early and opened the curtains to find a bright golden dawn greeting the tiny village of Lovedale.

I took a deep, contented breath and gazed at the acres of Appleby Farm stretching up to Colton Woods, across to Willow Farm and down the valley into the distance.

In *The World According to Freya*, everything is doable. And I genuinely believed that. Not in some airy-fairy motivational mantra way. More of a conviction that if it feels right, I should go for it.

And as crazy as it seemed last night, now, as I faced a fresh new day, my idea to open the Appleby Farm Vintage Tea Rooms felt absolutely right.

Chapter 17

Gradually we all settled into a new normal life of sorts. Uncle Arthur was home and convalescing, much to his and Auntie Sue's relief. Banning him from attempting to do any work had not been the issue that we'd envisaged: by the time the poor chap had eaten breakfast, had a bath, shaved and put on clean pyjamas he was worn out and needed another lie-down.

With Lizzie and Ross's help I'd given the farm office a mini makeover and now it was a much more welcoming and fragrant place to work. The smelly old carpet had gone and we'd scrubbed the old floorboards, the walls had been painted a cheerful shade of pale primrose, Ross had sanded down an old sewing table I'd found abandoned in one of the sheds and I'd tucked it into a corner to use as a desk. On it stood my sparkly new laptop, a jug of bluebells and . . . drum roll, please . . . a wireless router. YAY! I'd had broadband installed so I could Skype, FaceTime and iMessage to my heart's content.

Other than a quick spritz with some beeswax furniture polish, I hadn't touched Uncle Arthur's desk. After all, it was still his office and I was looking forward to his return to work, probably as much as he was. I was coping with the farm correspondence for now, but there was still so much about the running of the farm that I didn't have a clue about.

It was Friday morning at the end of May and I was filling in forms for the Vintage Tea Rooms planning application, humming happily to myself when Auntie Sue appeared at the office door with my lunch, closely followed by a hopeful Madge.

'It's all very hi-tech in here now, isn't it?' Auntie Sue marvelled, sliding a plate of cheese on toast and a mug of tomato soup on to my desk. 'All these new wires and things. We'll be catching up with Willow Farm at this rate.'

'Mmm, delish, thank you!' I bit into the crunchy toast and wiped the cheesy stringy bits off my chin.

Madge licked her lips longingly and I accidentally on purpose dropped a piece of crust on the floor for her.

'Who's running Willow Farm these days?' I asked. 'I've seen Harry from a distance, but not had chance for a chat.'

'Harry manages it. We see quite a lot of him as a rule. Nora and Jim retired to Bournemouth a few years ago, lucky pair.' Auntie Sue sighed wistfully. 'Do you remember how Jim got really bad arthritis when you were in your teens?'

'Er, sort of.' I stirred my soup and frowned.

'Well, the doctor's advice was to retire as soon as they could and move down south. Apparently, it's done wonders for Jim's health. Tough on Harry, though, having all that responsibility at such a young age.'

I nodded. 'It must have been.' I'd managed to escape responsibility until I was twenty-seven and I was still finding it hard to cope.

Auntie Sue perched her bottom on the edge of Uncle Arthur's desk. 'I'm surprised you've not been to see him.

You two used to be thick as thieves. In fact, Nora and I used to think the two of you would start courting at one time.'

I laughed. 'No, we were just mates and that was years ago. I don't suppose we've got much in common these days! Anyway, I'm sure I'll bump into him soon.'

Not that I was complaining but with all the paperwork for the barn conversion, unravelling Uncle Arthur's invoicing system, market research for the menu, putting mood boards together for the décor and sorting out the broadband, I'd barely had time to see anyone over the past few weeks.

'He's a grafter, that boy, and making a good job of it, by all accounts. Mind you, he's got it all computerized up there and he's expanded. No wonder he's still single. Perhaps he's still carrying a torch for you?' She raised her eyebrows knowingly.

I tutted at her. 'Stop stirring, you! Besides, we'll have our farm records computerized soon. I'll have to show you how to use the internet, Auntie Sue. You'll be able to find all sorts of lovely recipes online.'

She harrumphed and shook her head. 'I'm perfectly fine with my Delia and Mary Berry books, thanks all the same.'

'Well, *they've* both got websites and, look at this . . .' I dropped my toast back on the plate and tapped at the laptop, sprinkling crumbs liberally on the keyboard. 'Ta-dah! So have we!'

'Good gracious,' exclaimed Auntie Sue when the holding page for Appleby Farm Vintage Tea Rooms appeared on screen. 'Can you order a cup of tea on there?'

'No,' I laughed. 'But customers will be able to get directions, check out the menu and drool over your cakes before they even get here. I might even set up a webcam in the chicken run so that people can see exactly how free range our eggs are.'

The website was still under construction but I could already tell it was going to be fab. It was a going-away present from Anna, who had proved yet again to be an amazing friend.

She had boxed up the remainder of my meagre possessions ready for Charlie to bring to Lovedale. And when I'd called to thank her for all she had done for me, she wouldn't hear a word of it.

'You dropped everything and moved your life to Kingsfield for me and Mum when she broke her ankle,' she'd argued. 'It's no surprise at all that you're doing it again for *your* family. I will miss you, though,' she'd added softly.

'Aw, ditto, Anna,' I'd replied. 'But you've got an open invitation to visit and I hope you will.'

There was a pause down the line.

'You know what I'm like: happiest at home. And I've decided to help Mum out at the café on Saturdays. I'm doing the breakfast shift with Amy, the new girl, so she can have the morning to herself. Amy has turned out to be a star; you did a good job training her, Freya.'

We'd ended the call with her offering to build me a website for my tea rooms and giving me the name of someone who could do me a good deal on a laptop. Which I'd taken advantage of.

'This isn't all too much for you, is it, Freya?' clucked Auntie Sue, frowning gently. 'Your uncle and I are very grateful . . .'

'I know,' I stood up and wrapped my arms around her. 'You keep saying. Every five minutes.'

Her soft body shook with a chuckle as she acknowledged I was right.

'But I promise you, I've never been happier. Yes, I'm living in a bit of a whirl, but I like whirls – they're exciting. Besides which, Charlie and Ollie will be here in a few hours for the weekend and I can't wait for you to meet them. And if Charlie were to love the farm as much as I do, well . . .' I shrugged, not wanting to tempt fate.

My head was all over the place at the moment. One minute I was trying to imagine a future for Charlie and me at the farm and the next I was reminding myself that my current career as manager of Appleby Farm was just a temporary role.

Mind you, there was a fire station four miles away from Lovedale . . . that had to be a possibility, hadn't it? A transfer from Kingsfield to Cumbria?'

'Ooh, yes, I meant to ask . . .' She blinked rapidly, poked at a loose thread on the sleeve of her cardigan and two pink spots appeared on her cheeks. She was blushing, which was odd. 'What should we do, bedroom-wise? I need to go and make up some beds.'

'I thought they could go in the bedroom next to yours with the twin beds, in case Ollie wakes in the night or something,' I said, picking up my soup.

'Right,' said Auntie Sue, looking relieved. 'Only we wouldn't have minded, you know, if you and Charlie wanted a double bed . . . Your uncle and I have already discussed it.'

'Gosh, this tomato soup is hot,' I mumbled, hiding my face in the mug.

Eek! My turn to blush. I was twenty-seven and a woman of the world and not at all prudish about my sex life, but the thought of the two of them discussing it made my toes curl.

I cleared my throat. 'Anyway . . .'

'So what are you up to this afternoon, love?' she asked.

177

I smiled gratefully at the change of subject. 'I'm learning about beef farming with Eddy.'

It was a bit of a chicken-and-egg situation, or rather cow-and-calf, I supposed. What I still needed to get my head round was how Auntie Sue and Uncle Arthur could ever retire while they still had the herd.

The business was simple enough: the eighty head of beef cattle produced calves that Uncle Arthur reared on the farm and then sold. The sale of the calves paid the feed bills, the vet's bills, Eddy's wages and all the other farm costs. The question was, if the farm stopped breeding calves, then surely there would be no major costs, would there? So they could retire. But then what would happen to the herd? Could they be sold, perhaps? And without knowing the ins and outs of my aunt and uncle's finances, would they have any money to live on?

One thing was for certain: Uncle Arthur's health had to come first and running a busy farm could really not be the best way for a seventy-five-year-old man with heart disease to be spending his days.

'Ooh, I'll have to tell your uncle,' she said, breaking into my reverie. 'He will be pleased to hear that. He loves those animals like his own children.' She rolled her eyes. 'He's already started mithering about being allowed to see them.'

And there was me plotting to sell them off. My stomach flipped uneasily as I shared the last of my cheese on toast with the dog. Auntie Sue swooped on my empty plate and mug and headed for the door with Madge at her heels.

'Well, I think I'm better suited to the tea rooms really,' I said with a rather forced laugh, 'but there are one or two things I want to know.'

'Fair enough, love. And thank you for suggesting that we

subcontract out the silage this summer. And . . . well, help-ing out with the debts. It's a load off your uncle's mind.'

'Glad to help,' I said, feeling a rush of love for the pair of them. I'd paid off the seed supplier, the tractor loan and the tax bill, and there was still money left to pay for some extra help this summer and leave them a bit in the bank to cover any unexpected bills. 'Now, I'm off to find Eddy and learn about the Hereford herd. Do you think I'll need rubber gloves?' I giggled.

As it turned out Eddy drove me up to Oak Field in the Land Rover, so no close contact was required. What a relief! As docile as they looked, I was still quite nervous of the huge creatures and happy to stay within the confines of the vehicle.

The herd was split into three groups. This particular batch was made up of about thirty cows and their calves, dotted around the middle of the field under the dappled shade of three oak trees. We circled the group slowly, bump-ing about over the deep ridges in the field. The windows of the Land Rover were wound down and the sweet smell of fresh grass mixed with the more pungent aroma of cow pat filled the air. A few of the calves were suckling, some of the cows were lying down, others were grazing and one cow, rather embarrassingly for me, was humping another.

'Lovely sight, in't it?' Eddy pulled to a halt a few metres away from the nearest animal.

I flicked a glance at him, unsure whether he meant the two putting on a performance worthy of the *Discovery Channel*, but his sharp grey eyes were examining each and every animal carefully.

'Lovely,' I agreed.

'I like to see cows with calves at foot. When we were

a dairy farm, the calves were brought up in pens without their mothers. Which is how it's got to be, of course. Nice to see the little 'uns on grass, though.'

'So what do we need to do for the herd today?'

'Just a check for now. When we turn 'em out into the fields in spring, we let the bulls run with the cows. This group of lucky ladies has got Dexter.'

Eddy pointed to the middle of the group where a huge brown and white bull with a pink nose and little white curls on his forehead was chewing the cud and staring at us intently.

'Very handsome,' I agreed.

'About now – May, June – they'll be getting pregnant again. And then we'll start having calves February, March next year.'

I swallowed. Busy life for a cow! And I also realized with a jolt that next year's crop of calves could already be in production, so to speak. 'How can you tell if they're pregnant?'

He shook his head. 'You can't at this stage. She's in season, though,' he said, pointing to the cow that'd been thoroughly romped by her friend. 'We need to get the vet round for a routine pregnancy test. And we've got the TB test at ten o'clock tomorrow. Assuming the last bill's been paid?' He raised an eyebrow at me warily.

'All paid up,' I reassured him. Paying the bills had used up a good chunk of my money, but at least Uncle Arthur could stop worrying for the time being.

'Good. By June most of the herd will be pregnant,' he said. The knuckles of his left hand had a line of scabs along them as if he'd grazed them along a wall. He scratched at the edge of one of the scabs until it flicked off on to his lap. He picked it up off his moleskin trousers and dropped it out of the window.

I turned my head away so he didn't spot my wry smile. *Remind me again why you're single, Eddy*, I thought to myself.

He gave a great shuddering sigh and I looked back at him. 'Is Arthur finished with farming, do you think?'

My stomach flipped and for a moment I wasn't sure what to say. *The truth*, I decided, *just tell him the truth*.

'Gosh, Eddy, I don't know. He doesn't want to finish, but I worry about him, so does Auntie Sue. Things are going to have to change, I do know that. One bit of good news, though: Uncle Arthur has agreed to subcontract out the silage this summer.'

Eddy puffed out his cheeks. 'That's a bloody relief. Most of the land's ready for mowing, except the higher fields. We'll have to move fast — it starts to lose its nutritional value quickly once it's gone to seed. Want me to make some enquiries?'

'Would you? Thanks.'

He put the Land Rover into gear and we drove to the left-hand side of the field where one cow was dozing in the sunshine, her calf curled up beside her.

'Want to know what I'd do?' he said gruffly, gazing out at the pair of animals.

'Go on.' I nodded.

'Advertise half the herd for sale. Now. While they're out in't field all summer. It's much harder work looking after pregnant cows through winter. That's what I'd do, if I was Arthur,' he finished quietly.

'Thanks, Eddy.'

I reached over and squeezed his hand.

His eyes met mine and I wasn't surprised to see that they were a bit misty. Neither of us spoke. It was obvious what this would mean. If the Appleby Farm herd were to be sold there would be no job left for Eddy. And yet that was his advice. What a kind and selfless thing to say.

'Anyway . . .' I said brightly, patting his hand. I nodded out of the window, keen to steer the conversation back into safer waters. 'Are you happy with this lot, then?'

'Aye, although I'll think we'll move 'em on to the next field. The grass is mostly eaten off in this one.'

'What?' I squeaked, gripping the door handle as a vision of the two of us flapping our arms at the herd popped into my head. 'Move them how?'

Eddy chuckled and shook his head. 'Watch this.'

He put the Land Rover into gear and we began to creep forwards. When we were nearly at the open gate he leaned out of the window and whistled. Really loudly.

'Come on!' he bellowed and then whistled again. 'Come on. Hup, hup, hup.'

I turned round to look behind us. The herd was on the move; some actually running towards us, others clambering clumsily to their feet. 'Wow! Can I have a go?'

Eddy sucked in a breath. 'There's quite a knack to it.'

I hung out of the window and hollered for all I was worth: 'Come on! Come on. Girls; and you, Dexter. That's it, keep going! Hup, hup!'

Oh yes, I thought, settling back in my seat once the herd had all moved into the next field, *I'm a natural*.

I grinned all the way back to the farmyard, at which point I saw a car I recognized in front of the house and my happiness setting went into overdrive.

Charlie and Ollie had arrived.

Chapter 18

You know when things are going so well that you have to pinch yourself so you know you're really awake? That life has somehow or other gone from scarily worrying to deliriously perfect? Well, that was how I felt today.

I was stretched out in the sun in front of the farmhouse next to a swathe of deliciously scented lavender, looking at second-hand coffee machines on eBay. I'd positioned myself strategically so that I could still get a WiFi connection, manage to keep an eye on Uncle Arthur, who was sitting in the shade teaching Ollie how to whittle a stick, and steal surreptitious glances at my shirtless boyfriend all at the same time.

I closed my eyes for a second and lifted my face to the sun.

Charlie was digging Auntie Sue's veggie patch, which ran along the side of the farmhouse. She'd supplied him with a barrow-load of manure and a pile of bamboo canes, and he was cheerfully planting out her peas and French beans. She was now perched in a deckchair, supposedly peeling potatoes but I kept catching her peeking at Charlie's tattooed and tanned torso.

Not that I blamed her. I hadn't realized just how much

I'd missed him until he'd scooped me up and swung me round on Friday. I still couldn't quite believe he was here, nor how quickly he and Ollie had been absorbed into the Moorcroft family in the last forty-eight hours.

Things weren't absolutely perfect, of course: Uncle Arthur was still weak and had a grey tinge to his skin, Ollie had cut his finger twice on the penknife, I'd got sunburn on my nose and Charlie had stumbled into a patch of stinging nettles a moment after stripping his shirt off. Ouch! Plus there had been an awkward moment after Ollie had gone to bed last night when Auntie Sue had gushed that I'd make a wonderful mother, but maybe I was being oversensitive and perhaps it was only me who'd felt awkward . . .

Even so, if I could bottle my happiness this afternoon, I would be a millionaire. Fact.

Ollie was, as usual, keeping up a constant barrage of questions mixed in with snippets about his own little life, much to my uncle's amusement.

They were both sitting down: Uncle Arthur in his armchair, which Charlie had carried outside for him, and Ollie on a little stool at his knee. On the ground between them was a pile of willow sticks, they each had a penknife and their knees were covered in wood shavings. It was hard to tell who was having the most fun, but I'd certainly not seen my uncle look so relaxed since I'd arrived at Easter.

'You'd like *Cars*, Uncle Arthur,' said Ollie solemnly. 'It's even got tractors in it. I've brought the DVD with me. Shall we watch it later?'

Uncle Arthur chuckled. 'Appleby Farm has got real tractors, Ollie, but sadly no DVD player.'

'You can watch it on my laptop,' I suggested, rolling my eyes. Auntie Sue and Uncle Arthur were the only people I knew still with a teetering stack of videos next to the TV.

Uncle Arthur paused from his whittling to wink at me. 'Thank heavens for that, hey, Ollie.'

'At Beaver Scout camp we're allowed to melt marshmallows over the fire. Next time I'm going to show all the other boys how to whittle our own sticks. Do you like marshmallows?'

'I do,' said Uncle Arthur, holding up a fat stick that he'd carved Ollie's name into. 'Here you are, son. But I like cooking bread on sticks over the fire. Have you ever done that?'

I smiled at them both; I used to love doing that, too.

Ollie opened his eyes wide and took the stick from my uncle. 'Wow! Never. Can we do that later?'

'If your dad says so.'

'Dad?' yelled Ollie.

Charlie stood up straight and wiped his arm across his brow. He caught my eye and we both laughed. 'If Uncle Arthur is up to it, yes.'

'Cool!'

I patted the grass next to me and Charlie came and sat down.

'Anyone for ice cream?' called Auntie Sue, staggering to her feet with a huge pan of peeled potatoes.

'Me!' cried Ollie, abandoning his stick and penknife and following Auntie Sue into the kitchen.

'You can come with me to milk the cows later, if you like,' I heard her say. 'Then you can see where the ice cream comes from.'

'Cool!'

Uncle Arthur let out a sigh and closed his eyes. 'It's lovely to have a youngster about the place again. Tiring, though.'

I leaned against Charlie. Heat was radiating from him as he wrapped his arm around my waist and he smelled all

185

manly: sort of lemony and earthy and a tiny bit sweaty. He had a smear of soil on his chest, which somehow added to the appeal, and it was all I could do not to lean back on the grass and pull him on top of me.

'Do you think your aunt would mind babysitting tonight?' His lips were right next to my ear and my hormones suddenly went into overdrive.

'She'd love to. What have you got in mind?'

I met his blue eyes and we both giggled as he waggled his eyebrows seductively.

'Say no more. It's a date,' I said, sealing the deal with a kiss.

We left Ollie with Auntie Sue, making bread dough to cook on the bonfire that Charlie had started for them at the edge of the orchard, and drove out to Lake Windermere for a walk along the western shore in the evening sunshine. It was beautiful and peaceful; just him and me, the occasional family of ducks and the sound of waves lapping gently at the shingly shore.

I so wanted him to love it and he did.

'It's a beautiful place, Freya,' he said as we crunched across the stones to the water's edge. 'It must be like being on a permanent holiday.'

My heart soared. That was exactly how I wanted him to feel.

'And you know something else?' He slid his eyes to mine briefly before bending down and picking up a pebble.

I shook my head.

'You're even more gorgeous than ever. I know that absence makes the heart grow fonder and all that but . . .' He shrugged and skimmed the stone across the water. It bounced three times before disappearing into the lake. 'I

186

can't put my finger on it. Your face, your hair, even your freckles . . . you've always been a beautiful girl, but now, I don't know, you just seem to shine.'

'Oh, Charlie, that's the sweetest thing ever. I'm not sure that any of it's true, but I do know that I feel more alive when I'm here and it's like I've found my perfect job.'

'I see . . .' He pinched his lips together and a big frown appeared in his forehead.

Eek, how insensitive was that!

'Oh, Charlie! I'm so sorry, that's me all over, speak first and think later, or not think at all in some cases . . . Oh God.'

He grinned and hugged me to him and I realized he'd been trying hard not to laugh. 'It's OK, go on, hit me with your new "more alive" life.'

I looped my arm round his waist and we carried on walking away from the water's edge and rejoined the path through some trees.

'Well, I'm outdoors a lot of the time, and I'm flitting from one thing to the next, which I find really exciting. Like this afternoon, for example, one minute I'm learning how to make chocolate ice cream from Gloria and Gaynor's milk – oh, you should have seen Ollie's face earlier when Auntie Sue let him watch her milk them, by the way. He couldn't believe it when the milk started pumping through the tubes – and the next minute I'm on the phone to a hobby farmer who wants to know if Uncle Arthur has any heifers for sale. And the best thing is, Uncle Arthur said that yes, maybe he did and she's coming up from Gloucestershire some time next week. And that is exactly what Eddy wanted to happen, so that's . . . What? Charlie, are you laughing at me again?'

'No, well, yes, I'm just . . .' He shook his head indulgently.

'I'm not going to pretend I'm happy with you being so far away. But do you know what? When I see you like this, so full of it and fired up, I can't help but be happy for you.'

'And that's why I love you,' I murmured. 'For letting me be happy.'

'Right, that's it,' he said, glancing round to check we were alone. 'That deserves a kiss.'

He tugged my hand and ran, and suddenly we were off the path and kissing behind a tree, then in the bushes and getting covered in bark and leaves and each other.

'Thank you,' I said, when we finally came up for air. 'For everything.'

'I know, I'm a hero.' He grinned. 'How are you ever going to make it up to me?'

'Well, shall we start with a pint at the pub,' I suggested, 'and then take it from there?'

Sunday night and the White Lion was busy.

'Where do they all come from?' Charlie was amazed as I pulled him through the throng towards the bar. 'There are hardly any houses in Lovedale and the place is packed!'

'I know! Tourists, a lot of them: campers, people in holiday cottages, plus us farmers.' I gave him a twinkly smile. 'And it's a bank holiday weekend, don't forget.'

Ross was already at the bar, chatting to Lizzie, who was rushed off her feet as usual, pulling pints, handing out change and keeping her eye on who was next in the queue to avoid any arguments.

'Lizzie, Ross – meet Charlie,' I beamed proudly as soon as Lizzie had a free millisecond.

'Cor.' Lizzie grinned, running an approving eye over him. 'She said you were gorgeous.'

'Oi,' said Ross. 'I heard that. Can I get you both a drink?'

Charlie began talking to Ross and I pulled up a stool and chatted to Lizzie in between her serving customers.

'He is one majorly gorgeous man,' she hissed in an impossible-not-to-hear whisper.

'I know.' I grinned, turning pink.

I reached across and pinched one of Charlie's crisps. I always forgot what an appetite he had; after two platefuls of Auntie Sue's pot roast and a dish of sticky toffee pudding, he was apparently hungry again and had bought two packets of ready salted and a bag of peanuts.

'How are things with your sister?' I asked.

'Actually, Victoria's been all right,' said Lizzie, looking amazed, as if the thought had only just occurred to her. Her hair was caught up in a high ponytail and it swished from side to side as she talked.

'She was in here yesterday. Her job is amazing and they all love her at the radio station – her words, not mine. And she says she's got her eye on someone, she didn't say who. So, thank the Lord, Ross is safe. In fact, she only annoyed me once.'

'Oh?'

'Cheeky moo said she was going to help me get a better job.'

I looked across at Bill, the landlord, who had suddenly paused whilst pouring a pint of Jennings.

'Apparently they're looking for junior office staff at Radio Lakeland. I mean, for starters, how humiliating would that be, being the office junior when my sister is the talent? Allegedly. And for afters, I could never work in an office!'

At that moment, Charlie and Ross tuned back in to our conversation.

'Me neither,' we all said at once.

Bill's shoulders sagged with relief and he trotted off to deliver his pint to a customer.

Charlie looped an arm around my shoulders and I leaned my hip against him. I saw Lizzie mouth *Aww* to Ross and I pressed my lips together in a smile. This was lovely; the four of us. Shame Charlie had to leave again on Wednesday.

'What will you do for a job, Freya, when you come home?' Charlie asked out of the blue. 'You won't go back to the café, will you?'

I blinked at him. 'Ooh, gosh, I haven't thought that far ahead yet. I mean, I need to get the Vintage Tea Rooms set up first,' I said, feeling all hot and bothered. 'So it could be a while yet.'

'Oh.' His mouth did that upside-down smile thing and I could have kicked myself.

Lizzie put her hand in the air. 'I'll help you!' She pulled a face and folded her arms. 'Not that I get much time off but at least it'll give me a good excuse not to see Victoria, plus I can boast that I'm involved with a new business venture. Office job, my bum,' she chuntered.

'Thanks.' I swallowed, still looking at Charlie. 'There's loads to do. We're supposed to be clearing the barn out tomorrow, if that's OK?'

'Yeah, of course.' Charlie smiled, but his smile didn't quite reach his eyes.

'I'm seeing the planning officer at the council on Tuesday after the bank holiday and hopefully she'll give me the verbal go-ahead.'

'And you've got your builders sorted,' added Ross.

'Correct.'

I'd thought sourcing tradesmen would be difficult but all I'd had to do was stand at the bar in this very spot, utter the words 'reliable builder' and everyone had said 'Goat', and pointed towards a man sitting in the corner on his own.

Goat was a clean-shaven, squarely built man with a bald head balanced, it seemed, directly on to broad neckless shoulders. He had one leg longer than the other, a trait that had become quite obvious when he'd walked over to introduce himself. And I'd noticed he tried to hide his leg imbalance by standing on a slope or hitching one foot on to a stool when he spoke to me. Actually, he didn't talk much at all but his quotation was reasonable and he had drawn me up plan of how he thought the Vintage Tea Rooms could look, which matched my ideas exactly. I was a bit worried about how he coped with climbing ladders with his dodgy legs but didn't like to ask.

'I'll have to start sourcing crockery soon,' I said. 'I'm looking forward to that. I'm thinking pretty, mismatched china.'

I remembered my little battle with Shirley over the white mugs in her café. This time I would be able to indulge my love of colour.

'Ooh, lovely!' cooed Lizzie, pulling the cork out of a bottle of red wine for a customer.

'And at some point I'll have to employ someone to run it for me, I suppose.'

Lizzie looked over her shoulder to check Bill wasn't in earshot.

'Me!' she hissed. 'I mean, you can give me a proper interview and everything, but that would be my dream job. Seriously, Freya. Me, me, me!' She stared at me, eyebrows raised, willing me to give her a chance.

'Well . . .' I laughed awkwardly. Upside: I liked and trusted her. Downside: I couldn't quite put my finger on it but—

'There you go, Freya. Sorted. You'll be back in Kingsfield

in no time.' Charlie downed the last of his pint and thumped his glass down on the bar.

Lizzie clapped her hands and Charlie kissed my cheek.

'Yeah,' I said, forcing a brightness that I didn't feel. 'Lovely!'

And Lizzie would make a great manager. When there was something to actually manage. So why had my stomach gone all fluttery?

'Anyway,' said Charlie, looking at my nearly empty glass meaningfully, 'lovely to meet you but we left my son with Freya's aunt and uncle cooking bread on poky sticks over a fire, so we'd better get back.'

'Oh, damper bread!' exclaimed Ross and Lizzie at the same time.

'Ha-ha! Jinx. Padlock!' cried Lizzie, jabbing Ross in the ribs.

Charlie stared at me, bemused, and I shrugged, laughing. 'Let's go,' he whispered.

We left Lizzie and Ross giggling at each other and stepped out into the cool air. Slowly we wandered along the road and turned up the track to the farm. A few midnight-blue clouds darkened the night sky but even so a sliver of moon and a billion distant twinkling stars glittered above us.

'You don't get starry nights as stunning as this in Kingsfield,' he whispered. 'Too many street lamps.'

'I know,' I agreed. *And that's just one of the reasons I love this place so much*, I added to myself.

We got as far as the farm gate and he turned to face me. He circled my waist with his arms and I reached up to stroke the soft bit of his neck just under his cropped hair.

'I'm so glad I came to the farm. Now I'll be able to picture where you are and what you're doing when we're apart.'

I tightened my arms around his neck and he stepped closer until every inch of my body was pressed against his. 'And you'll visit again, won't you? I quite like showing you off.'

'Of course. If you want me to.' He dipped his head to meet mine and kissed me slowly.

'Yes, please.'

I closed my eyes and moved a hand round to feel the stubble on the side of his face, committing every touch, every scent, every detail of him to memory.

'Come on,' he said, grinning wickedly, 'I want you to show me the barn again. Remind me where everything in your tea rooms is going to go.'

'You've seen it,' I said, puzzled. Plus it was too dark and I didn't have a torch with me.

'True.' He started nuzzling at my neck and I shivered. 'But we had Ollie with us then. This time it'll be just you, me and the hay bales.'

'Oh, in that case,' I giggled, breaking into a run, 'catch me if you can.'

He did catch me. But only because I let him.

Chapter 19

Tuesday, the day of my meeting with the Cumbrian planning department, soon rolled around. I was the last one down to breakfast and everyone was at the table when I pirouetted into the kitchen.

'Ta-dah! How do I look?'

Charlie whistled, Ollie clapped and I kicked one heel up playfully.

'Ooh, you look a picture, lass. Doesn't she, Artie?' gasped Auntie Sue, pressing her oven-gloved hands to her cheeks.

Uncle Arthur looked up from his bowl of muesli. He was grimacing, which I hoped was a reaction to his new high-fibre diet rather than to my outfit. 'You're a stunner, love. You'll knock 'em dead.'

I was more of a tomboy-jeans-and-Converse girl at heart but today I was all about the Appleby Farm brand – I know! Get me and my marketing jargon! So I was vintage all the way from the knitted flower clip in my hair down to my kitten-heel shoes with the bows on the front, not to mention my ditsy floral dress and cute little cardigan, borrowed from Lizzie. Actually, I felt fab.

'I could get used to this look,' I said, peering at my rear view in the mirror above the fireplace.

'Me too.' Charlie grinned.

'Sausages?' Auntie Sue cocked an eyebrow at me as she slid sizzling plates of food in front of Charlie and Ollie.

'No, thanks. I'll have muesli, I think, if Uncle Arthur doesn't mind sharing?' I sat down beside him and nudged him playfully.

'Finish it up.' He shoved the cereal box my way with a wink. 'Please.'

'I collected the eggs this morning, Freya. By myself. Are you sure you don't want one?' Ollie said, squeezing a small mountain of ketchup on to his fried egg.

'I'll save mine until lunch, I think, Ollie.' I tipped some muesli into a bowl and sipped at a glass of water. 'I haven't got much appetite this morning. But thank you, anyway.'

'What advice did your dad have, lass?' asked Uncle Arthur.

I'd phoned my parents last night to tell them about my meeting. Mum had told me to look the part and not dress too casual or too businesslike.

'You need to present the face of Appleby Farm,' she'd said. 'People are sold on the detail; a pretty dress is an absolute must.'

And Dad had given me a pep-talk about buzz words.

'These bureaucratic types will have criteria for approving planning applications: tick the right boxes and you'll be in. Pepper your application with things like "job creation", "farm diversification", "rural enterprise" and "sympathetic renovation" and you'll stand a much better chance. Oh, and "visitor experience", they'll love that, too.'

I'd probably never remember all that but I did manage the dress and at least I knew they cared. Which was lovely but didn't stop my stomach churning like Auntie Sue's ice-cream machine in full raspberry-ripple mode, partly with nerves – that was only natural, I supposed – but mainly with excitement. The Vintage Tea Rooms was the first thing that had ever been truly mine and I was brimming with ideas and plans. I just hoped the planning officer would share my vision.

'Freya?' Charlie's teasing voice eventually penetrated my thoughts.

Everyone was staring at me and I realized I hadn't answered my uncle's question. 'Gosh! Sorry, I'm a bit pre-occupied this morning. Um, he sent his love and wished me luck.'

Was it my imagination or did Uncle Arthur just make some sort of grunting noise?

'So. What's everyone else up to today?' I asked, pushing my bowl to one side. I was siding with Uncle Arthur: the muesli reminded me of the special woodchip bedding that Lizzie had started using in Skye's stable.

'We're off for a picnic and a walk around Tarn Hows, aren't we, Ollie? Have a splash in the water?' said Charlie.

I reached for his hand across the table. 'Oh, I want to come! It's lovely there, very romantic.'

'Yuck,' Ollie muttered and we all laughed.

'And it's a busy day here.' Uncle Arthur sighed. He'd made it out of his pyjamas today and was wearing an old pair of overalls. 'Vet's due back to check on the TB test and Eddy says he's sorted someone to start with the silage. So I'd better—'

'Sit back down and finish your breakfast,' Auntie Sue finished for him.

'Is TB still a problem, Arthur?' asked Charlie.

'Oh yes, not as big as it was but it's devastating when it hits,' Uncle Arthur replied. 'In fact, a farmer on the Scottish border lost his whole herd last week.'

'Touch wood, we've never been through it at Appleby Farm,' said Auntie Sue with a sharp intake of breath. 'And I hope we never do.'

'Why, Auntie Sue, what happens?' Ollie asked.

'Well,' she said, ruffling his hair and shooting Charlie a worried look, 'the vet gives the cows an injection and if any of them react by getting a swollen lump, they have to be put to sleep by someone called a slaughterman.'

Ollie seemed to accept that answer and went back to his sausages.

'Seeing them being collected for slaughter must be awful,' I said with a shudder.

'Doesn't bear thinking about,' Uncle Arthur said, shaking his head. 'And then you've got a waiting game for at least six months before you can get the all-clear for the rest of the herd. Until then, you can't move any cattle on or off the farm. Ruins your business.'

'Is there any insurance money?' asked Charlie. 'Or does the farmer lose his herd and his investment, just like that?' He snapped his fingers.

Uncle Arthur sighed and folded his arms across his chest. 'There's a compensation scheme, but it doesn't pay full market value, I don't think. I heard of this one fella . . .'

Auntie Sue and I exchanged smiles. This subject would probably keep him occupied for hours.

'Blimey! Look at the time,' I said, checking my watch. 'I'd better be off. Wish me luck!' I stood up and gathered my folders and papers from a pile on the coffee table.

With my cheeks covered with kisses and my ears ringing with well wishes and Uncle Arthur still explaining the rather unpleasant ins and outs of bovine tuberculosis to Charlie, I left the farmhouse and crossed the yard to my trusty campervan and clambered in.

I inhaled a big calming breath. 'Come on, Bobby, adventure awaits!'

Four hours later the future of Appleby Farm Vintage Tea Rooms was as good as 'in the bag' and I was on my way home to the farm, singing my head off rather aptly to 'Tea For Two' by Doris Day on Radio Lakeland. I only knew the chorus but happily hummed the rest, accompanied by the tinkling of china from the passenger footwell of the campervan.

The sky was wall-to-wall turquoise, the fields were a hundred shades of green and the hedgerows were full of birds tweeting merrily. Well, I might have imagined the latter, but you get the picture . . . I was fizzing with excitement and ultra-appreciative of my beautiful surroundings on the journey back to Lovedale.

The planning lady who had met me – a sprightly old thing with spiky grey hair and coral-coloured lipstick, who must have been well past retirement – was my new best friend. Her name was Patience Purdue. And with a name like that how could she be anything but utterly charming? She was so enthusiastic about my plans that at one point I thought she was going to hug me, or was that me who was going to hug her? Not sure now, it was all a bit of a blur.

Patience couldn't give me a formal 'yes' at the meeting – my plans were to be submitted at the next meeting – but she did give me an informal nod and a wink, and even the address of a delightful second-hand shop down a tiny street in Kendal that specialized in retro tea sets – hence the rattling of cups and saucers next to me. In her view, as long I was preserving the buildings and making mainly internal structural changes, then we should be 'Vintage Tea Rooms *à gogo*'. At which point I got a bit carried away and joked that

I'd get my builder to cancel the wrecking ball straight away. But we soon cleared that up. And I learned a new buzz word – 'sustainable tourism'.

Must remember to tell Dad that, I thought to myself, giggling, as I indicated to turn into Appleby Farm.

Ahead of me I could see a pick-up truck that I didn't recognize pulling to a halt in front of the barn. In fact, the yard was busy today: both Eddy and Ross had parked their cars plus there was a black Range Rover with mud splashes on it by the side of the cowshed. I wondered if the vet had arrived already.

Car parking for the café, I added to my mental to-do list as I parked Bobby behind the pick-up, scooped up my papers from the passenger seat and put my shoulder against the door to open it.

'Arrghhh!' I yelped.

A man's face grinned at me through the window and in the blink of an eye I was whizzed straight back in time about sixteen years, to the day when the two of us tried to build our own zipwire in the orchard. The rope snapped and we were stranded up a tree until Eddy rescued us. I'd been scared to death then, too, and he'd grinned. Just like he was grinning now.

'Harry Graythwaite! You frightened the life out of me,' I cried, pushing open the door and jumping down beside him.

'Freya Moorcroft, still as feisty as ever, I see.'

Harry leaned forward, hands on my arms, and kissed my cheek.

'And proud of it,' I smirked back at him.

He stood back and looked at my dress and shoes. 'You're all grown up,' he said softly.

I felt my cheeks redden. I was only eighteen the last time

I saw him. It was the summer after I finished sixth form, my last long summer at Appleby Farm, my last summer of childhood really, I supposed.

'Yeah, I bet you never thought you'd see me in a dress?' I laughed. 'Anyway, we both are.'

His jaw was more chiselled and he had a day or two of stubble along it, but the rest – the tousled light-brown hair, the full lips and the dancing chocolate-brown eyes – was still the same. And when he smiled – like now – he still had a dimple in his chin.

He folded his tanned arms and leaned back against the wall. I couldn't help noticing how much broader and more muscular in the shoulders he had become since I last saw him. 'And you've seen the world now, I take it, seeing as you're back in the Lake District?'

I smiled at him. His words triggered a vague memory that I couldn't quite grasp. 'Not quite the whole world, but a decent chunk. Anyway, the farm is my priority for the next few months, so I'll be staying put for a while. What are you doing here? Not that you're not welcome,' I added. 'It's just a surprise. I've been meaning to come and see you ever since I arrived.'

'Since you yelled at me up at Knots Hill in the rain, you mean?' He rubbed his chin and looked down at his boots, chuckling away to himself.

Actually, I meant since I'd seen him in the pub, the time I'd fallen into a pothole thanks to Uncle Arthur's dubious torch skills and arrived slightly worse for wear having narrowly escaped an ice-cream bath, but I decided not to remind him of that.

'Yes, sorry, I was under a bit of stress at the time. Not to mention wet through.' I coughed. 'So?'

'I see.' He grinned. 'I'm looking for Eddy. I'm going to

take on the grassland contract for the season. I need him to ride round the farm with me and identify the fields so I can get cracking on the mowing as soon as possible. I've got a list of the fields from him but I'm not sure which is which without a map.'

'Well, that's a good idea of his. I approve.' I grinned, thinking what a good choice Eddy had made. It would be great to have Harry round the farm. Like old times, in fact.

'Thank you,' he smirked. 'I've helped out before, especially at harvest time, but this'll be the first time I've taken on an official contract.'

The sun was high in the sky and I shielded my eyes with my hand. 'Well, I appreciate it. Uncle Arthur will be out of action all summer and I think Eddy was starting to panic. Eddy must be with the vet, I think.'

'Yes, I recognize the Range Rover. No worries, I'll wait.'

'In that case, let's go inside. Would you like a cup of tea?'

Harry nodded and we walked side by side towards the farmhouse.

'Talking of tea, I've heard about your plans for the tea rooms. I think it's brilliant. I'm all for diversification. My mum told me,' he added, laughing at my bemused expression.

'But she lives . . .' I frowned.

'In Bournemouth, yes, I know. I think Hilary in the post office phoned her.'

We were still giggling about everyone knowing everyone else's business when I stopped in my tracks and touched his arm. 'It's just dawned on me, I can show you which fields are included in the contract. No need to wait for Eddy.'

I turned and walked back to his pick-up truck.

'What about the tea?' he called.

'Come on,' I laughed. 'You can earn it first.'

Chapter 20

Climbing up into the pick-up truck in a dress and heels was no more difficult than getting into my own vehicle, except that Harry was doing the gentlemanly thing by holding the door for me and I was doing my best to look ladylike and not launch myself into the seat as I normally would.

We set off out of the yard, with me clutching the list of fields that were to be included in the contract and Harry drumming his fingers against the steering wheel, like he'd always done, to some song that only he could hear.

It was odd and yet easy being with Harry again after such a long time. I'd missed him, I realized. Funny how someone can be such a big part of your life one day and gone the next. But that's what happens, I supposed. At eighteen we leave school and our world changes; we go off to work or uni or travelling and life takes a new path. There was only a handful of people I was still in contact with from school these days. Harry was different, though. I should have made the effort to stay in touch with him but those last few weeks of summer had been strained between us for some reason and then I flew to somewhere or other on my round-the-world trip and eventually when I did want to contact him I felt like it was too late.

'What's this one called, then?' said Harry, breaking into my thoughts as we drove slowly along the field behind the orchard.

'Clover Field,' I answered, pleased that I'd memorized all their names. I consulted the sheet of paper. 'And it's not on the list.'

'Sorry, Clover,' he called out of the window, 'you're not on the list.'

I giggled. 'Hey, do you remember Uncle Arthur giving us a driving lesson in this field in his Land Rover?'

Harry aimed the truck for the gap in the drystone wall into the next field and grinned. 'I do. You were rubbish if I recall and Arthur said he'd have to take us to one of the bigger fields next time.'

I punched his arm. 'That is so not true. I was just a more confident driver than you.'

He threw his head back and laughed. 'For confident read speed-demon. I think you aged your uncle ten years that summer when you turned seventeen and could start learning to drive.'

I tapped the tip of my finger on my cheek. 'Um, now, which one of us passed their test first? Let me think . . .'

I laughed as Harry rolled his eyes.

'Anyway,' he continued more seriously, 'it was good of him to teach me. My dad's arthritis was getting worse by then and he wasn't up to giving me lessons.'

'I know, poor Jim.' I reached across and touched Harry's arm. 'How is your dad? Auntie Sue said he's better now he's down south.'

'He's doing OK, thanks.' He smiled and rolled his

eyes. 'Still manages to boss me about, though, even from hundreds of miles away.'

Ten minutes in his company and it was like we'd never been apart. *That's the beauty of a true friendship*, I mused, glancing at his profile as he concentrated on the bumpy path across the farm, *you can just pick up where you left off*. We might have been ten years older but inside we were still exactly the same.

'Hey, please tell me you're not still into moody man bands?' I teased.

Our conflicting musical tastes had always been a standing joke between us. Whereas I was the world's biggest Backstreet Boys fan, he was into what I used to call 'music to break up to'.

'And I'm guessing you still have absolutely no taste whatsoever?' Harry raised a dark eyebrow.

'For your information, I'm a Take That fan these days.'

Harry snorted. 'I rest my case.'

'What happened to your drumming career, then?' I quipped. 'I thought you were going to be the next . . . what was his name?'

He grinned and shook his head. 'Dave Grohl, from Nirvana. And for your information, Miss Moorcroft, I *am* a drummer. Me and a couple of mates are in a band called The Almanacs.'

'Are you?' I beamed at him. I was all for people fulfilling their dreams. 'Good for you. Head down there, by the way, towards Bottom Field.'

'Yeah,' he nodded nonchalantly, 'we don't do many gigs, but our stuff goes down pretty well.'

'I don't suppose it'll be my cup of tea, will it? All rock stuff? You're right, I am still a pop fan.'

'Actually,' Harry cleared his throat and rubbed his nose,

'we do some pop stuff. We play at weddings and birthday parties; cover-versions, you know, a mix for all ages. You should hear us belt out "Valerie" – you can't move on the dance floor, believe me.'

'Really?' I smirked. 'You'll have to tell me when your next gig is, I'd like to hear you play.'

He shoved his sleeves up above his elbows as he drove. 'Steve, the guitar player, and his wife have just had a baby so we're having this year off, but I'll let you know. Anyway, tell me about you.'

We caught up on ten years' worth of news. His took ten seconds – Harper Adams University studying agriculture for three years and then back to Willow Farm so that his dad could retire. Mine took ages. Mainly because he kept interrupting with silly anecdotes from our teenage past.

'OK,' said Harry, stopping the truck fifteen minutes later, 'have I seen all the fields that need mowing?'

'Er, hold on.' I consulted the list. 'All except Crofters. Follow the line of the tree at the edge of Colton Woods,' I said, pointing ahead, 'and that's Crofters Field. It's our biggest, I think, nine acres.'

'Ah, the wonders of Lakeland farming,' said Harry, rubbing a hand over his stubble. 'A mate of mine further south has got fields of twenty acres or more. These small fields are so restrictive.'

'Oh, but they're all so pretty with their little walls and wooden stiles. It's what makes Cumbria so special.' I sighed, enjoying the view all the way down the valley towards Lake Windermere.

'Aye, true enough, young Freya,' said Harry, doing an impressive impression of Eddy and making me laugh.

'Although last time I was up here it was to remove a dead

badger from the edge of the field and that was not a pretty sight, I can tell you,' I added.

'Really?' Harry flashed his brown eyes at me sharply. 'They carry TB, you know, badgers. Have the cattle been in here?'

'I'm not sure.' I shrugged. 'Not for a while, I don't think. Harry, it's our vet visit today about TB, we should be getting back. Plus I want to tell everyone the good news about my planning meeting.'

'Sure.' Harry nodded, turned the truck around and set off in the direction of the farmhouse.

A few minutes later we arrived back in the yard and Harry turned off the engine and climbed out. As he wasn't looking, I decided to jump to the ground rather than climb out daintily.

Big mistake.

As my feet hit the cobbled yard I felt my dress tighten around my thighs and I knew instantly that I was stuck. I glanced behind me and my heart sank. The hem of my dress was caught on a lever at the side of the seat. The dress, or should I say, *Lizzie's* dress, didn't have a particularly full skirt and the fabric was so strained between me and the seat that when I tried to yank it free I heard it tear slightly. I could hear Harry's footsteps coming round the truck towards me. I looked down. The fabric had ridden up and my thighs were inappropriately bare. I tried jumping up and down and wriggling to free the hem but it didn't work. It was no use . . .

'Harry!' I squeaked, my face bright red as he appeared from the back of the truck. I tugged the front of the dress down to preserve what little shred of my dignity remained. 'Help, I'm stuck.'

He took one look at me and burst out laughing. Hands

on hips, shaking his head, eyes crinkling with amusement.

'It's not funny,' I remonstrated, 'and it's not even my dress.'

He seemed to find that even funnier and laughed harder. He leaned on the side of the truck, helplessly trying to speak, at which point I joined in and the pair of laughed until tears streamed down our faces.

'Sorry,' he spluttered. 'Not funny at all.'

'Not in the least,' I replied breathlessly, wiping away my tears. 'Now don't just stand there, do something!'

He tucked his phone in his pocket and walked towards me. 'OK,' he said, doing his best to keep a straight face and failing dismally. 'I'll lift you in the air and see if that does the trick.'

'Good plan,' I agreed, taking a deep breath to calm myself.

I wrapped one arm around his neck and he picked me up effortlessly. The skin on my arm grazed the soft hairs at the back of his head and I involuntarily inhaled the smell of him: grass, fresh laundry and lemons. I felt my face heat up. Harry and I were friends, just old friends, but I couldn't help feeling a frisson of electricity at being in a handsome man's arms. *I'm only human*, I thought; *this is a perfectly natural reaction*. Our faces were millimetres apart and we were both still grinning at each other.

'This is why I should stick to jeans,' I giggled, breaking the moment. 'Now, let's see if I can . . .'

I stretched behind me but couldn't quite reach the lever to free the fabric.

'Move closer to the seat, Harry,' I suggested.

'Sure. Hurry up, though, you weigh a ton,' he sniggered.

As I finally managed to release the hem of my dress, I heard a car door slam and the sound of small feet running towards the farmhouse.

'Quick, put me down,' I said excitedly, wriggling in his arms, 'that sounds like Ollie. Charlie must be back.'

'All right, keep your hair on,' he chuckled and released me from his arms.

A low voice made us both spin round. 'Too late, I am back.'

Charlie, arms folded, was standing at the end of Harry's truck. He looked from me to Harry and back again. My heart sank. To an outsider that must have looked really, really bad.

'Oh dear,' Harry murmured under his breath.

'Charlie! Hi!' I gushed, smoothing down my dress. 'This is Harry Graythwaite, my mate from Willow Farm next door. Harry, this is Charlie. My boyfriend.'

Harry raised a hand in greeting but Charlie ignored him.

'Looks like you've had a fun morning,' said Charlie coolly, scanning my face.

'Not really, we've been discussing fields until I got my dress stuck and Harry came to my rescue,' I said, feeling flustered, which was ridiculous because I hadn't done anything wrong other than be completely useless at exiting vehicles gracefully. 'Anyway, tea, anyone?'

'Blimey,' said Harry, pointing towards the black Range Rover, which was now reversing out of the yard, 'the vet's been here a long time.'

We exchanged worried looks.

'And there's Eddy,' I murmured, pointing to where he had appeared from the handling pens at the back of the cowsheds and was now striding purposefully towards us, his lips pressed into a grim line.

'Looks like there might be a problem.' Harry frowned. He slammed the passenger door shut and began to walk across the yard. I followed close behind him.

Eddy wasn't alone; my uncle and aunt, hand in hand, walked behind at a slower pace. Auntie Sue looked on the verge of tears and Uncle Arthur was ashen.

A surge of fear ran through my body and I rushed over to them.

'What is it? What's wrong?' I cried, leaping forward to take Uncle Arthur's arm as he stumbled over a loose cobble.

He looked at me and shook his head, his chest rattling noisily. I met my aunt's worried gaze as I waited for him to catch his breath.

'The Herefords have got TB.' His eyes were moist as he leaned against me and his shoulders sagged. 'Nearly half the herd. They'll have to be slaughtered. We're finished, lass.'

'No!' I gasped, feeling my knees go weak.

That couldn't be true, not after all we'd already been through this year.

I felt Harry's hand grip my shoulder and despite being in full view of Charlie, I didn't push him away. If I was going to help Auntie Sue and Uncle Arthur get through this new crisis at Appleby Farm I would need all the support I could get.

How could we possibly survive this?

Where the Heart Is

Chapter 21

From the spinning gallery of the barn – the barn that with any luck would soon be the most amazing vintage tea rooms ever to open in the history of the Lake District – I had a bird's-eye view across Appleby Farm.

It was mid-June and two weeks since the hideous day when forty cows had to be slaughtered because the vet found they had bovine tuberculosis. It was also the day when Uncle Arthur descended into what Auntie Sue termed 'one of his glooms' – he was still in it – and Charlie left the farm a day early, saying that he didn't belong and that he felt as though he and Ollie were in the way.

To an outsider the vista from here wouldn't have changed much from then to now. But things *had* changed at the farm. In a massive way. And I wasn't sure that Appleby Farm or the people who loved it would ever be the same again.

That wasn't to say I didn't still absolutely love every chicken, cow, horse, dog, cat, ancient stone wall, rickety building and dear person here. I adored them. And I was so glad I was going through this traumatic time with them, to support them. I just wished I didn't need to. While Benny and Björn hadn't turned a whisker since all the shenanigans,

Madge had taken to sitting at the gate in whichever field the Jersey cows were in during the day like a small bristly sentry. I was convinced she was trying to protect them from unwanted guests – like infected badgers, for instance.

I leaned on the smooth wooden railings of the spinning gallery, filling my lungs with sweet summer air and watched the tractor pulling a wide mower through the long grass in Beech Field. It made its way methodically in straight lines from one end to the other and back again, leaving a mounded row of cut grass in its wake. It was like watching the slowest tennis match ever.

That was new for a start. The tractor wasn't ours and neither was the driver. They had come from Willow Farm next door. And although I hadn't seen him arrive, I presumed it was Harry at the wheel. The grass wasn't being cut to make silage for Appleby Farm either; Harry was taking it in payment for doing the job.

Because silage is animal feed and with only half the Hereford herd remaining we wouldn't need so much feed this winter.

The depleted herd was up to my left in Crofters Field. Uncle Arthur, Eddy and even Ross, bless him, had taken the slaughter of the infected animals very badly. Only two weeks ago the herd had been split into three groups and spread across the farmland. Now there was one group and the cowshed had pens of orphaned calves inside it.

The calves had cried and cried that first night after they had lost their mothers. It was the most heartbreaking sound I've ever heard. I'd had a good cry myself that night.

Strictly speaking, I had loads to be getting on with and no time for daydreaming up here on this nineteenth-century version of a balcony. I gazed out over the fields and ran through my options.

I could write down all the things I needed to do before opening up the tea rooms. That would keep me busy for an hour or two. Or I could do a mood board for the interior décor; I was thinking rustic, mismatched and shabby chic (i.e. cheap). Or maybe I could take the campervan out for the day, drive around the beauty spots of the Lake District and have tea and cake in as many of them as I could manage. And in case you're thinking that sounds greedy, it's not – it's market research.

Anything. Anything would be better than tying myself in knots thinking about Charlie and our long-distance relationship, which was feeling more distant by the day. He had left before I'd had chance to properly explain how I'd managed to hook the bottom of my dress on the seat adjustment lever during my ungainly descent from Harry's truck. And then with the whole TB business, mine and Auntie Sue's priorities had been to prevent Uncle Arthur from getting too stressed. While we had made him a cup of tea and comforted him, Harry had helped Eddy and Ross to segregate the affected cattle from the healthy ones and Charlie had packed his and Ollie's bags. What had started off as such a lovely day had ended up disastrously . . .

'Freya, Freya, Freya!'

Aaannnd I was back in the room – or gallery – as Lizzie, dressed in jodhpurs and a strappy vest, her glossy dark fall of hair flying behind her, came scooting across the yard towards me, pulling me out of my thoughts.

She scrambled up the slate steps, trying to miss out the most worn ones, squeaking, panting and groaning simultaneously.

'So unfit!' she gasped. 'Listen to this.'

She had a little radio in her hand and turned up the volume so we could both hear.

'My sister is interviewing Harry Graythwaite on the radio.'

'Really? I thought he was in that field.' I glanced back over to the tractor in the distance. It must be one of his staff, then. Shame. I quite enjoyed bumping into him and having a chat.

Lizzie shook her head. 'He can't be; this is live. Shush.'

Sooo, you're listening to Radio Lakeland and I'm delighted to welcome farmer Harry Graythwaite from Lovedale into the studio. Good morning, Harry, and thank you for joining me.

'Listen to her. All gushy. She *so* fancies him,' Lizzie whispered. 'I knew she'd got her eye on someone. Poor sod. We *have* to save him.'

Hi, Victoria. Thanks for inviting me.

I couldn't help smiling when I heard Harry's voice. I could just imagine him in the recording studio, tugging at his shirt collar nervously and dropping dried mud and bits of straw from his boots all over the floor.

Victoria laughed in a tinkly way and Lizzie tutted. *So you're bringing your family's traditional Lakeland farm right up to date, isn't that right, Harry?*

I suppose so, he said.

Do tell us more, trilled Victoria. *I'm fascinated!*

Are you? Right. OK. Well, farming is in my genes, I suppose. I can't imagine doing anything else. Since I took over Willow Farm when my father retired, I've been putting my own mark on the farm, investing in farming for the future to . . .

'How did this interview even happen?' I said to Lizzie. Harry sounded a little bit confused, as though he wasn't quite sure how he'd found himself on the radio.

'She collared him in the pub. This will be all part of her master plan to seduce him. She's starting with flattery. If that doesn't work she'll stalk him until he caves in.'

Evidently Victoria didn't find Harry's answer all that

fascinating because after about three seconds she interrupted him. *So farming is booming, then?*

Not exactly, but the population is, he replied.

Oh, Harry! You are funny. Victoria gave a high-pitched laugh. *So all those single mums with eight children are just what you rich farmer types need, then?*

Lizzie groaned. 'She is unbelievable.'

Er . . . British farmers are trying to keep pace with the demands of our customers, produce good quality food on our own soil. Lower imports, lower carbon footprint. Healthier, fresher food. As the population grows, the world needs more food.

Oh, I don't know, Harry, Victoria sniggered. *Perhaps if the world had less food then there wouldn't be so many fat people . . . ooh, I think . . . yes, I'm being told to play some music. Don't go away, peeps, this is 'All Together Now' by The Farm!*

'Brilliant!' Lizzie snapped off the radio and grinned.

'Was it?' I blinked at her. I must have been missing something. 'I was mortified for her and I don't even like her.'

Actually, that was a fib; I had nothing against the girl, I just said that out of allegiance to Lizzie. It was Victoria who'd unwittingly given me the idea for the tea rooms and I couldn't help but feel a bit grateful. In secret.

'She has just dissed virtually the entire world! At least one person is bound to ring in and complain, surely? Then she'll get the sack, disappear in shame under the cover of night and I won't have to see her again until Christmas.'

'Maybe. Or she'll become infamous for her insults and people will come from all over to hear her and the ratings will go up,' I suggested.

'Whose side are you on?' Lizzie stuck her tongue out and then looked out at the view. 'What are you doing up here, anyway? Spying on who you thought was Harry?' She nudged me in the ribs.

'I came to check out these.' I ignored her and gestured to the old double doors behind us. There must have been some sort of lowering mechanism here at one time, but now if you stepped through the doors, you'd fall to the floor of the barn about four metres below.

'I'm going to replace them with glass.'

'Gorgeous. It's lovely up here, isn't it? Very romantic. Romeo, Romeo . . .' She began waving her arm over the wooden banister. 'Talking of romance, heard from Charlie recently?'

'Charlie? Um, yeah.' I shuffled my feet on the wooden floorboards and examined my thumbnail intensely.

'Oh, look, your auntie's over there.'

I leaned past Lizzie to look across the yard. Auntie Sue was at the farmhouse gate, scanning left and right around the farmyard.

Phew. I wasn't ready to confide in Lizzie that these days my conversations with Charlie were about as animated as the Shipping Forecast. And that whenever I came off the phone from one of them, I had a physical pain like I'd just swallowed dry bread and it had got stuck somewhere south of my oesophagus.

Charlie and I never used to shut up, each competing to get in there first with our news and funny stories. We still talked: he asked me if Uncle Arthur was OK and about the herd and how my tea rooms were coming on. I asked him about his allotment and Ollie and whether his fire-fighting crew had saved any lives that day. But it was what we didn't say any more that worried me. He'd stopped telling me that he loved me and I'd stopped promising I'd be back soon. I really needed to see him before the problem became any worse than it already was.

'Cooeee, looking for me?' I waved and Auntie Sue beckoned me down.

'Freya, have you got a minute?'

'Sure.'

I started to climb down the stairs and Lizzie caught hold of my arm. 'Invite Charlie back up to the farm. Without Ollie. Just you and him.'

'I've been thinking exactly the same thing myself.' I sighed.

I carried on down the stairs and smiled at Auntie Sue.

'What's up, Suzie?' I asked, looping my arm round her neck as we headed back indoors.

I'd just see what she wanted and then I'd call Charlie. He might even be able to come this weekend if he wasn't looking after Ollie.

'Cheeky madam,' Auntie Sue chuckled. She had a turquoise T-shirt on today that made her eyes sparkle and set off her fluffy white hair. 'Your uncle's waiting in the kitchen. Come and have a chat.'

Uncle Arthur was sitting at the table behind a fat pile of farming magazines and a thin folder marked 'Retirement'. He looked up when we entered with a half-smile, half-sigh. It was his default greeting these days.

The cardiologist was apparently 'astounded' by my uncle's recovery after his heart attack in April, using words like 'cast iron' and 'indestructible'. I thought the man must be blind; it was obvious to me that Uncle Arthur's heart was broken after losing half of his beloved livestock.

'Sit down, Freya.'

Uncle Arthur patted the chair at the head of the table. I sat down and Auntie Sue squeezed in next to me opposite her husband.

I looked at them both. 'Blimey, this sounds serious. Have I left a tea bag in the sink again?'

There was a pause. Short, but long enough to tell me to ditch the jokes.

Auntie Sue reached for my fingers. Uncle Arthur reached for my fingers.

'Freya, thank you for all you've done for us over the last few months. We couldn't have managed without you,' he began, his eyes looking rheumy and sad.

'And we don't just mean the money,' said Auntie Sue, patting my hand. 'You've been a ray of sunshine.'

'That's sweet of you to say.' I held my breath. There was a 'but' coming . . .

'But the farm can't carry on as it is.' Uncle Arthur stroked the cover of his retirement folder and Auntie Sue coughed.

'I mean *we* can't carry on as we are,' he corrected. 'And losing half the herd is devast—'

'Gives us an opportunity,' Auntie Sue cut in, 'to think about taking it a bit easier.'

'That's brilliant. I'm so glad you're thinking positively about the future.' I leaned across and kissed both of them. Auntie Sue had been angling for Uncle Arthur to retire for ages. Finally it looked as though she might be getting her way.

'So we're going to look at our options . . .' he went on.

'Cut back, sell the rest of the herd, make everything as simple as we can on the farm and then see what happens at the end of the year,' added Auntie Sue.

Simple? My heart plunged somewhere down near my knees. 'So . . . you don't want the tea rooms to go ahead after all?'

They both started protesting at once.

'No, no, that's not what we mean!'

'The tea rooms are a great idea!'

'But it's not simplifying things, is it?' I said, focusing hard on not sounding petulant. It was their farm and who was I to scupper their plans, but the Appleby Farm Vintage Tea Rooms was the first venture I'd ever felt truly excited about. It was my only venture, come to that.

Uncle Arthur opened one of his magazines and jabbed a finger at the page. 'Look, there's an article here about a farm that has opened up a children's adventure park. All farms are spreading their wings into different areas to stay afloat. And there's nowhere around here for a decent cup of tea.'

'Or a slice of my cake,' chuckled Auntie Sue.

'And at the end of this year either we stay here, keep the house and garden, and subcontract out the farmland and the tea rooms,' said my uncle, 'or we sell.'

'And buy a bungalow,' Auntie Sue said quickly.

'We'll get compensation from the government for the loss of the herd, which will give us a little lump sum to pay you back,' he continued.

'Or put down a deposit on a bungalow,' muttered Auntie Sue.

Uncle Arthur looked at me. 'I'm getting a subliminal message from your auntie. Do you hear it?'

We both laughed and Auntie Sue folded her arms and hitched her bosom closer to her chin.

'But why sell the rest of the herd?' I frowned. 'Couldn't the next farmer – whether he or she buys or rents it from you – take on the Herefords?'

'She?' Auntie Sue sat up in her chair. 'Is that your way of expressing an interest, lass?'

'Sue!' Uncle Arthur waggled his eyebrows at her. 'Possibly, love. We just thought it might make it a better proposition for someone. You know, coming in to a blank canvas. Or an empty field . . .' His voice sounded far away and my heart squeezed for him.

'So.' I slapped my palms down on the table. 'By the end of the year, come what may, you're going to retire?'

They both nodded. And I nodded. 'I can work with that,' I said, pushing myself up from the table.

'Where are you off to, lass?'

The pair of them stared at me uneasily.

'I've got builders to organize.'

I marched off to the office to ring Goat.

As Auntie Sue had put it, this was an opportunity. I had six months to make a success of the tea rooms. The decision from the planning department was due any day and it would be just my luck if I rang Goat next week and he said, 'Oh, sorry, I've just taken on a contract to build a hospital and I can't do your little barn for another year.' OK, that was a bit unlikely, but you get the picture.

Whatever happened, I couldn't fail. I had something to prove. To my dad, of course, because he'd lent me the money and had put his trust in me for the first time ever, but more importantly to *myself*. I'd always shied away from responsibility in the past and this was my chance to show myself what I was really capable of.

I sat down at my little sewing-machine-table desk and looked for Goat's number with Auntie Sue's words rattling round in my head: *Is that your way of expressing an interest, lass?*

There was zero chance of me being able to run the farm on my own. Nor would I want to. I'd always known I couldn't stay for ever; I knew I'd have to leave once the tea rooms were up and running.

But while it lasted, I was going to savour every moment.

Chapter 22

The next day got off to a rocky start when I woke up at seven o'clock with Benny on my chest. We both yawned simultaneously, which meant that my waking breath smelled of cat yawn.

'Oh, Benny, haven't you heard of dental floss? What have you been eating?' I groaned, sitting up suddenly.

My mood took a deeper nosedive when I got downstairs to find my big brother Julian sitting at the head of the kitchen table, drinking black coffee and fending off Auntie Sue's attempts at feeding him. Uncle Arthur was sitting in his armchair, hiding behind his newspaper. He lowered the paper when I came in, waggled his eyebrows and grinned.

Despite my shock and horror at seeing Julian, I couldn't help but smirk. My aunt can wear down the most reluctant eater to accept food. It usually starts off innocently enough with the offer of a biscuit. And if she gets turned down, she'll offer cake (homemade – just a sliver?), then a poached egg on toast (although strangely she calls it 'a buttered egg') and finally back to the biscuit.

'Fine,' muttered Julian through gritted teeth. 'A biscuit would be lovely.'

Auntie Sue sighed with relief and slid a plate piled high with shortbread fingers up to him.

I realized I was still hovering at the door. 'Morning, all. Hello, Julian.'

I came forward, touched his shoulder briefly in lieu of a hug and went and sat down a bit further along the bench.

We eyed each other warily. No one would ever suspect that we were siblings. In fact, at this precise moment, you'd be hard pressed to mistake us for the same species: me in my PJs with bed-head hair, gritty-eyed and still queasy from the cat yawn; Julian in an expensive linen suit and dark hair like Mum, although now he was in his forties, it was a bit on the sparse side and flecked with silver. He had darting brown eyes, narrow shoulders and his knees bounced perpetually under the table. He reminded me of a stoat.

Julian made a point of checking his watch. 'Morning, sis. I was wondering when you'd make an appearance. Dad said you were having an extended holiday up here. Nice work if you can get it.'

'Actually—' My lungs filled with indignation and I was about to give him both barrels when I felt a hand on my shoulder.

'Isn't this a lovely surprise?' exclaimed Auntie Sue, handing me a mug of tea.

My brother's eyes met mine and he sniggered.

'We-e-ll,' he drawled, shoving the biscuits out of his way. I took one and dunked it in my tea. 'I was at a conference in Edinburgh until the early hours and I thought rather than sleep in a hotel I'd drive through the night and pop in here for breakfast.'

I rolled my eyes. Next he'd be saying that sleep is for wimps.

'Breakfast? Ooh, how about a bit of bacon?' Auntie Sue began again.

'Christ on a bike, Sue,' muttered Uncle Arthur, giving his newspaper a thump to straighten the pages.

'And I wanted to see how you are, Uncle, after your heart attack,' said Julian smoothly.

'Which one?' I asked innocently. 'The first one at Easter or the second one seven weeks ago?'

He ignored me, took his phone out of his pocket, tutted and slipped it back in. 'I must say, I'm surprised to see you up and about, Uncle. I hope you're not overdoing it?'

I wasn't buying it. Julian didn't do social calls. He wanted something. Fact. I kept quiet and sipped at my tea.

'I'm fine, lad, thanks for asking. Did you say bacon, Sue?'

'No, Artie. Come and have your muesli.' Auntie Sue pinched the newspaper out of his hands and gave him a look that said 'and make more of an effort with your only nephew'.

'Cholesterol, Uncle.' Julian slapped his non-existent stomach. 'I avoid it like capital gains tax. You need to look after your heart if you're going to, er . . .' He pursed his lips to sip at his coffee. 'Retire.'

My eyes narrowed.

I'd phoned Dad yesterday to give him an update on my uncle and aunt's plans to leave the farm at the end of the year. I'd said that they hadn't decided whether to sell up or rent out the land and I'd asked if I could delay repaying the money I'd borrowed until then. And one day later, hey presto, the Master of Opportunity comes a-knocking.

Coincidence? I snorted into my tea. Not likely.

Julian didn't come rushing to our assistance in April, did he, when I called and asked for help? Oh no. He must have an ulterior motive and I wasn't leaving this room until I'd found out what it was.

Uncle Arthur shuffled from his armchair to the kitchen bench and began ploughing through his daily bowl of sawdust. 'How long are you stopping for?' he asked in a not altogether welcoming way.

I shunted up the bench towards my uncle to show solidarity.

'You'll be due back in London, I expect?' I asked hopefully.

'Sure, sure.' Julian frowned. 'But first I wanted to speak to you both.' He looked from Uncle Arthur to Auntie Sue and then pointedly at me. I folded my arms.

Auntie Sue poured herself a cup of tea, slipped a tea cosy over the pot and sat down next to Julian. 'What about, love?'

He patted her arm with his stoaty hand and left it there. 'I don't mean to pry and you certainly don't have to confide in me,' he gave an unconvincing self-deprecating laugh, 'but have you thought about who might inherit the farm?'

I gasped. 'Julian!'

The cheek of the man! Why didn't he just come straight out and ask how much they'd left him in their will while he was at it?

'We have.' Uncle Arthur tilted his chin up. There was a patch of stubble on his jawline that he'd missed with his razor. It gave him an air of vulnerability that made me want to hug him whilst simultaneously punching Julian right between the eyes.

Julian swallowed.

'We'd always hoped it would stay in the family, love.' Auntie Sue sighed.

Uncle Arthur dropped his spoon into the bowl and milk

splashed on to Julian's linen jacket (ha!). 'But we may not keep the farm for our retirement, we might sell.'

Auntie Sue shimmied her shoulders. 'And buy a bung—' She noticed Uncle Arthur's scowl and snapped her jaw shut.

'Excellent!' my brother cried, banging the table and making us all jump.

'Julian, much as we have loved you popping in like this,' I began impatiently, 'I don't see what business it is of yours, poking your nose—'

He flapped a hand. *Flapped.* Like I was a fly getting in his ointment.

'I might have a buyer for the farm.' He sat back and stretched his thin lips into a smug smile. 'Lock, stock and barrel. Why wait until the end of the year when you could start your retirement now?' He hitched up a narrow shoulder and grinned meanly at me.

There was a moment of silence during which my pulse speeded up so much I feared my poor heart would explode.

'A buyer?' breathed Auntie Sue.

I looked from one to the other: Auntie Sue's eyes had glazed over in wonderment and Uncle Arthur was nodding thoughtfully.

No, don't nod!

I forced myself to breathe. This had to be their decision. A quick sale, money in their pockets, completely stress-free living. They were bound to be tempted. But me? There were tears pressing at the back of my eyeballs and I was rapidly going into full panic mode.

What about my Vintage Tea Rooms? I wanted to shout. I'd got the next six months all mapped out. *And besides, this is my home*, I wanted to howl. But I didn't. I clamped my lips together with great difficulty.

'I know,' said Julian, laughing as if he didn't quite believe it himself. 'What are the chances?'

Precisely, I thought, sipping my tea. What *are* the chances?

'One of my fellow business angels is interested. Made his millions in television cables. The market for cables tripled in the noughties. Digital. That's where the money is.' He sniffed and rocked back on his chair. 'Anyway, now he fancies himself as a farmer, living the good life.'

'Well, isn't that a . . . thing?' exclaimed Auntie Sue.

'Now don't get too excited,' said Julian. 'This place is in pretty poor repair and mightn't be worth what you'd hoped.'

'Funny that,' I muttered.

He scanned the room greedily and I could just imagine him reporting back to Cable Man: 'Needs gutting, the whole place, top to bottom. But definitely got potential.'

This was a terrible development. *Terrible.*

'But if you do the deal direct, you'll avoid estate agents and all that nonsense, and you'll be saving yourself a lot of money.'

'It's a kind offer,' began Uncle Arthur tentatively, 'but we weren't planning on going just yet, were we, Sue?'

'Artie, we need to be realistic. Chances like this don't come along every day,' she said quietly, taking his hand.

Thank goodness for that, I thought. I couldn't stand the stress if it did.

'Right, well, let me know within the month,' said Julian, standing up, as if the deal was as good as clinched.

'A month!' I yelped at the same time as Auntie Sue said, 'Well, that sounds reasonable.'

I gave Uncle Arthur a pleading look. He stood up, too, and a little wave of love came over me when I noticed how much shorter than Julian he was. He'd shrunk since Easter, I was sure of it.

'I'm not committing myself to a time limit, son. This farm has been in the Moorcroft family for over a hundred years. Me and your auntie need to talk about it. Think things through.'

'He won't hang around, I'm warning you.' Julian sighed, shaking his head. 'People like him never do.'

Uncle Arthur eyeballed his nephew. 'And I won't be rushed.'

Go, Uncle Arthur! I just about managed not to punch the air.

'So be it.' Julian frowned and fiddled with his phone again.

There was something dodgy going on here; I just couldn't put my finger on it.

'Julian,' I said sharply. He lifted his eyes reluctantly from the screen of his phone. 'I'm confused. I only spoke to Dad last night about Auntie Sue and Uncle Arthur's plans to retire. And in the last twelve hours you've managed to find someone who wants to buy a farm. *In the Lake District*. All while you were at a conference. *In Edinburgh*. It's all very convenient, isn't it?'

'Indeed!' Julian laughed and put a snake-like arm around Auntie Sue's shoulders. 'It's obviously meant to be.'

'But how—' I huffed.

My brother spoke over me. 'Any chance of a quick tour of the farmyard before I go? I'll take a few pictures to show my contact. He's going to love the place as much as you do, I know he will.'

'Sure, sure,' said Uncle Arthur, making his way to the door hastily.

'I'm about to milk the cows, Julian, you can come and watch,' smiled Auntie Sue.

'Great,' said Julian, not entirely convincingly.

'I'm going to get dressed,' I announced. 'Then I'll do the hens, shall I?'

But no one heard. They were all fussing round, finding wellingtons to fit Julian so as not to ruin his poncy shoes, so I sloped off to my room feeling all crotchety.

Half an hour later I was back down in the kitchen, showered and altogether in a better frame of mind. If – and only if – my aunt and uncle wanted to sell to Julian's rich cable man, then who was I to stand in their way? It was their farm, their home and ultimately their future. Just as long as Julian didn't mess them about, that was my only worry.

There was a rattle at the letterbox and I got there just in time to snatch the letters up while Madge snapped in vain at the air, trying to bite the postman's fingers off through the flap.

'Junk, junk, junk,' I mumbled, flicking through the little pile of post. Eek! Except this one.

My stomach lurched as I dropped the rest of the envelopes on the table and kept hold of the large brown one.

It was from the Cumbrian planning department. I held my breath as I slipped my finger under the edge of the envelope. This was it. The decision on whether I'd be allowed to open the Appleby Farm Vintage Tea Rooms. In my heart of hearts I was expecting a yes – my friendly planning officer, Patience Purdue, had as good as told me so. But there was always a chance . . .

Actually, on second thoughts – I stopped tearing the paper and sprinted out of the kitchen and back along the hall to the office – I'd sit down at my desk first. Just in case it was bad news.

As my hand reached for the door handle, I froze. Julian was in there, talking quietly on the office phone.

'The old dears have as good as agreed. Yeah, yeah, I know . . . a goldmine.'

I clapped a hand over my mouth to stop myself yelling out. The absolute scumbag.

I knew it was too good to be true. *Fancies himself as a farmer, living the good life.* Yeah, right.

I pressed my ear closer to the door. My breathing was so loud, I could barely hear Julian's slimy voice. I caught something about demolition and was just about to burst in on him when the kitchen door banged open and interrupted me mid-eavesdrop.

Someone whistled tunelessly, presumably to attract attention, then called, 'Hello? Anyone home?'

It was Harry.

I dived back to the kitchen door, making him jump, and shushed him fiercely.

'Sorry, is someone asleep?' he said, twisting his mouth into a bemused smile.

'Shush! Listen to this,' I hissed.

Touching my forefinger to my lips to secure his silence, I grabbed his arm and hauled him along the hallway. We both pressed our ears to the office door.

'They've no idea what it's worth,' Julian laughed.

'Who is it?' murmured Harry, frowning with curiosity. 'What what's worth?'

'Julian,' I murmured back, shaking my head, 'and Appleby Farm.'

Squashed together like this, I was aware of the warmth of his body through his shirt and the faintest smell of mint on his breath. I felt hot all of a sudden and brushed a curly piece of straw from his sleeve.

'Yeah, luxury hotel, holiday village, country retreat . . . the sky's the limit,' Julian boasted.

Harry and I exchanged shocked looks.

'This deal will put me on the map. Julian Moorcroft has arrived.' And then he did an evil sort of laugh and ended the call.

'Quick!' I yelped under my breath.

I scrambled up the first flight of stairs, dragging Harry by the hand behind me. We flattened ourselves to the wall as Julian came out of the office and went back out into the farmyard, humming to himself.

I met Harry's bewildered gaze and let out a long shuddering breath. To my astonishment I found I was still clutching the letter from the council in one hand and Harry's fingers in the other. I let go of his hand, sank down on the worn stair carpet and dropped my head into my hands.

Harry squeezed in next to me, his thighs pressing against mine as he wrapped an arm around my shoulders.

'Freya, what's going on? I only came in to get the tractor keys and I feel like I've stumbled into an Agatha Christie mystery,' he said softly.

Despite my anger at Julian's underhand behaviour, I couldn't help smiling.

'Either that or an adult game of sardines,' he added, 'which, by the way, has a lot going for it.'

I picked at the corner of the envelope and felt the tingle of tears at the back of my eyes.

'Oh, Harry, as if we haven't got enough to deal with at the moment, what with TB and the movement restriction. Then Julian turns up unexpectedly and claims to have found a buyer for the farm. Auntie Sue and Uncle Arthur want to retire and I'm all for helping them do it,' I shook my head, 'but I can't believe Julian would try to cheat his own family out of the proper value of the farm.'

Harry raised an eyebrow. 'Sure about that? I've only met your brother a couple of times over the years, but I know you've never seen eye to eye over money.'

I sighed. 'Good point.'

'It would be a travesty to see the farm replaced by a hotel,' agreed Harry. 'Anything I can do to help, you will let me know, won't you?'

I felt my heart swell with gratitude. 'Thank you. I need a friend right now.'

We smiled at each other for a few seconds and it was all I could do not to sink against him.

'What's the letter, by the way?' asked Harry, breaking into my thoughts.

'This?' I said, a smile twitching at my lips. 'Let's have a look, shall we?'

I ripped open the envelope from the planning department and held my breath as I scanned over the page.

Planning application approved.

'Fantastic! Appleby Farm Vintage Tea Rooms can go ahead!' I exhaled with relief.

'Congratulations, I'm really pleased for you.' Harry grinned. 'So what's your next move?'

I stood up and caught sight of my reflection in the landing mirror. I felt my heartbeat, strong and defiant against my ribcage.

I'd always described myself as a fun, fearless female and Julian was undoubtedly a strong opponent. But I had right on my side and this was one battle I was not prepared to lose to my big brother.

'Right now? I'm going to fight Julian. I'm not going to let him take Appleby Farm from me, and certainly not from Uncle Arthur and Auntie Sue.'

*

By the time I'd found the tractor keys for Harry, splashed cold water on my face and made it outside to the yard, Julian was sitting in a sleek black sports car with his window wound down, chatting to Auntie Sue and Uncle Arthur.

'Leaving without saying goodbye, were you, Julian?' I said, forcing a smile as I bent to face him.

'Can't wait all day for you to get dressed,' he scoffed.

'Has Julian been telling you about his development ideas for a *luxury hotel* at Appleby Farm?' I smiled sweetly, not breaking eye contact with him and adding air quotes to 'luxury hotel'.

He pinched the bridge of his nose with one hand and punched the steering wheel with the other. 'Freya—'

'Or possibly a holiday village and – what was the other one? Oh yes, a country retreat.' I turned to face Auntie Sue and Uncle Arthur, who both looked bewildered. 'The sky's the limit, apparently. Isn't it, Julian?'

'All right, all right. Get out of the way,' said Julian, opening the car door and pushing me to one side as he climbed out. His foot landed in a puddle and muddy water splashed up his leg.

'So, there is no TV cable man?' Auntie Sue automatically stepped towards her husband and linked her arm through his. I felt guilty all of a sudden. In my haste to expose Julian for what he was, I hadn't considered how they might react.

'Yes, yes, of course there is.' Julian scowled, rubbing his wet trouser leg uselessly.

'There's just no good life,' I added. I put my arms around my uncle and aunt and hugged them tight. 'I apologize on behalf of my devious brother. He's trying to pull a fast one, I'm afraid.'

'Julian?' gasped Auntie Sue.

'Is that right, son?' said Uncle Arthur coldly.

'No!' Julian dragged a hand over his red face. 'Look. This is a bit awkward. I admit, I should have come clean. I do have a buyer interested, but he's an investor and not a would-be farmer. I just thought you might not want to see the farm as a development opportunity.'

'Not to mention a gold mine, eh, Julian?' I said quietly.

Julian made a show of checking the time. 'I've really got to get back to London.'

I smirked at him. How convenient.

'But would you consider it? If I offer you market rates?' he continued.

'No way!' I huffed, folding my arms. 'On your bike.'

Uncle Arthur put his arm round my waist. 'Freya, we're not in a position to turn offers down flat at the moment,' he murmured and then added more loudly, 'I don't like the way you've conducted yourself so far, Julian. But I will consider a sensible and honest proposal. Any more underhand business and you'll be shown the door. Is that clear?'

'Perfectly,' muttered Julian. 'How long—'

'And as I said, it'll be in my own time.' Uncle Arthur extended a hand, drawing the discussion to a close and Julian reluctantly shook it.

The car engine roared into life and within seconds it had disappeared, taking Julian with it. *Thank God*. My aunt and uncle tottered back inside and I stood soaking up the farm: the charm, the history, the aroma, the sounds and, more than anything, the overwhelming sense of home.

I was so privileged, I thought, being able to share this little corner of England for however long it stays in the family. But the thought of losing all this heritage filled me with horror.

All of a sudden a tingling sensation crept over me. It

began at the backs of my knees, flickered its way up my spine, along my arms and swirled around my head until every little hair on my skin stood on end.

I had no idea how little old me could keep Appleby Farm out of the hands of investors, but I was going to give it a good go.

Chapter 23

I had set a date for opening the vintage tea rooms. The first of August, which was five weeks away. Gulp. If I said it fast it didn't seem so scary.

It was hugely ambitious, admittedly, but Goat and his team were in the barn now, knocking seven bells out of it, and, as he said, it was mostly cosmetic (if you didn't count the toilets, plumbing, electrics and flooring). It was the new glazing that would take the longest time and that was already on order. And I'd started buying second-hand equipment and storing it in the shed.

Summer would be the busiest time of year and getting the tea rooms open to take advantage of all these potential visitors to Appleby Farm was my number-one priority. Besides which, with the whole 'leaving at the end of the year' plan, plus paying Dad back, not to mention Julian snapping at my heels, I had to crack on and make a profit sharpish.

Today was an inside day for me, partly because I needed to work on the menu and partly because the rain had been falling as sharp as needles since last night.

It's an unwritten rule that no one is allowed to complain about the wet weather up here because the Lake District

237

wouldn't be so green and lakey without it. That doesn't mean I enjoy it, though.

Harry had taken Uncle Arthur on a gentle jaunt to the weekly cattle auction. Officially Arthur was advising Harry on the purchase of some calves but I suspected that Harry was doing it out of the kindness of his heart to cheer my uncle up. Bless him, my uncle had been looking forward to a day out and a chin-wag with other farmers all week, and had been ready an hour early this morning. Auntie Sue was getting to grips with gluten-free flour for our 'special dietary requirements' offering and apart from the odd grumble emanating from the kitchen such as 'the damn stuff is like dust' and 'will this sponge ever rise?', the farmhouse was silent.

So when the phone on the desk next to me rang, I leaped into the air like a scalded cat.

I clutched at my heart. 'Appleby Farm,' I gasped.

'Hey, Green Eyes.'

'Charlie!'

I sat up straight in my chair as love and guilt played ping-pong somewhere above my head.

I hadn't phoned him to invite him up as Lizzie had suggested. In fact, I hadn't phoned him at all. I'd been totally immersed in my own little bubble, bouncing from one job to the next. Some – like choosing the lovely glossy tiles for the new loos – were fun, others – like booking a visit from the environmental health department – less so. I'd hardly had time to think, let alone talk.

And now he'd phoned me.

'Listen, this is just a quick call, I'm on duty and I might have to dash off at any minute.'

'My hero,' I laughed. 'Well, it's lovely to hear from you while it lasts.'

His voice was sexy and boyish and full of energy. There was the sound of men laughing somewhere in the distance behind him and I imagined the other fire officers teasing him for making a call to his girlfriend at work.

'There's a charity barbecue here at the fire station on Saturday night. There's a band playing, a few stalls, raffle and, you know, the usual. Vic, our cook, is doing the food, so it should be good. So what do you say? Fancy it? You could come home for the weekend?'

My heart sank. It sounded such fun and I could tell by his voice that he really, really wanted me to say yes. But I couldn't possibly go.

The builders were working over the weekend, digging the new drains for the plumbing in the tea rooms. I had to be on site to check everything was in the right place.

On the other hand, I hadn't seen him for weeks. Perhaps I could travel down on Saturday, go to the barbecue, then we could spend the whole of Sunday in bed together having fun and only getting up to make toast like we used to, when fun was my main goal in life. But now I had new goals. I had a business to get up and running.

What to do . . .

'Freya?'

I pictured the disappointment on Charlie's face and suddenly the miles between us seemed impossible to bridge. If I could just reach out and touch him, feel his hand in mine, this would be so much easier.

'I can't,' I blurted, feeling absolutely wretched. 'I'd love to but I just can't.'

'Right.' Flat, final and not a hint of his previous good humour.

'Charlie, I'm sorry . . .'

I told him all about my opening deadline, the builders

and the drains, and how if I didn't comply with three thousand regulations the environmental health inspector wouldn't give me a certificate. To be fair to the poor love, he did 'mmm' and 'I see' quite a bit while I was justifying my position as World's Worst Girlfriend.

'I get it, Freya. You're doing a brilliant job. But please come, you can't work every day of the week.' He sighed.

'That's what farmers do.'

'You're not a farmer,' said Charlie, 'you're my girl. Who I love. And miss. And if I don't see you soon I'll have completely forgotten what you look like.'

'I'm exactly the same. Only with frizzier hair at the moment because of all the rain,' I said softly, willing him to smile again. 'And I love you.'

Charlie sighed down the phone. The seconds ticked by and I became increasingly desperate for him to say something.

'Look, I'll try to get back soon, or you could come up to me. It'll only be for six months.'

'Six months?' he said, sounding shocked.

Oh God. I hadn't told him, had I?

I was all swollen-tongued with nerves but I explained about Uncle Arthur and Auntie Sue's retirement plan for the end of the year, adding that it might get cut short if they sold the farm to Julian's evil investor but that, for me, would be a travesty.

And when I stopped talking there was nothing. Not a sound from him.

'You don't want to come home, do you?' he said eventually. And bless him, his tone wasn't even harsh or mad. It was just sad.

I thought about it for a moment. *Home*. That was the problem. Kingsfield had never really felt like home. It was a nice place and all that, and of course it had its attractions – Charlie and Ollie, Anna, Tilly, Gemma and all the Shenton Road Café crew.

Be honest, Freya. Tell him the truth.

'I do want to see you, Charlie. But . . . remember when we were walking around the lake and I said that I felt more alive when I'm here?' I began.

'Yeah, I do. And I suppose I knew then, really.'

'Knew what?' My heart was pounding, as if it guessed that something really bad was about to happen, even though my brain was in total denial.

'Me here, you there. It was never going to work for long.'

'That's not true,' I gasped. Although even as I said it I wondered if I was just kidding myself. 'Charlie? Are . . .' My mouth suddenly went dry and I croaked, 'Are you saying what I think you're saying?'

'Babe, I think about you all the time. "I must remember to tell Freya," I say to myself. Or I'll walk past the café and automatically look for you. Or I'll sniff that T-shirt that you wore in bed the night before you went to Paris.'

'Oh, Charlie, you are a sweetie,' I said, remembering the night I'd spent in his flat before going to see my parents. That was before Appleby Farm had got under my skin like it had now, though. Now I barely had time to think about anything other than the tea rooms. An idea occurred to me suddenly.

'Look, what about tonight? We could each drive halfway and meet in the middle. At least then—'

'No, Freya, I can't do this long-distance thing,' Charlie continued softly. 'Between your crazy hours up there and my shifts in Kingsfield, we're never going to have time for each other. I'm sorry, babe, but it doesn't work – for me or for you. So yes, I think it's best if we stop seeing us other.

Because I think deep down you're where you want to be and there's nothing I can say or do that will change it.'

I hadn't realized I was crying until I felt the tickle of a teardrop on my chin.

'I'm so sorry, Charlie,' I gasped. 'You're right: I need to be here at the moment.'

'Hey, you've got nothing to be sorry for. Life just got in the way for us. Two different lives, in two different places. I still stand by everything I said before; I'm proud of you, Freya. Keep me posted, won't you?'

We said our goodbyes and did all the promising to keep in touch stuff and all the time I was shouting at myself inwardly to stop it, to not let him go, to argue that we could make it work and that six months, in the grand scheme of things, was *nothing*. And that this was crazy!

And then he was gone. I put the phone down and stared at it. Did that really just happen?

I laid my head down on the desk and prepared myself for a huge sob-fest but the door opened and Goat waded in without knocking, brandishing a can of spray paint. 'Where do you want your sockets, then?'

I spent a good hour with Goat, shuffling from wall to wall and spraying a dot of paint where I guessed I'd need an electricity point (two dots for a double) and if he noticed me sniffling every so often, he didn't mention it. It was very soothing, actually, and by the time I emerged into the yard it was eleven o'clock and the tears and the rain had stopped.

No point trying to work on the menu now, it would soon be lunchtime, courtesy of Auntie Sue's gluten-free experiments. There was, however, time for a restorative ride on Skye, so I took myself off to the stables.

I was still some way away when I heard the unmistakeable tones of Lizzie belting out a grunty version of 'Don't Cha'.

Lizzie was sponging Skye's body with a sweet-smelling lavender wash, swinging her hips to the chorus.

I coughed and she clutched at her throat.

'Jeepers creepers, Freya! Hey, what's with the swollen eyes? Hayfever? Do you want an antihistamine? I've got one in my bag, somewhere.'

She dropped her sponge back in the bucket as I held my arms out and started to cry.

'I need a hug.'

Lizzie was a great hugger. In fact, even Skye got in on the act, pushing her brown and white splodged nose in between the two of us as I relayed the whole story. And even though I was sobbing again, it felt nice to be able to talk to someone about it.

After a few minutes I noticed that Lizzie wasn't breathing.

'Lizzie?' I disentangled myself from her arms, which I'd just realized had got quite tight.

She screwed up her face and fanned her hand in front of her eyes.

'We're doomed,' she said in a strangled voice.

'Who?' I held on to her shoulders, a bit bewildered.

'Me and Ross.'

'Why?'

'Because if you and Charlie can't make it long distance, how can we?'

My eyes darted to Calf's Close, the field behind us, where Ross was mending fences both literally and metaphorically.

Yesterday there had been a bit of an incident.

At about nine o'clock Harry had raced into the yard while I was collecting the eggs. I'd beamed, waved and put

243

my egg basket down. He called in most days for something or other and I enjoyed our chats. We generally shared a sparky bit of banter at each other's expense but there was always a more tender moment, too, when he'd ask me for news on Julian or how Uncle Arthur was and whether there was anything he could do to help.

But yesterday he hadn't stopped to make small talk.

'Is your uncle in?' he'd shouted, jumping out of his pick-up truck, looking all serious.

I'd wiped the smile off my face, sharpish. 'He's having a rest. Can I help?'

There wasn't much I didn't know about the detail of the farm now. I knew what was in each field, I knew which crops had been sprayed with what and I knew the plans for harvesting. I had an up-to-date file of all the Herefords' details and I could lay my hands on Gloria and Gaynor's milk yield in a nanosecond.

Harry obviously hadn't thought so, though. He'd stared at me, a glimmer of a smile playing at his lips. 'I'm sure you can. Your cows have escaped and they're running free on Lovedale Lane. Can you give me a hand to round them up?'

Ah. So maybe I didn't know how to do everything.

'I'll get Uncle Arthur,' I'd said hastily.

In hindsight I wished I'd videoed the carry-on – we'd have made a fortune on one of those funny film-clips programmes. One cow had ended up on the village petrol station forecourt, two had trampled through Hilary-in-the-post-office's garden, we found one paddling in the beck and a couple of others had, very honourably, turned themselves in at the handling pen. We had all helped to round them up but Harry had been our hero: calm in a crisis and totally unfazed by holding up the traffic as he drove a line of panicky cows up the middle of Lovedale Lane back to the farm.

Anyway, Ross had spent this morning going round the village making good the damage, and, at this precise moment, was only a very *short* distance away from Lizzie mending the bit of wall through which the herd had made their escape.

'Yeah, I know he's there now,' she said, pressing a finger under each eye to blot her tears. 'But come September he'll be miles away at uni in Shropshire. For a *year*! Surrounded by clever types. He'll forget all about me.'

'He won't,' I cried. 'Besides, it's a student year, don't forget. They have their own separate calendars. Their months are like one of our weeks. In fact, their holidays are longer than their terms. And he'll spend all his holidays with you, I know he will, and weekends probably.'

'Do you think?' she hiccupped.

She gazed over at Ross through tear-filled eyes and I put my arm around her.

'Deffo. Anyway, you're not doomed because . . . because . . .' I gulped in some air and Lizzie blinked at me, waiting for me to finish.

I'd been trying to pin down my thoughts since I got off the phone from Charlie and they'd kept escaping me. Suddenly, there they were, laid out in a row in front of me like a batch of Auntie Sue's perfectly formed scones.

'Charlie and I are different,' I said, holding up a finger as Lizzie opened her mouth to object. 'But you and Ross are the same.'

'Huh?' Lizzie frowned.

'Think about it,' I said. 'You love farmers, he loves farms and you both want to live in The Lakes. You two are on the same path.'

245

'True.' She nodded.

Whereas Charlie and I, I realized with a sharp jolt, whilst we had a great time together, were on totally separate journeys. We were like something astrological – meteorites or asteroids perhaps – that had collided, sparked along together for a while and then bounced off on completely different trajectories. It was bound to happen . . . written in the stars, even.

At the end of the day I wasn't Charlie's perfect match and he wasn't mine. I wanted a home in the country, filled with my own children; he wanted to stay in Kingsfield and was content with Ollie.

And these things were deal-breakers. For both of us.

On some level, I'd always known this and suddenly it all made sense. He was a great friend and I wanted it to stay that way. Maybe in the future when I didn't feel quite so emotional about it, he could be the sort of big brother that I'd always wanted.

'Hey, Lizzie, there's something I've got to do. I'll see you later.'

I leaned back against the damp bench in the orchard, circled my tense shoulders and read through the letter one more time. It had taken me three attempts to get the tone right, but I thought I'd finally cracked it.

Dear Charlie,
The six months I spent in Kingsfield were great. The four months I spent in Kingsfield <u>with you</u> were amazing.
I am a lucky girl to have had you as my boyfriend since Christmas. You are a wonderful human being, a gorgeous man and a fantastic role model for Ollie.
Today when you ended our relationship it felt like a piece of

my heart was being torn away. But I just want you to know
that I think you did the right thing. A kind and brave thing.
And I'll always thank you for that.
 We had fun, didn't we?
 Love and hugs
 Freya xx

PS I hope you still think of me when your Outdoor Girl toma-
toes are ready x

I still felt sad and lonely, and I knew it would be a
while before I stopped missing him and before I stopped
thinking 'ooh, I must remember to tell Charlie' whenever
something funny happened, but I felt better. I folded the
letter and sealed the envelope.

And that, as they say in the American TV shows, was
closure.

Chapter 24

I was still sitting in the orchard, holding my letter to Charlie and wondering whether we could do something with all these apples in September (organic cider being my favourite idea) when Uncle Arthur lowered himself on to the bench beside me.

'Word has it that you've had a rough morning.' He patted my thigh. 'Everyone's in the kitchen gluing their jaws together with your auntie's gluten-free biscuits and Lizzie passed on your news about Charlie. I'm sorry to hear that. Feel a bit responsible, too. Me and my dicky ticker,' he tutted.

I slipped the envelope into my pocket and leaned my head on his shoulder.

'You mustn't feel guilty. I'm here because I want to be. I made my own choices. And you know what?' I smiled shakily at him. 'I don't regret a single thing.'

'That's my girl.'

We sat in companionable silence. The birds were singing again and directly above us the sun was beginning to tunnel its way down through the swollen clouds.

'I love this orchard.' I sighed. 'It's so peaceful and pretty, and there's something timeless about it.'

'I know what you mean. I remember climbing these trees

when I was still in short trousers. They're bigger now, of course.'

'What are – the trees or your trousers?' I teased.

He waggled his eyebrows. 'Well, if you're still making jokes, you'll survive.'

'Oh, I'll survive all right.' I nudged him with my shoulder. 'So. Is it just apple trees or do you have any pears?'

Uncle Arthur's body began to shake and I peeled myself off him to find him chuckling.

'What?'

'You asked me that when you were eleven!'

'Did I? And what did you answer?'

'I said no, we had no pears. But I planted a pear tree especially for you and for three years nothing happened. Not a single pear. And the next year – whoosh. We had tons of them. I'll show you.'

We stood up from the bench and made our way past some pecking hens to the smallest tree in the corner of the orchard.

'Oh, yes,' I laughed, 'I remember now. Don't remember a bumper crop, though.'

'No. That was the summer you didn't come to the farm. You went to visit your parents in Australia when you were about fourteen.' His warm eyes met mine. 'It was a quiet one that year.'

I thought of the two of them picking pears with no one to eat them and my heart pinged with love. And suddenly I had an urge to hear more stories – happy ones, preferably – about the farm. I felt as if time was running out and I needed to collect all his memories and store them up, like when you collect shells from a beach and later turn them over, one at a time, in your hand and remember just how perfect the day was.

I glanced back up at the tree and looped my arm through his. 'There's loads of fruit on it this year and I'll definitely be here to eat them. Come on, fancy taking a walk round your farm with me?'

His face lit up. 'I'd like that very much.'

We decided to take a route across the fields rather than back through the farmyard and along the track, and as I unlatched the gate into High Field I turned and noticed a great ball of greenery in the centre of one of the apple trees. And in the tree next to it and . . . all the trees except the pear tree, in fact.

'Is that ivy, up in the trees?' I asked.

Uncle Arthur squinted to follow my pointing finger. 'Mistletoe. Grows in big clumps like that. It's a nuisance really.'

'Oh, how lovely! The orchard must look so romantic in winter when the trees have lost their leaves.'

'I suppose so. But not the most romantic place on my farm,' he chuckled, ushering me through the gate.

'Really! You mean there's somewhere more romantic than this? Lead on!' I smiled, mentally adding 'sell mistletoe at Christmas market' to my growing list of new business ideas.

We reached the edge of Oak Field where some of the cows were grazing and stopped for Uncle Arthur to get his breath back. He took a bottle of water out of his jacket pocket and sipped at it.

'Look at those little fellas,' he chuckled.

Two calves were frolicking around, kicking up their back legs and headbutting one another.

'Cute!' I took my phone out and snapped a couple of pictures. They'd do for the Facebook page. When we had one.

'Probably sounds daft, but my animals are like family. I'll miss seeing cattle in my fields when they're all gone.' He sighed. He pocketed his water and we carried on trudging uphill.

'How was the cattle auction?' I asked, trying to keep the conversation light.

'Good. Well, good to be part of the action again and see livestock changing hands. Harry didn't spot anything he fancied. I had my eye on a lovely Hereford bull, but . . .' He shrugged and pushed his hands deep into his pockets. 'I suppose my days of buying beasts at auction are behind me.'

I put my arm lightly around his waist and hugged him.

No animals were allowed to enter or leave the farm whilst the TB movement restriction was still in place. But even without that, Uncle Arthur had no use for a new bull; from the end of the year, he wouldn't be farming beef any more. It seemed such a sad end to his career.

I scanned the fields around me and my heart squeezed. What would be here in twelve months' time? The idea of no Appleby Farm was too awful to contemplate.

'But you don't have any regrets, do you, about being a farmer all your life? I mean, who wouldn't want to own this?' I spread my arms out.

'You never really own land, lass. If anything it owns you – your soul, at any rate. You can be its guardian but that's about all.'

He stopped and bent over, resting his hands on his thighs, and my stomach lurched.

'Are you OK?' I asked, touching his arm.

He stood up and stretched. 'I'm fine. But my heart attack was like a tap on the shoulder to remind me that every day is a gift. And this farm . . . it's a gift, too, and one day soon

251

I'll have to pass it on. Farming is a young man's game. And you know what?' He blinked at me and I shook my head. 'I felt old at the auction today. There were only a few old men like me left. Harry knew everyone.'

'That's because everyone else your age is already retired,' I laughed, hoping to cheer him up. I tucked my arm through his and we began to walk again. 'Like Harry's parents, living it up on the south coast. Taking it easy and enjoying themselves.'

He chuckled. 'All right, then. Come on, last one to the top is a donkey. I've still got to show you the view before it rains.'

The top of the hill, where Colton Woods met the field, was the furthest point from the farmhouse and also, on a good day, had the best view. Today the visibility wasn't great but the view was still spectacular.

'There's more rain on its way.' Uncle Arthur nodded to the sky behind me and sure enough an army of charcoal clouds was marching towards us, urged along by a sharp wind.

'We should go back,' I said.

Too late.

Seconds later the heavens opened and we had to flatten ourselves against the hedge while we pulled up our hoods. Mine only partially covered my hair. I touched the ends tentatively; it would have quite possibly crocheted itself into a blanket by the time I was back inside.

'Can you see that hut?' Uncle Arthur shouted above the deluge.

I scoured the landscape until I spotted a dilapidated wooden hut tucked into the corner against the drystone wall (a misnomer at this precise moment if ever I heard one). I nodded. We both lowered our heads to protect ourselves and made our way towards it.

As we reached the hut, I helped him clamber up and we stumbled, relieved, out of the rain. There was no door and the roof was riddled with holes. But it was much drier than outside and there was even a wooden bench to sit on.

'What is this place?' I asked, out of breath from heaving Uncle Arthur up the step. 'I remember playing inside when I was small. I always wondered why it was here.'

'Shepherd's hut. Left over from when we farmed sheep. Derelict now, of course. The shepherd used to spend the night out here during lambing season.'

It was derelict. But it was also very sweet. There were windows at each end and a door in the centre. One half appeared to be for sleeping, or sitting as we were, and the other half was the kitchen end. There was even a little stove, although the chimney was missing. The hole in the roof was still there, though, and the rain was bucketing through it.

'Is this the only shepherd's hut you've got?' I asked, feeling a tingling of excitement along my spine.

He wiped the raindrops off his face with a dry handkerchief and passed it to me. 'No. There's one other at the far side of the woods. Why?'

My brain had a new idea zipping about. Forget the cider. This was huge.

I grinned at him. 'Uncle Arthur, have you ever heard of glamping?'

For the next few minutes I told him all about glamorous camping and how amazing this little hut could look if it had a facelift. He told me that Eddy was a dab hand with wood and if anyone could restore the old relic it was him. Before we knew it I'd imagined the opening of the Appleby Farm Glampsite and the rain had almost stopped.

253

What better place to wake up in the morning with these views? So romantic! I almost wished I'd known about this when Charlie . . . I exhaled quickly, blowing away my daydreams.

'Hey!' I grinned, slapping the bench as a thought occurred to me. 'Is this the most romantic spot on the farm, then?'

'No, lass.' Uncle Arthur groaned as he stood – a sharp reminder that he was supposed to be taking it easy and not hiking uphill in the rain, gulp – and beckoned me to the window. There was no glass in it and the wind blew spray into my face.

The view from the window looked straight down the valley and although the day was wet and wild, it was pure 'Lakes', from the grey stone walls criss-crossing the landscape to the shiny slate roofs, vivid green and yellow fields, and the tiny ribbon of road snaking into the distance.

It completely took my breath away.

'See that little lake?' he said. 'Right at the far edge, near the boundary with Willow Farm?'

I nodded. Harry and I had spent many a summer's day fishing in that lake. 'I see it.'

'That's where I met your auntie. She came up from the next village with a group of her friends. Middle of winter it was, the trees were laced with thick frost and the lake had frozen over. Now that's the most romantic place on the farm.'

His face had glazed over with a warm smile. He had such a friendly face, my uncle. I'd have loved to have known him when he was a young man. I bet he would have been quite a catch.

'Sounds absolutely magical.'

'That was exactly what she said. She told me that she'd

254

never been ice-skating before and would I mind holding her hand. So I helped her on to the ice.'

'What a gentleman.' I smiled, pulling him back from the window and making him sit down.

'Sue clung on to me and chatted nineteen to the dozen all the way round. She told me that she used to pass Appleby Farm on her way to school and always thought how lovely it was. And then she looked at me with those beautiful blue eyes and smiled, and I was a goner.' He sighed wistfully.

'Love at first sight,' I breathed dreamily.

'It was,' he said proudly. 'And that's why the lake is my favourite spot.'

Where would my special place be? I wondered. And who would be The One, now that Charlie was no longer in my life?

'I was a farmer's son and not used to chatting up pretty girls,' Uncle Arthur was saying. 'I don't know what came over me, but I asked her to go to the local dance. I couldn't believe my luck when she said yes.'

'Tell me about the secret sign,' I urged. I'd heard this story a hundred times – it was part of family folklore – but I loved hearing it.

'Again?' he chuckled, scratching his chin. 'All right.'

My heart was melting as he told me again me how he had fallen in love with Auntie Sue at that dance and even though he had been quite shy, he had decided that he had to tell her how he felt. So he squeezed her hand three times.

'What was that for?' she'd asked him.

So he'd squeezed her hand again saying, 'I love you' – one word with each squeeze.

'Arthur Moorcroft,' she'd replied, 'you are the sweetest man I have ever met.'

'We were married a few months after that and from then on whenever we wanted to tell each other how we felt, we used our secret sign and no one around us knew a thing. And I'll let you into another secret,' he leaned towards me and winked, 'we still do it.'

'Such a gorgeous story.' I pressed a kiss to his whiskery cheek. 'You were so in love and so happy.'

He looked away quickly but not before I saw a flicker of sadness cross his face.

'We have been happy but . . .' He swallowed. 'Not having any children has been a great sadness. For us both.'

My heart twisted for them and I remembered how Auntie Sue had said that it hadn't mattered so much to him. It seemed as if his pain was just as great but perhaps he'd kept his feelings hidden from her over the years. I scooted closer to him on the old wooden bench.

'Auntie Sue showed me the nursery. It must have been heartbreaking for you both.'

He tucked my hand into his and we both stared at the floor.

'We lost three babies, you know. Two boys and a girl. All buried at the church over the hill.'

'Oh, no.' Three! I pressed a hand to my mouth as tears sprang to my eyes. 'Auntie Sue never mentioned that, she just said "baby". I can't begin to imagine how awful that must have been.'

'Each time your auntie fell pregnant we were so excited, so hopeful that we'd have a family. This time, we thought, this time it'll work out all right. But each time the loss got bigger, the desperation worse. And the terrible thing was that no one could give us a reason.'

'That's so unfair; you'd have made brilliant parents,' I said, tears streaming down my cheeks. I stopped and flung my arms round his neck. We stood and hugged, each wrapped in our thoughts.

'I know it's not the same,' I said finally. 'But you've got me.'

'And I thank my lucky stars every day that we do,' he said softly, wiping my tears away with his rough thumb.

I smiled and took a deep breath. 'Now unfortunately, I think we'd better brave the weather and make our way back to the house or Auntie Sue won't be telling either of us that she loves us.'

Back out in the field, the rain had died off but the grass was wet and slippery underfoot. We were both wet too and I was worried that Uncle Arthur would catch a chill if I didn't get him home soon. I tucked his arm through mine and forced myself to slow down to his pace.

'Look at that,' he tutted, pointing down to Bottom Field. 'Part of that barley crop is as flat as a pancake. The rain must have really given it a battering. That won't please Eddy.' He chuckled. 'He's been boasting that this will be the best yield yet out of that field.'

'Won't it spring back up when it dries?'

He shook his head. 'No, it'll stay like that. So we'll get a lower yield. Oh, well. Not a lot we can do about it.'

'Is that Eddy, there?'

Coming towards us, rolling across the grassland was the Land Rover.

It stopped beside us. Harry was in the passenger seat and Eddy was at the wheel. Harry waved at me.

'You're soaked.' He grinned. 'Get in. I've brought you a dry towel.'

'Thanks,' I said, with a shiver. The cold had seeped through my clothes and I was covered in goose pimples.

Eddy wound the window down as I opened the door. His eyebrows were knitted together and he looked even more dour than usual. 'The barley in Bottom Field is buggered. It's always the best crops that g'down,' he grumbled.

And he glared at us when Uncle Arthur and I bent double laughing.

We climbed into the back and Eddy drove the Land Rover towards Oak Field. Harry produced a bar of chocolate from his pocket and offered us all a piece.

I broke off a square and let it melt on my tongue, starving all of a sudden as well as freezing.

'Harry's asked for a look at Dexter,' said Eddy.

'I've been thinking about pedigree cattle, Arthur,' Harry said, turning round to face us. 'Perhaps rather than buy calves, I could buy your Hereford bull from you once the movement ban has been lifted in November. Start my own herd?'

Uncle Arthur beamed. 'I'd like to think that there'd still be Herefords in Lovedale from my herd. And I'm sure we could do you a good deal on price, eh, Eddy?'

Harry gave him a stern look. 'Market value, Arthur, or no deal.'

Uncle Arthur chuckled. 'You'll do for me, son.'

I caught Harry's eye and he winked at me. The hairs on the back of my neck prickled. I got the feeling he was doing this to help us out, just as he'd promised. I felt a warm rush of affection and smiled my thanks back at him.

What a difference from Julian's way of doing business.

Eddy slowed the vehicle down and pulled alongside the cows.

'Not that I can see too much when they're all lying down, but they're looking healthy to me. What do you reckon,

Eddy?' asked Uncle Arthur, winding his window down and leaning out.

Without exception all the remaining cows were pregnant. Everyone was holding their breath that the next TB test in July would prove negative so that no more of these lovely animals would have to be destroyed.

'One's got a touch of mastitis and the daft 'un who made it as far as the petrol station got a sore foot for her trouble. Apart from that they're fine,' Eddy agreed.

'And Dexter looks a very fine chap,' added Harry.

Uncle Arthur sat back, drew a deep breath and reached for my hand.

'This is what Appleby Farm is all about, lass. A Lakeland farm – the land, the animals, even the flat barley.'

I heard Eddy harrumphing at that.

'And I'd give my right arm for it to stay just the way it is,' he continued. 'Not with some bloody hotel on it, or a holiday village or the other thing.'

'Country retreat.'

'That's the one.' He shot me an anxious look. 'Your posh camping stuff is all right, though.'

'Posh camping?' Harry raised an eyebrow.

'Our Freya reckons people will pay to sleep in our field in the shepherd's huts,' Uncle Arthur explained.

'I do,' I said, ignoring Eddy's snort of mirth.

'Interesting.' Harry nodded thoughtfully, furrowing his dark eyebrows.

'I think so, too,' said Uncle Arthur.

'Thanks.' I squeezed his hand and met his eyes. Just for a second. And then I looked away and made a silent promise that if I, Freya Moorcroft, had anything to do with it, Appleby Farm would stay exactly as Uncle Arthur wanted it to.

Chapter 25

Auntie Sue and Uncle Arthur lifted their breakfast mugs in unison. 'Happy birthday, love!'

A whole thirteen days had whizzed by since Charlie and I split up, and a showery June had given way to a warm and sticky July. This morning was no different, except it was my birthday and despite my protestations that I was too busy to be doing with birthday bother, nobody had listened.

'Thank you, both.' I scooped up a mouthful of pancakes (served American-style with crispy bacon and maple syrup – Auntie Sue had insisted on something special and even Uncle Arthur was excused his muesli for the day) and turned my attention to the stack of birthday cards.

There were several with a Kingsfield postmark on them and I opened them carefully, flattered that Tilly, Gemma and Shirley, who hadn't even known me this time last year, had remembered my birthday. Anna's card was a rude one, which made me snort, but I passed it round the table anyway. Uncle Arthur choked on his bacon and Auntie Sue asked what funbags were.

'This is from us,' said Auntie Sue, pulling out a large parcel from one of the kitchen cupboards.

I tore through the flowery wrapping paper to reveal a pile of folded thick fabrics and oilcloths.

'I know it's not very birthday-like,' she said, chewing on her bottom lip.

'They are perfect,' I squealed, lifting an apron from the top of the pile and holding it against me.

If someone had told me that I'd be so excited about getting aprons for my twenty-eighth birthday, I wouldn't have believed them. But these were in pale-blue oilcloth with our new Appleby Farm Vintage Tea Rooms logo (my birthday present from Anna) across them and they were impossibly beautiful.

'That's good, then.' Her voice was casual, but her face was beaming with pride.

'Aprons and matching tea towels,' I said, kissing my aunt and uncle warmly. 'We're all going to look fantastic.' I'd picked out some features in the barn in duck-egg blue paint and the contrast with the oak, the exposed brick and the white tables and chairs was stunning.

It made it all seem so real. Which was just as well because we opened in less than a month. Eck!

There was a knock at the door and in trooped Lizzie, a delivery man, Eddy and Harry, chorusing 'Happy Birthday'. Correction: Lizzie and Harry were singing; the other two shuffled in a bit awkwardly.

Eddy shoved a posy of roses at me. 'Many happy returns. From the garden, like.'

I inhaled them. 'Oh, they're heavenly. Thank you, Eddy.' I grabbed him for a kiss and just managed to graze my lips against his cheek, which smelled of disinfectant, before he escaped.

'Sign here, please,' said the delivery man, sliding a large wooden crate on to the table and holding out an electronic signing gadget whilst endeavouring to shake Madge off his leg.

'It's from Paris!' I cooed and Lizzie gasped.

The delivery man departed, looking relieved. Eddy and Uncle Arthur disappeared off to the office and Harry, who had been loitering by the door, stepped forward and kissed my cheek.

'Hello, birthday girl,' he said, pulling a slightly creased card from his back pocket. He looked smarter than usual: jeans that seemed too nice for the farm and a bright white T-shirt that set off his tan.

'Hello.' I flushed. The last time I'd had a card from him was for my eighteenth birthday. He'd kissed my cheek then, too, and at the time it had seemed like a massive turning point in our friendship. From children to young adults in one swift kiss . . .

'Come on, hurry up and open this parcel,' Lizzie demanded, bouncing on her toes.

'All right, all right,' I tutted.

The four of us gathered around the table and I levered open the crate with a knife.

Inside was another box and lying on top of it was a birthday card from my parents. Tucked inside that was a handwritten note from my mum.

I thought you might like these for the tea rooms — just bits and bobs I've collected from all the countries I've been to. It's a bit of a passion of mine. I hope they give you as much pleasure as they've given me.
Love, Mum xxx

'Sounds very intriguing. Thanks, Mum,' I said aloud, tearing open the box.

'Flippin' eck!' I gasped. We all hung our heads over the crate, even Harry.

Inside, carefully cocooned in bubble wrap, were forty or fifty pieces of delicate china: cups, saucers, milk jugs, sugar bowls and I even spotted the spout of a couple of teapots. They were all different colours and patterns, from pinks and reds, to silvers and golds, yellows and greens, blues and blacks. My eyes filled up for the second time.

'Wow,' breathed Lizzie, 'these are too good for the tea rooms! What if they get broken?'

I shook my head. 'I don't believe in keeping things for best. These are too beautiful not to show off.'

'Agreed,' said Auntie Sue firmly. 'My mother left me her Wedgwood dinner service when she died. A wedding present. She'd never used it once. What a waste,' she tutted sadly.

'My present next,' declared Lizzie, adding, 'although it's not new or a surprise.'

She handed me a soft parcel, delicately wrapped in tissue paper and tied with ribbon. It was so beautiful that I couldn't bear to tear into it. Lizzie was chomping at the bit by the time I'd removed the ribbon and curled it into a ball on the table.

Inside was the pretty tea dress that she'd lent me to wear to my planning meeting in May.

'It looks better on you than me.' She shrugged as I gave her a big thank-you hug. 'There's the tiniest tear in the hem at the back. Don't know how that happened, but I'm sure you could mend it.'

I heard a snort from Harry and didn't dare meet his eye.

'Oh, I'm sure I can,' I said breezily, 'and it's a lovely dress. Aww, thanks, everyone, for your presents and cards. I feel like a princess.'

'Hey, you haven't had my present yet!' Harry arched his eyebrow mysteriously. 'And before you ask, no, it's not a fawn.'

Our eyes met and we both burst out laughing. Lizzie and Auntie Sue looked bemused, or possibly confused.

'I can't believe you're still going on about that!' I said, wiping a tear from my eye. 'You have the best memory of everyone I know.'

'Oh, come on, who could forget that?' He laughed. 'There was a TV programme on one Christmas about reindeer,' Harry explained to the other two. 'Having her own fawn was all Freya could talk about for the next week.'

I'd forgotten how much I used to share with him when we were growing up. I'd confided all my dreams and he, as good as gold, would listen and tell me how great my ideas were.

'I remember!' exclaimed Auntie Sue. 'Didn't you ask for one for your birthday the following summer?'

'She did. She was going to open her own reindeer farm,' Harry added.

'Sanctuary,' I corrected, still giggling, 'not farm. I wouldn't have wanted to eat them.'

'You are so cute.' Lizzie sighed. 'But back to the present. Come on, Harry.'

'OK. Strictly speaking it's more of an experience than an actual gift.'

'Oh,' was all I could manage. No idea why, but I was suddenly overcome with embarrassment, like an 'experience' with Harry was something rude. The nudging and winking going on between Lizzie and Auntie Sue didn't help either.

'And, er,' he looked at his watch, 'we should get going.'

'Now?' I gulped.

Everyone nodded. All with huge grins on their faces.

'But I've got work today.'

Lizzie rolled her eyes. 'Always working, Freya! Put some fun back into your life.'

'Right,' I mumbled.

'And wear the dress,' added Auntie Sue, hitching up her bosom and winking at me.

'Definitely,' said Lizzie, giving a pointed look at my old shorts and T-shirt combo.

'Yes,' agreed Harry, 'wear the dress. It's too beautiful not to show off.'

An hour later and we were scooting along country lanes towards Hawkshead, having left Lovedale and a long to-do list behind. Any guilt about not getting on with my jobs had completely evaporated in the sunshine somewhere by Lake Windermere.

'So this is all very mysterious.' I glanced at his smiling profile as we turned into a narrow tree-lined lane signposted Rigg Farm Café, Campsite and Sculpture Garden.

'I thought you'd be interested to see how another farm has moved with the times,' said Harry, displaying his dimple as he grinned at me.

'Oh, so it *is* work. At least I don't have to feel so guilty about taking the morning off.'

'I suppose not. But there will be birthday cake involved. I know how much you girls like cake.'

'Huh! That's a very sexist attitude. I think you'll find . . . what?' I said all huffily. He was laughing at me.

'Sorry, couldn't resist it; you always were easy to wind up.'

I folded my arms and pretended to look offended. Thank goodness I hadn't insisted on staying at home to work. This was way more fun.

Harry pulled into the car park and we drove round looking for a space long enough to take his pick-up truck.

'Rigg Farm belongs to the family of an old friend of mine. His parents are sheep farmers, but he and his two sisters wanted to get involved with the business in some way, so they each started their own venture on the farm. Here we go; I'll park on this end.' He grabbed the back of my seat while he reversed into the space. 'Alice is an artist and she's added a garden, which has won some award or other, and she holds sculpture exhibitions here all year round. My mate Tom is a chef – and coincidentally the lead singer in The Almanacs. He runs the café and oversees the farm shop where they sell their own lamb. And the other sister Tessa, the youngest, has just started a yurt campsite business.'

I stared at him. 'Oh, really? Just like my glamping idea!'

Harry turned off the engine and removed the key. 'Yes, that was what made me think of bringing you here. And if you're still keen, there are two more shepherd's huts at Willow Farm you're welcome to have to add to the collection.'

I swallowed a lump in my throat as I climbed out of the car, taking care to keep the skirt of my dress with me this time. What a thoughtful . . . thought.

'Thank you, Harry,' I murmured, shaking my head, 'that's very generous of you.'

'Freya, for my family, farming is all we've known. Except Mum has taken up body-boarding, apparently.' He rolled his eyes and we shared a smile.

'But anyway. I can't imagine not keeping Willow Farm in our family and if I can help keep you in Lovedale . . . the Moorcroft family, I mean, then just ask.'

The car park was all stony and I was conscious of Harry's

hand hovering at my elbow as I tried not to stumble. By the time I'd made it to the path the soles of my feet were burning and I was bitterly regretting wearing my posh shoes.

'What do you want first: to explore or cake?'

'Explore, definitely.' I was still a bit full from my pancakes. Although not that I was going to admit it, Harry was right; there was no way I could turn down cake. Especially on my birthday.

The café and farm shop were located in a long, low wooden-clad building. Two chalkboards advertised the special offers of the day. Next to the café was a map of the place, so we consulted it and set off towards the gardens, Harry shortening his long stride to match mine.

'Sorry to hear about you and Charlie, by the way. We didn't get off to a good start but he seemed like a good bloke,' said Harry.

I felt my face heat up at the memory of Charlie finding me in Harry's arms, albeit innocently.

We were walking through a neatly manicured section of lawn with a frill of lavender around the edge. Every so often a stone-carved woodland creature was visible through the purple fronds. I was enchanted and glad to have something to focus on rather than look Harry in the eye.

'He was. Is. But . . .' I hesitated, not wanting to get into the details. 'These things happen. And another six months apart was too much to ask our relationship to bear.'

'Is that how long you're staying, then? Only six months?' He furrowed his brow as he tweaked the head off a lavender flower.

'Yes. No. I don't know, really.' I felt all flustered.

The path narrowed and we bumped into each other.

After a few 'after you, no, after you's I took the lead along the path.

'I love it in the Lakes, adore it. And I didn't realize how much Lovedale is a part of me until I came back as an adult.'

'I can relate to that.' Harry laughed softly. 'Although, of course, I've never lived anywhere else – except my three years at uni. And I couldn't wait to leave there.'

We reached a wrought-iron gate at the end of the path and he stepped ahead to open it for me. I smiled my thanks as I passed him.

'At least you know that Willow Farm will be your home as long as you want it to be. Auntie Sue and Uncle Arthur are definitely retiring at the end of the year, whatever happens. And if the farm changes hands, then . . .' I shuddered at the thought of leaving Appleby Farm. 'Well, then I don't suppose there will be anything here for me.'

'Nothing?'

'Well, no.' I shrugged.

'I see.'

Something in the way he said that made me whirl round to look at him; he'd almost sounded insulted. But his face gave nothing away. What had I said?

'Um, anyway, half of me thinks that opening the tea rooms is a great idea,' I continued, 'and the other half worries that I'm grasping at straws. What do you think?'

I looked over my shoulder again to see what his face was doing. He stopped and I stopped.

'Oh, Freya,' he said softly, so softly that a flurry of goosebumps ran down my back. He opened his hand and sprinkled the purple lavender flowers on the ground.

I held my breath, completely unsure how to read Harry's response.

'Whether it's a success financially, only time will tell, but I think it has given your aunt and uncle something positive to cling on to while they're still reeling from Arthur's heart attack and the TB outbreak. So I'd say that means it's already a success.'

I nodded. 'Thank you. I hadn't looked at it like that.'

He held my gaze for a couple more seconds and then cleared his throat. 'And if you're only going to be here for another few months, then I'll just have to make the most of it, won't I? I mean, *you*. Won't *you*?'

I was a bit confused about who was supposed to be making the most of what but for some reason my heart was racing and my mouth had gone dry.

'Yes,' I stuttered.

'You're staring.' He arched an eyebrow at me.

'Sorry.' I laughed, feeling my cheeks redden.

'Well, walk then, or you'll never get your birthday cake.' His eyes flicked to the path head.

'Yes, boss.'

Rigg Farm was gorgeous and despite all the new additions, looked completely unspoilt. The canvas yurts were just visible through the trees along with plumes of wood smoke, and the sound of children playing filtered through the woods. The sculptures were dotted here and there throughout the gardens and even amongst the trees, and each time we came across one it was a lovely little discovery. No two pieces of art were alike and each one complemented its surrounding perfectly: a wire fairy with dainty wings hanging from a tree; a huge stone sundial set inside a maze of low hedge on the brow of a hill; and my favourite: a pair of sheep made from polished copper near the entrance to the café.

We had walked in a full circle and arrived back at the café's chalkboards before I knew it. Amazingly I found I did indeed have room for a slice of cake.

I left Harry flicking through a display of leaflets and walked towards the chalkboard (nice touch – handwritten) to consult the menu. I was just taking my phone out of my bag to take some pictures of it when I heard a shrill but familiar voice.

'Harry! What a coincidence!'

I turned to see Lizzie's sister Victoria sail up to Harry, kiss his cheek and flick her foot up behind her like a Disney princess. She was wearing huge sunglasses and a long, clingy black dress that showed her pointy hip bones. Over her shoulder was a big pack of some sort of equipment and she was carrying a microphone.

'Are you stalking me?' she purred. 'Oh, you've gone red! Didn't mean to embarrass you, darling. And don't worry,' she leaned in and hissed, 'I've secretly always wanted a stalker.'

I walked over to join them. 'Hey, Victoria.'

Was it my imagination or did her lips just do a cat's bum impression?

'Hi, Freya. Isn't that Lizzie's dress? Very feminine – you should try it more often. Anyway, it looks better on you – Lizzie's hips are far too wide for it.'

'Thank you,' I said, wondering if I meant it. There were more back-handed compliments in that speech than I could shake a stick at.

'What brings you here?' asked Harry, folding his arms awkwardly.

Victoria flashed him a smile. 'It's for my new feature: "Victoria's Secret Gardens". I'm planning a whole series of them, Victoria's Secret something or other – shops next, probably. Really it's so I can make people think of sexy underwear when they hear my name. Brand association, you know.'

She looked back at me and paused. 'Victoria's Secret is a lingerie retailer, Freya.'

Rude! OK, so maybe Lizzie was right about her, although why she was acting like I was a threat was beyond me.

'I live on a farm, Victoria, not in the desert.'

Harry put his hand on my arm and nudged me towards the café. 'For the record, Freya's underwear is very sexy. Anyway, don't let us hold you up.'

Eek! Too embarrassing. I glanced down to see if any of my not-very-sexy-at-all undies were on display. They weren't. Victoria's jaw dropped like a stone and then, ever the professional, her smile was back on.

'Yes. Right. Better press on.' She beamed and then leaned forward, adding, 'Need to interview the public. Oh, here come some of them now, excuse me.'

We watched as she lay in wait for some new arrivals from the car park.

'She seems very keen on you,' I said with a sideways glance at Harry. 'Are you two . . . ?'

He raised an eyebrow. 'No, thank you, she'd eat me alive.'

I was happy with that answer.

Victoria switched on her microphone and lunged forward, thrusting the microphone into the faces of a smartly dressed couple who were passing.

'Hello, I'm Victoria Moon, reporting for Radio Lakeland. Can I ask you some questions for "Victoria's Secret Gardens"?'

As she said this last bit she turned to Harry and gave him an exaggerated wink.

'Sure, sure,' murmured the couple as they shot excited looks at each other. He circled his shoulders, she patted her hair and they both cleared their throats.

'So, I understand that entry to the gardens is free to old age pensioners,' she smiled sweetly, giving them her 'poor you' face. 'That must be a tremendous boon to people like you, barely living above the poverty line?'

We moved out of earshot, but not before I heard the woman gasp in indignation and her husband reply sourly, 'We wouldn't know. I'm only fifty-eight and my wife is even younger.'

'Really?' Victoria looked baffled as the couple swept past her, their faces thunderous.

Harry and I looked at each other, both on the verge of the giggles and escaped to the café.

'Love her or hate her, she's certainly entertaining,' said Harry, watching her approach another group of people.

Love her? I tried not to feel put out.

'Come on, birthday girl,' he said, taking my hand. 'Let's get you some cake and hope they can do better than Victoria Sponge.'

'Wait.' I stood my ground. 'What was all that about my knickers being sexy? You haven't seen my underwear.' Not recently anyway; there'd been plenty of times as kids but I rather hoped he'd forgotten about the pants that used to have the days of the week on them.

Harry gave me a mischievous grin. 'They were on the washing-line when I came through the garden this morning. At least, I assume they were yours. Pink ones with frilly bits. And a few weeks ago when you got stuck climbing out of my truck, I caught a glimpse then, and when you were about eighteen . . .'

I went bright red and pushed ahead into the café. 'All right, you win. Time for cake, Harry.'

It had been a hugely fun few hours but although I'd enjoyed seeing Rigg Farm and spending time with Harry,

I couldn't help feeling strangely unsettled. I watched him surreptitiously as we drove back to Lovedale, drumming his fingers on the steering wheel and whistling something unrecognizable under his breath. I studied the details of his face, marvelling at how he'd changed from a boy to a man in ten years; the stubble on his jawline, the curve of his mouth, the pulse in his neck just below his ear.

His mouth twitched and he turned to look at me as if he'd known all along that I'd been staring. And in that moment my stomach fluttered and I realized what had unsettled me: the boy I'd played with, confided in and shared my dreams with had turned into a man who could give me goose-bumps with a single look.

Chapter 26

There was less than a week to go until the grand opening of the Appleby Farm Vintage Tea Rooms. I say 'grand'; it was more likely to be what Anna termed 'a soft launch'. This was what she did with her dating websites, apparently: let the thing go live without making too much of a song and dance about it so you could iron out all the wrinkles in private. She'd learned her lesson after the huge advertising campaign that launched Crack of Dawn Dating dot com, a niche dating website for early risers. Unfortunately there was a bit of a misunderstanding about this niche and the first eager beavers to upload their profile photos were all called Dawn – and let's just say you couldn't see the colour of their eyes from *those* pictures.

Anyway, on our launch day Uncle Arthur was going to cut the ribbon and Auntie Sue was going to cut the cake. All I had to do between then and now was make sure we were ready to open.

Arrghhh!

Since my birthday I had ploughed my way – with the help of Anna in Kingsfield, Lizzie and Auntie Sue – through the most enormous heap of jobs. We had had the thumbs-up from the council's environmental health people, the website was up and running, we'd finalized our food offering, a second-hand coffee machine had arrived from an Italian coffee shop in Kendal that was closing down and I'd ordered twenty different types of tea for our 'Lovely Cup of Tea' menu.

Of course, the barn itself still looked like a war zone: stacks of timber waited to be transformed into skirting boards and door frames; chandeliers still in their boxes needed to be hung; the kitchen units were in but had no doors; piles of rubble and debris sat in every corner . . .

The list was scarily endless. Goat was adamant that he was on schedule but that didn't stop me having a minor panic attack every time I stepped into the place. And there was still a mountain of jobs to be done by me, or at least it felt like it, but today I was having a few hours off because reinforcements were arriving in the form of the lovely, calming influence of Tilly Parker.

And I couldn't wait.

Bobby the campervan and I had made it to the train station in excellent time. I parked up and walked across to the platform a couple of minutes before Tilly's train was due in.

I positioned myself near the 'Welcome to The Lakes' sign and waited.

That sign had been the first thing I'd seen when I'd arrived three months ago at Easter. And now here I was, welcoming someone else, setting up my own business and living the Lakeland dream.

I was just on the verge of coming over all emotional when the station announcer piped up with the 'next train to arrive at . . .' message. Passengers immediately surged forward, the train came into view and ground to a halt and then I was surrounded by noise and people with their pushchairs, luggage and excitement. I stood on my tiptoes and searched for Tilly. She soon appeared, beaming and waving through the crowd, dragging a purple wheeled suitcase behind her.

'Tilly!' I leaped up and down on the spot.

'Freya! It is so lovely to see you!' she cried, letting go of her case as we flung our arms round each other's necks. 'And I could murder a nice cup of tea.'

'Now *that* is easily arranged.' I took charge of her suitcase and guided her to the car park.

'What would you like: Darjeeling, Rooiboos, English Breakfast, Earl Grey, *Lady* Grey . . . ?'

By late afternoon I'd given Tilly a tour of the farm. She'd stroked the noses of Gloria, Gaynor and the calves, we'd walked through the orchard, I'd pointed out the Hereford herd and told her the sad story of losing half of them, and she'd brought me up to date with everything that had been happening in Kingsfield. Neither of us had paused for breath and now that the builders had knocked off for the day we were sitting in the barn on crates, having yet another cup of tea.

'I think I'm in love with Appleby Farm already.' Tilly sighed dreamily. 'No wonder you abandoned us. I think I'd have done the same given half the chance.'

I winced. 'I know, it was all a bit sudden, wasn't it? To be honest, most of my moves have been like that. I've always had itchy feet.'

The sound of whistling interrupted us and we both looked over to the doorway where Harry was walking in backwards, straining under the weight of a stack of chairs, piled up on a hand trolley. My heart pinged at the unexpected sight of him.

'Oh goodness, Harry, let me help you,' I cried, jumping to my feet, feeling hot all of a sudden.

He rested the trolley on the floor, rubbed his forearm across his brow and puffed his cheeks out with exertion. 'You can get cream for that, you know.'

I looked at Tilly, whose mouth and eyebrows were already twitching with curiosity. She shrugged her shoulders.

'Cream for what?' I asked.

'Itchy feet.' He grinned.

'Ha ha,' I said, hands on hips.

'Sorry, couldn't resist,' he chuckled. 'Anyway, where do you want these?'

I'd picked up a job lot of pine chairs and tables at auction for a song, and Harry had offered to fetch them for me a few at a time in his trailer whenever he had a spare half-hour. Between the three of us we unloaded the trolley and stacked the chairs at the side of the room while I made the introductions.

Harry went back out to the yard to reload the trolley and Tilly poked me in the ribs.

'He is lovely,' she whispered.

I nodded. 'He's our next-door neighbour. I've known him for years and he's like a son to my aunt and uncle.'

Harry poked his head back in. 'Can you two give me a hand with this table?'

Tilly and I went out to the trailer. Ten minutes later the furniture had all been unloaded and Harry went on his way.

'Actually, I think I've changed,' I said, pouring us both a fresh cup of tea. 'I don't have that restless urge any more.'

'I can see that.' She smiled. 'You're still the same ball of energy that you've always been, but there's an air of purposefulness about you now.'

I sipped my tea and smiled at her wistfully. 'I can imagine being happy here for the rest of my life. Does that make me sound really boring?'

'It makes you sound happy,' said Tilly, squeezing my hand across the table. 'I tell you who'd absolutely love it here – Aidan. Did I tell you about his new TV show, *Woodland Habitats* . . . ?'

I grinned as she began yet another story about her boyfriend Aidan and his job as a TV director. Not that I minded. I was thrilled for her.

Charlie had met Tilly on her first day at the allotments and he'd told me what a delicate thing she had been, with a face as pale as a ghost and a pain behind her eyes that had been impossible to miss. By the time I'd met her in November she had started to heal, but it wasn't until she fell in love with Aidan that she really came back to life. Now she was as sunny as a daisy and the only remaining signs of her painful past were the fine silvery scars down her shins from the car accident that had made her lose her baby and had taken her husband James's life so tragically early.

It was amazing what love could do to a person, I thought, watching her eyes light up as she told me about the house she and Aidan had found together.

'Now, then.' She arched her eyebrows at me sternly. 'I thought you were going to be working my fingers to the bone and apart from moving a few chairs, I've been sipping tea like the queen. What can I do to help?'

I lifted my hair off my neck, twisted it up into a bun and let it fall again. 'Blimey. Where to start? OK.' I sat up straight. 'Be honest, what do you think of the décor? Is it "vintagey" enough?'

She had already told me she loved it when we'd walked in. I loved it too, with its duck-egg-blue shelves behind the counter ready to be stacked with all my colourful china as soon as the builders had gone and the collection of bevelled mirrors I'd hung in the darkest area of the barn. There were other little things still to be done too, like hanging the floral bunting and adding old-fashioned glass bottles to each table to hold posies of fresh flowers. But the barn was so cavernous that I was worried we didn't have enough big stuff to make a 'vintage' statement.

Tilly took her time to look round the barn, tapping her finger against the end of her nose thoughtfully.

'Oh,' she pronounced suddenly. 'Art. That's what's missing in here. All these lovely exposed stone walls are crying out for some adornment. A few big pictures dotted here and there would finish the place off. Maybe some of those retro advertising posters, or "Keep Calm and Have Another Cupcake" type of thing?'

'Ooh, yes, you are spot on, Tills!' I beamed at her. This was exactly what I needed: a fresh pair of eyes on the place. I was so close to it that I was pouring cups of tea in my sleep at the moment. 'They'll have to be cheap, though. I'm running out of money fast.'

The two of us stood up and were trying to work out how many pictures we should have and how big they needed to be when Lizzie arrived.

'Tilly!' she squealed, jumping in between us and squeezing us in a rugby-scrum-style hug. 'I'm Lizzie over the Moon to meet you.' She released us and beamed from one ear to the other. 'We are going to have so much fun together. We can be like Charlie's Angels!'

Awkward moment. Tilly looked down at her fingernails, I blinked at Lizzie and she clapped first one and then the other hand over her mouth.

'I could slap myself,' she muttered eventually. 'In fact,

279

you slap me, Freya, I'm so stupid. I nearly said Three Musketeers, too. Why didn't I say Three Musketeers?'

'It's fine.' I laughed. 'We can't keep tiptoeing around it. Charlie and I are finished and that's that. How is he, Tilly?'

I'd wanted to ask before, but hadn't in case he was really miserable and then I'd feel terrible.

Tilly frowned and gazed up to the ceiling. 'Er . . . he'll be fine. He's just moping a bit at the moment. Whenever I go to the allotment, he plonks himself down on my bench and just sits there, watching me. And he says he's not entering the Allotment Annual Show next week and he's always up for that. You know how competitive he gets about his runner beans.'

I swallowed and nodded. Poor Charlie.

'He needs to start dating again,' said Lizzie sagely. 'Get back in the saddle.'

'You're right,' I said, and I meant it. 'He deserves someone lovely. Rack your brains, Tilly, who do we know?'

Tilly and I exchanged looks. It was a bit of an odd conversation; she'd fixed him up with me and now I was asking her to do it again, albeit with someone else. This must be the ultimate milestone in an amicable break-up, I realized.

'Funnily enough, I suggested to him that he should start dating again.' Tilly shot me a nervous smile. 'But he said he only meets firemen at work, there's no one suitable at the allotment and that he never goes anywhere else.'

'I'll ask Anna for advice; she could introduce him to internet dating. She's the expert in that area,' I said and instantly my pulse began to race. Anna the homebird. Anna, who had no intention of leaving Kingsfield, ever. Anna, who had always had a bit of a soft spot for Charlie . . . Goodness, that was something to think about. 'Now, can we change the subject, please? Fixing my ex up with a new girlfriend is making me feel a bit weird.'

'Absolutely.' Tilly clapped her hands. 'Let's think artwork for these walls.'

'Ooh, I know!' Lizzie put her hand up. 'Make some frames out of that wood,' she said, pointing to the pile of timber. 'Buy a roll of vintage-style wallpaper and frame it.'

Tilly and I blinked at each other. Perfect.

'You,' I said, plonking a smacker of a kiss on Lizzie's cheek, 'are as clever as you are crazy.'

Auntie Sue's veggie patch was in full 'summer excess' mode at the moment, so dinner was a huge freshly picked salad with warm roast chicken, followed by mixed berry Eton mess. Everything was from the farm, even the chicken, although I whispered to Uncle Arthur to keep Tilly in the dark about that bit.

'That was so delicious, Mrs Moorcroft,' gushed Tilly as we settled ourselves in the garden in the warm evening sun with a bottle of wine. 'You'll have to give me the recipe for that pudding.'

Auntie Sue flapped a hand. 'Call me Sue, please. And that's not my recipe; I got it off the web.' She tried to pull off a nonchalant smile, but she looked like she might burst with pride. 'Are you a keen cook, Tilly?'

'What I lack in skill I make up for in enthusiasm.' She smiled, sipping at her wine. 'But the kitchen in our new house is lovely, so I'm planning to do a lot more entertaining.'

'Tilly and Aidan are buying a house together, Auntie Sue,' I told her.

'How lovely!' She clasped her hands together. 'Your first house. I remember moving into our first place like it was yesterday.'

'Wasn't it the farm?' I asked.

'Oh no, lass! Your grandparents were still alive then. Uncle Arthur was just a farmhand in those days. We had a cottage in the next village.'

'Tell us all about it, Auntie Sue.' I wriggled happily in my chair. I was a sucker for old stories, especially romantic ones, and judging by the sparkle in my aunt's eye, we were in for a treat.

'Right,' she chuckled. 'Well, in those days you didn't move in together until you were married.'

She glanced sideways at Tilly, who blushed daintily.

'But the cottage was all ready for us to move into when we arrived back from our honeymoon abroad.'

'I thought you went to Wales for your honeymoon?' I said.

'We did.' Auntie Sue nodded earnestly.

Tilly and I exchanged giggly smiles.

'Anyway,' she continued, 'we got off the train and had to catch two buses back to the village, and the second bus dropped us half a mile from the cottage. There was no such thing as suitcases with wheels in those days and Arthur, being a gentleman, insisted on carrying both of the cases all the way.'

At that moment Uncle Arthur appeared, wearing a clean shirt and his best summer flat cap, holding the dog's lead.

'Just taking Madge for a stroll,' he announced. It was code for 'going for a pint at the White Lion' and it didn't fool Auntie Sue for a second.

'Oh, Artie, I was just telling the girls about when we moved into Forge Cottage.'

'And you were a proper gentleman, we hear.' I grinned.

Uncle Arthur took a seat and waggled his eyebrows. 'In that case I'm going to stay and listen. Make sure you get your facts right.'

'So anyway,' she continued with a chuckle, 'by the time we reached our new front door, he was out of puff and he'd lost the feeling in both of his arms.'

'It was you with all those shoes in your case,' Uncle Arthur grumbled. 'We only went for four days!'

'A girl can never pack too many shoes,' said Tilly solemnly.

'But despite the pins and needles in his arms, he was most definite about carrying me over the threshold. So I opened the door and he set the cases down.'

'She was only a slip of a thing in those days,' he hissed, ducking quickly out of Auntie Sue's reach, as she swiped at him.

'So Samson here hoisted me up in his arms. He just about had time to kiss me and then, boom. His arms gave way – down we went like skittles, hitting our heads on the stair banister as we came flying into the front room and landed on the floorboards with him sprawled on top of me.'

'Oh, no! That's terrible,' I said, biting my bottom lip.

'It gets worse.' Uncle Arthur's shoulders started to shake.

Auntie Sue covered her cheeks with her hands. 'All our friends and family had hidden inside the kitchen to surprise us but when they leaped out, the first thing they saw was us on the floor in a compromising position. They all went silent except my mother who walloped Artie with her handbag and screamed, "It's broad daylight and you've not even closed the door, you filthy animal!"'

We all burst out laughing at poor old Uncle Arthur's treatment at the hands of his new mother-in-law until he stood up to leave for the pub. He leaned across and kissed his wife's cheek.

'But I managed to get my beautiful wife over the threshold and I've thanked my lucky stars ever since.' And with that he ambled across the yard with Madge.

Aww! 'I can laugh about it now,' chuckled Auntie Sue, getting to her feet. 'But at the time it was a month before I could show my face at the Women's Institute.'

She wandered off into the kitchen, leaving Tilly and me to finish the wine.

'We're not planning to get married just yet,' Tilly giggled. 'But I'll bear that story in mind for the future.'

I smiled but inside I felt a pang of loneliness. Seeing Tilly so loved-up and hearing Auntie Sue's romantic stories made me feel more alone than I had since splitting up with Charlie. I missed being half of a couple, missed having someone to make memories with.

I thought I was doing a fair job of keeping my feelings hidden until Tilly nudged me and whispered, 'Why don't you call him? It's obvious that you want to.'

'No.' I shook my head, hoping that my face wasn't as red as it felt. 'As far as he's concerned I'm still the scrawny kid with the skinny legs who used to beat him playing conkers. He doesn't even think of me as a woman.'

Tilly burst out laughing. 'You and Charlie used to play *conkers*? Or is that a euphemism that I've never heard of?'

Charlie. She meant Charlie and I'd automatically thought of Harry. Eek. Now I was truly blushing.

'What? Oh. Sorry.' I shifted in my seat and was saved any further embarrassment as Lizzie came running across the yard towards us, holding her hands out as if she was about to conduct a full orchestra.

'Guys, guys, guys.' She checked to make sure we were both listening. 'I bring news. She might be an absolute nightmare, but my sister does have her uses.'

Lizzie paused, flashing us a beaming white smile to lend a touch of drama to the announcement. 'Victoria has agreed to give you an on-air mention on the day of your grand opening! Ta-dah!'

'Yay!' I yelled, jumping up and punching the air. 'Thanks, Lizzie!'

How amazing was that! PR on our opening day would kick us off to a brilliant start. *Knickers to the soft launch idea*, I thought. *Why not start off as you mean to go on: loud and proud?* And anyway, what could possibly go wrong?

Chapter 27

Twenty-four hours to go and counting!

Deep breaths, deep breaths . . .

Yep. Only twenty-four hours to go until the Appleby Farm Vintage Tea Rooms opened its doors for business. At this precise moment, it didn't have any doors to open. But Goat and his crew were on the case. It wasn't just the new glass barn doors that were being fitted; the loos were having their cubicle doors hung too. At the moment the toilets were bright and clean but a little on the open-plan side for most people's tastes. This was the builders' last job and then, as promised, they would be finished right on schedule.

I had barely slept for the last few nights and I think it was only adrenalin that was keeping me going. To be fair, we were all slightly speeded-up versions of ourselves today, tackling our jobs with a zeal normally associated with caffeine overdose: Auntie Sue was stocking up our lovely ice-cream counter, which was right at the front of the tea rooms; Eddy was making some big picture frames from spare bits of timber; Tilly was in charge of final decorations, including hanging bunting, picking sweet peas for all the tables and sticking wallpaper into the frames as soon as

Eddy had made them. And Lizzie had taken a couple of days off from the White Lion to help us out and was giving all the crockery a final polish before stacking it behind the counter on the lovely duck-egg-blue shelves.

Numerous delicious cakes had been baked by Auntie Sue and this afternoon, Lizzie, Tilly and I were going to decorate them. That would just leave the scones to make at the last minute so that they would be as light as air on our opening day.

Right now my job was to help Ross position the new signs outside. We had already sorted the ones for the car park (previously known as Clover Field), we'd carried a seven-foot oak post, a bag of ready-mixed concrete, a shovel and the sign itself down the farm track to Lovedale Lane and Ross was digging a hole for the post.

'I reckon that's deep enough,' said Ross, wiping his forehead on his arm and ramming the shovel into the ground like a spear.

I peered down the hole. 'Agreed. Shall I hold the post while you pour the concrete?'

Ross nodded. We positioned the post and I held it firm while he tipped the concrete from the bag. 'You're a real inspiration to Lizzie and me, you know, Freya,' he said, concentrating on his work and avoiding my eye.

My heart squeezed at his 'Lizzie and me' – they were such a cute couple and I'd loved seeing them grow close since I'd been at the farm. 'Oh, Ross, aim higher than me to be inspired!' I laughed, flattered none the less.

'No, seriously.' He raised his face to mine and stared at me earnestly. 'Breathing new life into a Lakeland farm is exactly what I want to do when I have my own place.'

'Hey, Ross!' I exclaimed. 'Why didn't I think of this before? You should make an offer on Appleby Farm. You could use your inheritance! You could take over, build the herd back up and run it as it is. Then Eddy could stay too.' I gave him my best eager smile.

I'd been worrying a lot about Eddy recently. He was nearly sixty and he'd worked here all his life. I couldn't see him being happy working anywhere else.

'Nice idea, Freya.' Ross grinned shyly. He picked up a splint and nailed it to the bottom of the post to support it while it dried. 'But the money I inherited from my mum won't buy a farm this big. Anyway, I want to finish uni first and then get a bit more experience working with someone else before I invest in somewhere of my own.'

'Fair enough, it was just a thought.' I sighed. 'Right. The moment of glory.'

I picked up the wooden sign and unwrapped it from its protective plastic covering. It was a thing of beauty: duck-egg-blue painted wood, with our lovely logo picked out in black. I handed it to Ross.

'What if you get a customer today before you're ready?' he asked, stretching up to reach the hook on the post.

I laughed. 'That's a nice problem to have! Um . . . I suppose I'll give them a cup of tea on the house and invite them to our opening tomorrow.'

'Good answer.' He grinned. 'OK. Done.'

We both stood back to admire the new sign: *Appleby Farm Vintage Tea Rooms*.

Just looking at it made my stomach flip with pride. It dawned on me all of a sudden how far I'd come since my waitressing days in Kingsfield. I had my own business!

But for how long?

Julian had taken to phoning Uncle Arthur every week to ask if he'd reached to a decision about selling the farm. So far Uncle Arthur had refused to give him a definite answer, but how long would it be before he caved in? I'd worked so hard to get to launch day, I couldn't bear to let Julian come along and ruin it now.

My shoulders sagged and I couldn't help a little sigh escaping.

'Fantastic,' said Ross, mistaking my sigh for a happy one. 'What a team.' He put his arm round my shoulders and squeezed.

'Tha— Arrrgh!' My thanks morphed into a scream as a car came to a sudden stop behind us and tooted its horn.

Ross and I turned as one to see Victoria in a little red open-top sports car, grinning at us wickedly at the roadside.

'Now, now, you two.' She tutted slyly, pushed her sunglasses on to the top of her head and wagged a finger. 'I'm not sure Lizzie would entirely approve of that sort of conduct in public.'

'What do you think of our new sign?' I said, ignoring the jibe.

Victoria squinted as if she couldn't read it clearly. 'Very rustic. Now, where should I park?'

Er?

I looked at Ross, who just shrugged.

I must have looked blank because Victoria rolled her eyes dramatically. 'Lizzie *did* tell you I was going to feature you on my radio show, didn't she?'

I swallowed. *A mention*, I thought, *just a mention. Nobody said anything about a visit*. 'Yes, but . . .'

'Oh, car park!' She pointed at the newly nailed-up sign. 'I'll park up, grab my stuff and see you in a mo.'

And with that she accelerated up the farm track in a haze of dust.

'EEK!' I squealed. 'What are we going to do? We haven't even got any cake ready to offer her!'

'Er . . .' Ross frowned.

This was our one chance to be on the radio. I could not afford to cock it up. *Think, Freya, think.*

'Gimme your two-way radio,' I demanded.

Ross handed it over and I started to run up the farm track back towards the barn, speaking into the radio as I went.

'Eddy, is Auntie Sue there?'

'She is.'

'Tell her to drop everything and get over to the house and bake some scones. Small ones so they cook quicker. Victoria Moon is on her way. Repeat, Victoria Moon is at the farm. Ooh, and tell the builders to hide when we come in.'

My pulse was racing but I had a plan. And far from being nervous, I felt excited and elated. I *loved* this sort of challenge. I would give Victoria a tour, take her round the whole farm, hand her the press pack I'd prepared for the local paper, which I hoped would be coming tomorrow, show her some of my 'before and after' photos of the barn and just generally fob her off until Auntie Sue's scones were out of the oven.

Sorted.

By the time I reached the car park I was ready to meet my first guest and conduct my first ever radio interview.

'I'm massively grateful to you for this, Victoria,' I said, rushing in case she needed help with the big recording pack thing that I'd seen her with at Rigg Farm. But she only had a small handbag with her. Odd. 'It will give us such a boost on opening day.'

'So you should be,' she murmured, sliding her oversized sunglasses back in place. 'You'll be the first in my series of "Victoria's Secret Cafés".'

'That's great!' I said, taking deliberately slow steps to

290

make the journey from the car park to the farmyard as long as possible. 'How did the "Victoria's Secret Gardens" feature go?'

She waved a hand. 'I canned it. Well, as I said to the head gardener at Highfield Hall, once you've seen one garden you've seen them all.'

I knotted my eyebrows, doing my utmost not to laugh. 'Highfield Hall? Haven't they just won an award from Cumbria Tourism for their sunken gardens?'

'Really?' She paused to stare at me. 'That's odd because they've just pulled all their advertising from the radio station. If they had half a brain they'd ramp it up now that they're award-winning to bring in the punters. Fools. Look, I haven't got all day. Can we get on with it?'

'Sure!' I beamed. 'I'll give you the tour.'

It was my finest hour. There was not a single detail of Appleby Farm that I missed out.

I took her into the orchard and pointed out the organic fruit that went into our apple juice and apple tarts. We leaned over the wall into Calf's Close where the Jersey cows were grazing, and then I showed her the dairy where Auntie Sue made all our own butter and ice cream using their milk. I took her through Auntie Sue's veggie patch and explained about our strawberry and raspberry homemade jam. We sat on a bench in the orchard and she had a cursory flick through the press pack and my photographs. I told her all about my love of vintage tea sets as we walked through the yard towards the barn.

Behind me in the distance I could hear Goat barking orders to his team. I spotted that the barn doors had been fitted and I saw Tilly creep past, bent double with handfuls of sweet peas, but so far there was no sign of Auntie Sue and her scones.

And I'd run out of things to show Victoria. I ran a finger around the neck of my T-shirt nervously, before having a brainwave.

'Shall we do the interview now? I could tell you about—'

Victoria put up her hand. 'Pur-lease, Freya. No more. I'm barely awake here. Now can we see inside the tea rooms? And I presume you'll offer me a cup of tea? I'm gasping!'

My eyebrows shot up but, to my credit, the rest of me remained calm.

'Of course.' I laughed a little too loudly. 'Follow me.'

Right on cue, Auntie Sue appeared on the kitchen doorstep bearing a tray covered with a gingham cloth. She bustled across the yard and darted into the barn just in time.

My heart was beating like a drum as I ushered Victoria inside ahead of me and I had to stop myself from gasping aloud at the sight.

I'd only been away from it for a little over an hour and I had lived and breathed the place for the last few weeks, but now it was as if I was seeing it through someone else's eyes. The barn in my absence had truly been transformed into the Appleby Farm Vintage Tea Rooms.

My eyes filled with tears as they moved from the English-rose wallpaper, which Tilly had framed and mounted, to the polka-dot bunting strung around the walls. The scrubbed-pine tables were adorned with fresh flowers in their pretty little bottles, and the air was filled with the scent of summer. Lizzie stood in front of the shelves, which groaned under the weight of the exquisite cups and saucers, adding a bright pop of colour to the otherwise pastel palette of the room. Auntie Sue, slightly pink from baking, stood behind her ice-cream counter, and Tilly, with twinkling eyes and a wide smile, pulled back a chair and gestured for Victoria to sit. I couldn't see or hear the builders, so they'd obviously obeyed orders to make themselves scarce, bless them. The whole effect was magical.

It was too, too perfect. And for a moment, I didn't trust myself to speak.

I glanced at Victoria. She too was silent, her eyebrows raised and her mouth turned down at the corners in what I read as a 'grudgingly impressed' face.

'Tea?' I managed in a strangled voice.

'And scones?' added Tilly, racing back to the counter.

Victoria made a show of looking at her watch as she took a seat. 'No carbs after one o'clock for me,' she announced primly. She cast her eye disapprovingly over the rest of us, adding, 'I prefer the lean look.'

'For the love of Pete!' muttered Auntie Sue, jabbing her hands on to her hips.

'No carbs after one?' scoffed Lizzie. 'Since when?'

'Choose your brew,' I boomed, shoving the tea guide into Victoria's face to distract her from her critics. 'We're aiming to offer the widest range of teas in the Lake District.'

'Oh, anything,' said Victoria, looking bored, or annoyed – it was hard to tell with those sunglasses on. She waved the leaflet away. 'I'm not fussy when it comes to tea.'

Hold on a minute! I felt a knot of tension twist my insides. It was Victoria who'd given me the idea for the tea rooms in the first place, after complaining about the tea in the White Lion. But I bit back a retort and smiled sweetly as Lizzie brought over a pot of English Breakfast tea.

'Thanks, Lizzie.' I smiled as we exchanged knowing glances.

'Here you are, *madam*,' said Lizzie. 'A pot of unfussy tea.'

'Bloody hell!' Victoria spluttered, crashing her tea cup down into its saucer. 'What on earth is that?'

I followed her stare upwards to where Goat had installed

293

a glass panel high up in the barn wall from the spinning gallery. Four builders' bums were squashed up against the glass, as the men bent forward to lean on the wooden balustrade.

So that was where they were. Gulp.

It was enough to put you off your Belgian buns.

'So,' I said brightly, resisting the urge to snap my fingers in her face to drag her attention back to me, 'what do you think?'

'Nice.' She nodded distractedly.

Nice? Surely she could do better than that. *Nice?* My hackles were well and truly up. And to think I used to come to her defence when Lizzie moaned about her.

Think of the publicity, Freya. That's all that matters. Grin and bear it.

'Thank you for those kind words,' I said gaily. 'Now do you think you have everything you need for your feature? I notice you haven't written anything down?'

'No need,' she said, getting to her feet. She tapped her temple. 'I have amazing recall for detail; it's all stored up here.'

I stood too. It looked like she was leaving, thank goodness. 'Right. Good. I'll show you to your car.'

'I thought I might see Harry today, working on the farm. Sad face,' said Victoria, with a little pout when we reached the door.

I shook my head. 'His work is finished here for the moment. He won't need to come back until mid-August for the next mow.'

'Oh, silly me,' she trilled, rolling her eyes, 'he did mention that last night at the restaurant. It must have slipped my mind.'

She shot me a sideways look and I mustered up a smile in

294

return. If she was trying to make me jealous, it didn't work. I was intrigued, that's all, and maybe a little disappointed. I thought Harry would go for someone less shallow, someone more deep. Deeper, I mean. Anyway. I sniffed mentally. His choice. None of my business. Whatsoever. Although I'm sure I remembered him saying that she'd eat him alive . . .

'Freya? Wakey wakey.' Victoria snapped her fingers. 'I'll see myself out.'

She marched off into the yard and I let out a sigh of relief. She turned and did a little wave.

'And be sure to tune in tomorrow, won't you?'

'Will do!' I called, raising my hand in goodbye.

'Well done, you!' said Tilly, wrapping an arm round my waist. 'Although I must say, she seemed a bit passive-aggressive.'

'Huh, welcome to Family Moon!' grunted Lizzie, joining us. 'You're a threat to her, I'm afraid, Freya.'

'But why?' I frowned.

Lizzie and Tilly exchanged looks. 'Harry,' they said in unison.

'It's obvious. Even to me and I barely know him,' said Tilly.

'Harry and I are just old friends,' I said, reddening under their scrutiny.

'Anyone for freshly baked scones?' called Auntie Sue, plonking the makings of afternoon tea for an army on a table in the middle of the room. 'I don't want them to go to waste after all that palaver.'

'Yes, please!' I answered with relief. 'And I'll shout the builders down to join us. That's assuming they'll eat carbs after one o'clock,' I sniggered.

We finished the lot. No surprises there.

Chapter 28

Extra-wide ribbon to tie across doors – check.

Big fancy gold scissors from Auntie Sue's sewing box – check.

'Wish you were here at Appleby Farm' postcards to hand out to visitors – check.

My old Freya keyring in my pocket for good luck – check.

I had done everything I could; I'd thought of everything, or at least tried to. I crept out of the tea rooms and closed the door as quietly as possible. I was quivering with nervous energy and didn't quite know what to do with myself. I inhaled the dewy air deeply and closed my eyes, letting my ribcage rise and fall as I gradually found peace.

The farmyard was silent: the hens were still cooped up in their house, the calves asleep in their pens; there were a few soft snorts coming from the field beyond the orchard where Skye was standing up, probably still asleep, and I felt like the morning belonged only to me.

I consulted my watch: five a.m.

I really should go back to bed . . .

By nine o'clock I had showered and dressed in our agreed uniform of jeans and a white vest top under my special polka-dot apron, and I'd eaten a banana for breakfast. I stood in the kitchen armed with a battle plan for our grand opening.

'Right, everyone, listen up.'

I looked around at my team of Lizzie, Tilly, Auntie Sue and Uncle Arthur, and felt my throat constrict with love. Everyone was at the kitchen table except Uncle Arthur, who was buried under the newspaper in his armchair.

They were all so kind, hard-working and supportive. I couldn't have done any of it without them and I really, really wanted to tell them, but my emotions were so close to the surface right now that if someone as much as touched me, let alone said something kind, I would dissolve like a sugar lump before their very eyes.

And I couldn't afford for that to happen.

I exhaled sharply, blinked and cleared my throat. *Keep it together, Freya.*

Tilly, Lizzie and Auntie Sue would be helping in the tea rooms all day. Uncle Arthur, once he'd cut the ribbon, would retreat to the house and man the phone in case we had any press enquiries. The *Gazette* was invited, as was the local TV station (well, why not – if you don't ask you don't get!) and our glossy monthly magazine *Cumbrian Homes* had hinted that they might come, too. Besides which, Uncle Arthur had been doing a bit too much recently and the community nurse who'd popped round had told him off. A day sitting in the office would do him good.

I began to run through the arrangements for the day but before I'd got past the ribbon-cutting ceremony, Madge jumped to her feet and started barking. There was a knock at the door and I opened it to see the wiry little man from Lakeland Flowers who'd delivered a bouquet to me back in the spring. At least I think it was the same man; the bouquet of exotic blooms was so huge I could only see the top of his head.

'Miss Moorcroft?'

'That's me!' I beamed. 'Who would be sending me flowers?'

'Charlie?' suggested Lizzie, clutching her hands to chest.

'Or Harry?' Tilly speculated breathily.

'Read the card!' cried Auntie Sue, getting into the swing of it.

Tilly, Lizzie and Auntie Sue stuck their faces into the flowers while I signed for them.

'There's no card,' said Auntie Sue, disappointed.

'Isn't there?' The little man frowned. 'Wait a tick, I'll check the van.'

'You've got a secret admirer, lass,' chuckled Uncle Arthur.

Which was a bit worrying, seeing as the only men I saw these days were Eddy and the vet. Neither of whom you could call 'a catch'.

The delivery man dashed outside, hotly pursued by Madge, and trawled through a stack of paperwork on his front seat. He returned two minutes later looking apologetic.

'Sorry,' he said, pressing his lips together. 'There isn't always a card, especially if they're from a secret admirer. Call the shop; they'll have a record of it.' He winked, handed me a business card and jogged off.

'Told you. Secret admirer. Any more tea in that pot?' Uncle Arthur held up his mug hopefully.

Lizzie got up, slid the kettle on to the Aga hotplate and made him a fresh cup.

'Never mind,' I said, tucking the card in my apron pocket, planning to deal with it later. 'They will look gorgeous on top of the counter next to the cash register. Auntie Sue, you're good at flowers,' I said, handing them over. 'Can I leave them with you?'

'Yes, love.' She immediately started unwrapping the cellophane and separating out the stems.

'I have to say, Freya, you're very good at delegating these days,' Uncle Arthur pointed out, slurping his tea.

'Hmm, well, I've learned from the master.' I grinned, catching Auntie Sue rolling her eyes. 'Right. Where were we?'

'Ribbon-cutting ceremony,' Tilly reminded me.

'Thanks, Tills.' I reached out and squeezed her hand.

Tilly had been a boon and I would be very sad to see her leave this evening. But leave she must, because Aidan was whisking her off to Venice to some swanky hotel in the morning. And I'd offered to give her a lift to the station as soon as we'd cleared up for the day.

'OK, so I'm expecting my friendly planning officer to turn up and someone from Cumbria Tourism, too, so—'

Just then Madge skittered across the floor to the door and whined to be let out.

'Madge, for goodness' sake! I'm never going to get through the agenda,' I said testily, stomping over to let her out.

'She'll be after her morning egg, Freya, you know what's she's like,' chuckled Auntie Sue.

I glanced at the clock. Sure enough it was half past nine. A wave of fear washed over me. We opened at eleven.

Tilly giggled. 'I can't wait to tell Aidan about this.' She shook her head. 'A dog that knows exactly when it's nine thirty and trots off to—'

'Oh my life, Freya!' shrieked Lizzie. 'The radio. Victoria's show. She said it'll be on at nine thirty.'

It took us four and a half minutes to locate the radio and

tune it in to Radio Lakeland, by which time I had beads of sweat the size of golf balls popping out on my forehead and it took all my self-control not to wail with frustration, convinced that the 'Victoria's Secret Cafés' feature would have been and gone by now.

We gathered around Uncle Arthur's radio, which he called a 'wireless', and listened in silence while the weather man informed us in an overly jaunty voice that we were in for some light showers later on. Then, finally, Victoria came back on air.

And the time is nine forty a.m. and you're listening to Victoria Moon. Now all my regular listeners will know that I love nothing more than getting out and about, and talking to local people in my series called 'Victoria's Secrets', uncovering some of the most secret locations in The Lakes and bringing them to your attention.

'Brillo pads!' squealed Lizzie. 'We didn't miss it after all!'

'Shush!' I shushed.

And today in the first of a new series, 'Victoria's Secret Cafés', I visit a rather unusual venue in an old farmyard barn in Lovedale.

A shiver ran down my back and I glanced up at Lizzie.

Call it a sixth sense, but there was something in the way Victoria lingered on the word 'unusual' that made me fear for what was coming next.

And by the look on Lizzie's face, she was sensing it too.

'We're on, Artie. Are you listening?' Auntie Sue hissed.

'Yes, love.' He leaned across and took her hand. A look passed between them and I guessed that he'd just squeezed her hand three times. 'It's exciting, isn't it?' he said, hunching up his shoulders.

I dragged my eyes back to the radio, a smile on my lips.

Appleby Farm Vintage Tea Rooms is, as the name suggests, situated on a farm, and guess what? They open to the public today. Yes, that's right, lucky little me was able to get an exclusive preview of what owner Freya Moorcroft claims will serve the widest range of teas in The Lakes! Although I must say, she gave a tinkling laugh, *when I was there all they offered me was boring old English Breakfast tea. Hardly very imaginative.*

'The cheeky moo!' gasped Lizzie, flaring her nostrils.

I placed a calming hand on her arm. 'Let's hear her out,' I murmured. Although to be honest my spirits were taking a bit of a nosedive.

So my verdict? I wasn't able to sample any of their advertised homemade cakes, unfortunately. She sighed. I caught Tilly's eye and shook my head. This woman was unbelievable. She had turned down Auntie Sue's homemade scones . . . *However, I can tell you that the interior is more rustic than vintage at the moment, but who knows, things may improve once the tea rooms are finally finished. The builders were very much in evidence when I was there.* That grating tinkly laugh again.

I looked at the rest of my team. Lizzie had her head on the table, Tilly looked very pale, while my aunt and uncle were staring at each other in a state of confusion.

I reached across to turn the radio off. I'd heard enough, but Victoria piped up again before I had chance.

Oh, one teensy word of warning, peeps. A little bird told me that poor Appleby Farm has recently suffered an outbreak of a terrifying contagious disease, so if you're in any way concerned – my advice? Leave it a month or two before popping in for a cuppa. Now, let's play some music . . .

A rush of nausea surged from my stomach to my throat and I swallowed hard.

I lowered the volume of the radio and looked round the table at the stunned faces of my dear friends and family.

'We're ruined,' whispered Auntie Sue, two channels of tears forming down her cheeks. 'Who's going to come now?'

Uncle Arthur put his arm around her shoulder and she sobbed into his neck.

'We keep having bad luck, Artie. When's it going to end? Let's just sell up. Start our retirement before it's too late.'

Lizzie clapped her hands over her mouth. 'Oh, Freya, I'm so sorry. I should have known. I should have seen this coming. I blame myself.'

Tilly stood up to try to comfort me, but I shook my head, unable to speak. I strode from the kitchen and stumbled out into the yard, gasping for air. How could she? Why would she? And . . . and . . . what was I supposed to do now?

I pushed open the farmhouse gate and dropped to the floor, perching my bottom on the step. I'd worked non-stop all summer towards today. Overcome all sorts of little problems. But nothing like this . . . attack from Victoria. I suddenly felt drained and heavy-limbed.

Brushing tears of frustration from my eyes, I spotted a small white envelope on the cobbled ground. I blinked and stared at it. *Freya*. I could definitely read the name 'Freya' on the front of it.

I reached forward and grabbed it. It must have fallen out of the bouquet of flowers and fluttered under the van. I slipped my finger under the edge of the envelope and tweaked the card out, wondering and hoping . . .

I held my breath.

Congratulations on the opening of your tea rooms. I'm sure you'll make a success of it. Sorry I can't be there.
Your proud Dad xxx

A bubble of laughter fizzed up inside me. I hadn't expected that.

Oh, Dad. I held the card to my chest. He was proud of

me. And here I was whimpering on the doorstep like a sad puppy. *Thank you, Dad*, I thought, *your timing was absolutely perfect*.

I jumped to my feet, bursting with energy. He was right. I *would* make a success of it.

'Right, folks,' I yelled, running back up the path towards the kitchen. 'Come on. One hour till party time!'

Chapter 29

I bounded back inside, wreathed in smiles, took a big breath and dug deep for inspiring words. Tilly, Lizzie and Auntie Sue blinked at me expectantly.

'Yes, it is a setback. Yes, we could have done without that poisonous review.' I hesitated and pulled a face. 'Slight understatement there.'

I attempted a laugh but it emerged more like a squawk.

Blank faces stared back at me.

I tried again. 'Come on, chaps, don't look so down. I believe in what we're trying to do and I know you do too. And once people come through the doors they will love it. Fact.' I jabbed a finger in the air to drive home my point.

It took me a few seconds to notice that Uncle Arthur was no longer sitting down but standing in the doorway to the hall. His eyebrows were knotted and he rocked on his tiptoes, jingling the coins in his pocket.

'Tell her, Artie,' Auntie Sue whispered.

'What? What is it?' I swallowed and the hairs on my arms stood up.

Uncle Arthur coughed, folded his arms and looked down at the floor.

'You just missed your brother on the phone.'

I groaned. 'Not again. Tell him to leave us alone. Especially today. We're too busy to listen to . . .' My words dried up as I noticed everyone's nervous faces. 'What is it?'

'He's found a buyer for Appleby Farm, lass,' said Auntie Sue quietly, a pink blush creeping up from her neck to her cheeks.

'Another farm wants to take it on,' added my uncle, stroking his chin. I hadn't seen his pallor so grey since his heart attack.

'But . . .' Words failed me. I sank down on to the bench at the kitchen table. Nobody spoke.

I had a contingency for every eventuality today, or so I thought: an umbrella stand if it rained; outdoor tables and chairs if it was sunny; a bucket of carrots and little bags of corn for children to feed the animals; vegan, gluten-free, nut-free and diabetic treats for special diets and even, much to Auntie Sue's disgust, some non-dairy ice cream! The one thing I didn't anticipate was an eleventh-hour sabotage attempt from my big brother.

Tilly and Lizzie scooted up along the bench and slung their arms round me, muttering condolences.

What was the point in even opening the tea rooms now? Even if people did turn up – and that was looking unlikely, thanks to Victoria – who knew whether we'd even still be here in two months' time?

I class myself as a happy-go-lucky sort of person, but at this moment, my powers of optimism were being well and truly tested.

The radio was still on but I was too distracted to notice which song was playing. However, I did tune in when I heard Victoria's voice. In fact, my whole body did, tensing like a tight rubber band poised to go ping.

Ooh, she trilled, *we've got a caller on the line. Hello there, you're live on air speaking to Victoria Moon!*

Um. Hi, said a youngish male voice. *I just heard your review of Appleby Farm Vintage Tea Rooms and I—*

My ears pricked up. That voice sounded familiar . . .

Hold your horses! Tell the listeners your name and where you come from, giggled Victoria.

Oh. Sorry. It's Harry Graythwaite and I'm from Lovedale.

My heart went boom at the sound of his voice. What was he up to?

'Harry?' Tilly hissed. 'Is that your Harry?'

I nodded rapidly. Lizzie nudged me and I realized what I'd done and turned scarlet. My Harry.

Well, he-llo, Harry. Again. More giggling.

I gritted my teeth. The woman was such an outrageous flirt.

Lizzie shot me a look. 'I'm going to kill her,' she muttered.

Yes, well, as I was saying, I'm calling about Appleby Farm Vintage Tea Rooms.

I loved the way he gave it its full name like that.

And I was a bit confused when I heard your review. He chuckled.

You and me both, I agreed silently.

Because I was there the other day and had the most amazing chocolate fudge cake, washed down with a pot of lapsang souchong.

Auntie Sue and I exchanged looks and shrugged. That was news to us!

Really? said Victoria incredulously. *Well—*

And the views from the barn. In a word. Wow. Breathtaking. On a clear day you can see right down the valley from Lovedale all the way to Lake Windermere, sparkling like a sliver of sapphire in the distance.

You make it sound so romantic, said Victoria breathlessly.

At last, I thought, something she and I agreed on. I looked round the kitchen and bit back a giggle. It looked like we all agreed. Tilly and Lizzie were chewing their bottom lips, Auntie Sue was clutching her bosom and even Uncle Arthur had gone dewy-eyed.

It is, Harry replied and then lowered his voice. *And on a serious note, you didn't get your facts straight. It's true that Appleby Farm was hit by TB a while ago but it poses no threat to humans and I'm delighted to say that the vet tested the herd last week and gave them the all-clear.*

Auntie Sue and Uncle Arthur gave each other relieved smiles and I crossed my fingers; only one more test to go in September and if that was clear as well, life could go back to normal.

Really? Gosh, I didn't know that, stuttered Victoria.

And Appleby Farm needs our support now more than ever. We're all part of a unique community here in Cumbria. The Moorcrofts are doing what they can to preserve a traditional Lakeland farm and I think that should be applauded and supported. Don't you?

Well, I—

And what better way for children to learn about our heritage than to see a working farm in action while enjoying freshly made produce. And I've heard that the first fifty children to visit today will receive a free cookie.

Eek! I looked at my watch. Time until launch: one hour. Number of cookies baked: zero.

'We don't have any cookies!' Auntie Sue whispered anxiously.

I shushed her as Victoria asked Harry whether he would be coming to the launch. I held my breath.

Sadly I can't make it. One of my sows has gone into labour and she had eight piglets last time and one of them got his head stuck—

Whoa, thank you, Harry, family show, et cetera . . .'

So, if you're listening, Freya, sorry I—
Clunk.
Oh dear, said Victoria swiftly, *we seem to have lost Harry. Let's play some music . . .*

I snapped off the radio and stood up, head in the whirliest whirl ever. I was struggling to take everything in: Julian's call, Victoria's scathing attack and now Harry's heroic attempt at damage limitation, which was so amazing and kind and completely unexpected. Our little team had been through the wringer this morning and it was up to me to get everyone back on track.

I put on my best encouraging smile. 'OK. The way I see it is this . . .' *Julian is a tossy-tosspot and I hate him,* was what I thought, but instead I said, 'Whatever happens, whether you do decide to sell to Julian's farm person, Uncle Arthur and Auntie Sue; whether two or twenty people turn up today after Victoria's glowing review, one thing is for absolute certain: Appleby Farm Vintage Tea Rooms are opening today. We have guests arriving in one hour and Harry Graythwaite has thrown us a lifeline. So let's go out there and give our visitors a huge Appleby Farm welcome.'

Tilly and Lizzie whooped and clapped their hands.

'Oh,' I laughed, 'and does anyone have a recipe for cookies?'

'I do!' yelled Tilly. 'I make chocolate chip cookies with the children at school all the time.'

'Fabulous!' I beamed. 'Right. Action stations. Auntie Sue – scones please. Lizzie – over to the tea rooms and set up cups and saucers on every table. And I'm going to prep the fruit for the ice-cream sundaes. OK, chop, chop.' I clapped my hands and they all leaped into action.

And suddenly we were back on track, full of vim and vigour, and brimming with purpose. The kitchen filled with clouds of flour and the aroma of chocolate as Tilly and Auntie Sue started their baking. Uncle Arthur began to slope off to the office and I ran out to the hall and caught him up.

'Uncle Arthur!'

He turned and I grabbed hold of his hands. You could never mistake him for anything other than a farmer: the sleeves of his check shirt were rolled up as a concession to summer, although he still had a flat cap on, and he was wearing braces to keep his baggy trousers up now that the results of his new diet were beginning to show.

'I know how important it is to the two of you to retire. And I am all for that. Truly. No one deserves to take it easier in their old age more than you.' I grinned at this last bit.

'Oi, less of the old,' he chuntered, raising an eyebrow.

'I just . . .' I swallowed a lump in my throat, suddenly unsure of myself. Was I being fair? Should I simply let them retire, sell up and let the farm go, make it as easy as possible for them?

Or fight for it? Because once land has gone, it's gone for ever. Fact.

'I don't want you to sell the farm,' I blurted out. 'Just give me a chance to make a go of it.'

Uncle Arthur's shoulders sagged. 'Freya, lass, there's no one I'd rather see staying on here, keeping the Moorcroft family at Appleby Farm, than you. You know that.'

I nodded hopefully. He cupped a rough hand round my cheek and rubbed away a tear that I hadn't realized was there.

'Look, Uncle Arthur, I haven't got enough money and I haven't quite got my head round what I'd do with a huge farmhouse and a hundred and fifty acres of land. But I just have this feeling here.'

309

I pressed a hand to my heart.

'It's doable. I know it is. I just haven't worked out how yet. Do you have to sell? Can't you stay in the farmhouse and rent out the fields?'

He lifted his cap and scratched his head.

'Your brother has come up with a good offer from another farm. We haven't talked money yet, I know,' he admitted, 'but at least the land would stay as farmland, which is a big plus in my book. And your auntie can have that bungalow she's after.' He peered into my eyes and we shared a smile.

'Two months,' I pleaded. 'Please. Give me two months to make a proper go of the tea rooms and to come up with an alternative plan before you give Julian an answer.' Even as my mouth was forming the words, I was aware how ridiculous it was. Short of winning the lottery, what could I possibly conjure up in that time?

'All right,' whispered Uncle Arthur, shooting a worried look towards the kitchen. 'But it's just between you and me. Don't tell your auntie or she'll have my guts for garters.'

I grabbed hold of his whiskery face and planted a smacker on his cheek. 'Thank you, thank you, thank you. Now, I must dash. I've got tea rooms to open.'

By eleven o'clock quite a crowd had built up outside the tea rooms. The great and the good of Lovedale and the surrounding villages were there, as well as the delightful Patience Purdue from the planning office, the *Gazette*'s photographer and a mousy lady called Jayne from the local tourist information office. Quite a few families had arrived and I would be eternally grateful to Tilly for baking the biggest mountain of cookies I'd ever seen to hand out to the over-excited children.

The place was buzzing. *I* was buzzing, come to that, and despite all the drama of the first part of the day, I was having a ball. Ross and I had tied the huge blue ribbon across the locked barn doors into a big bow and it looked fabulous. Then Lizzie realized she'd been locked in and pressed herself up against the glass from the inside, yelling for help until Ross reminded her that she could escape through the fire exit. But now all of us were ready for the grand opening.

I beckoned Auntie Sue and Uncle Arthur to join me at the ribbon and handed them the gold scissors.

I cleared my throat and mothers and wives shushed their children and husbands respectively.

'Good morning, everyone, and welcome to Appleby Farm Vintage Tea Rooms. Thank you all so much for joining us on this very special occasion. I hope that the tea rooms will become a real hub of the community in the months to come and that you'll all become regular guests.'

I crossed my fingers behind my back praying that this would be the case and that Julian's sale would simply evaporate into thin air.

'So without further ado . . .'

My eye was suddenly distracted by a taxi speeding into the yard and grinding to a halt in a cloud of dust. A tall elegant woman emerged, slammed the door and ran as quickly as her heels would allow towards the crowd.

'Mum!' I cried.

'Freya! I'm not too late, am I?'

'Over to you, Uncle Arthur.' I grinned and dashed through the crowd to give my mum a hug.

'I'm delighted to declare the Appleby Farm Vintage Tea Rooms well and truly open,' said Uncle Arthur, doing his best to hack his way through the thick ribbon with Auntie Sue's sewing scissors.

The doors opened, the crowd surged forward and Tilly, Lizzie and Auntie Sue fought their way inside to take their places at the counter.

'This is such a lovely surprise,' I squealed, kissing Mum's cheek.

'You didn't really think I'd miss my little girl's big day, did you, darling?' She laughed, her brown eyes shining happily.

'I'm so glad.' I fanned my face to fend off the tears. 'Come on, let's go inside and see if we can find you a table.'

'A table? You must be joking,' she said, slipping off her jacket. 'You can find me an apron, please, I'm here to help!'

My mum had flown in from Paris to be my waitress. My chest heaved with happiness.

'Thanks, Mum.'

Chapter 30

At five minutes past five the last group of customers left the tea rooms.

'Bye, thank you for coming!' I waved them off towards the car park, stepped back inside and pulled a victory elbow-into-the-hip punch.

'Right. Beer and bubbles!'

Tilly uncorked bottles of prosecco and I passed round glasses and bottles of beer, specially stashed in the fridge for this moment, and a merry little crowd toasted our first day's trading. As well as my staff (loved, loved, loved saying that!), I'd asked Goat and his men to join us for a celebratory drink. Eddy and Ross came along too and a party atmosphere soon kicked in.

I worked the room, making sure everyone had a drink, thanking each person for their help and dispensing either a hug or a kiss as I deemed fit.

My beautiful mum was leaning against the ice-cream counter in conversation with Auntie Sue and Uncle Arthur. She had worked like a Trojan for me, clearing tables and washing up, ferrying dirty and clean crockery backwards and forwards to the kitchen in the farmhouse where there was more space. She still looked elegant and fresh, despite having had to leave Paris at some ungodly hour this morning. I, on the other hand, through a monumental slip-up on my part, had forgotten to train anyone else to use the coffee machine and so had steamed myself to within an inch of my life all day making cappuccinos and lattes. Any make-up I did have on had slid off several hours ago. On the plus side, I wouldn't need a facial for a while.

'Mum, have a top-up.' I sloshed some more bubbly into her flute glass. 'Mum?'

Her eyes were glittering and huge tears threatened to break loose any second. She threw her arm round my waist and kissed my face noisily. 'I just want to say, darling, that I'm *so* proud of you. The tea rooms are beautiful and it's almost impossible to imagine this space as an old barn.'

'Aww. Thanks, Mum.' I basked in the golden glow of her praise for a second or two. 'But everyone helped. And I couldn't have done it without Dad's loan.'

'Where is Rusty?' Uncle Arthur frowned. 'Surprised he didn't come with you.'

Mum's hand fluttered to her string of pearls. 'Important meeting at the bank. Couldn't get out of it, I'm afraid.'

Uncle Arthur tutted and I pushed back the familiar pang of hurt. Work would always come first with Dad; it was the way he was. But he *had* sent me those gorgeous flowers. I leaned my head on Mum's shoulder.

'But you're here and you can tell him all about it. I'll give you a menu to take back to show him, and some cake.'

'Which reminds me, we've run out of scones,' said Auntie Sue. 'I might make some different types tomorrow. What do you think, Freya?'

'Ooh, yes, someone did ask if we'd got any without fruit in. So maybe some plain ones.'

'And I've written the chocolate chip cookie recipe down

for you, Sue.' Tilly popped her head into the group and handed Auntie Sue a folded piece of paper. 'Freya, can I have a word?'

Tilly pulled me to one side. 'I really don't want to leave, I've had such a lovely time, but it's nearly time to get my train.'

I gave Tilly a hug. 'Bloomin' good job you *were* here to make those cookies! Trust Harry to make a grand gesture like that.'

I rolled my eyes, but truthfully I couldn't wait to see him in person to thank him. Maybe people would have come to our grand opening anyway, but those things he'd said about Cumbria being unique and us needing people's support, and the way he'd described our valley with such warmth made my eyes well up every time I thought about him.

'I only met him briefly but if I'd known what a hero he was I'd have sat him down and grilled him about his prospects.' Tilly pressed her lips into a knowing smile.

'He is a hero,' I agreed, 'and I would have liked him to come to the launch so I could thank him properly.'

'Yes, such a shame about the pig.'

Lizzie joined us, pulling the pins out of her bun. She shook her hair loose and it looked immaculate. How was that even possible? Both Tilly and I had put our hair in a bun, too. It had been our agreed 'look'. I now had a halo of frizz all around my hairline and most of Tilly's bun had escaped in straggly clumps at the back of her head.

Lizzie grunted. 'You leave the pig to me. She's gone too far this time.'

I snorted into my prosecco. 'I think Tilly meant Harry's pregnant sow, not your delightful sister.'

Tilly nodded and burst out laughing. 'And we were so

315

right about Victoria. She has definitely got it really bad for Harry.'

'Don't,' I muttered. 'It makes me feel ill just thinking about it.'

Lizzie and Tilly exchanged smug smiles. 'Oh, so you admit—' began Tilly.

'Nothing,' I finished for her, holding up a hand. 'But he's my friend and I want him to meet someone lovely, someone who shares his passion for the countryside, someone who looks across Lovedale valley and feels her heart soar.'

'At the sliver of Lake Windermere, glinting like a sapphire in the distance?' Lizzie quipped, tongue visibly wedged in her cheek.

'Oh, bog off.' I pressed the bottle of chilled prosecco to my face and I swear I heard it sizzle.

'We are, actually.' Lizzie grinned and flung an arm round each of us. 'Ross is coming with me to a friend's engagement party in Kendal. Lovely to meet you, Tilly. See you tomoz, Freya. Mwah. Mwah.'

Noisy air kisses for both of us and she went off to round up Ross.

'I'll go and say my goodbyes, too,' said Tilly, setting her empty glass down and making a beeline for Auntie Sue.

I'd only had a drop of bubbly for toasting purposes as I was driving Tilly to the train station. I was scanning the table, looking for some water to top my glass up with, when Uncle Arthur appeared at my side and slipped his hand into mine.

'You've done a marvellous job today, lass. You were born to run your own business. You're a good leader and didn't lose your nerve when things went a bit wobbly this morning.'

'Thanks, Uncle Arthur. I think I've finally found my niche.'

We shared a secret smile as Tilly came back, kissed Uncle Arthur goodbye and then the two of us set off for Oxenholme railway station.

It was early evening by the time we arrived at the station and the light showers promised by Radio Lakeland's jolly weatherman were looming at the edge of the horizon. I nabbed the widest spot in the car park, retrieved Tilly's case from the back of the campervan and ran round to the passenger side to say goodbye.

'You will come and visit again soon, won't you?' I said, hugging her tightly.

'Oh, my goodness! Try stopping me.' Tilly beamed, wide-eyed. 'And next time I'll bring Aidan with me. He'll love it just as much as I do. In fact, as soon as I get on the train I'm going to call him. I really think he'd be interested in Colton Woods for his *Woodland Habitats* programme.'

'Do! I can show him round. I used to play in those woods when I was a kid.'

'With Harry?' she said slyly.

'Yes. With Harry,' I tutted. 'It's full of wildlife. We used to sit and listen to owls hooting in the trees in the evening. Down the hill on other side of the woods is a little church and in the spring we used to collect bunches of bluebells and sell them to people coming out of mass for ten pence.' I paused. 'Actually, that was me. Harry refused.'

'You see!' She pressed a kiss to my cheek. 'You were a budding entrepreneur even then. I'd better go.'

'Have a fab time in Venice!' I yelled through Bobby's open window as I climbed in.

I watched her go, dragging her little case on wheels along the pavement in the wrong direction towards platform two, which would take her to Scotland. I giggled to myself and waited. And then I watched her reappear, pink-faced and breathless, and this time head off to platform one for all trains south. Phew.

As I started the engine my phone buzzed into life as a text message came through. I quickly looked at my phone and grinned. It was from Charlie.

> Hi Freya, hope your opening went well. Give me a
> call when you can. Charlie x

Bless him, he'd remembered it was my big day. I'd call him from the farm later. I stuck the phone back on the passenger seat and manoeuvred Bobby out of the car park.

I drove back towards Lovedale in silence. Normally I entertain myself by singing along to the radio at full volume, but today I needed some thinking time.

The clock was ticking: I had eight weeks to come up with a plan to prevent the farm from falling into the hands of a new owner.

Over the last couple of months I'd come up with a series of wacky ideas to make money from Appleby Farm: turning it into a campsite, renovating the shepherd's huts, making cider and selling mistletoe at Christmas. And there were other things I could do, too, like hiring the tea rooms out as a venue for parties or developing Auntie Sue's Jersey ice cream into a proper brand and selling it in places other than just the White Lion.

The problem was that although the notion of running lots of different projects under one roof was my idea of heaven (I mean, seriously, I would never complain of being bored again!), I wasn't sure whether I could pull them all together into one cohesive business.

It started to drizzle and I switched on Bobby's windscreen wipers, feeling a bit drizzly myself.

And if I couldn't come up with a sensible plan, it was hardly going to be much of a proposition for my uncle and aunt, was it? Ooh, let's see . . . a buy-out offer from another farm versus a Mary Poppins handbag full of schemes from the butterfly-minded Freya.

However exciting my business ideas were (to me at least), I couldn't see a way for them to happen *and* still give Auntie Sue and Uncle Arthur the financial freedom that they were after.

Oh, sod it. My brain was aching, I'd already been awake for fourteen hours and I'd had a massive, massive day. I didn't want to think about it any more.

I reached for the radio button, cranked up the volume and began to belt out the words to Beyoncé's 'Single Ladies'.

Although, I pondered, turning the music back down again, I *could* go and talk to Harry about it. He might have some bright ideas and I *did* want to thank him for coming to my rescue on the radio earlier. On the other hand, he still might be up to his neck with a sow in labour (yuck, now that was a picture I'd have trouble dismissing).

Despite that, all of a sudden there was no one I wanted to see more than him. Here was me feeling all alone with no one to confide in, when the perfect confidant was literally at the end of my garden.

I had reached Lovedale already and the turning to Willow Farm was looming. Before I had a chance to think it through properly (and if I *had* have thought it through I would have pulled over and at the very least given my hair a brush), my finger hit the indicator switch and Bobby was bumping slowly along the lane over the potholes towards Willow Farm.

In a couple of minutes I would see Harry. Which was good because today I'd realized just how important he was to me.

The way he'd leaped to my defence on air had made my heart twist with happiness. But now that I thought about it, it wasn't just today; it was the way he remembered little things about me, like fishing for minnows in the beck and wanting a fawn for my birthday. It was the way he listened when I told him my crazy ideas and it was the way he felt the same as I did about our family farms.

He just . . . got me.

We were two peas in a pod, two halves of one whole. We shared a love of the same things in a way that Charlie and I had never done.

All of these things brought me to a conclusion that had been gathering momentum in my heart for days, weeks, possibly even months . . .

'I love Harry,' I gasped, gripping the steering wheel tightly. 'I love Harry Graythwaite!'

I laughed out loud at myself in wonderment, relieved that the tiny niggle deep in my brain had finally worked its way to the surface. But after about twenty seconds my happiness faded.

Obviously he didn't feel the same way, or he'd have done something about it.

No man would actively choose to just be mates with a girl they fancied the pants off, would they? No. They'd make a move. Or at least ask them out on a date.

And Harry had never asked me out on a date.

A little voice cleared its throat and reminded me that he had, in fact, taken me to Rigg Farm, and so in theory that constituted a date.

I batted the voice away. That was different. It had been

320

my birthday and anyway, it had been a trip to demonstrate farm diversification. And learning about farm diversification cannot, under any circumstances, be construed as the setting for a date.

Even if you had fun? asked the little voice slyly.

Even then, I retorted firmly. But regardless of my non-reciprocated feelings for him, he was the best friend a girl could have. And I would tell him as much.

I hadn't been to Willow Farm for years, but I remembered the layout. I had to turn off this lane into a driveway. The farmhouse sat at the end of the drive and all the farm buildings were in blocks behind the house rather than around a central yard like at Appleby Farm.

There was a car parked up ahead on the lane and as it came into focus, my breath caught in my throat and my heart started to beat thunderously. It was Victoria's little red sports car.

What was she doing here?

I stopped the campervan next to a broad oak tree and climbed out. The rain had worsened and I wished I was wearing something more substantial than a vest top. Feeling like some sort of secret spy, I hopped up the lane to the end of the drive to see if I could see anything or, more accurately, any*one.*

I inched forward, holding my breath, making sure that I stayed hidden behind a clump of trees. Eek – there they were! I jumped back and peered through the leaves.

Harry was standing in front of the farmhouse. *With Victoria bloody Moon hanging round his neck.* Their noses were almost touching and he was holding his hands out at the side of her head as if he were about to scoop her face up to meet his.

I couldn't bear to watch.

I clapped my hand over my mouth, ducked my head and ran back to Bobby. I jumped in and reversed all the way back down the lane.

It was only when I reached the main road that I realized my hands were shaking. It was one thing to accept that Harry only regarded me as 'friend material', it was quite another to accept that those two were an item.

I could kick myself. Of course they were. All the signs had been there.

I thought back to our trip to Rigg Farm and how we'd bumped into Victoria then. Coincidence? I think not. Plus he'd gone into the studio to be interviewed on her radio show *and* she'd dropped into conversation that she had been to a restaurant with him the night before she visited the tea rooms. She had pursued him relentlessly and her dedication had paid off.

But *Victoria Moon*?

The discovery of the two of them had sucked all the joy out of my day.

He deserved someone better than her. And if that was the sort of woman he went for, well, he wasn't the man I thought he was.

But I was not going to cry. I wound down the window to let the damp air in and inhaled a big breath.

The track leading to Appleby Farm came into view. I turned in, parked up in the yard and walked wearily up the path to the farmhouse. There was no one about and for once I was grateful not to have to make conversation. I was about to go upstairs and run a bath when the phone rang.

I flopped down in the office and answered it.

'Freya? This is Aidan, Tilly's boyfriend. She's just called me from the train. This might sound crazy, but I've got a proposal for you.'

My face broke into a weary smile. 'Go ahead, I love crazy.'

Thirty minutes later, I lay in the bath with a cold glass of wine, my head spinning with ideas. Aidan had sworn me to secrecy. His proposal was crazy – but brilliant crazy – and I couldn't wait to talk it over with Tilly. But even more exciting than that, I had the makings of a plan to keep Appleby Farm in the Moorcroft family. And it just might work.

Love Is in the Air

Chapter 31

Until I moved back to the Lake District, Sunday mornings (or the tail-end thereof, which was all I used to see) went like this: wake up, grope for my glass of water, take that first sip that tastes like nectar, make yet another fervent promise to myself never to drink flaming sambuca again and then ease myself in to the day, praying that the pictures of me twerking like Miley Cyrus haven't made it to Instagram.

Not any more.

Now you're far more likely to find me at my converted sewing table in the office by eight o'clock, ordering tea or napkins or something equally glamourous. Or I might be checking the website for hits, replying to emails for party bookings and jotting down things on my new wall planner. And do you know what? I totally love it. My life isn't perfect, whose is? But for the first time I feel as though I'm exactly where I should be, doing exactly what I want to do.

Home. Such a tiny little word. And yet at the same time, it means so much.

On this particular Sunday morning, the weather outside the office window was bright, sunny and as crisp as an autumn apple. It was the middle of September, with two weeks to go until some very important dates, and fourteen weeks until – drumroll please – the wedding of Tilly Parker and Aidan Whitby. YAY!

And what was even more heart-claspingly joyful was that their nuptials were only going to be bloomin' well celebrated at Appleby Farm. Double YAY! Yes, I had been given the very great honour of being in charge of their special day and I was so overwhelmed by them placing their trust in me that I kept having to pinch myself!

It all started when Aidan called me on the day of the tea rooms' opening. He was whisking Tilly off to Venice the following day and had planned a secret marriage proposal. What he also wanted to do was take all of the stress out of organizing the wedding for her so that it was as different as it possibly could be from her wedding to her first husband. I didn't know Aidan that well but by the end of that phone call not only had I agreed to host their wedding at Appleby Farm, I also absolutely adored him; he was possibly one of the sweetest, most thoughtful, romantic men I'd ever met.

Tilly had phoned from Venice the morning after Aidan proposed and in between the squeals and sobs I managed to work out that he'd arranged for a gondolier to pick them up from the jetty of their canalside hotel just before sunset. Under the Bridge of Sighs on the Rio del Palazzo, Aidan had asked Tilly to make him the happiest man in the world and marry him. She'd replied that she would be honoured to, as long as he got back up off one knee because the gondola was wobbling furiously and it was making her nervous. Aidan had slipped a ring on her finger, the gondolier had popped open a bottle of champagne and the gondola had glided magically through the water to a *bacaro* (which is Italian for wine bar), owned by the gondolier's sister, where they whiled away the rest of the night feeding each other warm crostini and drinking bubbly.

What an absolutely gorgeous proposal!

And they were such a gorgeous couple that I only felt the smallest twinge of jealousy at Tilly's current state of euphoria.

'The thing is,' Tilly had gushed, 'as soon as I got on the train after leaving you in the Lake District, I phoned him and told him all about the farm and the woods, how beautiful it was, and you selling bluebells to the people coming out of church, and he asked for your number. I was convinced he wanted to come and shoot his new TV show *Woodland Habitats* in Lovedale. But this is even more exciting, I'm so happy!'

And I was happy too. Their wedding was to take place on the twentieth of December at the church on the other side of Colton Woods with the reception in the tea rooms. I was literally counting down the days. Tilly had said she was happy to leave the flowers, the catering, the photographer, the wedding car . . . in fact, everything except her dress – to me. It would be a small wedding – close friends and family only – and she had asked whether I minded that Charlie would be coming. 'Not at all!' I'd reassured her, 'Charlie and I have both moved on; it'll be fine.'

Given that things hadn't worked out as I'd planned between Harry and me, that wasn't strictly true. But Charlie at least seemed to be making progress on the relationship front.

He'd sent me a text on the opening day of the tea rooms asking me to get in touch. Which I did. He'd wanted to let me know that he had been thinking of me on my big day. We'd got chatting about this and that and I'd wheedled it out of him that he'd been feeling a bit lonely. I spotted my chance and persuaded him to go for breakfast at the Shenton Road Café when I knew Anna would be working.

And the very next weekend he went along and took Ollie with him, too.

Unbelievably, the three of them had got chatting and Ollie, bless him, asked Anna to come to the park with them to fly his kite. And then, according to Anna, who called me later that day, 'one thing led to another'. They were taking it slowly, she'd said, and it was still early days. But she had wanted to tell me straight away in case I heard the news from other sources and did I mind?

We'd both had a girlie sob down the phone, but I'd promised whole-heartedly that I was delighted for them. They'd be good for each other, I just knew it. Besides, Anna was so happy that it would have been selfish of me not to have given them my blessing. It was just, you know, still a bit new so, for the moment, I was doing my best to keep both men – Charlie and Harry – out of my thoughts.

Staying away from Harry was proving difficult. He seemed to spend more time at our farm than his own these days. He'd handled the barley harvest for us and this week he'd been helping Eddy prepare the cowsheds ready to house the cattle over winter. I hadn't seen Victoria at all – thank goodness – and so luckily hadn't had the misfortune of seeing the pair of them together since I'd spied on them at Willow Farm.

Lizzie doubted that there was anything going on between them. 'Except in Victoria's head.'

'But I've seen them,' I insisted. 'They were on the verge of kissing.'

And we'd both shuddered at poor Harry's fate.

When Harry was here on the farm working, he usually popped into the tea rooms at some point. But this week I'd hardly seen him. Once, his visit had coincided with a hen party that'd arrived for afternoon tea – he only stayed for thirty seconds. And the following day a huge group of silver-haired ramblers had descended on us in need of refreshment. I'd been too busy to chat, which was sad because I missed his smiley face, his bad jokes and his teasing reminders of my teenage antics.

And I missed that little frisson of excitement that I felt whenever he was near.

Anyway . . . So, back to the wall planner.

I picked up my special marker – blue for a booking – and jotted down the date that had just come in via email: a birthday celebration afternoon tea. General trade at the Appleby Farm Vintage Tea Rooms was steady, but the party bookings were starting to come in thick and fast. We were proving to be a big hit with the mother and toddler brigade, who adored buying the little Appleby Farm bags of corn and feeding the hens.

My eye fell on the last day of September where 'TB' was written in black. It was D-Day for the cattle. This was the second round of tests since the TB outbreak in May. Hopefully this time, the vet would give us the all-clear and then Uncle Arthur could decide what he wanted to do with the beef herd. Whatever he did would bring him and Auntie Sue a step closer to their retirement.

But the day after was the biggie: the first of October was marked with a big black cross. That was the date by which Uncle Arthur had promised to give Julian an answer about selling the farm to his buyer.

My stomach lurched. I'd got ideas – plenty of them – I just couldn't quite get them to stack up financially. I was reaching into the drawer in my makeshift desk for my little – and unfortunately, I mean little – folder of business plans that might prevent the farm falling into this secret buyer's hands, when there was a sharp rap at the window. I looked up with a gasp to see Lizzie sitting on Skye's back. The two of them were outside the office window, standing between the raised beds that Charlie had made in Auntie Sue's veggie patch.

'Flippin 'eck! You frightened the life out of me!' I cried, opening the window and leaning out to rub Skye's white and chestnut nose.

'Freya Moorcroft, it's your lucky day. I, Lizzie Moon, will work in the tea rooms with you today for free.' She flashed a bright smile at me but it didn't quite reach her eyes. It was the kind of smile I used when someone asked – as they did a lot round here – if I was courting and I pretended I didn't have time for all that business.

'Fab! Thank you. In that case, while you take Skye to the stables I'll make us some breakfast. I haven't eaten yet.'

She stuck out her bottom lip. 'Don't you want to know why?'

My heart melted for my friend. 'Is it because Ross has gone back to uni?'

She leaned forward until she was lying flat against Skye's mane and tutted. 'Know-all. He called this morning. Says he's already missing me. But I can't stop imagining that he's having a great time with the other students, and so I thought a day washing up and buttering scones would take my mind off my heartbreak.'

'Well, I can definitely help there by keeping you busy all day, and you can help me sort out my ideas into a proper business plan for two weeks' time.'

'Why, what's happening in two weeks?'

I held up my folder of ideas. 'I need a cunning plan to foil my brother.'

'Right you are. Make mine a fried-egg sandwich and I'm all yours. Come on, Skye.'

Lizzie clicked her tongue against her teeth, tweaked the reins and clip-clopped off to the stables.

I closed the window, gave the folder a last look before tucking it back in the drawer and set off in search of breakfast.

I was working on the principle that as the days ticked by and I was really down to the wire, I would have a brainwave and I'd come up with a rescue package that would knock spots off my brother's farm proposal. I mean, his proposal didn't make sense. An existing farmer who wants to take over Appleby Farm? Surely it could only be someone local and we hadn't heard a dicky bird. I was convinced it was actually some shady development company pretending to be farmers, who would concrete over the entire farm and turn it into luxury holiday apartments as soon as our backs were turned. Well, whatever, or whoever, this mystery buyer was, they weren't getting their hands on the farm at least until after the wedding. If I had my way, they wouldn't get their hands on it at all.

Auntie Sue and Uncle Arthur had just finished their breakfasts and, judging by Auntie Sue's lack of apron and Uncle Arthur's best trousers, it appeared that they were on their way out.

'Morning, everyone,' I said, kissing them briefly and pressing a hand to the teapot in search of a brew. 'Are you going somewhere?'

The kitchen table had its usual stacks of papers on it, although I noticed these days that the pile of old farming magazines had been replaced with assorted listings from all the local estate agents.

'Morning, lass. Yes, we are, but don't worry, your scones are already made and cooling. Have you got that brochure, Artie? Let Freya see where we're going.'

Uncle Arthur sighed and made a show of sifting through the papers on the table.

I took a frying pan down from the hook above the Aga while I waited, set it on the hotplate, melted a knob of butter and broke four fresh eggs into the pan.

'What do you think of this, love?' asked Auntie Sue, wrestling a brochure from her husband's grip. She joined me at the Aga and pushed the open pages towards me while I loosened the eggs from the bottom of the pan with a spatula. '"Oaklands Retirement Development, exclusively for the over sixties." It's got a social centre, a medical centre and a gym, and—'

'What do I want with a ruddy gym?' growled Uncle Arthur. 'I've got a hundred and fifty acres of space to walk about here, right on me own doorstep. I want fresh air and views, not living cheek by jowl with a load of geriatrics.'

I cleared my throat to smother a giggle. If they let sixty-year-olds in, there was a good chance he'd be fifteen years older than some of the residents. I bit my lip and said nothing.

'But we won't have all those acres, will we, Artie? Not if we sell up.'

'I'm working on the menu for Tilly and Aidan's wedding today,' I said, changing the subject diplomatically.

It did the trick. Auntie Sue sank back down on the bench next to Uncle Arthur and squeezed his hand. 'Oh, lovely.' She sighed. 'I can't wait to see the tea rooms all dolled up for the wedding.'

Lizzie let herself into the kitchen and sat down just as I slid our double-fried-egg sandwiches on to the table.

'I'm trying to come up with something delicious, unique and easy enough to feed a crowd,' I said.

'Yum,' said Lizzie, smothering her eggs with ketchup. 'Morning, all. How about spag bol?'

I pulled a face. 'Falls down slightly at the unique hurdle, don't you think?'

She puffed out her cheeks. 'Have you ever tasted my spaghetti bolognese?'

'No, true, but I was thinking something a bit more . . . British. Something to celebrate local produce.'

Uncle Arthur coughed. 'Just a suggestion, but you are on a *beef* farm . . . Roast beef? We can send one to the butcher specially.'

I sat down next to Lizzie and grinned at him. 'Genius! A roast dinner on a December day will warm everyone up.' I hesitated. 'As long as it's not one of the cute ones.'

'Freya!' Lizzie, Auntie Sue and Uncle Arthur tutted in unison.

I blushed and bent over my plate. 'I know, I know.'

Auntie Sue stood up and held out Uncle Arthur's tweed jacket. 'Up you get. We'll be back at lunchtime, Freya. Don't forget your cheque book for the deposit on an apartment, Artie.'

'Eh?' Uncle Arthur paled.

'Joke! Come on.'

They left the farmhouse, still bickering, and Lizzie and I finished our breakfast.

'This wedding's going to be so cool,' said Lizzie, pouring herself a mug of tea. 'I can't wait to meet Aidan. He must be really trendy.'

I laughed. 'Why?'

'Wanting a rustic wedding at a farm. It's *the* thing at the moment. Six of my friends are getting married next year and four of the receptions are on farms. He's bang on trend.'

'Is he?' A spark of something that could just be my

long-awaited brainwave fizzed in my brain. I glanced at my watch. 'Ooh, come on, Lizzie, it's nearly opening time. Can you grab the milk and I'll carry the lemon drizzle cake.'

'Sure.'

We both stood up and cleared away our dirty plates. 'By the way, Harry made a rare appearance in the pub last night and he said—' Lizzie began.

'What are your thoughts on ginger cake?'

Lizzie blinked at me. 'Meh, that's what I think. I also think you're changing the subject.'

'I agree,' I said, opening the fridge and handing Lizzie two cartons of milk.

'Do you?'

'Yep.' I packed the fresh scones into a plastic box and tucked them and the lemon cake under my arm. 'Ginger is the Marmite of cakes, or possibly coffee cake. Coffee cake definitely has its share of enemies.'

Satisfied that I'd nipped the Harry and Victoria conversation in the bud, I headed for the kitchen door, only to be stopped in my tracks by the office phone ringing.

'Can you go on and open the tea rooms? I'll get that.'

I put down the cakes and scampered back to the office, hoping that it would be another booking for a baby shower. We'd had one the week before and it had been a roaring success. The women had got through the biggest mountain of cupcakes and, considering there had been zero alcohol involved, had been extremely raucous.

'Appleby Farm Vintage Tea Rooms; Freya speaking.'

There was an exasperated huff down the line followed by a mumbled expletive, which immediately told me who was calling.

'Julian,' I said unenthusiastically.

'Still playing at tea parties, I see? Sorry, Freya, but there'll be no more fannying about. We need to move forward with this deal. Is Arthur there?'

'No, they're both out. Gone to look at . . . a horse.' No way was I going to let him know they'd gone house-hunting, he'd have the For Sale sign up before they even got home. Or worse, a Sold sign.

'A horse? At their age? For God's sake. All right, tell them there's a rural property surveyor coming to value the farm tomorrow morning. If they've got a problem with that, they'll have to call me.'

'Hold on a minute. We've still got two weeks,' I fumed.

'For what? A miracle? The buyer wants to get things in motion; plans have already been drawn up. They've waited long enough and I can't . . . I mean, Arthur can't afford to lose this deal.'

Plans? That sounded ominous. What did a farmer need plans for?

'Is there anything in the world more important to you than profit, Julian?'

'Don't be naive.'

The line went dead. I headed back through to the kitchen, collected the cakes and stepped out into the cobbled farm-yard. I was instantly calmed by the autumn sun on my face.

Perhaps Julian was right. Maybe I was naive and maybe I'd never be rich but I knew how to be happy. And I was pretty sure that true happiness had somehow passed my brother by.

Chapter 32

Later that evening, I pulled on my wellies and overalls, and joined Auntie Sue out in the milking parlour as she led Gloria and Gaynor in for milking.

There were fourteen stalls in all, seven down either side of the parlour, each with their own milking equipment connected up to a big milk tank left over from the days of dairy farming. The two cows swayed amiably into stalls next to each other and plunged their heads straight into their feeding troughs.

The parlour was, of course, a bit pongy, but its walls were made of the same moss-covered stone as the barn. If it didn't have all this paraphernalia in it, it could have just as much potential as the barn I'd converted for the tea rooms. A farm shop, perhaps, or—

'Ooh, I'm stiff tonight,' Auntie Sue groaned, breaking into my daydream as she bent towards Gloria's under-carriage and wiped her udders.

'I'll help.'

I jumped down to the lower part of the floor that ran down the centre of the milking parlour. Auntie Sue turned the pump on and I attached the cups to each teat on both of the cows. It was easy enough to do – the suction in the cups did most of the work, I just had to aim straight.

Auntie Sue came and stood next to me, and for a couple of minutes we stayed silent. It was mildly hypnotic listening to the 'suck-release-suck-release' of the pump and watching as the ivory milk squirted thinly through the plastic tubes on its way to the tank.

'So, come on.' I nudged her. 'Spill the beans about today.'

Relations between her and my uncle had been a bit strained when they'd arrived back from their house-hunting at lunchtime. This was the first time I'd got her on her own since then and I wanted the full story.

'Well, that was a disaster,' Auntie Sue had huffed, flipping up the bin lid and dropping the Oaklands Retirement Development brochure into it. 'Rabbit hutches, the lot of them. And the kitchens, Freya! You couldn't swing a cup let alone a cat. Where would I put my Aga? No storage inside and barely enough room to sit in the garden. Where would we put all our furniture?'

I'd been about to point out that downsizing meant moving to a smaller house until I caught sight of her face – fierce. I'd kept my opinions to myself.

Uncle Arthur hadn't been so sensible. 'I was pleasantly surprised.' He'd picked up another brochure, this time for 'Sunset Living Luxury Residencies' and sunk into his armchair.

Auntie Sue had begun slicing bread for sandwiches with unnecessary force. 'Yes, well. I could see that. We'd only been there five minutes and you were off playing dominoes in the social centre with some other old reprobates.'

Uncle Arthur had winked at me and shown me a handful of coins: ill-gotten gains, presumably.

'And talk about busy!' she'd ranted. 'It was right on the

main road, cars hurtling past every second of the day. I'd never get a moment's peace. No,' she'd shaken her head firmly, 'it wasn't for me.'

'What about this one?' Uncle Arthur had suggested, holding up the brochure. 'They've got an indoor swimming pool and sauna.'

She'd tugged it out of his hand and replaced it with a cheese and pickle sandwich.

'I want to live in a nice quiet bungalow, not a bloomin' holiday camp.'

At that point I'd told them about Julian's phone call and the appointment with the surveyor in the morning, and all talk of retirement homes had been instantly forgotten.

Now, in the milking parlour over the throbbing of the machinery, Auntie Sue checked over her shoulder furtively and took a step closer.

'I've found a bungalow,' she hissed. 'Converted stables on the edge of farmland. It'll be perfect for us when it's finished. I knew it as soon as I saw the details. Two bedrooms, a big kitchen with room for an Aga. Only two miles from here. On a bus route for if ... when, you know ...'

I nodded. I knew. If anything happened to Uncle Arthur, she would be stranded without access to public transport.

'I only took him to that Oaklands Retirement place as a sort of test. Show him somewhere he'd loathe and then he'd be so grateful not to live there that he'd agree to anything. That backfired, didn't it?'

She smiled at me wanly.

I stuck my arm round her. 'You silly sausage. He loves you so much that he'll agree to anything.'

Her eyes twinkled. 'I know.'

We both laughed.

'So you're happy to move somewhere smaller, then?'

She nodded. 'And I'm tired of all these stairs.'

'What about all your, you know . . . furniture?' I stared at her.

In the nursery was what I meant. The hand-painted characters on the wall and the old wooden cot.

I think she understood because her eyes softened. 'It's time to let go of our old life and start enjoying a new one. Things that weren't meant to be, well . . . Artie always says if we'd had a son this, if we'd had a son that . . . But nothing's for certain, is it? We could have had a son or daughter who'd wanted to be a doctor or join the army. And we could still have ended up like this with no one to take over the farm.'

But I want to take over the farm.

My latest business idea was brilliant – though I said so myself. It would make money, it was bang on trend and it would use the farm and buildings, and some of its land sympathetically. But two things stood in my way: it wasn't farming and I didn't have a lump sum of money to buy the farm from my aunt and uncle.

Which probably meant that my brilliant idea was a non-starter.

'That's the end of that, I think,' Auntie Sue said briskly.

'What?' *How did she know?* 'Oh, the milk!' I laughed, as Auntie Sue switched off the pump.

I released Gaynor from the milking machine, Auntie Sue did the same for Gloria and we led them back across the yard to the field.

'I'll miss the girls when we're in our new bungalow,' said

Auntie Sue, fastening the gate behind us. 'And the hens. But it'll be nice to pop back and see them when the new owners have moved in.'

My heart sank. As far as she was concerned, the farm sale was as good as complete. She was ready to move out and had already begun to imagine life without the farm.

Funny how things turn out. Six months ago, Appleby Farm was a place of sepia-tinted childhood memories for me and now it was my entire world. And I *so* couldn't bear the thought that that world might end.

I took a deep breath and painted on a smile. 'Fancy a walk down to the honesty box with me?'

She nodded and looped her arm through mine. 'I've still got to finish up in the milking parlour, but go on then.'

We headed across the yard, me slowing my pace to match hers. The arthritis in her knee caused her to favour one side so we waddled rather than walked down to the road.

The honesty box had done really well this summer. During July and August we'd done a roaring trade in salad potatoes, fresh peas and soft fruit, and now we were selling big bags of apples alongside cobs of corn and, of course, our eggs.

'Do you think the new owners will let me keep the tea rooms at Appleby Farm?' I asked, emptying the money tin into both our pockets.

Auntie Sue blinked at me. 'Of course, lovey! We'll make it a requirement of the sale. I expect the new farmer will love to have visitors to the farm, just like we do. Why wouldn't they?'

I shrugged, feeling tearful all of a sudden.

Because Julian was involved and for some reason I couldn't envisage him having lined up a tweedy farmer with an apple-cheeked wife as buyers for Appleby Farm.

She patted my hand. 'Anyway, we'll see what tomorrow brings, Freya.'

I couldn't help shuddering. We would indeed.

Mr Turner, the surveyor, arrived at nine fifteen the following morning in a smart estate car. Auntie Sue invited him into the kitchen for a cup of tea, introduced everyone and gestured for him to join Uncle Arthur and me at the table.

Madge was lying under the table and she gave a low growl as Mr Turner took a seat. I was with Madge; there was something sinister about him. He had hair the colour of mushrooms, one eyebrow permanently raised and an odd tendency to jut his chin out before speaking.

'Have you come far?' trilled Auntie Sue.

Jut. 'Lancaster. Straight up the M6.'

He placed a small laser beam measuring device, a camera and a clipboard on the table in front of him.

'Where does the farmer live now?' Uncle Arthur asked.

Jut. 'Farmer?'

'Yes, the potential buyer. Is he or she local?'

Mr Turner dipped his chin to consult his clipboard. 'It's not so much a "farmer" as a farming organization.'

A wave of dread washed over me. *I knew it.* This was classic Julian. There was no jolly farmer; it was just a ruse to get Uncle Arthur to sell up. I glanced at my uncle; his thick eyebrows were bunched up warily.

'What sort of organization?' I asked rather more aggressively than I'd intended.

Mr Turner paled. 'I'm sorry. I don't have the details.'

By which he meant he wouldn't reveal them.

'Thank you for the tea, Mrs Moorcroft.' He stood up and gathered together his equipment.

It was a damp, cold day and Uncle Arthur looked quite

relieved when Mr Turner requested that he be allowed to 'get on with it' unaccompanied. The three of us watched him leave in silence.

'What do you think Julian's up to?' Auntie Sue asked, wringing her apron between her fingers.

Uncle Arthur grunted. 'Don't know, Sue. We'll have to wait and find out.'

I sprang up off the bench, darted to the door and pulled on my wellingtons.

'I'm not waiting,' I said and ran out into the yard after Mr Turner, Madge scampering beside me.

I spotted him by the dog kennel with his back to the chicken run, taking pictures of the cowsheds.

'Mr Turner,' I yelled, 'I want to talk to you.'

The next moments flashed by in a blur and everything seemed to happen at once. A chicken flew out of the kennel and pecked the surveyor in the back of the leg. Mr Turner leaped into the air with shock. He clung on to his camera but dropped his clipboard. Madge, presumably thinking that this stranger had designs on her freshly laid egg, which was no doubt waiting for her in the kennel, began to bark viciously. Then she flew at him and tore a chunk out of his trousers – at least, I think it was only his trousers. The startled man stumbled backwards, landing in a sprawling heap on the kennel.

'Ow, my back,' he yowled, rubbing his spine. 'Call this bloody dog off.'

Luckily Madge didn't need calling off: she'd obviously remembered the egg and slunk off into the kennel to retrieve it. Which was just as well because the papers on Mr Turner's clipboard had come loose, an architect's drawing unfolding on the yard. I was so shocked by what it revealed that words completely failed me.

I knelt down on the cobbles, pinned the drawing flat to the damp ground with both hands and stared. The large piece of paper depicted a very different-looking Appleby Farm to the one I saw before me now. Gone were the barns, the tea rooms, the lovely old stone buildings, the fields nearest the house with their ancient drystone walls . . . In fact, with the exception of the farmhouse itself, this new layout was almost unrecognizable.

Mr Turner clambered to his feet and tried to prise the drawing from my fingers. 'You have no business looking at that,' he bellowed.

'Actually, I have every business,' I said indignantly.

At that moment Auntie Sue and Uncle Arthur appeared and the tractor chugged into the yard with Eddy at the wheel.

'What's all the commotion?' cried Auntie Sue from the farmhouse gate.

'Don't speak to my niece like that,' barked Uncle Arthur at the same time over her shoulder.

Eddy climbed off the tractor seat and marched towards us. His boots made such a clatter on the cobbles that I looked up. New boots and clean jeans. I blinked. Unheard of!

Anyway, I ignored Mr Turner and held my ground. As I tried to make sense of the drawings I could literally feel the blood drain from my face. Four long cattle sheds, a maternity unit, a hospital unit, two huge milking parlours, offices . . .

'This isn't farming, it's . . .' I floundered, searching for the right word.

Mr Turner jutted his chin out as far as it would go. 'It's intensive dairy farming,' he finished for me.

There was a collective gasp.

'Is that right, Arthur?' Eddy glared at his boss, his face puce. 'You're selling out to an intensive dairy – where cows never feel the sun on their backs, never get to graze in paddocks?'

Now I was no farming expert, but I did know from the odd snippet I'd seen in Uncle Arthur's magazines that intensive dairy farming was highly controversial and a million miles away from the way Appleby Farm had been run since it had been in our family.

'Now, now, Eddy,' my uncle countered. 'I've agreed to nothing yet.'

Eddy nodded grimly. 'But you're not denying it.'

'I'm seventy-five, Eddy, and this is a cash offer.' Uncle Arthur shrugged weakly. 'What choice do I have? I could have another heart attack and—'

'Don't say that!' wailed Auntie Sue and she clapped her hands over her ears.

What? I blinked at Uncle Arthur. Surely he wasn't *still* considering Julian's offer? Not after finding out what the intensive farming company had planned. Why did everything come down to money? I felt sick.

'Excuse me,' interjected Mr Turner, 'but I've still got a job to do and who's going to pay for these trousers?'

I examined his trousers. One bare white knee was poking through a large hole and a flap of trouser material hung almost to the floor. It was all I could do not to grab it and rip for all I was worth.

'Your job's finished,' I snapped. 'And you can send the trouser bill to your client. I'm sure he'll pay up. Now go.'

Auntie Sue looked on the verge of tears. Uncle Arthur put his arm round her shoulders.

Mr Turner jutted his chin. 'This has got quite out of hand. It was all that hen's fault.'

'No, it wasn't the hen's fault,' I replied coldly. 'It was my brother's fault. And I'm going to phone him right now and tell him what I think of him.'

I pushed past everyone, leaving them arguing amongst themselves, and ran back into the farmhouse to the office.

Maybe I should have taken a few moments to collect myself, build a rational argument and approach my brother calmly. But I didn't.

'How could you?' I spat, when he answered my call.

'The surveyor has been, I take it?' asked Julian smoothly.

'This intensive dairy farm of yours would ruin the landscape and destroy our beautiful Lakeland farm. And what about animal welfare? What about the lives of those poor cows?'

'Oh yawn, yawn,' Julian groaned, sounding bored. 'Wake up, dearie. Farming isn't all about baby calves frisking about in the meadow. Arthur doesn't breed pets, he breeds meat. Farming is a form of industry and this development is no different, except it's investing millions in developing food production for twenty-first-century Britain.'

'Well, they can stick their millions. We don't want them.'

I slammed the phone down so hard that the desk shook and I sat with my hand still on the receiver, getting my breath back. The phone rang again almost immediately. I picked it up and braced myself for a further onslaught.

'Appleby Farm Vintage Tea Rooms, Freya speaking,' I muttered through gritted teeth.

'Freya, darling! It's Mum. Dad and I are at Manchester airport. We're stopping off for lunch and then we're making our way to the farm. Will everyone be at home this evening? Your father and I have got some news.'

'Mum! Right.' I swallowed. 'How exciting! Yes, we'll be here.'

My heart was still thumping as I put down the phone. My father hadn't visited Appleby Farm for decades. What was he up to now?

Chapter 33

By six thirty, when Mum and Dad's taxi rumbled into the farmyard, the rest of us had reached some sort of uneasy truce. By which I mean that we had all agreed to disagree.

Auntie Sue had taken my uncle off to the next village in the afternoon to visit the bungalow she'd fallen in love with and he had declared it 'not bad', which she took to mean 'perfect'. It was part of a small development and wasn't quite finished, which according to Auntie Sue made it even more appealing; they would be able to make some of the final decisions and put their own stamp on it.

Eddy had spent most of the day moping about in the tea rooms, where, between serving customers, I had had a long chat with him, confiding in him how much I really wanted to buy the farm.

'Aye, well, you'll need three-quarters of a million pounds for that, lass,' he'd replied, which more or less put paid to that idea.

And he'd confided that he had a new lady friend who lived on the coast in Morecambe. She had a fresh fish business, selling out of the back of a van, and had started calling in at the White Lion once a week. They'd struck up a romance after he'd complimented her on her potted shrimps and now she was dropping hints that she wanted him to get a Monday-to-Friday job so they could spend more time together at weekends.

'I'm thrilled for you, you dark horse!' I'd hugged him and he'd blushed and not even shoved me off – it must be love. 'That explains the new boots and the ironed jeans.'

'Yes, well, she's made me smarten up a bit.' He shrugged. 'But I wasn't going to leave Arthur in the lurch, what with his heart attack and everything. But now . . .' He puffed out his cheeks and shook his head sadly.

I nudged him sharply. 'Hey! Not that I want to stand in the way of you and your love life, obviously. But this Moorcroft,' I tapped my own chest, 'isn't ready to give up on the farm just yet.'

And then he'd gripped my hand, kissed my cheek and said anything he could do to help, I only had to ask.

So when Mum and Dad began to haul enormous suitcases (rather unnervingly) out of the boot of the taxi, everyone was in a slightly better, if apprehensive, mood. The taxi drove off and Uncle Arthur and my dad walked towards each other hesitantly. I racked my brains but I couldn't remember ever seeing them together before. I held my breath as Uncle Arthur extended a hand towards his younger brother. Dad took it and then pulled him closer and slapped him on the back.

Auntie Sue and my mum smiled at each other indulgently as they kissed each other's cheek.

My dad looked up at the farmhouse. 'It's good to be back. The place looks exactly as I remember it; it hasn't changed a bit. Our old dad would be proud of you, Arthur.'

Uncle Arthur mumbled something about that being debatable and extracted himself from Dad's grip.

Oh, God. I felt a lump swell up in my throat and didn't dare meet anyone's eye. I wrapped my arms tightly round my mum's neck instead, breathing in her familiar perfume.

'That's a lovely welcome,' laughed Mum.

I shook my head gently. 'I am so glad you're here.'

'Does that include me?' said Dad.

'Of course,' I said, kissing his cheek and rubbing my face where his bristly moustache had tickled it.

'Planning on moving in, are you?' I pointed to their luggage.

He opened his mouth to answer but Auntie Sue clapped her hands. 'Come in, come in,' she cried. 'Let's not stand on ceremony.'

Ten minutes later we were all ensconced around the kitchen table with teas and coffees. Once all the 'milk?' and 'pass the sugar' pleasantries had run their course, a palpable tension, as heavy as a storm cloud, descended over us.

'We're leaving Paris and thinking of coming back to England,' Mum blurted out, the first to cave in under the pressure. 'Rusty is retiring at last. With immediate effect.'

'Really? That's fantastic! Where in England?' I asked. *Please say nearby.* I nearly said that out loud but remembered I might not be living round here myself for much longer so I kept my mouth closed.

'Well . . .' Mum began, flashing me a nervous smile.

'Retiring? Just like that?' Auntie Sue's shoulders visibly sagged. 'Oh. We're so jealous, aren't we, Artie?'

Uncle Arthur grumbled something about chance would be a fine thing and slurped his tea noisily.

'It's not quite . . . I wouldn't . . .' My dad shifted in his seat as if his beige slacks were bothering him before admitting,

'I've been pensioned off. The apartment comes – or should I say goes? – with the job.'

'He's got a golden handshake.' Mum patted his hand gently. 'To thank him for all his hard work.'

Dad grunted and folded his arms.

'I'm chasing after a golden handshake myself.' Uncle Arthur sighed, mirroring Dad's arm-folding. 'But it's feeling more like a Judas kiss.'

'Now, now, Artie.' Auntie Sue patted *his* hand. 'Your health comes first, not the farm. This place will be the death of you.'

Mum frowned at me enquiringly across the table and I grimaced and mouthed, *Later*.

'Do you know, Arthur,' Dad said, running a hand over his bald head, 'now that I've left the bank, I feel like my entire life's work has vanished into thin air. I envy you having this place. No matter what happens, Appleby Farm will always be here. I hadn't realized until I came back how much I've missed it.'

I stared at him open-mouthed until Mum cleared her throat and looked pointedly at me. Well, *this* was new. It seemed like Dad felt the same way about the farm as I did and yet he had never ever had a good word to say about farming before now. What happened to 'British farming is a money pit' and 'you start the year with nothing and you finish the year with nothing'?

Uncle Arthur scratched his chin. 'But you couldn't wait to get away from Appleby Farm, Rusty. And you've never been back since.'

I gave my dad a stern look. 'That's true, Dad.'

'There was never a role for me here,' Dad answered morosely.

He dug a clean spoon into the sugar bowl and began

grinding the crystals against the side of the bowl. I recognized the habit: I did that myself. Shirley at the café had always been telling me off for it.

'I was always the studious one,' he added. 'You were bigger, stronger and older than me, the one Dad always shouted for when he needed help with anything. So I left.'

Uncle Arthur shook his head slowly. 'Mam was heartbroken after you left. You were always her favourite.'

'Was I?' Dad looked so dejected and my heart melted for him. And bizarrely I knew just what he meant. I'd always felt like the unwanted child; Dad had always seemed to favour Julian. Weird how history seemed to repeat itself.

'I devoted my working life to the bank.' Dad hesitated. 'In fact, I devoted *all* my life to the bank, and now what have I got to show for it, for my *life*? Nothing.'

'You've got me,' I said quietly, sliding the sugar bowl out of his reach, 'and Mum.' Technically he had Julian, too, but I didn't want to think about him at the moment.

Dad stared at me blankly for a moment and then tutted at himself. 'I'm sorry. Of course I have. And I'm fully aware that I haven't been the world's greatest dad.'

Now *I* was patting his hand.

'What I mean is . . . I went in on Friday to collect some paperwork and there was a new chap at my desk. No one even looked up. I'd been instantly replaced. And after making Paris our home, we get a letter informing us that we need to leave the apartment. Just like that.' He snapped his fingers.

Mum smiled reassuringly. 'Darling, that Paris office was tiny when you arrived. Now it's thriving. And anyway, look on this as an opportunity. A fresh start, time together. Just think – we can have a home! Our *dream* home, somewhere cosy, not some fancy rented place.'

'That's just what I said to Artie, Margo, when the herd came down with TB. This is an opportunity!' cried Auntie Sue.

At that moment Benny the cat jumped on to Mum's lap and rubbed his head against her chin, as if demonstrating the benefits of a cosy home.

Dad got up from the table and stood, hands on hips, looking out at the view of the fields through the window.

'I was so wrong about you and your dedication to the farm, Arthur. Yes, I've got money in the bank, but you've got this.' He nodded at the outside world. 'This is your legacy. While I've been absorbed in the pointless pursuit of profit, up to my eyeballs in stress, you've spent your life enjoying the simple pleasures, looking after the land, preserving our heritage for future generations.'

'Stop!' Uncle Arthur pressed his hands to his face. 'You're making me sick with all your airy-fairy good-life rubbish. You think you've cornered the market in stress? Well, you know what they say, don't judge a man until you've walked a mile in his shoes.'

'Calm down, Arthur,' Auntie Sue pleaded. 'Think of your blood pressure.'

Uncle Arthur growled, pushed his chair back from the table and stood up to face Dad.

'I've served my time as a farmer, Rusty. And yes, I've loved every minute of it, but Sue and I haven't seen the world like you.'

'Maybe not, Arthur, but when you've got scenery like this on your doorstep,' Dad sighed contentedly, 'who needs the rest of the world?'

'I'm seventy-five and I can't remember the last time we went on holiday,' snapped Uncle Arthur. 'And if I hadn't had two heart attacks, I probably wouldn't have had a day off this year. And although we've got some savings tied up, we've had the cash flow from hell this season. If it hadn't been for our Freya and you bridging the gap till we sell this spring's stock, we'd have got into even deeper debt. If you don't think that's stressful, you're a bigger idiot than I thought.'

'Now hold on a minute,' Dad chided gently, 'I think we're talking at cross-purposes here.'

Uncle Arthur jabbed a finger at my dad. 'And if *my* only chance at a golden handshake is to sell out to a big dairy outfit, then for once in my life I think I'm going to put us first and not the land. Pursue my own bit of profit, buy my wife *her* ideal home.'

'Sell?' gasped Mum.

There was a startled silence broken only by the sound of Uncle Arthur's panting. This was the moment I should have spoken up, declared my beleaguered intention to prevent Appleby Farm from falling into the hands of the intensive farming company, but before I could do so Uncle Arthur straightened up and took a deep breath.

'Yes, Margo, sell. So put that in your pipe and smoke it.'

With that he rammed his cap on his head and stormed out of the house. Auntie Sue made a mewling sound and clapped a hand over her mouth, and Mum and Dad exchanged bewildered looks.

This was awful. I had never seen my uncle so upset. Auntie Sue wasn't much better, I thought, watching as Mum tried to comfort her. I had to do something.

I joined my dad at the window. He was stroking his moustache pensively.

'Uncle Arthur's not really mad with you, Dad. He's angry at the situation he's in. He wants to secure the farm's future as well as his own and it's not proving easy.'

He nodded. 'Poor chap. He's not had an easy year. And there's me blundering in with my "lucky old you" attitude.'

He turned back to Auntie Sue and Mum. 'I'm sorry, Sue. Shall I go and find him?'

Auntie Sue looked up and shook her head. 'He'll be having a minute with the cows; he'll be all right. Don't worry, it'll blow over.'

'In that case, Dad, can I show you the tea rooms?'

His eyes met mine and he broke into a smile, the tension easing for a moment. 'I thought you'd never ask. Lead on.'

We walked across the yard slowly. I unlocked the big glass doors to the tea rooms – tricky with sweaty palms – and stood back to let him go in first.

I'd spent years pretending to myself that I wasn't bothered what my dad thought about the way I lived my life. I realized now that it was a form of self-defence. Dad's approval of the Appleby Farm Vintage Tea Rooms meant the world to me and my heart was absolutely pounding.

I held my breath as he walked around the interior in silence, shaking his head in what I hoped was wonder rather than disappointment, stopping to peer up at the window on to the spinning gallery and shooting me looks of surprise every few seconds. He was certainly thorough: he examined the bunting, the framed wallpaper, the ice-cream counter, the chalkboard menu and even went behind the serving hatch to inspect the cups and saucers that Mum had sent me.

Come on, Dad, I'm dying here.

'Well?' I blurted out finally.

'I love it,' he stated simply and then laughed. 'Your

mother said you'd done a good job. Frankly I'm stunned.'
He shook his head again. 'And to think I used to play in
this barn when I was a boy.'

'Phew!' I beamed. 'Thanks, Dad. You don't think it's too
rustic?' *Like Victoria Moon did*, I recalled bitterly.

'No!' he exclaimed. 'It's charming.'

'Look at this.' I darted over to fetch the visitors' book.
'People have left some lovely comments. It was supposed to
be for suggestions, but most customers have just left compliments.'

I was fully aware that I was showing off but I'd never
really had my father's full attention before and I was
revelling in it now that I had it.

'Sit down and I'll make you one of our special teas.'

Dad held up a hand as he took a seat at one of the tables.
'I'm swimming in tea. Have you got anything stronger?'

There were some beers tucked into the back of the fridge
left over from our opening party in August and I flipped
the lids off two bottles.

'Ah!' Dad smacked his lips appreciatively and cast an
eye over the tea rooms. 'Do you know, you might be able
to reproduce this venue elsewhere? Have you thought of
opening more?'

I hadn't. It was a damn good idea, though. 'Do you really
think so?'

He swigged his beer and nodded. 'You could propose it
to other farms.'

I shuddered. 'It's this farm I'm bothered about, Dad.'

Dad frowned. 'Mmm. I couldn't help noticing that we
seemed to have walked in on a bit of an atmosphere.'

'Understatement.' I quirked one eyebrow.

I filled him in on what had been happening at the farm,
about Julian's relentless quest to push Uncle Arthur into

selling Appleby Farm and the proposals for an intensive dairy farm.

'Good God.' Dad blinked at me. 'Is Julian putting pressure on the old boy?'

I puffed out my cheeks. 'Massively so. I think Uncle Arthur feels like if he turns down Julian's offer, he might never get another and Auntie Sue is desperate for him to ease up and retire.'

Dad got up, walked to the glass doors and stared out at the view, just as he had in the kitchen. 'I can't imagine all these lovely old buildings being replaced by industrial units for the sake of profit. That would be a travesty.'

'Absolutely,' I agreed.

I could hardly believe it: just as the blinkers were falling from my father's eyes about the beauty of Appleby Farm, Uncle Arthur was preparing to throw in the towel. I cleared away the empty bottles, walked over to Dad and together we left the tea rooms.

'I know that farming has to move on. It's an industry like any other and you can't hold back progress, blah, blah, blah, but . . .' I shrugged. 'Surely there's a halfway house? A way of farming that's still true to the traditional way of doing things?'

Dad's shoulder brushed against mine as we headed by unspoken agreement towards the orchard. It was the closest father and daughter moment we'd ever shared and my knees had gone a bit wobbly.

'Appleby Farm means a lot to you, doesn't it?' said Dad.

I swallowed and nodded.

'What would you like to happen to the farm?' He watched me closely, waiting for an answer. He was genuinely interested in my opinion, I realized, and I felt my face heat up with pride.

'I've got some ideas,' I said, crossing my fingers behind my back and hoping he didn't ask to hear them this instant.

We'd reached the orchard and Dad picked us an apple each from the nearest tree. I bit into mine; it was sweet and juicy and I remembered my idea of making cider. I made a mental note to look into it.

'This retirement thing has taken me by surprise somewhat and I must confess I'm dreading it. I wonder . . .' He tapped his chin. 'How about this? If you can come up a viable plan to run the farm profitably, I'll finance it.'

Go into business together? I hadn't seen that one coming. *Say something, Freya.*

'Coolio.' I groaned inwardly. *Coolio?* Just what every businessman wants to hear.

'Your mum and I are staying at the Gilpin Hotel this week, so we'll have plenty of time to talk. Does that sound like a plan?'

I closed the gap between us with one step and hugged him tightly.

'Thanks, Dad.'

Chapter 34

I was on a massive high when I waved off Mum and Dad. After leaving me in the orchard, Dad had gone off to find his brother and the two of them had disappeared to the White Lion to clear the air. They had returned several pints later, arms round shoulders, with a renewed respect for each other, which was so heartwarming to see.

It was going to be wonderful having them in Cumbria for the week and Mum had already promised to come and help in the tea rooms as much as she could. But what had warmed my soul more than anything was that Dad had listened to me – really listened. For the first time in my life I felt as though he saw my potential and valued my opinion, just like Auntie Sue and Uncle Arthur had always done. We might never see eye to eye completely but I definitely felt closer to him already. And it felt amazing.

So amazing, in fact, that I had too much energy for my body. My brain was whirring and I was beside myself with enthusiasm to finally pin down a proper, grown-up business plan that Dad could buy in to.

I decided to saddle up Skye and take her out for a ride to clear my head. On my way to the stables I spotted a familiar figure in the orchard, halfway up a tree, trying to reach a big red apple.

'Lizzie!' I bowled up to her, waving my arms in the air.

'What's up with you, matey?' She laughed and jumped down empty-handed. 'Got gnats in your knickers? What's new?'

I hugged her, noticing her jodhpurs and fleece. 'Loads! How long have you got?'

'Five minutes. I'm just picking an apple for me and Skye and then we're going for a hack through the woods before it gets dark.'

'Oh no! I was going to take her out. Please let me, Lizzie. I need to get off the farm for a bit, I'm desperate.'

She rolled her eyes playfully. 'Go on, then. But I'm so bored. Bill has given me the night off because his daughter's back from her gap year and she wants to work behind the bar tonight. I think she wants a permanent job, you know. So if you were still thinking about a manager for the tea rooms . . . ?' She eyed me hopefully before tweaking a smaller apple from a lower branch and biting into it.

I'd love Lizzie to work for me. She was a grafter, great with people and she already *did* work for me for free, but I couldn't offer her a job. Not yet. But before I had chance to tell her about my conversation with Dad, she leaped up in the air, startling me.

'Oh, Freya! I cannot *believe* I nearly forgot this nugget of news. Guess what.'

'Spray that again,' I said, wiping apple juice from my face.

'Oops, soz!' She giggled. 'Victoria has got the sack from Radio Lakeland. She's managed to get her old job back at Liver FM. God knows how. And she's going back to Liverpool! She, of course, is claiming that her job on Radio Lakeland was only a six-month secondment and that she couldn't wait to leave, but I heard that she got the boot after she put her foot in it good and proper with Miss Cumbria, live on air.'

I grabbed hold of Lizzie's hands and we did a little celebratory jig. 'That's fantastic! I know she's your sister, Lizzie, but . . .'

She shrugged. 'No worries. Glad to see the back of her. Apparently she announced that after the next piece of music, the beautiful Miss Cumbria would be joining her in the studio. Then she played the track but forgot to turn off her microphone and broadcast herself declaring that Miss Cumbria had hands and feet the size of a shire horse and she wouldn't be surprised if underneath all that make-up she was actually a man.'

'I suppose she had to leave.' I grinned. 'She must have run out of people to insult!'

'Mmm,' Lizzie huffed. 'I just hope people don't think that I'm like my sister.'

I hugged her. 'Don't be daft. Everyone loves you.'

Seriously, what was it with siblings? Lizzie was warm, kind, fun and full of empathy, whereas Victoria was . . . not. And Julian and I? We might share DNA but that was where it began and ended. Thank goodness.

'I know I shouldn't be happy about other people's misfortunes,' I said, 'but I can't say I'll miss her.' A thought struck me suddenly. 'What about Harry?'

Lizzie paused from munching her apple and smiled. 'I saw him last night in the village. He said he hadn't wanted to say too much, because he likes me, obvs.' She batted her eyelashes. 'But apparently she was getting to be a bit of a stalker, turning up at his house and crying all over him, saying that he was the only one who understood her and she had no one else to talk to.'

I narrowed my eyes. 'According to Victoria, they've been out to dinner and I've seen them together with my own eyes getting very cosy on the doorstep of Willow Farm.'

Lizzie lifted a shoulder. 'Perhaps that was just one of the times she turned up at his house?'

My heart skipped unexpectedly. Perhaps that was true. Maybe I'd been seeing more than there was to see?

'Do you know what? If you really don't mind me borrowing Skye, I might ride over there. Just say hi.'

'Just say hi?' Lizzie raised a perfectly arched eyebrow. 'You fancy him, don't you?'

'No.' Did my voice just jump an octave? I coughed discreetly and tried again. 'He's just . . . I don't know. I need someone to bounce farmy-type ideas off and he's a good listener. And very comforting.'

Put like that I almost believed it myself.

Lizzie stared at me, a smile tweaking her lips upwards. 'Yeah, right. *Apple pie* is comforting,' she pointed out. 'If we're talking desserts, Harry Graythwaite is more like tiramisu: dreamy and delicious, deep and dangerously potent, buff and—'

'Anyway,' I interrupted hurriedly, feeling a little hot under the collar, 'can I take Skye? It'll look more natural if I just turn up on a horse.'

'So you *do* fancy him?'

I lifted one shoulder non-committally and aimed a half-hearted kick at a fallen apple.

'Nah, I don't mind. I might make an apple pie instead,' said Lizzie, pulling a plastic bag out of her fleece pocket. She selected a few healthy-looking windfalls off the ground. 'Ross is home at the weekend and . . .'

'He needs comforting?' I finished for her.

'Tiramisuuuu,' she cooed after me as I charged off to the stables to fetch the horse.

Willow Farm had been in the Graythwaite family even longer than Appleby Farm has been in ours. It was slightly further from the centre of Lovedale along the valley and I decided to go the cross-country route, through the fields and up and over Knots Hill.

Harry's dad had been a sheep farmer before he'd retired and I recalled their fields being dotted with white blobs all year round. I also remembered one fantastic snowy February school holiday when Harry and I had been allowed to stay up all up night to watch the lambs being born. We'd then bottle-fed two little rejected lambs and I'd really felt part of something special that night. Now the fields were green and blobless, and it suddenly dawned on me that I hadn't got a clue what sort of farmer Harry was.

As Skye and I approached the farmhouse along the bridleway, I started to get a bit shivery. Not sure why, though. If anyone was going to understand my burning desire to keep Appleby Farm in the family it would be Harry.

The path I was on led me straight through the farm buildings. I was surrounded on both sides by large open sheds, some stone and slate, and some built from new bricks with corrugated metal roofs. They were all full of cream and bluey-grey coloured cows.

A flock of hens scattered at the sound of Skye's hooves on the yard but apart from that there was no one about, although I could hear a dog barking inside somewhere. I climbed down off Skye, attached her reins loosely to a gate-post and looked out across the fields.

I opened my mouth to shout hello but closed it again;

the view across the valley back towards Appleby Farm completely captivated me. It was a magical sight. Low cloud either side of the valley smudged the lines of the hills, the greens and browns of the fields, the russet leaves on the trees and tiny pops of colour from distant buildings all painted the perfect autumnal scene.

I stepped up on to the bottom bar of the wooden gate, leaned my chin on my forearms and just drank it in. *Glorious.*

Skye shuffled restlessly. Without turning, I reached a hand up to her nose to calm her and my fingers touched more fingers.

I yelped, whirled round, snatched my hand back and jumped down off the gate all within a second.

'Jesus!' I panted. 'Where the hell did you appear from?'

Harry's eyes twinkled. 'Says the girl creeping through my farmyard unannounced.'

In his olive-green waxed jacket, jeans and tall welling-tons he looked perfectly suited to his surroundings in a hot, masculine, sexy sort of way.

Did I just think the word 'sexy'? I felt my face heat up.

'Sorry, I should have called first. Spur-of-the-moment thing.'

He raised his eyebrows. 'I'm only joking. It's lovely to see you. And I didn't mean to make you jump. You looked so peaceful there enjoying the view. I was enjoying it myself actually.'

He chuckled and I wasn't sure whether he meant the landscape or me standing on a gate sticking my bottom out.

'I never tire of that view,' he said, nodding towards the fields. 'I'm a lucky man, I know.'

Not my bottom, then. Shame. *Floozy.*

I cleared my throat. 'I was just thinking to myself how

glorious it is. Fields as far as the eye can see. How long before it all gets concreted over in the name of progress?'

Harry pretended to recoil in horror. 'Hey, I don't know who's been giving us modern farmers a bad name but progress doesn't have to be negative, you know. It's all about finding your niche.'

'Now niches, I like the sound of,' I beamed. A niche, in fact, was what I was after myself.

'Come on, I'll show you round.' He produced a carrot out of his jacket pocket and fed it to the horse.

'Wow. Cool trick. Have you got anything in there for me?' I laughed, eyeing up his pocket.

What am I saying?

He gave me a sideways glance and laughed softly to himself. 'Nothing else in here, I'm afraid,' he said, patting down his pockets, 'but I can show you my piglets?'

Now everything sounded rude.

'Piglets?' I snorted.

Harry chuckled. 'Come on.'

He led me through the farmyard and past the chickens.

'I only keep about six hens,' he said, 'not like at Appleby Farm. But I like to see them pecking round the yard. A farm's not a farm without them.'

I told him about the hen that lays an egg in the dog kennel for Madge every day and we were both laughing when we reached a field with three large huts in it. Three fat black sows were snuffling around, surrounded by little piglets. It was difficult to be exact because they were so wriggly, but I counted at least eighteen little ones.

'They're lovely! Are any of these the ones born on the day the tea rooms opened?' I looked sideways at him. 'The ones you told Victoria about?'

'Good memory.' Harry nudged me in the ribs. 'Yes, these

are my Berkshire pigs. One of my niches. I've got a boar, too; he's got his own sty down past the cattle.'

I could hear the pride in his voice and had to stop myself from hugging him. He hadn't reacted at all when I said Victoria's name, but I still had to be sure.

I took a breath. 'Harry, Victoria mentioned that you went to a restaurant with her? Is that true? Were the two of you . . . seeing each other?'

'God, no!' He quirked his eyebrow. 'I saw her at a restaurant opening in Kendal once. Remember my mate Tom from Rigg Farm?'

I nodded, feeling stupid and relieved already.

'He gets invited to all those sorts of things and we've been at a loose end in the evenings this summer so I went with him. She was there for the radio station, I think.'

'Loose end?'

One of the sows trotted over to Harry and he bent over the wall to scratch behind her ears.

'Normally The Almanacs rehearse once a week and play a gig every couple of weeks but Steve, the guitarist, wanted to take a year out to enjoy fatherhood; Tom's the lead singer.'

'And you whistle along, presumably.' I giggled.

'Ha ha, very funny.'

I watched him make a fuss of the pig and chunter to her under his breath. I grinned.

'It's a bit different to the flock of sheep your dad had,' I said.

'I'm still finding my feet, really, but I wanted to do something different. My plan is to invest in more rare breeds. A few years ago there were only a handful of Berkshires in the entire country. If they died out it would be a catastrophe.'

'Well, it looks like these three girls have added to their numbers.' I smiled.

Harry nodded earnestly and leaned a little closer. 'It might sound a bit soft – and I wouldn't repeat this to my bank manager – but I feel like a guardian; not just of the land but of the livestock, too. And I'm definitely going to breed pedigree beef next year, like Arthur. As soon as his bull gets the all-clear, I'm going to make your uncle an offer for him.'

I inhaled his scent: wax jacket, fresh air and autumn leaves. Who knew that particular combo could smell so intoxicating.

'Thanks, Harry.' I sighed. 'I know you could buy a bull now instead of waiting for Dexter to become available. I do appreciate it, you know.'

He shrugged. 'Farmers help each other out; it's the way it's always worked. And Arthur will be glad to know his prize bull has gone to a good home.'

You are so lovely, was what I thought, gazing up at him.

'You're like Noah,' I said breathily, 'looking after the animals.'

He threw his head back and laughed. It was such a genuine, infectious laugh that I joined in, too.

'Freya Moorcroft,' he shook his head, 'no one has ever made me smile as much as you. You're bonkers, you know that.'

'Me? Thanks. I think.' I grinned back at him and then wrinkled my nose at the smell. 'Can we move away now, please? I thought cow manure was bad but these bad boys stink.'

'Don't listen, pigs, I think you smell lovely,' called Harry. 'Let's walk past the cattle, then, if the lady prefers cow muck.'

We set off towards the cowsheds at a slow pace, him humming and me wondering when I should broach my plans for Appleby Farm. It was different for him, I thought. It had always been on the cards for him to be a farmer; he'd been learning what to do since he was little. I was still playing catch-up.

'You've always known what you've wanted out of life, haven't you?' I said, breaking the silence. I had a sudden sharp image of the two of us riding in the tractor, him at the wheel, aged about twelve, telling me how he was going to be a farmer just like his dad.

Harry nodded and smiled, his brown eyes crinkling at the corners.

I touched his arm lightly. 'I'm glad you got your dream. I'm a tad envious, to be honest. You've always completely belonged here, whereas I've drifted from place to place, a bit rudderless.'

Although right at this moment I felt pretty at home. With Harry.

He stopped walking, looked down at his feet and shook his head. 'And I envy you your freedom. You're right. This is the life I chose, the life I wanted, and while I wouldn't swap it for the world, I didn't actually have any choice in the matter. Sometimes . . .' He lifted his eyes to mine and I felt my heart race. 'Well, sometimes it feels a bit small. But ever since you came back you've made me wonder. What if?'

My breath caught in my throat. I held his gaze and waited. What if what?

'What if I'd done some of the things you've done with your life – travelled the world, done all sorts of jobs, and met hundreds of people? I know that Cumbria will always be my home, but sometimes I feel trapped. Do you know, I haven't had a holiday in five years? There never seems to be the right time or the right person to go with me.'

'Oh, Harry, come travelling with me,' I blurted.

It was the saddest thing I'd ever heard and reminded me so much of something Uncle Arthur had said. I took a tiny step towards him, wrapped my arms round his neck and hugged him. And for a second or two he hugged me back.

I shut my eyes and wondered, *What if? What if I kiss him now? What would he do?* Was I just an old mate to him, or could I be something more? My heart was thundering in my chest and being so close to him was making me feel light-headed.

Harry took a step back, looked straight into my eyes and for one heart-stopping moment I thought he was going to kiss me. He stroked my face with the back of his finger and my stomach fluttered at his touch.

'And that's exactly it, Freya,' he said flatly. 'You'll be off again soon on another adventure; the next stop on your world tour. And I'll still be here, left behind.'

He smiled at me sadly – *sadly* – which had to be a positive sign, right? Particularly as I had no intention of leaving.

'Ha! Funny you should say that. I am at the start of a new adventure. But this time it's a bit different. I've got plans, Harry, big plans.' I gave him a sparkly smile but he sighed, a shadow passed across his face, and he turned away. And then suddenly he shook himself and carried on as if he hadn't heard me.

'I suppose I'm on my own adventure, too,' he said breezily, as if the moment that was still making my heart pound hadn't happened. He nodded in the direction of the nearest cattle shed and we began to walk again.

'So you're a beef farmer, too?' I asked, as we came to a halt and a group of inquisitive cows started jostling for position to get a good look at us.

'We finish beef here, rather than breed,' said Harry, patting the neck of the nearest animal. 'That means we buy in cattle and keep them for around four months until they are ready for the table. During that time each animal is individually looked after, they're weighed regularly and their diets are designed to produce the healthiest animals possible. I'm building a good reputation.'

'Good for you,' I said, giving him my brightest smile. And I *was* impressed; I was just more interested in the finger-face-stroking business, which had made my legs tremble.

'But there's other exciting stuff, too,' he said, leading me back along the yard towards Skye. 'We're trying willow coppicing next year.'

'Oh, for biofuels?' I asked, glancing sideways at his strong profile. How glad was I that I'd started reading Uncle Arthur's old farming magazines?

I was rewarded by seeing Harry's face light up and he stopped in his tracks. 'Exactly. It's a long-term project but I'm hoping it could be the start of something big for us. Or it would be if I could get my hands on some more land.'

'What do you mean?'

'I still need fields to grow food for my livestock, so I've got limited space.'

Oh my God. My entire body began to tingle.

I whirled round to face him. All of a sudden my mind started to race. So this was it. This was it!

'Freya?' He stared at me intently. 'Are you all right?'

I started to laugh. An excited, jackpot sort of laugh. The missing piece of my puzzle was standing right here in front of me with his tousled hair, brown eyes and just the right amount of stubble to be sexy without being beardy.

'Harry.' I grabbed his hands.

'Yes.' He stared at me with a quizzical smile.

'I could kiss you.' I twinkled my eyes at him. It was a figure of speech, but deep down I really, really meant it. There was nothing I'd rather do. Fact. God knows what he was going to say to that. Poor chap.

The smile vanished from his face and he gazed at me earnestly. 'Go for it.'

Which took me completely by surprise.

Go for it.

I inched forward, threaded my hands through his hair and pulled him towards me, arching my back to bring our bodies nearer together.

'I will, then,' I said softly.

I stared into the eyes of the man I'd known as a boy, but there was nothing childish about his expression now. His eyes were full of a fierce emotion that stole my breath and made my heart race.

Harry groaned. 'Freya,' he whispered as his arms circled my body and drew me against him.

This felt so right, I realized, as if it was always meant to be, as if even though we had parted as friends ten years ago I had carried him in my heart. Maybe I'd needed to go away to understand how much I wanted to be here. My heart wasn't just bursting with love for Lovedale and Appleby Farm, but for Harry too.

I was going to do it.

My lips finally reached his and for the tiniest moment we were kissing.

But as suddenly as it had started the kiss ended. Harry pulled away and loosened his grip on my waist, leaving me breathless and dizzy.

'Freya, this is not . . . I can't do this.' He gazed down at me and the torment in his eyes made my stomach churn with fear.

'What? Harry, what's wrong?' I lowered my hands from his neck and laid them on his chest. 'What is it?'

'I'm sorry.' His expression had changed, as though a door had slammed in his brain. He cupped my chin in his hand and stroked his thumb against my cheek. 'I can't do this.'

'Harry, why is kissing me so terrible?' Tears of humiliation began to threaten and I blinked them away.

'You mean too much to me. There's too much to lose.' He took a step backwards and his arms fell loosely to his side. 'Lovedale, the farm, me . . . it'll never be enough for you.'

'That's so not true, I'm not going anywhere,' I gasped, trying to get a handle on what was happening. My head was churning with emotions and my body felt hollow, as if my heart had been scooped away.

He looked away into the distance and then back at me, shaking his head sadly. 'There's nothing to keep you here if the farm is sold. You said so yourself. And I can't be just . . . a bit of fun.'

My face turned scarlet. 'Harry, you are far more important to me than that.'

'And you are to me,' he said.

He reached a hand out to stroke my cheek and we stared at each other, my heart pounding with disappointment.

'You'd better get back; it's getting dark.' His voice was low and soft.

I nodded, staring into his eyes, looking for an explanation for his sudden mood swing. But no matter how hard I tried, I couldn't understand what had just happened.

I mounted Skye and he untied the reins from the gatepost and handed them to me.

'You're probably the best friend I ever had, you know,' he said with a smile.

So that was it. I was destined never to be more than Harry's friend. I swallowed the lump in my throat and pasted on a bright smile. 'Me too.'

Chapter 35

Auntie Sue was giving me a hand in the tea rooms the next morning. There were only two tables of customers, which was just as well: I hadn't had much sleep because I had been mulling over my business plans and of course my humiliation at Willow Farm and I kept getting people's orders wrong. Somehow someone had ended up with a bowl of ketchup with their scone instead of strawberry jam and I'd filled a teapot with hot milk by accident.

Auntie Sue tutted at me. 'You need a break. I heard you in the office last night until God knows what time. Were you working on your business plan for your dad?'

'Yes,' I said, exhaling morosely. 'Sorry if I disturbed you.'

She pinched my cheek just as she used to do when I was small. 'Don't talk nonsense, Freya, you're an angel.'

She tucked my arm through hers and led me to the far table nearest the doors. 'Sit yourself down, lass, and I'll bring you a cuppa.'

I sipped at my tea, leaving my aunt to chat to our guests, and surveyed my little venture with a critical eye. Appleby Farm Vintage Tea Rooms was looking even more vintage-y these days. We'd received a few 'thank you' notes from customers who'd made the effort to send retro cards. I'd tucked them into a lovely old padded noticeboard criss-crossed in satin ribbon that I'd found in a junk shop. And behind the cash desk, I'd hung some old black-and-white photos of the farm from the 1940s, all in different types of frames to give the display an eclectic look.

I was just wondering if Auntie Sue would let me have the old pine dresser to fill a bare corner when Lizzie came in, poured a cup of tea and helped herself to a meringue – our new line. They were huge, crunchy and chewy, and had delicious chunks of pistachios in them. Free tea and cake was Lizzie's perk for being my unpaid waitress.

She sat opposite me and bit straight into her meringue, closing her eyes as it melted on her tongue. 'If your auntie stops making these when she retires I'll camp outside her door and sob.'

'So will I,' I said, helping myself to a piece off her plate. Finding another cake baker was on my to-do list. I could still knock up a batch of decent scones, but I didn't have the time or skill for much else.

Lizzie stared at me. 'I feel as grumpy as you look.'

Great. If my poor customer service didn't put the punters off, my miserable face would. I attempted a smile.

'Better?'

Lizzie raised a shoulder half-heartedly. 'Bill's daughter Natalie has rearranged all the fruit juices in the fridge. I can't find a thing now. She says it looks prettier by colour instead of by brand. I think she's trying to psych me out so I'll leave. Took me ages to find the Appletiser this morning.' She paused to slurp her tea. 'So did you get any tiramisu last night?'

I glanced over to Auntie Sue; she was giving directions to the steam railway to a customer.

'I got the tiniest taste,' I hissed, flashing Lizzie a keep-your-voice-down stare.

Her mouth formed a perfect O as she abandoned her meringue and clapped her fingertips together silently. 'As in actual kissing action?'

I nodded, a smile hovering at my lips momentarily. Despite how badly it ended, I couldn't help recalling what a magical moment it had been.

Lizzie pulled her bottom lip between her teeth. 'I knew it! This is going to be ace. Me and Ross, you and—' She stopped, noticing my fed-up face. 'What?'

'He pushed me away. Said he couldn't do it and that I didn't understand.'

Lizzie's face fell. 'Eh?'

'One kiss, which barely even got going, and then he sent me home. Please don't be nice, Lizzie, or I might cry.'

She nodded, wide-eyed, and drank her tea without saying a word.

I shrugged helplessly. 'Maybe some things are better left in the past. Perhaps Harry thinks that those golden days of childhood when we raced to the little shop with a pound and came back weighed down with sweets were too good to mess with. Perhaps he's right.'

'Rubbish. You two are spot on for each other. It doesn't make any sense at all.' Lizzie tapped her cheek with her finger pensively. 'And I can't believe you were buying sweets at eighteen. What about the last holiday you spent here? What did you do then?'

Funny she should have asked that. I'd been going over that myself in bed last night. Things had changed between us that summer. Harry had been getting ready to leave Lovedale for university and I was planning my gap year. He'd asked me when I'd be back and I'd said not until I'd seen the world, which seemed to put him in a dark mood that I hadn't been able to shake him out of. Last night he'd mentioned something about feeling trapped at the farm and he seemed convinced that I would be leaving again at the first opportunity. He didn't seem to appreciate that leaving Appleby Farm would break my heart.

'You're right,' I smiled, 'we were regulars at the White Lion by then and I'd swapped the sweets for cider. Anyway, I've got to move on and put last night's rejection down to experience. There's a good chance we could be working together in the future, so maybe it's best if we stay just friends or things could get messy.'

Lizzie gazed at me, lips pursed, and I could almost hear her brain clunking away.

I put on what I hoped was my brave face and passed her the menu to change the subject.

'Now, what do you think we could add to this?'

'Oh, now,' she wriggled in her seat, 'I'm so glad you asked. Fresh crêpes. You could get one of those crêpe pans. Perfect to serve with the ice cream. And a children's menu. I know you do cakes but,' she raised her eyebrows and pulled a cute face, 'imagine tiny little fairy cakes and biscuits and sandwiches.'

I nodded. 'Two good ideas.'

'Really?' She sat up tall. 'Do I get the job?'

'Yes.' I laughed. 'If there is a job, it's yours.' But my words were muffled because she'd dived across the table and was squeezing the living daylights out of me.

'You're looking better,' Auntie Sue beamed, collecting our empty plates and cups. 'Are things coming together a bit for you now, Freya?'

'Fingers crossed, Auntie Sue,' I said, getting to my feet. 'I just have one phone call to make.'

*

Five minutes later I settled myself down at my desk and dialled the number that I knew off by heart.

He answered almost immediately.

'Willow Farm?'

'Harry, it's Freya.' My voice trembled with anticipation and I ran my tongue over my teeth.

There was a slight pause on the line and then we both said at once, 'About last night . . .'

'Please,' I said hurriedly, 'let me go first.'

'OK,' he chuckled.

I pressed the phone to my ear and I could hear him breathing. And waiting.

'Harry, I just want to say that I'm deeply embarrassed about my behaviour last night and I promise sincerely that it will never happen again.'

'Freya, there's no need—'

'Yes, Harry, there is. Because I want our farms to work together.'

'Oh?'

'On your biofuels project. And for that to happen there needs to be no awkward feelings between us, OK?'

He let out a long breath. 'Of course.'

'Good,' I said with a shaky laugh. 'Right, now that that's cleared up, I think I may have a solution to your land shortage.'

'Really? *You* have a solution?'

'Don't sound so surprised,' I laughed. 'Are you free at seven thirty tomorrow evening?'

I held my breath.

'I am.'

'Excellent.' I exhaled loudly. 'Can you come to Appleby Farm then and I'll explain everything? And while you're on the line, do you think The Almanacs would play at Tilly and Aidan's wedding on December the twentieth?'

He laughed. 'You are full of surprises, Freya. I'll check with the others, but I don't see why not. It's about time Steve's paternity leave came to an end.'

'Yay! See you tomorrow.'

I put the phone down and pressed a hand to calm the butterflies in my stomach.

Two birds. One stone. Go, me.

I'm normally such a carefree sort of person; I breeze through life with a smile, a shrug and barely a backwards glance. But now I looked down at my hands – shaking like leaves.

It's because you care, said a little voice.

I swallowed and looked at the expectant faces gathered round the farmhouse table. I did care. More than I'd ever cared about anything in my life. I'd come a long way since recklessly declaring that I'd save the farm back in the spring. But I'd meant it then and I was still determined to do it now. I just hoped my family liked my ideas . . .

It was seven o'clock, the remains of a chicken pie had been cleared and replaced with a tray of coffee and a box of after-dinner chocolate mints. I had set up my laptop at the head of the table, pages of hastily scribbled notes at my side. Auntie Sue and Uncle Arthur sat on one side, Mum and Dad on the other.

'Thank you, everyone, for coming,' I said nervously. Which was a bit ridiculous seeing as fifty per cent of my audience lived here. Blimey, it was a good job this wasn't *Dragons' Den.* My palms were sweaty, my face had already gone pink and I hadn't even started yet.

Mum beamed at me encouragingly. She looked different

this evening. Her hair was in loose waves, she was wearing a pink soft-cotton shirt and jeans, and she looked more relaxed than I'd ever seen her. Dad didn't look quite so sergeant-major-ish either. They sat squished up together, holding hands like teenagers. Must be something in the air.

Uncle Arthur popped a chocolate into his mouth and put his hand up. Auntie Sue slid the box over towards my dad out of her husband's reach.

I pointed at him. 'Yes, Uncle Arthur?'

He chuckled. 'Thanks for everything you've done this year, love. But I don't want you to feel responsible for what happens to us and the farm.'

He paused to reach out for the chocolate box again, but withdrew his hand under Auntie Sue's reproachful, beady-eyed glare.

'I blame myself,' he continued. 'Filling your head with fanciful notions of the farm being a gift, and what not. But I'm an old man now. I have to accept that things are done differently these days.'

'Modern farming doesn't have to be so different,' I said. 'Progress needn't mean losing our link to the past.' I thought of Harry last night and how he felt he was a guardian of the land, a twenty-first-century Noah. I felt my chest tighten with sadness and then remembered that he would be here in a few minutes and I really should get a move on.

I took a deep breath. 'Now, hear me out and please keep questions until the end.'

I'd laboured over this presentation, deliberated over each word and injected, I hoped, the right balance of business strategy for Dad and my deep love of the farm for my aunt and uncle. I'd hesitated over announcing my plans *en masse*, but at the end of the day, the farm and my future plans for it were a family affair and I wanted everyone to approve.

'Appleby Farm,' I began, making sure I made eye contact with each one of them in turn, 'is the most old-fashioned place I know. It probably looks the same now as it did two hundred years ago. Most of the equipment belongs in a museum, there are tiles missing off every roof and the shepherd's huts out in those fields have more holes in them than Swiss cheese.'

My family members were silent; I think it was a mixture of indignation, intrigue and interest.

'So how best to bring it into the twenty-first century? Well, I'll tell you.'

I stopped talking, tapped on the keyboard of my laptop and the screen filled with the name of my new business: Appleby Farm Vintage Company.

'We leave it exactly how it is,' I announced.

'Oh, darling!' sighed Mum, her hand fluttering to her pearls. 'I love it already.'

Dad patted her knee. 'Calm down, Margo,' he muttered. 'I can't see how doing nothing is going to achieve much.'

I ignored him.

'I've known nothing but love here at Appleby Farm and that's thanks to you two.'

Auntie Sue beamed at me and pushed the chocolates back to Uncle Arthur.

'And at the risk of sounding a little bit cheesy, my plan involves sharing that love with others.'

Dad tugged his moustache sceptically.

'Don't worry, Dad,' I said, 'the Appleby Farm Vintage Company has three objectives at its heart: keep the farm in the Moorcroft family; help Auntie Sue and Uncle Arthur retire in comfort; and diversify to keep the farm profitable, embrace progress and respect its heritage. So how do I do that . . . ?'

I explained how my new company would have four divisions: hospitality (which at the moment was just the tea rooms), holidays, food and drink and, finally, my pièce de résistance: weddings.

'What sort of food and drink?' asked Dad.

'Dad,' I tutted, 'questions at the end.'

'Sorry,' replied Dad, looking suitably chastised.

I told them about my idea to develop the ice-cream brand and find stockists throughout the Lake District, and my (admittedly slightly whacky) plan to make cider. I reckoned we could make at least twenty gallons this year alone. I told them about Rigg Farm and their woodland yurts and how successful they were at attracting corporate bookings.

'We are going to renovate the shepherd's huts and turn them into holiday accommodation, and not just with our two huts. Harry has got two we can have and eventually I'm going to buy a few more and fill a whole field with them. Imagine "Back to Basics" farm holidays. Dad's banking contacts would love it!'

I explained how I'd convert the old dairy into retail space, expand the vegetable garden to grow produce to sell, and change the honesty box into a proper farm shop.

'Weddings?' grunted Uncle Arthur. 'And that wasn't a proper question so don't tell me off.'

I nodded excitedly. This was my favourite bit; I really wanted them to like this idea. 'According to a recent survey – of Lizzie's newly engaged mates, no need to go into detail – nearly seventy per cent of brides-to-be are considering a vintage farm wedding for next year. It's a booming industry.'

'Really?' said Dad, hoiking a still dubious eyebrow. 'Always good to join a new market early on.'

'And we're holding our first wedding here in December

383

for Tilly and Aidan, so we'll have lots of photos for the brochure and website. And I also want to get my hands on a carriage and my own horse, so we can offer vintage transport to the church. Ooh, they could use Bobby too, I hadn't thought of that!'

I jotted myself a note before I forgot.

'But the point is,' I said, jabbing my finger on the table, 'it will all look the same, it will still have its quirky charm, it will still be Appleby Farm. If future generations of Moorcrofts want to be dairy or beef or sheep farmers, they can. It will all still be here.'

Mum, who had been nodding throughout my entire presentation, gave a polite cough. 'Darling, it all sounds wonderful, but what about you? It sounds like a huge business empire to me. There won't *be* any future Moorcrofts if you're not careful.'

Chance would be a fine thing.

'Mum, when I'm ready to settle down, you'll be the first to know.'

'Will I?' she beamed. 'Oh.'

We shared a secret smile. She and I had come a long way this year. Auntie Sue caught my eye, too, and gave me an approving wink.

Eddy had his own section in my presentation: I proposed that we offered him the job as farm manager to oversee the maintenance of the land and buildings, work on the shepherd's huts and hopefully set us up with a cider press.

The animals had a mention too: the pets, Benny, Björn and Madge, would of course move with my uncle and aunt, but I wanted to keep the Jersey cows and learn how to look after them myself. I loved them as much as Auntie Sue did and needed their milk for ice cream. And I wanted to keep the hens. A farm's not a farm without hens, I said, echoing Harry's words from last night.

Auntie Sue was delighted. 'That's a relief, lass. There's only room for one or two chickens at that bungalow and certainly no cows.'

'I didn't know you wanted a bungalow?' teased Uncle Arthur. 'Why didn't you say?'

She cuffed him round the ear.

'I'm going to keep Kim but sell Kanye,' I announced, 'and as soon as we've got the all-clear from the vet, Uncle Arthur, I think we should sell the beef herd to give you a bit of a nest egg. Ooh and by the way, Harry definitely wants Dexter.'

Uncle Arthur sighed. Our eyes met and I faltered. Here I was blazing through his farm like a tornado. Was all this a step too far? He reached out and squeezed my hand. 'Carry on, lass,' he mumbled.

'Talking of money, Freya?' said Dad.

I swallowed. 'Yep. Just coming to that.'

This was where my whole plan could come crashing down round my ears. I'd made some massive assumptions. I just hoped I'd got it right. I looked at my watch: seven twenty-nine. Harry would be here any time now.

'Mum, Dad, how would you like to live at the farm?' I held my breath.

'Good gracious!' Dad exclaimed.

The pair of them blinked like bears coming out of a cave into sunlight. Which, frankly, was better than I'd expected. These were people who'd lived a life of opulence abroad for twenty-five years. Appleby Farm was a lot of things, but none of them was associated with luxury.

At that moment the phone began to ring.

'Damn it, just as things were getting interesting,' Auntie

Sue groaned, hobbling off on her arthritic knee to the office.

There was a knock at the door and I hurried towards it, leaving my parents to stare at each other with bewildered expressions.

I opened the door and there was Harry, a breath of fresh air, full of vitality and curiosity, in jeans and a T-shirt despite the cool autumn evening. My heart hammered as I searched his eyes for traces of our awkward encounter at Willow Farm, but there was nothing to see except warmth.

'Not late, am I?' he said, brushing his lips against my cheek.

'Perfect timing, actually.' I ushered him to the kitchen table where he shook hands with the men and kissed my mum. 'I've just asked Mum and Dad if they'd consider living here.'

I looked at my parents' faces. 'Just for a few years – say, five. Until I can afford to buy it myself. If you bought the farmhouse and buildings and twenty acres—'

'Only twenty?' began my uncle, until I held up a finger to shut him up.

'I reckon that will be plenty for my business. But this is where Harry comes in.'

Harry leaned his forearms on the table and nodded. 'I've got plans for expansion and the most cost-effective way to do that is locally. Freya thought that you might be able to help me out.'

'Do you see, Uncle Arthur?' I said, giving his shoulders a hug. 'You can rent the rest of the land out to Willow Farm; Harry is desperate for more acres. It keeps it in the family and gives you an income.'

'Is that right?' marvelled Uncle Arthur, a huge smile threatening to split his face in two.

Harry nodded. 'I must say it does sound like a good solution. Come over to Willow Farm, Arthur, and I'll show you my plans for biofuels.'

'Will do, lad.'

'Well, we were thinking of relocating to the Lakes,' Dad said thoughtfully. 'What do you think, Margo?'

Mum's face was all furrowed, her eyes were shiny with tears and her bottom lip was wobbling furiously. She opened her mouth to speak and a little squeak came out. 'It sounds wonderful to me.'

'You seem to have thought of everything, Freya,' said Dad, looking pink. 'I'm impressed.'

'Fantastic!' I jumped up and clapped. 'And in five years—'

'You'll be thirty-something,' Dad interjected. 'I must agree with your mother. This is a terrific undertaking for a single woman. Where's your life in all this? What about love?'

Harry shifted in his seat and I could have died with embarrassment. I tried to come up with a witty retort but all I could conjure up was the image of Harry's finger stroking my cheek last night and how for one moment I'd felt like my heart would burst.

Deep breaths, Freya.

Before I'd managed to reply, Auntie Sue stumbled back into the kitchen in a flap.

'There's a girl on the phone who says she's a friend of Lizzie's. She wants to come and look round our *wedding venue*.' This last bit required extremely wide eye-opening on her part. 'She says can she have her wedding photos with the cows?'

'Yeah. Why not?' I shrugged. 'Gloria and Gaynor will look lovely with ribbons round their necks.'

'I've heard it all now,' chuckled Uncle Arthur, elbowing Harry in the ribs.

'She also says she wants to see which room she and the bridesmaids will be getting ready in!'

I'd already thought of that. I got to my feet. 'Right. When's the wedding?'

'Next June.'

'Perfect,' I said briskly. 'The farmhouse's new reception room and downstairs bathroom will be finished by then. OK, I'd better talk to her.'

'Where's that going to go?' asked Uncle Arthur, scratching his head.

'Your office. And the office is moving to the hayloft above the milking parlour.'

I scampered out of the room, leaving Harry shaking his head in amusement and Mum and Dad arguing over which of them I took after the most. Both of them, pleasingly, seemed keen to claim me as a chip off their old block.

A couple of hours later I jumped into bed, head whirling with all the amazing things that had happened. Julian and his intensive dairy shenanigans had been well and truly kicked into touch. My parents had agreed to buy the farm and help me get the Appleby Farm Vintage Company off the ground. Auntie Sue had persuaded Uncle Arthur to make an offer on her dream bungalow first thing in the morning, and I would offer Lizzie a job as manager of the tea rooms. My eyes closed and I burrowed further under the blankets. The only thing that was missing from my perfect evening was someone to share my happiness with. As my body started to drift off to sleep, the last face I saw was Harry's.

Chapter 36

The next few weeks absolutely flew by and we all celebrated when the Hereford herd was officially cleared of TB. As soon as the movement ban was lifted, Eddy and Uncle Arthur took the calves off to be auctioned and Harry came along to collect Dexter, Uncle Arthur's prize bull.

In a matter of weeks, everything on the farm seemed to have gathered pace. I spent half my time in meetings with Patience Purdue at the planning department, talking about changing the use of some of our buildings, or with my new best friend Jayne from the tourism office, who in turn had told me about funding that the farm might be eligible for, which, of course, led to more meetings. Goat joked that with the amount of work I was putting his way, he might as well put a caravan in the farmyard to save him going home. At least we hoped he was joking.

I did have a short break at the beginning of October when I took my new tea rooms manager, aka Lizzie, away to the Yorkshire Dales for the night to stay in the most beautiful shepherd's hut on a hillside next to a stream.

Spending time in such tight proximity had made us closer and taught us things about each other. For instance, I found out that Lizzie is a bit OCD when it comes to cleaning work surfaces – useful to know and a very commendable trait in the catering profession. And she discovered that I laugh in my sleep – less useful, but at least she now knows she has a happy boss.

The following day we arrived back stuffed with English breakfast and, more importantly, ideas for our own Appleby Farm Vintage Holidays business just in time to see Harry supervising the delivery of one of his shepherd's huts. It was in even worse condition than ours and he and Eddy declared it a long-term project for the spring. Eddy was already getting stuck in to renovating our first hut, ready for Tilly and Aidan to stay in. It was to be vintage in style, of course, with a double bed at one end that converted into a little table and bench seats in the day, a kitchenette at the other and the world's tiniest log burner in the centre to keep them warm on their December wedding night.

Auntie Sue and Uncle Arthur's new bungalow was almost ready to move into and Auntie Sue was having a lovely time with the developer, picking out her tiles and colour schemes. Dad had had the farmhouse valued and between the four of them and the family solicitor they had agreed a price. I'd dreaded Julian's reaction to missing out on the deal but Dad had shaken his head.

'He won't dwell on it,' Dad had said confidently. 'He'll move on to something else. Projects like this fall through all the time.'

And he had been right; Julian hadn't seemed that bothered and claimed to be too busy negotiating a deal on some land to build a wind farm along the Norfolk coast. It did cross my mind, slightly uncharitably, that Julian's reaction was due to his assumption that one day he'd inherit the farm through Mum and Dad's will, but I wasn't prepared to lose sleep over that issue just yet.

By mid-October, and only a month into the job, Lizzie had managed to expand her role and assert herself in almost every area of the Appleby Farm Vintage Company.

'I need to be able to deputize for you,' she'd explained to me, as she packed up boxes of our new leaflets to take to a wedding fayre. 'And I want to be part of everything, not just the tea rooms.'

Which was why we were in the new dairy at eight o'clock one morning, making ice cream – Lizzie's first attempt. Maybe it was the white clogs or the long overalls or the white hair nets, I wasn't sure, but I never felt I looked my best when making ice cream.

I watched Lizzie as she poured fresh Jersey milk into the pasteurizer. With her olive skin and full lips she managed to look gorgeous even with her hair scraped back under a net. I felt like an ugly duckling standing next to her.

'I was thinking of holding a demo day,' she said. 'You know, invite some of the delis in Bowness and Windermere over. They can see how the ice cream is made, have a taste and then I'll see if I can tempt any of them into stocking it for next spring. We could invite someone from Radio Lakeland, too – someone nicer than my sister, obviously.'

'You,' I said, jabbing her in the ribs, 'are a genius. Fact.'

Lizzie had already suggested that we add a mezzanine level to the tea rooms, accessible via the spinning gallery, which would give us tons more space and allow us to do private parties without closing the tea rooms to the public. The barn had been crying out for the extra room and I'd already set Goat on to it; I just wished I'd thought of it myself.

I began to assemble the ingredients for today's batch of damson (home-grown, of course) and dark chocolate ice cream, and Lizzie started cracking fresh eggs into a stainless-steel bowl.

'Ooh, I nearly forgot. Tilly called last night. Aidan wants to know if we'll manage to cook all that roast beef for the wedding breakfast in the farmhouse kitchen or do we want to use one of his TV catering companies. They've got a mobile kitchen, apparently. But there are only thirty people; we could manage. What do you think?'

'Definitely use caterers,' said Lizzie. 'Not only will it give the farmyard a touch of glamour, you'll have enough to do on the day without sticking your head in and out of the oven – no offence, Freya, but your face does go a bit scarlet when you're stressed.'

'Cheers,' I said wryly, 'I agree. I'll book them, then. Mum said she'll help on the day, too, and is Ross still OK to be the wine waiter?'

'Oh yes,' said Lizzie, tapping her nose. 'All part of the master plan. I want him to start thinking about our wedding, pick up a few ideas. I shall be dropping some tiny subtle hints – so tiny he'll think he thought of it himself.'

I stared at her. 'Your wedding? You two have only been together for five minutes.'

'Six months, actually,' she said haughtily. She flipped up the lid of the bin with her foot and deposited a pile of egg shells into it. 'He'll graduate next summer and we can begin our lives together properly. He's The One. And when you know, you know. Why wait?'

I wouldn't know, I thought sombrely, but I did remember Tilly saying something very similar about Aidan months ago and look at them now, so I guessed it must be true. I put down the bowl of damson purée and pulled her in for a hug. 'I'm really happy for you,' I said, unable to keep the slight note of sadness out of my voice.

'Right.' Lizzie thrust her hands on her hips. 'Operation Date My Boss begins. I can't have you single any longer. It's too depressing and it's not good for business.'

I sighed and handed her a jug of cream to add to the pasteurizing machine. 'The problem is that I can't get Harry out of my head.'

'Mmm.' Lizzie frowned, handing me back the empty jug. 'I must admit, I did think you two would have got it together by now.'

'I don't understand what I did wrong. It was fine until I kissed him.'

'Wait – *you* kissed *him*?' she said incredulously. 'How bold!'

The worst thing about this white hair net, I now realized, was that there was nowhere to hide a blushing face. I bent down over the jug and stared into it for absolutely no reason.

'I thought he was keen and our faces were close anyway, so I sort of met him halfway. But he changed his mind. I regret it now. All those days spent climbing trees and building dens and catapults . . . I don't think he can see past that. He still sees me as a tomboy.'

Lizzie patted my arm. 'Oh, babe – I mean, boss – don't regret it. It sounds to me like you had masses of fun as kids. Anyway, you know what farmers are like. Not exactly in touch with their emotions, are they? Perhaps he needs some encouragement? Tell you what, Ross is home tonight, I'll get him to invite Harry to the pub for a pint, you get all dolled up – nice outfit, a bit of lippy – and turn up so the next time he sees you there'll be no mistaking that you're all woman.'

I sighed. 'I don't know . . .'

'Trust me,' she said, tapping me on the end of my nose with the damson spoon. 'Whoops.'

'Lizzie! Have I got a purple nose?' I gasped and giggled at the same time.

She scrunched up her face and gurgled with laughter. 'A bit.'

'Right. You asked for it.' I scooped up a spoonful of cocoa powder and began to take aim.

At that moment there was a sharp knock from behind me on the glass panel of the dairy door. Lizzie ducked and I flipped the spoon up into the air, sending a cloud of brown powder into my own face.

I squeezed my eyes tightly shut. 'Help, I've got chocolate blindness,' I squealed.

'Lizzie, hi,' said a voice, sounding too similar to Harry's not to be Harry.

Lizzie tried to reply but all I heard was a snort.

'I was looking for Freya. Is that . . . ?' Yep. Definitely Harry and presumably now pointing at me.

'Cloth please, Lizzie,' I said curtly, holding out my hand.

A few seconds later my blindness had gone, although I suspected that the chocolate powder would look like badly applied bronzer.

'Your uncle sent me over,' said Harry. His voice came out all strangled and muffled, and he'd covered his face with his hand. I could still see his eyes, though – twinkling with mirth. 'I'm taking him over to Willow Farm to show him my plans for the biofuels project. I thought – he thought – you might like to come, too.'

I blinked up at him. Out of the corner of my eye I could see Lizzie, gripping her sides, her face contorted in silent laughter. I shook my head and a shower of cocoa powder flew off my hair net.

'No, thanks, I'm busy.'

'I can see that.' Harry started to cough – at least, I think he was coughing – and slapping himself on the chest.

'Just give her five minutes, Harry,' said Lizzie, gulping for air. 'She'll be there.'

'Great,' said Harry breathlessly. 'See you in the yard.'

'Well, that was perfect,' I muttered as we watched Harry stride back across the yard.

'All woman. In a chocolatey, damsony way,' she whispered.

'I'm going to kill you,' I muttered through gritted teeth.

Willow Farm seemed to be a hive of industry compared to Appleby Farm in farming terms. Harry had three men there today: one bedding down the cattle with a huge machine called a straw blower; one ploughing the fields ready for winter barley to be planted, and the third operating a computerized feed mixer.

Harry, generously, hadn't mentioned my altercation with the cocoa powder to Uncle Arthur, so thankfully, apart from the odd smirk, the incident wasn't referred to when I joined them with clean clothes and a chocolate-free face.

'The farm's come a long way since your dad's day, lad,' said Uncle Arthur, looking impressed as we stopped off to check on Dexter in his new home. 'There's more machinery here than I've ever seen in my life.'

'I'm going for a quality product, Arthur. We don't breed cattle here yet, we just finish beef. But now I've got a pedigree bull, I'll be hiring him out for breeding straight away. And we raise Berkshire pigs, of course. I'm looking for a good profit margin in everything we do.' Harry smiled. His voice was neutral, but his face was unmistakably brimming with pride.

I was proud of him, too, and it was all I could do not to tell him as much. I looped my arm through my uncle's instead.

'Can we say hello to your horse?' I asked. 'I didn't see him last time.'

'Sure. Come and meet Storm.' Harry gestured towards the stables. 'He's the exception. There's no profit in owning a horse.'

'Good fun, though.' I smiled.

Harry's eyes met mine. He grinned and shook his head slightly. *You and your fun*, he seemed to be saying.

There was accommodation for five horses and Storm, a chestnut stallion with a white stripe down his nose, was in the end stall; the others were empty. He was gorgeous.

I reached up and patted his neck and Harry fetched a carrot out of his pocket, pausing to smirk at me before feeding it to the horse. This time I didn't ask if he'd got anything in there for me.

'That's it, I'm afraid,' he said. I had no idea whether he was talking to me or Storm but I studied the toe of my wellington boot just in case.

'Your sister was a great horse woman, I remember,' said Uncle Arthur.

'She was,' Harry agreed. 'These stables were always full when I was growing up. Do you remember, Freya? All four of us had a horse.'

I nodded. 'How is Jenny these days?'

'She's well, as far as I know. Don't see much of her, she lives in Scotland.' He sighed. 'If you remember she couldn't wait to get off the farm when she was growing up. Ironically, she married a salmon farmer. They've got two lovely girls.'

My heart ached at the forlorn expression on his face. It must be hard for him without any of his family nearby: parents on the south coast and his sister far away in the north.

Uncle Arthur shook his head. 'You Graythwaites seem to have all migrated and us Moorcrofts are all coming home to roost.'

Jenny was older by six years and she had had the most beautiful pony ever, snowy white and—

'Harry,' I said suddenly, 'didn't you used to have a carriage?'

He raised an interested eyebrow. 'Yes. Still got it in one of the sheds. Why?'

'Watch it, Harry, you'll be roped in to her wedding business before you know it,' Uncle Arthur chuckled, turning away from the stables. 'Now, come on, what about this land you're after?'

Computerized or not, Harry's office was far messier than Uncle Arthur's had been before I took charge of it. ('Needs a woman's touch,' Auntie Sue declared later when I told her about it.)

The smell was a bit ripe, too, but I forgave him that because the source of it, taking up a third of the floor space, was a wire pen containing a wriggling, yapping, tail-chasing litter of plump puppies, presided over by a red setter with a big smile on her face. I hadn't realized dogs could smile, but Harry's evidently could. One of the puppies bounded over to the edge of the pen towards me and in a flash I was in love.

I scooped up the puppy, held the squirming, yeasty-smelling body to my face and yelped as it started to chew a strand of my hair, which was the exact same colour as the puppy's fur.

'Look, it's me in dog form,' I laughed, holding the puppy up to my cheek.

'Really?' said Harry, scratching his nose. 'I hadn't noticed. The mum is called Belle, I haven't named the puppies.'

'Odd choice for a farm dog,' sniffed Uncle Arthur, drawn to Belle nonetheless. He stooped to ruffle her silky ears.

'I know,' admitted Harry, looking sheepish. 'I'd planned on getting something sensible, but when I arrived at the dog sanctuary I saw Belle and fell for her immediately. Apparently, she was too bonkers for the family who'd bought her and she needed re-homing. No one would take her on because she was pregnant at the time.'

Oh. How lovely was he? I realized my expression had gone all gooey and buried my head in the puppy's fur.

Uncle Arthur and Harry began poring over plans of their respective land and brochures about short rotation coppicing for biofuels, which I know I should have been interested in but, come on, what's more interesting than puppies? I tuned out and climbed into the dog pen. Belle stood up, stretched luxuriously and leaped out of the pen, leaving me in charge.

Twenty minutes later, I had been nipped, licked, climbed over and even weed on, and two puppies had fallen asleep in the crook of my arm. Meanwhile the two men – the new and the old face of farming – had come to a satisfactory agreement about Uncle Arthur's spare acres and were making moves to wrap up their meeting.

I reluctantly laid the puppies down in a much-chewed wicker basket, climbed out, hoping nobody noticed the wet patch on my jeans, and joined them at the door.

'This has been my biggest concern,' Uncle Arthur was saying, pumping Harry's hand up and down enthusiastically. 'Sorting out who would take care of my land after I'm gone. And you two have solved that for me. I can't thank you enough.'

My uncle rested one hand on my waist and the other on Harry's shoulder. I watched his Adam's apple bob up and down as he swallowed, and his old eyes filled with tears. Harry's gaze met mine, he smiled softly and just as I had that snowy night all those years ago when the lambs had been born, I felt a connection between us, like we were part of something very special.

Chapter 37

One morning in November I was in Clover Field, the small one at the back of the orchard, checking on the progress of the new shower block. There was a sharp wind whistling down through the valley towards Lake Windermere and although I was bundled up in layers, the cold was nipping at my extremities and I was looking forward to getting back into the tea rooms and thawing out over the steam of the coffee machine.

Clover Field was the chosen site for our shepherd's huts; it was hidden from the house by the orchard but was close enough for Goat to extend the farm's plumbing system so that guests wouldn't have to use the house.

'This one, I think,' I said, tapping a 1940s-inspired bathroom range in Goat's catalogue.

'My old gran had something like that,' said Goat, his tone implying that that wasn't necessarily an endorsement. He was standing on his long leg with the short one propped up on his toolbox. 'And she had one of those doll thingummyjigs with a knitted skirt to hide her loo paper.' He shuddered. 'Don't you think customers will want something a bit more modern in here?'

'Look at that, Goat.' I pointed over to where Eddy was

fixing a stainless-steel chimney into the first shepherd's hut. 'If they want modern, they've come to wrong place. We're vintage all the way, even down to our loo-roll holders. Good tip there, thanks.'

He rolled his eyes as I handed back the brochure and headed across the wet grass, off to visit Eddy.

I was greeted by the sight of Eddy on all fours inside the hut, dressed in a dirty khaki boiler suit with his bottom in the air. His little dog, Buddy, scampered towards me and stood on his hind legs for some fuss.

'Hey, Eddy, looking good.' I meant the hut, not his rear end, but once the words were out of my mouth, I didn't feel that I could correct myself. I gave Buddy a tickle under his chin and he padded back to his spot in the corner.

'A right pig of a job this has turned out to be,' grunted Eddy. He had his head in the log burner and his voice echoed through the flue hole in the top. 'I've cut the 'ole in't roof for the chimney in't wrong place.'

'Oh dear.'

I pressed my lips together to keep a laugh from escaping. Eddy didn't like us to think he was enjoying his new job too much. The truth was a different matter: he loved the shepherd's hut so much that on a fine day, he'd taken to eating his lunch out here, sitting on a camping chair and drinking beef tea from a flask.

And who could blame him? The hut looked amazing. The furnishings weren't in yet, although they were ready and in storage in the shed, but the kitchen was finished, the interior had been decorated and the tiles around the log burner were in place.

I'd toyed with the idea of plumping for an array of Cath Kidston-style colourful prints, but in the end had taken my colour palette from the view out of the hut windows: wood panelling for the walls, soft greens and dove greys for the fabrics, and I'd found a gorgeous range of enamel storage tins in pale blue for the kitchen. The effect was gentle, calming and extremely relaxing, which was exactly what I wanted my guests to experience when they stepped inside.

It didn't seem to be working for Eddy, though.

'Can't we just shunt the log burner up a bit?' I asked timidly.

He withdrew his head and scowled at me. He had black streaks down his face and looked quite menacing. 'I'll have to,' he muttered, 'but it won't be symmetrical then.'

I was saved further debate about the importance of a symmetrical fireplace by a sudden wheezing at the door of the hut. I turned to see Auntie Sue, dressed in Uncle Arthur's anorak and wellies, red-faced, wide-eyed and completely breathless.

'Ooh, is the buyer here?' I gasped.

Now that the cattle had all passed their TB test with flying colours, the Hereford herd was up for sale again, and the lady from Gloucestershire who we'd had to cancel in May was still interested in buying them. She was due at the farm that morning.

I glanced quickly at Eddy. That might explain why he was even more of a grump than usual. I rested a sympathetic hand on his shoulder and he patted it.

Auntie Sue shook her head, still panting. 'Freya, lass, it's your friend Anna on the phone. She says there's been a flogger on the interweb and we've had thousands of smacks!'

My eyebrows shot up. 'Is Anna still on the phone?'

Auntie Sue nodded. Her grasp of the internet was still a bit patchy and due to her breathlessness I wasn't sure if this news was good or bad.

402

'Thanks, Auntie Sue,' I yelled, jumping down from the hut and racing across Clover Field to my new office.

I scrambled up the wooden steps to the loft above the milking parlour. The office wasn't quite finished, but it had electrics, a phone line, a desk and chair, and my wall planner, so the plastering and flooring could wait for the moment.

'Anna!' I dropped into my chair and took a deep breath. 'Are you still there?'

'Oh my God.' Anna's voice was fizzing with excitement. Phew. The smacks must be of a good variety, then.

'Did you know you've had a YouTuber with three million subscribers to her channel at the tea rooms?' she shrieked. 'From BRIGHTON! All THE top vloggers are in Brighton.'

'No,' I laughed, 'I didn't know any of that. But it's a good thing, I take it?'

Come to think of it, the last hen party we'd had in was from Brighton. It must have been one of them. Waif-like little things, immaculately groomed and incredibly demure. Not one of them looked like they might be online A-listers.

'Well, she only vlogged from the tea rooms and stuck pictures of some cows on Instagram and this morning alone, you've had fifty thousand hits on your website!'

Anna continued to look after our website for us, add news, update the menu, that sort of thing. Her company also hosted it on her server, whatever that meant.

'What does that mean for us?' I asked.

Anna squealed with delight. 'It means the Appleby Farm Vintage Tea Rooms have arrived, Freya. It means you'll need to make more scones because your bookings are going to go through the roof, baby!'

'Really?'

'And, more good news . . .' Anna paused dramatically. 'I'll be seeing you soon. Charlie's bringing me to Tilly and Aidan's wedding.'

'Oh, Anna!' I squealed. 'I'm so pleased. No, actually, I'm more than pleased. This is brilliant!'

'Seriously?' she asked, sounding worried. 'Because the last thing I'd want to do is—'

'Anna, stop,' I insisted. 'Charlie is a love and so are you. I'm thrilled. Really.'

I did my happy dance round the office, she joined in in Kingsfield and we ended the call whooping with joy to each other. The phone rang instantly. I took a booking for a twenty-first birthday party. It rang again. Could we host an office party? Another hen party? Afternoon tea for fifteen? I switched the answer phone on and looked out of the window. The car park was busy – not just with the family hatchbacks and mumsy four-wheel drives, but with cute little Fiats and Minis.

I hurried to the tea rooms and had to push my way through the throng to the counter. Lizzie and Mum, cheeks flushed, looked at me with relief. I grabbed an apron and joined them.

'Yes, please?' I beamed at the person at the head of the queue. 'What can I get you?'

As soon as I'd had a chance I'd brought them up to speed with our YouTube début and the excitement of that and the evident increase in business had produced just enough adrenalin to see us through the day. By closing time the three of us were completely worn out and as soon as Lizzie switched the sign from open to closed, we collapsed in a heap.

'Best. Day. Ever,' declared Lizzie, from her spot on the

floor where she'd slid down the glass doors. 'Lots of today's customers were potential brides, you know. Your vintage company idea is going to fly, babes – I mean, boss. Hey!' she said suddenly. 'We could have a vintage festival here next year; we could be the vintage Mecca of the North West!'

'Right now I'm more concerned with cakes.' I frowned. I was leaning on the counter, surveying the sparse remains in the food cabinet. 'Auntie Sue is so busy packing for their move that she's only just keeping up with normal demand.'

'I'll help,' said Mum, scooping a pile of crumbs from the table in front of her into a napkin. 'I've wanted to suggest it for ages, but I didn't want to tread on Sue's toes. And if we're going to be baking more that gives me the perfect excuse to order a new oven.'

I clasped my throat, horrified. 'You aren't thinking of getting rid of the Aga, are you? A farmhouse kitchen needs an Aga.'

I pictured a basket of snoozing kittens in front of it and mentally added kittens to my growing list of the menagerie I planned on introducing to Appleby Farm at the earliest opportunity.

'No, it can stay; we'll need the extra capacity. But I thought we could get a large stainless-steel professional oven. I've always dreamed of one of those. The Aga is lovely, but I get the feeling it's in charge of me rather than the other way round. And if we continue to attract a younger crowd like today, I thought we could try a few more current recipes.'

Lizzie wrinkled up her nose. 'What. Like buns?'

Mum laughed and shook her head. Her hair was pinned up in an elegant chignon and she looked just as well-turned-out now as she had at ten o'clock this morning. My heart squeezed with pride. Not just because she was so pretty but because she had adapted from her life as a banker's wife in a luxurious Parisian apartment to a waitress in my tea rooms at a tumbledown farm in northern England, seemingly without a murmur. There was a lot more to my mum, I realized shamefully, than I'd given her credit for.

'No, Lizzie,' Mum replied, 'like macarons, or individual lemon tarts or a tiramisu slice.'

Lizzie winked at me at the mention of tiramisu and I shot her a warning look.

'That would be amazing, Mum, if you would.' I sighed gratefully. 'We might even have to source another supplier if things continue like this, as long as they follow our recipes for consistency.'

'Ooh,' Lizzie's eyes lit up, 'we could do an Appleby Farm Vintage recipe book!'

'You and your ideas, Lizzie,' I laughed. 'No wonder I'm shattered. I can't keep up.'

Lizzie got to her feet, hugged us all goodbye and set off for home. She was still living in a room at the White Lion and for once I envied her the tiny uncomplicated space. As soon as my parents moved in in a week or two they were transforming the whole middle floor of the farmhouse into a master suite with bathroom and dressing room. And the new downstairs reception room and bathroom hadn't been finished yet. The place would be in chaos right up until Tilly and Aidan's wedding and my head spun just thinking about it.

I must have sighed out loud because Mum appeared at my side and put her arm round me.

'Darling,' she said gently, 'as your mother, who loves you very much, I can't help noticing a distinct lack of social life, not to mention boyfriends.'

I laughed softly and leaned my head against her. 'I'm fine, Mum, honestly. Getting the business off the ground and being able to pay you and Dad back is my number-one priority at the moment. A social life can wait for now, as can men.'

Mum pressed a kiss into my hair and I felt the tension ease from my shoulders.

'Never put your career before love, Freya. Your job will never love you back, never share memories with you when you're old, never give me a grandchild to spoil rotten.'

'I'm not making a choice to be single, Mum; it just hasn't happened.'

'Do you know, I gave up my career for your father?'

I shook my head.

'I'd just finished a cordon bleu cookery course in Manchester and had accepted a trainee position at a pâtisserie in Paris starting in three months' time when I met him.'

'Mum!' I pulled away to stare at her, amazed. 'Why don't I know this?'

'I thought you'd be appalled.' Her hand fluttered to her pearls and she twisted them into a knot. 'Equal opportunities and all that. Such an old-fashioned thing to do these days. Different in the seventies, of course.'

'A pâtissière?' I marvelled. No wonder she was so flippin' brilliant in the kitchen!

'Your father was doing well at the bank at the time and was in line for promotion. There was no way he could have come to Paris with me. He said that even though we'd not been together long, we would have to stop seeing each other, that I already meant so much to him. He couldn't bear to fall in love with me, only to have his heart broken when I left. So I wrote and told them I wouldn't be coming.'

'Poor Dad,' I said, thinking that there was a side to him, too, that I hadn't been aware of. My spine was tingling at the thought of such love between them, but there was something else that I couldn't quite put my finger on . . .

'We got to live in Paris in the end, of course, and now it appears I'm about to become a pâtissière,' Mum continued happily. 'So I'm getting my career after all. A little belatedly.'

'I'm glad for you,' I said, kissing her cheek.

I suddenly thought of Harry and his reason for ending our kiss. *You mean too much to me* . . . His words echoed my dad's from decades ago. That was it! That must be why he couldn't kiss me, because he thought I would be moving on again and leaving the farm. But unlike my mum, I wasn't going anywhere. He had thought I was off on a new adventure. But my new adventure was right here. That had to mean we still had a chance. Didn't it?

Chapter 38

It was moving day. December. Not the ideal time of year to have your kitchen door propped open, exposing the house to the Cumbrian elements, but Auntie Sue's dream bungalow was ready and the pair of them wanted to get themselves settled before Christmas. I was glad we'd decided to close the tea rooms for the day; the removal men had arrived at seven thirty this morning in an impossibly big lorry that almost filled the farmyard and had been tramping in noisy procession backwards and forwards to the house ever since.

'Should I make more tea, do you think, lass?' worried Auntie Sue. 'Or offer the men some shortbread?'

Auntie Sue had been packed since last week, which meant her sole occupation this morning was to fret and flap.

I handed her a pair of scissors instead and led her outside. 'Why don't you go outside and pick yourself a bunch of winter foliage to arrange in a vase when you get to the bungalow?'

'Good idea,' she said breathily and disappeared into the shrubs, muttering about skimmia and euonymus and whether the birds had left her any berries on the holly. I sighed with relief. Flower arranging always calmed her down.

The lights were on in the tea room. I had taken on a new part-timer, Rachel, and she had come in to do some cleaning and tidying while we were quiet. She lived locally and arrived on her horse for work, which I thought had to be the best form of commuter transport ever. Lizzie was touring vintage shops to pick up last-minute props for Aidan and Tilly's wedding; we still needed something vintage for the wedding favours and I wanted a quirky way of presenting the seating plan. Mum and Dad had disappeared for a couple of days to a hotel.

'To give Sue and Arthur some space,' Mum had said, 'otherwise it will look like we're hovering.' She also confided that she'd planned to do some serious furniture shopping although, wisely, she had kept Dad in the dark about that part of the itinerary.

Goat was taking advantage of my parents' absence to decimate the first floor and no sooner had Auntie Sue and Uncle Arthur removed their toothbrushes from the bathroom, than he and another man began swinging lump hammers at the internal walls to make way for the new master suite.

By lunchtime the lorry was packed up and the removals men were ready to go. One of them guided the driver as he reversed all the way down the farm track and trundled off the short distance to the bungalow. The builders stopped work for their lunch break and I sent them over to the tea rooms out of the way. Almost at once a welcome peace reigned over the farm.

'Well,' said Auntie Sue, removing the doorstop from the farmhouse door and pulling it to behind her, 'I think that's everything.'

I gave her a hug. 'You OK?'

She pulled a cotton handkerchief from her coat pocket

and sniffed. 'Never better,' she said, dabbing her eyes.

The two of us stood on the doorstep, just as we had that dark night at Easter when I'd arrived. She still smelled the same – fresh bread and Nivea face cream – but so many other things had changed. The beef herd – what was left of it – was newly installed at a farm in Gloucestershire, the barn was now our vintage tea rooms and Clover Field would have holidaymakers in it next year instead of cattle. But it wasn't just the farm that had changed, we all had.

'End of an era.' Auntie Sue sighed.

'Start of a new adventure, too,' I added.

'Right,' said Auntie Sue stoically, 'where is Artie? I'm getting in the car.'

The Land Rover was staying at the farm; the ancient thing was better suited to romping over fields than roads, so Uncle Arthur had bought them a sensible little runaround.

I pulled on Dad's emerald-green jumper, which I'd recently appropriated. It swamped me but was the cosiest thing ever and, although I said so myself, it set off my skin tone perfectly. I walked Auntie Sue down to the car where Madge was already waiting. She'd taken one look at the lorry this morning and taken refuge on the driver's seat. Benny and Björn, sensibly, were nowhere to be seen; they were staying at the farm until Auntie Sue and Uncle Arthur had settled in.

'I'll find him,' I said, 'he won't have gone far.'

I ran back to the farmhouse and up to the top of the stairs calling his name, poking my head into every room, but there was no sign of him. I stopped at the nursery. Auntie Sue didn't keep the door locked any more. I walked in and stood in the centre of the room, absorbing the love from the sunny yellow walls and the perfectly painted nursery rhyme characters and my heart heaved with sadness.

New start for them, though, I thought, *a new happy chapter in their lives and who knows, one day, perhaps, there will be children at Appleby Farm*. But enough of the daydreams. I left the nursery behind and ran back downstairs; for now, I'd settle for locating my wayward uncle.

'Any joy?' Auntie Sue shouted as I came back outside.

I shook my head and darted off to check the farm buildings. I did a tour of the cowsheds, the stables, the barn, and even the sheds. Still nothing.

Auntie Sue, getting fed up, tooted on the car horn but he still didn't materialize.

I walked back over to the car.

'Did he have a favourite spot, Auntie Sue? Somewhere special where he may have gone?' I asked anxiously as she wound down the window.

She wrinkled her forehead and then sighed sadly. 'It was all his favourite, love. He could be anywhere. I'll get out and walk up the fields, see if I can spot him.'

'Not in those shoes,' I laughed.

She'd changed into her best shoes and wool coat to arrive at her new abode. Uncle Arthur had wolf-whistled when he'd seen her and joked that he hoped she wasn't expecting him to carry her over the threshold again.

'You stay here,' I said, racking my brains to think where he might have gone and which path to take.

I trotted down to the orchard with the intention of letting myself through the gate and into Clover Field, trying not to panic. Uncle Arthur was probably chewing the cud with Eddy, I told myself firmly; they'd be reminiscing about old times. It didn't work. My pulse was galloping like a racehorse.

412

Suddenly I spied him. He was at the far side of the orchard, slumped on the old bench facing Clover Field. I approached him from behind, smiling to myself at the tufts of grey hair visible over the collar of his winter coat.

'There you are!' I called. 'I've been looking everywhere for you. You nearly gave me a heart attack. Figuratively speaking,' I laughed.

Uncle Arthur didn't move. Or speak.

My heart thundered in my chest as I ran through the trees and raced to his side. *No. Not now. Not after all we'd been through to reach this moment.*

He turned and gave me a watery smile. 'Just saying goodbye, lass.'

My legs gave way and I collapsed down on to the bench beside him, clutching my heart. I blinked at him and took his hand.

'You OK?' I asked.

I thought we'd lost you.

He gazed at the fields that stretched out in front of us, acre after acre of grassland.

'Until I saw those fields empty I didn't quite believe my farming days were over.'

'I know it's not the same as seeing a herd out there grazing,' I said, 'but Harry will look after it, I'm sure.'

Uncle Arthur nodded. 'He's a smashing lad and you'll be here, too. I never thought there would be Moorcrofts at Appleby Farm after me and your auntie had gone. Thanks, love.'

He squeezed my hand and I grinned at him. 'Thank *you*, you mean. This farm is a gift. You told me that. And it's the best gift I've ever had.'

In the distance there was an impatient tooting of a car horn.

'We'd better go,' I said, helping my uncle to his feet. 'Your life of leisure awaits you.'

I waved and waved until their little car had bounced down the track and disappeared from view. And then there was just me.

So this was it.

I took a deep breath, feeling slightly overwhelmed.

Another generation of Moorcrofts had left the farm and I had been promoted to its guardian angel. Unbelievably, I had got my wish. Scary, though.

I turned with a shaky sigh to face the farmhouse and for a moment I stood and let everything sink in. Its cheery stone frontage with its nine sash windows and three chunky little chimney pots seemed to beckon me in and I felt my heart swell with a mix of anticipation and hope. Appleby Farm had a kind of magic all of its own and whatever the future held for me and my ambitious plans, I felt instinctively like it was on my side.

I cleared my throat to pull myself back to the present. Christmas decorations, I decided, that's what I'd do for the rest of the day. I'd go out and buy a tree, fill every empty corner of the farmhouse with fairy lights, glittery baubles and tinsel, and by tonight I would be so exhausted that I wouldn't even notice how lonely I felt.

I was about to go inside in search of the old box of Christmas decorations when the sound of a diesel engine approaching the farmyard stopped me in my tracks.

It was Harry in his pick-up truck. My spirits lifted instantly and my face was wreathed in a smile by the time he pulled up at the farmhouse gate and wound down his window.

'Just in time.' I grinned. 'You can help me look for something.'

'What, your hands?' His eyes twinkled at the long sleeves of Dad's jumper.

'Ta-dah!' I sang, producing my fingers from the depths of their woollen cocoon.

'So Arthur and Sue have moved out?' he said, serious all of a sudden.

I nodded. 'Their retirement began as of five minutes ago.'

'Great, great.' His eyes met mine and then flicked away again. 'You're staying, then, in Lovedale?'

I beamed at him. 'I am. Can you believe it? I'm back for good.'

'For good,' he said in a low voice, as though he was testing out the words for himself.

We stared at each other for what felt like ages. The atmosphere between us was so heavy that it was all I could do not to dive in through the window of his truck and snog the face off him.

Harry rubbed his hands together, breaking the spell. He grinned mischievously. 'Well, in that case, I've got something for you. Close your eyes,' he demanded.

'Yeah, right,' I scoffed. 'Last time you said that and I obeyed you, you tipped a pot of worms down my back.'

'Freya, the last time I said that I was thirteen,' he said softly.

So softly, in fact, that heat spread from the pit of my stomach to my face as quickly as a grass fire. I snapped my eyes shut and did as I was told.

I listened to him jump out of the truck and slam the door. My heart was beating like a drum and the urge to spring my eyes open was immense. I felt his presence in front of me and I inhaled discreetly, revelling in the earthy scent of him.

What has he got for me? I wondered. *Please let it be a kiss.* My lips were almost numb with the agony of waiting to be kissed again by Harry Graythwaite.

'Now put your hands out.'

Even as my spirits dipped at the realization that a kiss didn't seem to be on the cards, they instantly rose again as Harry deposited a warm furry body into my arms.

'A puppy!' I gasped, opening my eyes wide. 'You've brought me one of your puppies!'

A tiny ball of red fur, with ears that looked too long for its body, started burrowing into my jumper. I clamped my hands round its little pot belly and lifted it up to have a good look.

'Thank you!' I smiled. I stood on tiptoe and pressed a kiss to Harry's cheek. 'I love him, or is it a her?'

'Her. No farm is complete without a dog,' said Harry with a half-smile, stroking the puppy's back with his forefinger.

'Odd choice for a farm dog,' I said in a gruff voice, mimicking my uncle.

Harry threw back his head and laughed. 'Arthur's right and I didn't dare let on that the previous owners had named her Belle after the Disney princess. That would have ruined my macho image completely.'

Not with me it wouldn't.

I grinned at him. 'In that case, I'll call her Elsa after the princess from *Frozen*. Continue the family tradition. No one will ever know. Hello, Elsa.' I kissed the puppy on her nose and she instantly tried to lick my face.

'Ouch!'

Harry chuckled as the puppy sank her tiny teeth into my nose. 'I chose this one for you because she's a ball of energy, into everything, full of fun. Just like you.'

'I'll take that as a compliment.'

'You should.'

'Your timing is perfect, too. I was just contemplating the fact that I'm going to be all on my own tonight and the prospect really doesn't appeal.'

I risked a look at his handsome face, willing him to take the hint.

I could just reach out and pull him close, I thought, *and run my fingers through his hair.* Perhaps this time, he wouldn't push me away. But what if he did? I'd already made a fool of myself once. Did I really want to risk a second rejection? Far safer to let him make the first move. And then I'd know for sure.

I just hoped there would be a next time.

But before I had time to act, Harry grabbed me by the shoulders and turned me towards the house.

'Go on.' He shooed me and my new playmate up the path. 'Get her inside or she really will be frozen.'

'OK, OK, Mr Bossy Pants,' I giggled, scooting up to the door. 'Let's go and find a blanket or . . . Oh!'

I turned, expecting him to be close behind me, but instead he was back at his truck.

Harry cleared his throat. 'I'd better be off,' he said, his eyes clouded with an expression that I couldn't quite read. 'Give you two a chance to bond.'

'Right. Good idea.' My voice sounded stilted and I tried to soften my words with, 'Thanks again.'

He raised a hand in goodbye and disappeared in a cloud of diesel smoke just as Goat and the builders emerged from the tea rooms, all balancing their lunch boxes on their heads.

'Men,' I muttered to Elsa, 'are impossible to understand.'

417

Chapter 39

The rest of December flew by in a whirl of wedding planning, puppy training and building work. Before I knew it, the schools had broken up for the Christmas holidays and Tilly and Aidan's wedding party of thirty had descended on Lovedale.

On the day of the wedding I was up with the larks. Actually, I was up before the larks. It was still dark outside and the only sound in the kitchen, where I sat with Elsa asleep on my lap, checking the umpteen things on my to-do list, was the snuffling and snoring of bodies stretched out in their sleeping bags in front of the fireplace.

The weather forecast predicted temperatures barely rising above freezing and the possibility of light snow showers. This to me sounded perfect for a winter wedding.

Most people had arrived last night and we'd had quite a party until eleven o'clock when Tilly, very sensibly, had issued instructions for bed. Not everyone was staying in the farmhouse: Tilly's mum and partner and Aidan's parents were over in the White Lion; Tilly and her bridesmaid, Gemma, were staying in Auntie Sue and Uncle Arthur's spare room (their first guests – Auntie Sue had been baking and cleaning for them all week); Aidan's sister and family had taken over my room and the little nursery on the top floor; and the people in sleeping bags at the other end of the kitchen were Aidan's best man and his wife, and two teachers from Tilly's school. Various other guests were dotted around the area in rented cottages.

'Morning,' whispered Mum, tiptoeing into the kitchen. 'Tea?'

I nodded and she slipped the kettle on to the Aga and took out mugs and tea bags as quietly as she could.

'Couldn't you sleep either?' I asked softly as she slid a mug in front of me.

She shook her head. 'I've got the cake to finish. But I can't function until I've had my tea.'

The cake, currently boxed and on the kitchen table, was going to be a thing of beauty: a single tier covered in snowy white icing. She had bought two feathered lovebirds and made a tiny heart-shaped arbour, which the birds would nestle underneath.

Tilly's eyes had welled up with tears when she'd seen it. She'd also cried when she'd seen the tea rooms, already laid for dinner – vintage lace tablecloths, floral china, bunches of winter foliage arranged in colourful glass bottles along every table. The seating plan, which took the form of miniature bunting pegged on old-fashioned string, had also produced gasps of delight.

'You've put so much work into it, Freya,' she'd marvelled, fingering the retro bags of sweets we'd arranged at everyone's place. 'All the little details. It's even more beautiful than I imagined.'

Mum tightened her dressing-gown belt before sitting down beside me. Elsa instantly sprang up and leaped on to her knee. We shared a smile as the puppy wagged her entire

419

body at the sight of a new person before settling back into sleep.

'Let's have a look at your list,' she said, reading over my shoulder. 'Mistletoe, champagne, bells, ribbon – oh, very romantic.'

'It is, isn't it?' I smiled, kissing her cheek. 'Our first wedding, Mum.'

She sipped her tea and smiled. 'Exciting. And you've worked so hard, darling, I'm sure it will be a great success.'

'I know that marriage is all about celebrating love and life together, but the wedding is the start of the journey and I adore the thought that I'll have helped make Tilly and Aidan's day magical for them.'

We sat in the silence of our own thoughts for a few seconds when suddenly I wondered when I'd get my own magical day and a sigh slipped out.

'That's a big sigh.' Mum's eyes searched mine, full of concern.

Since we'd got closer, I'd told her about Charlie and how I'd thought at one time that he could be The One. However, I hadn't mentioned my feelings for Harry because she had a habit of going all girlie when he was around and I suspected she wouldn't be above a bit of well-intended match-making if she thought that would help. But now, in the quiet of the kitchen, just the two of us awake in the world, I had a sudden urge to tell all.

'I miss being half of a couple, Mum.'

She put her arms around me and pulled me to her side. 'Oh, Freya, you'll find the right man one day, I'm sure.'

'The thing is, I've got a major crush on Harry. But it's unrequited.' I shrugged helplessly. 'We're friends, which is lovely, but I want us to be more than that.'

'Oh, darling, I don't think it's unrequited.' Mum chuckled softly. 'I've watched him when you enter the room. He's like a brighter version of himself when you're around.'

I frowned. 'Really? Then why doesn't he say something or do something? I've given him loads of chances . . .' I giggled. 'That sounds like I've been virtually throwing myself at him at every opportunity.'

'You two have grown up together. Perhaps he's being cautious because there's so much at stake. You know, shared history.'

'But whatever happens we'd still have that.'

'Yes, but would you still have your friendship?'

I opened my mouth but my answer was cut short by the sound of a truck pulling into the yard. The caterers had arrived.

'Goodness,' said Mum, 'they're early!'

'Aidan suggested that as so many of us are staying here, they might as well arrive early and cook us all bacon sandwiches.'

Four people still cocooned in sleeping bags sat up immediately.

Phil, Aidan's best man, yawned and scratched his chin. 'Did someone mention bacon?'

At noon the church bells were chiming joyfully and a low sun was making the frosty churchyard sparkle. Everything had gone to plan – even the snow showers had held off this morning – and I was brimming with relief and excitement. I opened the church doors, breathless from all the running around, and looked for Lizzie. A hush had already descended on the surprisingly large congregation as I slipped into my seat at the back of the little church beside her and Ross.

'Tilly's arrived,' I whispered to her. 'You've done amazing things to her hair. She looks like a 1940s starlet.'

Lizzie flicked her hair over her shoulder and beamed. 'Thanks. Doesn't the church look pretty?'

I nodded.

The end of every pew was adorned with bunches of holly, mistletoe and ivy, tied with hessian ribbon. A plump Christmas tree festooned with children's hand-made decorations stood to one side of the altar and a beautiful wooden nativity scene to the other. Aidan, in the centre, looking handsome in a pale-grey suit, glanced over his shoulder every few seconds to catch a glimpse of his bride.

'And packed!' I exclaimed. 'I think the whole of Lovedale has turned up!'

Somewhere above us a pianist started to play a beautiful, magical piece of music. A few bars in, the double doors were opened by invisible hands and Tilly appeared on the arm of her mum. The sight of that alone had me blinking back the tears. Her dad had died years ago, I'd been told.

'Oh, bless,' breathed Lizzie.

'I know,' I whispered back hoarsely, sending up a silent prayer of thanks for having such a healthy dad of my own.

I'd assumed that as I was here in some sort of official capacity I would be too busy to get all emotional. Stupid, stupid me. I pressed a finger under each eye and hoped my mascara wasn't making them completely panda-like.

The congregation turned and smiled as one as Tilly, swathed in a bias-cut cream satin dress and faux-fur shrug, glided majestically past with her mum. I spotted Charlie for the first time, pressed up close to Anna halfway up the church on the opposite side. They caught my eye and waved in unison. Charlie had had a late shift yesterday and so they'd driven up this morning with Gemma's husband,

Mike, and I couldn't wait to catch up with them. I'd been a bit apprehensive about what it would be like to actually see them together for the first time. But now I realized as I waved back that I was OK. Everyone deserved to be happy, everyone deserved a special someone.

'What is this music?' I whispered, gruffly to Lizzie. 'It's breaking my heart!'

She tapped the order of service and I followed her finger.

'"A Dream Is A Wish Your Heart Makes" from *Cinderella*,' I read. Blimey, how lovely was that!

Gemma appeared next, looking stunning in cappuccino lace. 'OMG! Fairytale dot com!' she squeaked as she smiled and waved her way up the aisle.

'I want to get married here,' I heard Lizzie whisper to Ross.

I sniggered softly to myself. So much for the subtle hints.

The vicar, a middle-aged lady with short grey hair, chunky black glasses and pillar-box-red lipstick, welcomed everyone to the Lake District and launched into the service. Before long we'd reached the important bit.

'And now, Tilly and Aidan, I invite you to make your solemn vows to each other,' announced the vicar.

She took a step backwards towards the altar and Aidan and Tilly turned to face each other, both grinning wildly.

The silence was deafening as Aidan took Tilly's hands in his and spoke straight from the heart.

'I, Aidan, am honoured to take you, Tilly, to be my wife. From the moment I first saw you, you captured my heart. Your beauty, your soul and your loving heart fill me with joy and inspire me to be the best that I can be. This day, before our friends and family, I give you all that I am, all that I have. I promise to love you and cherish you for the rest of our lives. And that is my solemn vow.'

Even from the back of the church I could see the tears sparkling in Tilly's eyes. She took a few deep breaths and then gazed at him adoringly.

'I, Tilly, take you, my darling Aidan, to be my husband. Because of you I love, I laugh, I dream again. You are my silver lining, the sunshine in my day, and the bright stars in my sky. In this new journey of marriage, I promise to be beside you every step of the way. Your dreams are mine and I will love you for eternity. And that is my solemn vow.'

Not a single dry eye in the house.

'Tissue?' asked Lizzie, handing me the packet.

'Thanks,' I gulped.

Tilly and Aidan were declared husband and wife and, to rapturous applause, he not only kissed her but swung her round in the air. Impossible not to cry, absolutely impossible.

The service seemed to be over in a flash. Suddenly the church bells were ringing again and Aidan and Tilly, arms around each other's waists, were waving and blowing kisses as they skipped back down the aisle.

My next job was to get back to the farm and get the mulled wine and hot fruit punch ready for when the bridal party arrived.

As soon as I could, I zigzagged my way through the crowd and out of the church. It was snowing lightly and the cold air made me shiver as it touched my skin. My stomach flipped with happiness; this had to be the most romantic setting for a wedding ever. I ran down the path to where I knew the horse and carriage would be waiting with the driver.

And there he was. Harry. My poor heart skipped a beat. Dressed appropriately for the occasion in a tweed jacket, collarless shirt, braces and moleskin trousers, he looked amazing. His eyes widened when he saw me and he jumped down from the carriage and dropped a kiss on my cheek.

I'd persuaded him to let us repaint his sister's old carriage white and my mum had recovered the seat in red velvet. It was on permanent loan to us for all future weddings. I'd also twisted his arm into being chauffeur for the day.

'Hey,' I said, unable to keep the pleasure at seeing him out of my voice. 'Don't you look the part!'

'What of – village idiot?' He rolled his eyes. 'You didn't tell me that I'd have to dress up.'

'Sorry, did I forget to mention that?' I said, feigning innocence.

'I'm only joking.' He grinned. 'Mind you, I'm glad I put my dad's old thermal underwear on. '

'Don't blame you,' I said, trying to bat away the mental image of Harry in his undies. I wrapped my arms round myself. 'I could do with some extra warmth myself.'

'You look beautiful, Freya, almost as radiant as the bride.'

'Me? Get away.' I pressed a hand surreptitiously to my face in case by 'radiant' he actually meant red.

I'd opted for a long-sleeved vintage tea dress printed with tiny green flowers and teamed it with an emerald green wool coat and tan leather boots – dressy but practical enough for me to run around organizing things in.

'I'm delighted with the carriage. Thanks so much, Harry.'

Lizzie and I had spent a good part of yesterday decorating it. We'd used miles of white satin ribbon, millions of ivy fronds, hundreds of sprigs of mistletoe plundered from the orchard and piled some thick woollen blankets into the carriage for the happy couple to snuggle under on the journey to the farm. Even if I said so myself, it looked stunning.

'Glad to help,' he said softly.

His eyes locked on to mine so intensely that my heart suddenly felt too big for my chest and then for some inexplicable reason we edged closer to each other.

Harry swallowed and rubbed at his sexily chiselled jaw. 'Freya . . .' he began tentatively.

'Yes,' I answered breathily. Oh my God, this was it. This. Was. It.

He reached out and brushed the snowflakes from my cheek and my stomach quivered at his touch. 'Do you think—'

'Freya,' called Tilly, from the church steps, 'come on, we want you in some photos, too!'

Now? Seriously? I could have sobbed with frustration.

'Coming,' I called, waving to her. I turned back to Harry. 'You were saying?' I said, trying to keep the urgency out of my voice. 'Harry?'

'It can wait.'

'No, it can't,' I said petulantly, barely resisting the temptation to stamp my feet.

He threw back his head and laughed. 'Go,' he said, twisting my shoulders and giving me a gentle nudge. 'We've got all the time in the world to talk.'

I stumbled backwards towards the church path. 'Have we?'

He lifted one shoulder lazily. 'Of course.'

My legs were trembling as I raced to take my place in the wedding photo line-up. Harry caught my eye and winked. What was all that about? Lizzie was right about him, he was *so* tiramisu.

Chapter 40

The wedding guests had arrived back at Appleby Farm and were sipping mulled wine by the time Harry guided Storm and Skye and the fairytale carriage into the yard. Tilly and Aidan, wrapped around each other, blankets heaped over them, looked deliriously happy, if a little red-nosed. The snow had stopped and a light dusting remained – the fields, trees, rooftops and even the farmyard looked as if they had been sprinkled with confetti by Mother Nature for the occasion.

'Freya!' Tilly waved as Aidan helped her down from the carriage.

I skipped forwards and gave them both a hug. 'Congratulations, Mr and Mrs Whitby.'

Harry climbed down and shot me a cheeky grin before being instantly besieged by Aidan's niece and nephew who wanted to sit in the carriage. I watched out of the corner of my eye as he let them hold the reins and stroke the horses. He was so patient with them that my heart melted.

'Remember how we met?' Tilly grinned. 'In the café last winter and you came to my Ivy Lane Great Cake Competition?'

I laughed. 'My baking has improved since then, you'll be glad to know.'

Aidan meandered off to have a word with his best man, who was cackling with laughter at something Gemma was saying. Tilly looped her arm through mine.

'Look how far we've come in one year,' she exclaimed, planting a kiss on my cheek. 'Who'd have guessed then that this would be where we'd be now! Me getting married and you organizing the wedding!'

'I'm chuffed to bits for you, Tilly. Aidan will make the perfect husband. Now, you'd better go: I think you're wanted,' I said, releasing her arm.

Uncle Arthur had appeared, accompanied by the gentle clanging of cowbells as he led Gloria, the Jersey cow and her calf, Kim, dressed up in white ribbons and new bells around their necks (that had been a job and a half before breakfast, believe me!), into the yard. Everyone, including our official photographer Natalie, Bill's daughter, lifted their cameras in readiness for some vintage farm photographs.

Harry touched my arm lightly. 'I'll leave the carriage here, I think, for the kids to play in. What do you think?'

'Good idea.' I smiled up at him and let out a deep breath. 'Is it going OK, do you think? I'm so nervous something is going to go wrong any second.'

He grinned. 'You're a born organizer, Freya. Always were. The rest of The Almanacs will arrive about seven, the caterers are already doing a fantastic job if the smell of roast beef is anything to go by and Natalie is taking pictures like they're going out of fashion. Nothing will go wrong.'

He pressed a swift kiss into my hair and I blushed at the tenderness of his gesture.

'Thanks, Harry.' I sighed, feeling my shoulders relax.

'Um. What was it you wanted to say earlier?'

'Er . . .' His voice faded away as Charlie and Anna joined us, arms entwined.

'You've done a great job, you two,' said Charlie, shaking Harry's hand and kissing my cheek chastely. 'The tea rooms, the wedding business . . . the place is unrecognizable.'

'Nothing to do with me,' said Harry matter-of-factly. 'I'm just the carriage driver.'

Anna and I leaped into each other's arms and hugged wildly while the two men traded man-stuff.

'I miss you so much,' groaned Anna. 'You look so different, so . . . I don't know, together, settled, I suppose.'

'I am different.' I shrugged happily. 'I know where I'm going and I know what I want out of life.'

I couldn't resist sneaking a look at Harry as I said that and caught him staring at me. Whoops, now I was blushing and he had a big daft grin on his face.

'Are you sure you don't mind?' she whispered. 'About me and Charlie? Now that you've seen us. In the flesh, as it were.'

'Nooo,' I protested, meaning it, even though I was feeling the most single person on the planet right now. With the exception of Harry, who was also single as far as I knew, but whose fault was that?

Anna was still talking. 'I think I might be in love with Charlie.'

'Oh, Anna, that's brill. And I'm happy for you, really.'

'Do you miss Kingsfield even a little bit?'

'Of course I do!' I exclaimed. 'I miss you and my friends but Lovedale is home.'

'No more flitting round the country, then?' Anna raised an eyebrow in disbelief.

I pulled away from her side and flung an arm out in a grand gesture. 'Look at that view! Who needs the rest of the world when you have paradise on your doorstep?'

Harry covered his mouth with his hand and coughed, but it sounded suspiciously like a laugh to me. 'I'm going to get these horses back to the stables before they get cold,' he said. 'I'll see you later.'

'OK.' I smiled tightly. Were we ever going to have a moment to ourselves?

A loud gong sounded and the catering manager announced that dinner was served.

'Oh gosh,' I yelped, 'I'm supposed to be doing things!'

I scampered off to find my clipboard, my heart squeezing for them as Charlie pulled Anna towards him for a kiss as soon as my back was turned.

Four hours later, Lizzie, Ross and I shifted the tables to the edge of the room to make way for a dance floor while Harry, Tom and Steve did their final sound checks on our makeshift stage at one end of the tea rooms. My back was beginning to ache and my legs were shaky from not having eaten more than a mouthful of the delicious beef, but I felt absolutely elated. Tilly and Aidan's day had been a massive success and I'd even taken another booking for a spring wedding next year.

'Thanks for all your hard work, guys,' I said, hugging them both as we moved the last table. 'I don't think our first wedding could have been more perfect if we tried.'

'Oh, I don't know,' said Lizzie primly, 'I've made one or two notes for our wedding.'

Ross coughed.

'I mean our next wedding,' she corrected herself.

Ross and I looked at each other and shook our heads,

and then we all scattered to different corners of the room as Harry dimmed the lights and jumped on stage. Tom, The Almanacs lead singer, grabbed the microphone.

'Good evening, everyone.' Tom grinned. 'Can we have a huge round of applause please as Mr and Mrs Whitby take to the floor for their first dance?'

We all clapped and whistled as my beaming friend and her new husband appeared on the dance floor and wrapped their arms around each other. As the band began to play the introduction to 'Show Me Heaven' by Maria McKee, I caught Harry's eye and we exchanged a secret smile about blokes playing girlie stuff. Girlie or not, Tom was an amazing singer and The Almanacs did a great version of it. I'd never seen Harry play the drums before and now I couldn't take my eyes off him; he was so absorbed in his music and my heart quickened at being able to watch him unobserved from the edge of the room.

The music filled the old barn and goose bumps pricked at my skin. I leaned up against the wall under the as yet unfinished mezzanine, tucked out of view and watched Aidan twirl Tilly slowly around the dance floor, cupping her face as she laced her fingers behind his neck. The two of them were so wrapped up in each other that it was almost as if they were the only two people in the room and I felt tears spring to my eyes with happiness for them.

As they moved in time with the music, both of them closed their eyes and Tilly rested her forehead against Aidan's cheek. It was such an intimate moment that I felt bit like a voyeur but, even so, I was so moved that I couldn't turn away. The song finished and Aidan and Tilly's parents ran on to the floor and began hugging the happy couple. We all clapped again and my eyes welled up with tears for them.

431

Tom came back on the microphone. 'And now before we pick up the pace, by special request, we're going to do an acoustic version of a Take That number. This one's called "Back For Good".'

I sighed heavily as Tom began to sing; I adored that song. But in the absence of someone to dance with I turned away to go and do something useful and bumped straight into Harry.

My heart lifted at the sight of him and we smiled at each other.

'Hello, drummer boy.'

'You are the soppiest woman I know,' he teased, wiping away the tears that had just started their descent down my cheeks with his thumb.

'Says the boy who cried at *Titanic*,' I scoffed. Technically so had I, but he was a boy and he had been mortified when I'd spotted his tears and told him he should be impervious to the fate of poor Leo. And anyway, Kate had been lying on a massive piece of driftwood, if she'd truly wanted to save him, surely she could have—

'Freya?' Harry's voice was serious all of a sudden.

'Yes,' I said, startled out of my trip down memory lane.

'I requested this song for you. Will you dance with me?'

Words seemed to desert me so I nodded and then felt a hand in mine: warm and rough, a true farmer's hand. And my heart began to race as the hand I knew so well squeezed mine. Not once but three times.

I. Love. You.

Uncle Arthur's secret sign. The breath caught in my throat and I stared at him.

'It's true, Freya,' he murmured close to my ear, sending shivers down my spine.

'You remembered the secret hand squeeze?' I asked

shakily, as Harry wrapped his arm around my waist. He pulled me close and we began to sway in time to the music.

The nearness of his body sent a surge of electricity through mine. I looked at our fingers still entwined. I must have been about fourteen when I told him that story. Round about the time I was obsessed with falling in love; I recalled sighing a lot and professing everything to be 'so romantic'.

'Of course I do.' His eyes gazed at me with such warmth that it was impossible not to understand their meaning. 'I remember everything you ever told me.'

'Oh yeah?' I murmured, laughing softly. 'I'm not sure that's necessarily a good thing. Like what?'

He puffed out his cheeks, his eyes twinkling with mirth. 'Like the time you said if you had a baby boy you'd call him Nick after the one in the Backstreet Boys unless you actually *married* Nick from the Backstreet Boys, in which case you'd call him Howie.'

I clamped a hand to my mouth and giggled. I'd forgotten that. 'What else?'

His eyes locked onto mine as he pressed my hand to his chest. 'Everything. Every memory of you is in here, etched on my heart.'

My whole body melted with love. That was the most beautiful thing anyone had ever said to me.

'Oh, Harry.' I caught his other hand in mine. 'Do you mean,' I swallowed, hardly daring to believe I was saying the words, 'do you mean that you love me?'

His face softened. 'I've loved you all my life,' he said simply. 'Freya, will you tell me something?'

I nodded, overwhelmed by the intensity of his gaze.

He inclined his head towards the stage and grinned. 'Are you back for good?'

I beamed at him. 'Yes. I am.'

He closed his eyes and kissed my forehead. 'Thank God for that. Now stop talking and let me concentrate on the powerful lyrics of Gary Barlow.'

I giggled as Harry pulled me in tightly and for another couple of minutes the two of us circled in time with the music, cheeks pressed together. As the song drew to a close he leaned away from me and nodded to the door.

'Come on, let's go outside. I've waited hours to have you to myself.' His brown eyes twinkled mischievously and I laughed.

'What about the band? Shouldn't you be playing?'

'They don't need me for the next one.'

And hand in hand, trying not to look too obvious, the two of us escaped into the wintry night, closing the big tea room doors behind us.

'It's freezing,' I gasped, laughing as our breath billowed out in a cloud between us.

Harry wrapped his arms round me and rubbed my back to keep me warm.

'I've got an idea,' he said, pulling me to the carriage. 'Jump up.'

I was almost breathless with nervous excitement as the two of us sank down next to each other under the woollen blankets. There was a gentle twanging of guitars coming from the tea rooms, where the tempo had increased a little, and a louder twanging of my heart vibrating against my ribcage.

Harry slid an arm around my shoulders and pulled me close. I reached out a hand and traced a finger along his handsome face.

'I have to say, Harry Graythwaite, you've done a fantastic job of hiding your feelings for me.'

He tilted my chin towards him and stared at me intently. 'I thought you'd never see me as anything but a friend.'

'Same.' I smiled shyly. 'Especially after that disastrous kiss at Willow Farm.'

He groaned and ran a hand through his already messed-up hair. 'In all my wildest dreams about you, Freya, I never imagined that when I finally got the chance to kiss you I'd push you away.'

'So why did you?'

'The last summer you were here, when we were both eighteen, I felt like my whole life was planned out for me – uni and then back to the farm – and I felt trapped. You, on the other hand, were free to go wherever you wanted with whomever you wanted. And what I wanted more than anything was to be with you. You broke my heart when you left Lovedale that summer and being a bit of a coward, I didn't want to risk that happening again.'

I frowned at him. 'Harry, I'm so sorry. I knew that something had changed between us, but I had no idea that you felt that way.'

He shrugged. 'I know. I was going to tell you how I felt but then you said you wouldn't be back in Lovedale until you'd seen the world and I remember thinking: *That's that then, she'll never be back.*'

I nodded slowly, as the memory from that day came trickling back. I'd barely seen him after that conversation, he'd always made an excuse for not meeting up and then I'd left the farm and not seen him again for years.

'But I did come back,' I said. 'I came home. And I am so glad I did.'

He slid his fingers across my face until his hand was cupping the back of my head. We were so close now that I could feel the heat from his body.

435

'Me too. But even then I didn't think for one moment that you'd stay,' he said. 'I assumed you'd be off again on another adventure. And who could blame you?'

I shook my head firmly. 'Not this time,' I whispered. 'I'm not going anywhere. I love you, Harry.'

He lowered his face to mine. 'Really?'

His breath was on my lips and suddenly my body didn't feel cold any more.

'Really.'

Across the yard, lights glowed at every window of the old stone farmhouse. A canopy of stars twinkled high above us and we were surrounded by garlands of ivy, ribbon and mistletoe entwined around the carriage. It was the perfect place to fall in love and my heart swooped with happiness.

I slipped my arms around Harry's neck and he pulled me on to his lap, all the time holding my gaze.

Slowly he brushed his lips against mine and the moment seemed to hang in the air between us, as if time was standing still in order for us to savour our first kiss.

Harry kissed me and I kissed him back, gently at first and then deeper, as his arms tightened around me. I felt my body melt against his, no longer certain where I ended and he began.

His kiss tasted of home and I knew there would never be anywhere else I would rather be than in this man's arms. Harry was, I thought dreamily, my perfect match.

Our first kiss lasted for ages, which was absolutely fine by me. When we finally came up for air, Harry looked so pleased with himself that I laughed with sheer joy.

'I guess that means we're past the "friends" stage,' I said, leaning back as far as I could until we both tumbled down on to the velvet cushions.

'Freya Moorcroft,' said Harry, his voice gruff with desire, 'I've waited ten years for that kiss.'

And so, I realized, as I pulled him down to kiss him again, had I.

Paradise

A long weekend away in March was all we could manage to squeeze in. We were so busy, what with Harry's fledgling biofuels crops to look after and the start of the wedding season nearly upon us. Besides, neither of us wanted to leave Lizzie and Ross in charge of Willow Farm and Mum and Dad looking after Appleby Farm for much longer than that. But as Harry pointed out, a long weekend still constituted a holiday and as we had had an incredibly wet winter – even by Lake District standards – and he hadn't left the country for five years, we were both revelling in the Moroccan sunshine and savouring every precious moment together.

On our second evening we were sitting on our little mosaic-tiled terrace enjoying the soft breeze and the hazy sun, sipping at cold beers. My skin was tingling from so much unaccustomed sun. Somehow, despite using factor-fifty sunblock, I'd managed to burn both my knees and, attractively, one side of my face. Harry, of course, had turned a delicious shade of brown. He was sitting on the other side of the table, head tilted back, snoozing away, his beer resting on his bare chest.

I clunked my beer bottle on to the patio table decisively,

stood up and moved behind his chair, wrapping my arms around his neck.

'Are you tired?' I asked.

He opened one eye, raised an eyebrow seductively and sat up straight. 'No.'

'Good.' My lips twitched at the disappointment on his face as I popped a pen and postcard on his lap.

'That was sneaky,' he tutted.

'Oh, come on.' I laughed. 'We need to send them today or they won't reach England until after we're back.'

For a few minutes we sat in silence while we penned our postcards home. Correction – I was silent, Harry alternated between whistling under his breath, umming and ahhing, and complaining that he hadn't sent a postcard to his parents since he left school.

As soon as mine was finished, I laid it on the table triumphantly and picked up my beer.

'I'm done.'

Hey Lizzie

YAY! We're on holiday! Morocco is fab. Fact. You should come. But not for a while because I can't manage the tea rooms without you (sorry!).

The pool is lovely but the sea is FREEZING! And this morning we sat on the beach playing cards and a man walked up with a camel and sat down next to us to watch! Cray-cray, as you would say.

Anyway, you know that thing you said about Ross being The One and when you know, you know? Well, I totally get that now.

And that is all.

Love

Freya xx

PS I had tiramisu last night . . . delicious   ;)

Lizzie Moon

Willow Farm

Lovedale Road

Lovedale

The Lake District

England

Harry was still deep in concentration, pen poised.

'Come on, Graythwaite, what are you writing – *War and Peace*?' I teased.

Not that I minded; he looked completely gorgeous in his swimming shorts and I was more than happy to sit and look at him unobserved.

He tossed his postcard on to the table, took a long swig of his beer, shielding his eyes from the sun as he grinned at me. 'Done.'

'Can I read it?' I asked, interested to see what he'd said about me to my prospective in-laws.

He lifted a shoulder lazily, which I took as a yes, so I reached out and pulled it close enough to read and laughed as he murmured 'nosy' under his breath.

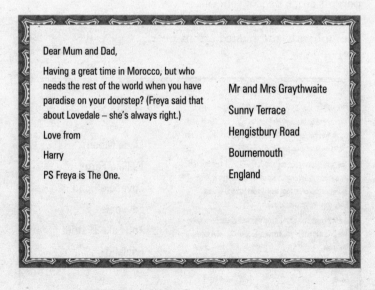

Dear Mum and Dad,

Having a great time in Morocco, but who needs the rest of the world when you have paradise on your doorstep? (Freya said that about Lovedale – she's always right.)

Love from

Harry

PS Freya is The One.

Mr and Mrs Graythwaite

Sunny Terrace

Hengistbury Road

Bournemouth

England

'Oh,' I said inadequately, brushing a stray tear from my face.

Harry stood up and leaned over me. He planted a soft kiss on my lips.

'Will that do?' he asked.

'Yes, Harry Graythwaite,' I smiled, as he scooped me up and carried me into our room, 'that's absolutely perfect.'

THE END

The Thank Yous

As always, thanks and much love to my family, Tony, Phoebe and Isabel, for all your cheering and flag-waving during 2014.

Appleby Farm covers topics that I really had no clue about and so I owe a huge debt of thanks to hordes of people for their kindness and generosity of time. You know how at the end of *The Archers*, they always mention an Agricultural Consultant? Well, I had lots of them in this book! My sincere thanks to David Prince of Wood Farm, John Hardy of Jericho Farm and Geoff Brown of Bluebell Dairy. And an extra special thanks must go to Charlotte Sharphouse and Joe White from the wonderful Old Hall Farm, a working Victorian farm in the Lake District which inspired the setting for *Appleby Farm*. Any farming inaccuracies are completely down to me!

To Gina McLachlan, thank you very much for planning out poor Uncle Arthur's health issues!

Thanks to Chris Hanbury for your musical knowledge of cheesy wedding first dances and for coming up with the name for Harry's band.

Many thanks to Julie Gregory, who let me cuddle one of her chickens (Mrs Fluffybum to be exact) and who showed me where her hens like to lay eggs. And a second thank you to farmer David Prince, whose egg-eating dog gave me an idea for a storyline!

Thank you to my agent Hannah Ferguson for your wise words of encouragement throughout the year and for keeping me writing when times were tricky. And editor extraordinaire Harriet Bourton, you clever clogs, you! Without your initial spark of an idea, this book wouldn't have happened at all!

As a marketing bod myself, I know how much hard work goes on behind the scenes to make things look effortlessly successful and so I consider myself truly fortunate to work with such an enthusiastic, supportive and passionate team of people at Transworld. Yes, I'm looking at you, Bella Bosworth, Sarah Harwood, September Withers, Laura Swainbank and Helen Gregory. Thank you, lovelies!

Finally, to some very special people. I am writing this after completing the *Appleby Farm* cover reveal promotion. Thank you to the wonderful bloggers and reviewers for your constant support and excitement for my books, it is a pleasure to know you: Jill Stratton, Dawn Crooks, Janet Emson, Louise Wykes, Ananda and Marina from @ThisChickReads, Erin McEwan, Jody Hoekstra, JB Johnston, Kim Nash, Sharon Goodwin, Kirsty Maclennon, Catriona Merryweather and Sonya Alford. You ladies are the best!

*Enjoy an extract from another charming
modern love story from Cathy Bramley*

Conditional Love

A takeaway, TV and tea with two sugars is about as
exciting as it gets for thirty-something Sophie Stone.
Sophie's life is safe and predictable, which is just
the way she likes it, thank you very much.

But when a mysterious benefactor leaves her an
inheritance, Sophie has to accept that change is afoot.
There is one big catch: in order to inherit, Sophie must
agree to meet the father she has never seen.

Saying 'yes' means the chance to build her
own dream home, but she'll also have to face
the past and hear some uncomfortable truths . . .

With interference from an evil boss, warring parents,
an unreliable boyfriend and an architect who puts
his foot in it every time he opens his mouth,
will Sophie be able to build a future on her own
terms – and maybe even find love along the way?

Read on for a sneak peek at the opening chapter!

Chapter 1

I woke up on the floor, wedged between the bed and bedside table. My hip bone was bruised, my skin was mottled with cold and I had pins and needles in my arm. Painted across my face was the smug smile of a woman who hadn't got much sleep the night before. Getting up was a priority; I was freezing and I really didn't want Marc to wake up and find me down here.

It took a full thirty seconds of grunting, shuffling, inelegant flailing of limbs and a carpet burn to my right buttock to wriggle free. Not a pretty sight.

I sighed with pleasure at the slumbering, golden-haired Adonis taking up the entire width of the mattress. He looked so peaceful. He was certainly a deep sleeper; he hadn't even woken up when he'd pushed me out of the bed.

Silently, I opened the drawer, took out the card I'd lovingly made for him with my own fair hands and slid it under the pillow. Then I slipped back under the duvet and perched on the edge, savouring the heat from his perfectly honed body. I propped myself up on my elbow and gazed at him.

It was Valentine's Day and I had a boyfriend.

I couldn't help grinning.

Last year – and the year before that, come to think of it – I had been single and I'd had to hibernate for a full twenty-four hours until the dreaded day was history and I could stop feeling marginalized by society. In fact, since Jeremy a few years ago – I shuddered at the memory of my controlling ex-boyfriend – I hadn't let anyone get close. But Marc was different.

He and I had been together for nine months and last night was the first time that he had stayed over. I'd invited him to before now but he had a stall on Sneinton market and usually had to get up for work really early and said he didn't want to wake me. But last night he'd said he didn't have to be there until nine, so he might as well stay. How romantic – to choose Valentine's Day as the first time to wake up next to me!

Right, let's get the party started.

I coughed lightly but there was no response, not a flicker of his golden eyelashes.

I coughed more sharply and this time he stirred and stretched, threatening my precarious position on the edge of the bed, and I grabbed hold of his arm.

Oh, those biceps!

'Morning, princess.' He yawned and gave me an almighty slap on the bottom.

I knew this was his idea of being affectionate but it was hardly the most romantic wake-up call. I replied with my own delicate yawn, and smiled in what I hoped was a 'Sleeping Beauty awakened by a True Love's Kiss' type manner.

He picked up his watch, swore under his breath and swung his legs over the side of the bed.

I flopped onto my back and pulled the duvet up, enjoying the extra room in the bed. Also enjoying the view of muscles rippling across chest as he pulled his jeans up over firm thighs. What a man!

Oh no, I was a bit slow on the uptake there, he was getting dressed! That wasn't first on my agenda of love.

Marc looked down at me, his face suddenly serious. Oh my giddy aunt! He was working up to something.

He cleared his throat. 'Sophie, we need to talk.'

He sat back down on the bed and reached for my hand. Darting eyes, heavy breathing, serious face . . . If I didn't know better, I'd have thought he was going to propose. Hold on a mo – it *was* Valentine's Day, what if . . . ?

'Wait!' I yelled, making Marc flinch.

If he was going to propose, I didn't want to be lying on my back like an invalid. I pushed myself up to a semi-sitting position and rested my arms on top of the duvet.

Oops! Never flatten your arms against your body. It adds at least thirty per cent to the surface area of each limb. I read it in *Heat* magazine in a feature on how to look good in photos.

I raised my arms off the duvet and smiled brightly.

Marc frowned. Poor love; this sort of thing must be so nerve-racking. Shame really, in this day and age all the stress shouldn't be loaded onto the man. Still, the woman usually ends up organizing the wedding, so it sort of evens itself out in the long run.

'Sorry! You were saying?' I nodded at him encouragingly.

Marc exhaled and gazed at me with his baby-blue eyes. That was the look of love. Right there.

'There's no easy way to say this, princess, but . . .'

What the fudge?

I gasped, but the nerves-induced accumulation of saliva in my throat created a strangled sort of gurgle. My spit went

449

down the wrong hole and I started to choke. Not attractive, nor in the least bit timely.

Marc, determined to finish now he was on a roll, carried on slashing my newly minted dreams of married bliss into ribbons, while simultaneously slapping me on the back. Hard.

By the time I had found the wherewithal to hold my hands up, beseeching him to stop, he had all but finished his 'Dear Sophie' monologue.

The message had been clear, but what had he actually said? Straining to hear over my own ear-splitting wheezing, I had only caught one or two words. I must have misheard; I thought he used words like 'different things', 'boring', 'freedom' and 'nice'.

He backed away from my single bed, from me and from our relationship towards the bedroom door, holding onto my fingers until the last possible second. It was quite a poignant moment: if I hadn't been puce and completely hoarse, I might have said something profound. But other than to wail 'Why? Why?' at him, words completely failed me. So I stayed silent, doomed to for ever hold my peace.

He winked and was gone.

Happy chuffin' Valentine's Day.

'Zombie-like' was the best way to describe my mood at work over the following ten hours. At my desk in the advertising department for *The Herald*, Nottingham's daily newspaper, I barely registered the banter of my colleagues or my overflowing in-tray. My hands simulated typing on my keyboard, but in reality I was simply going through the motions and I avoided the phone all day.

The bus ride home, normally quite an ordeal, was comparatively therapeutic. At least I didn't have to talk to anyone.

It was shaping up to be the worst Valentine's Day of my entire life. What was I saying – 'shaping up'? How could it possibly get any worse? By the time my flatmates had rallied round me this morning, Jess making soothing noises and placing a mug of sweet tea in front of me and Emma threatening to cut off Marc's balls and feed them to the squirrels, I had already pronounced the day an unprecedented disaster.

I was determined not to cry again. And that was no mean feat seeing as the evening commuter bus I was on appeared to be packed almost entirely with smooching couples and women with huge bouquets of flowers, cruelly serving to ram home my new single status.

Facebook! I was going to have to update my relationship status to 'single'. But not today; I couldn't face the humiliation of declaring myself single on the international day of love.

I shook my head, still struggling to comprehend what had happened this morning. I'd been convinced that today was the day that Marc would reveal his true feelings for me. Well he'd certainly done that. Be careful what you wish for, as the saying goes.

All my Valentine's Day dreams were in tatters. I thought of the little nest egg that I'd been building up for years, waiting for the right time, the right person to settle down with. I'd begun to think that Marc could be that person. Not that we'd ever discussed a joint future, although he did once ask to dip into my savings to get a new business off the ground and we were both in our early thirties, I'd assumed it would just happen one day; it was only a matter of time.

With a sigh, I shifted the dream of having my own home to the back burner, along with my other abandoned dreams; the property market was no place for single, first-time buyers at the moment – far too risky!

At my bus stop, a group of people – in twos, obviously – jostled against me as I tried to disembark. I was barely clear of the last step when the bus trundled off through a puddle, sending a spray of black slush up the back of my tights.

Marvellous.

How could snow – so white, so pure, so beautiful – turn so vile in only a few hours? It was clearly a metaphor for a love gone sour. I huffed up the steps towards home, feeling forlorn and uncomfortably wet.

The Victorian house we lived in had long ago been split into flats. I let myself in and flicked through the mail on the communal post shelf. No scented envelopes, huge bouquets of flowers or small square boxes with 'To Sophie Stone – love of my life' on them, then? No? Thought as much.

Tears welled up in my eyes and I brushed them away. Actually, why shouldn't I have a good cry? I was sad, might be properly sad for weeks, come to think of it. I loved Marc, he was so big and strong and unpredictable. Emma would say that this was a reason *not* to love him but he was exciting and I was going to miss having that excitement in my life.

For a moment, I considered sliding down the wall to the floor and succumbing to my sorrow. But it looked draughty and very public, far better to get home and let my lovely flatmates cheer me up.

I began the ascent to flat four, sniffing the air hopefully on the off-chance of catching any tantalizing aromas even though it was my turn to cook. Nothing. I waggled the key in the lock and pushed my way into the tiny hall.

'Oh, babes, are you OK? I've been worried about you

all day.' Jess threw her arms round me, crushing me to her bosom.

'I'm fine.' I swallowed hard, lying through my teeth, and pulled back to examine my plumptious flatmate.

Jess narrowed her eyes. 'Sure?'

I nodded. 'Why are you wearing a toga?'

'It's not a toga, it's a chiton,' she replied, releasing me to perform a twirl in front of the hall mirror. 'I'm doing Ancient Greeks with Year Five.'

Despite my crushing melancholy, I managed a smile. Jess was a born teacher and always threw herself wholeheartedly into every topic. And even in an old sheet she looked fabulous.

'Ah, of course it is, I can tell now.' I grinned. 'You look great, Jess.'

'Thanks, babes!'

Right, food. I left her measuring the circumference of her head with a piece of string and made my way into our uninspiring kitchen.

The fridge revealed nothing much except a pack of Marc's chicken breasts. I always liked to keep high-protein food in for him in case he popped in for a snack after the gym. They were slightly grey and slimy and was I imagining it, or did they have a stain of abandonment about them? I sighed loudly and dropped them in the bin.

There was nothing else for it; it would have to be 'three-tin surprise'. Not my favourite; in fact, no one was fond of it. I had gleaned all my culinary talents from my mother; it hadn't taken long. She was to cooking what Heston Blumenthal was to hairstyling: a total stranger. This particular concoction was like playing Russian roulette with your taste buds and suited my mood perfectly.

'Come to Auntie Em!'

453

I turned to see Emma holding her arms out. With her overalls, stripy T-shirt and long red plaits she looked like an over-sized Pippi Longstocking.

I dived into her arms, buried my face in her neck and felt tears prick at my eyes for the umpteenth time.

'How are you doing, kiddo?' she murmured.

'Oh Emma, I'm just . . . I can't . . . you know.'

'Yeah, I know,' said Emma, soothingly.

I knew her tongue would be bitten to shreds with the effort of not blurting out, 'I told you so.'

She had never been a huge fan of Marc and I was grateful that she hadn't started another character assassination tonight; I didn't have the energy.

Emma had been my best friend since college. She had been doing an art foundation course and I was studying A-levels.

She had been taller, louder and brasher than me at sixteen. I had been hovering timidly on the edge of college life until she plucked me out of the shadows and tucked me under her wing. I had stayed there ever since.

Now she was a self-employed silversmith with a studio in a trendy part of Nottingham. The stuff she designed ranged from contemporary fruit bowls through to intricate one-off pieces of jewellery. Ironically, the only jewellery she wore was a shell she'd found in Cornwall while surfing, threaded onto a piece of leather.

'I forgot.' Jess bounded into the room, her auburn bob now adorned with a headdress made from bay leaves stuck to a bra strap. 'A letter came for you.' She placed an envelope reverently on the kitchen table. 'It looks important.'

I abandoned the quest for tins immediately, my heart beating furiously as I grabbed the envelope. Perhaps all was not lost, perhaps . . .

'It's from a firm of solicitors,' said Emma, reading the franking label over my shoulder.

My heart sank and then immediately leapt up to somewhere just below my throat.

Solicitors?

Why did I automatically feel guilty even though, as far as I could remember, I had done absolutely nothing wrong? It was the same when I passed through the 'Nothing to Declare' channel at the airport; I would blush, let out a high-pitched giggle and start making jokes about the two thousand cigarettes in my bag. I don't even smoke.

'Hey! You don't think Marc has done something dodgy, do you, and implicated you in it?' said Jess, wide-eyed.

Emma gave her a sharp look. 'Of course not, it's probably something nice. Go on, open it!'

'Yes,' I said, trying to think positive, 'it could be um . . .'

Emma nudged Jess and winked. 'I know. It's a restraining order from Gary Barlow's people!'

Jess giggled and they linked arms, started swaying and launched into the chorus of 'A Million Love Songs'.

Despite my nerves, I couldn't help smiling. The two girls were more than flatmates; they were sisters, Jess being the elder by two years. I loved them both dearly and they treated me like a third sister, which in practice meant that they both mothered me and teased me mercilessly.

I prodded Emma in the ribs. 'Hey, leave me alone. I haven't written to him for ages.'

We shared a smile and I turned my attention back to the letter in my hands.

'Oh my Lordy,' I continued. 'Listen to this: "Dear Miss Stone, Whelan and Partners have been appointed . . . blah, blah, blah . . . writing to inform you that you are a beneficiary in the last will and testament of Mrs Jane Kennedy.

Please contact this office at your earliest convenience. Yours, blah, blah, blah . . .'

I plopped down into a chair, dropping the letter onto the table. The sisters picked it up and looked at it.

'Bloody hell, Sophie!'

'A mystery benefactor!' squealed Jess. 'How exciting!'

'Well, whoever she is, I think this calls for wine.' Emma darted to the fridge and poured three large glasses while I reread the solicitor's letter.

Jess sat down next to me at the kitchen table and patted my hand. 'There you go, you see. The day might have started badly, but this letter,' she tapped it with a sharp pink nail, 'might be the beginning of a whole new adventure.'

'Exactly,' said Emma, holding up her glass. 'Cheers!'

Just then Jess's stomach gave an almighty rumble. 'Ooh, excuse me! Who's cooking dinner?'

I didn't reply. I was still staring at that letter. *More to the point*, my brain cried out, *who's Jane Kennedy?*

Enjoy as an ebook now or available in paperback November 2015!

Or you could try the fresh, funny
and sweetly romantic . . .

Tilly Parker needs a fresh start, fresh air and a
fresh attitude if she is ever to leave the past behind
and move on with her life. As she seeks out peace
and quiet in a new town, taking on a plot at Ivy Lane
allotments seems like the perfect solution.

But the friendly Ivy Lane community has other ideas
and gradually draw Tilly in to their cosy, comforting
world of planting seedlings, organizing bake sales
and planning seasonal parties.

As the seasons pass, will Tilly learn to stop
hiding amongst the sweetpeas and let people
back into her life – and her heart?

Available now

And coming soon . . .

Wickham Hall

Holly Swift has just landed the job of her dreams: events
co-ordinator at Wickham Hall, the beautiful manor home
that sits proudly at the heart of the village where she grew
up. Not only does she get to organize for a living and
work in stunning surroundings, but it will also put a bit of
distance between Holly and her problems at home.

As Holly falls in love with the busy world of Wickham
Hall – from family weddings to summer festivals, firework
displays and Christmas grottos – she also finds a place in
her heart for her friendly (if unusual) colleagues.

But life isn't as easily organized as an event at Wickham
Hall (and even those have their complications . . .). Can
Holly learn to let go and live in the moment?

After all, that's when the magic happens . . .

Available in paperback January 2016!

Appleby Farm recipes

Cathy's Afternoon Tea Favourites

Victoria Sponge

For me, a slice of light and fluffy Victoria Sponge, filled with strawberry jam (preferably homemade) and dusted with crunchy caster sugar, simply cannot be beaten. The best one I have ever tasted was made by my daughter Phoebe, who overheard my Auntie Kath talking about her fail-safe method and then came home and baked the most perfect cake ever. The secret lies in the weight of the eggs . . .

You will need . . .

3 large eggs weighed in their shells (note this down!)

The same weight of caster sugar, self-raising flour and room-temperature butter

1 teaspoon baking powder

A pinch of salt

Strawberry jam

Extra caster sugar for dusting

Grease 2 x 20cm sandwich tins and line the bases with greaseproof paper. Pre-heat the oven to 180°C (350°F/ gas mark 4). Combine the butter and sugar and beat until really light and fluffy. Whisk the eggs together and then add them to the mixture gradually. Fold in the sifted flour, baking powder and salt (I usually use a spatula to do this part.)

Divide the batter between the two tins, spread the top to smooth it out a little and pop them into the middle of the oven for 25–30 minutes. Don't open the oven for at least 20 minutes! The sponge is cooked when a skewer inserted into the centre comes out clean.

Allow to cool in the tin completely and then transfer to a wire cooling rack. Choose the nicest one to be the top. Place the other one on a plate and smother it generously with strawberry jam (avoid big fruity lumps). Add the other sponge cake and sprinkle with caster sugar.

Serve as soon as possible for maximum fluffiness!

Scrumptious Scones

Dried fruit has its place: Christmas cake, for example, and mince pies. But I think scones are better unadulterated, just meltingly soft as soon as they are cool enough to slice and spread with clotted cream and a dollop of jam! According to Auntie Sue, the secret to perfect scones is in the mixing: over-mix and you've got yourself a batch of primitive weapons . . .

You will need . . .

225g self-raising flour

Large pinch of salt

50g of slightly salted butter

25g caster sugar

125ml buttermilk

4 tablespoons of milk

Flour for dusting

Clotted cream and jam to serve

Preheat the oven to 220°C (425°F/gas mark 7). Grease a large baking sheet (unless it's non-stick). Sift the flour into a mixing bowl and add the salt. Chop the butter into small cubes and add to the bowl. Rub the butter into the flour swiftly to make crumbs, lifting the mixture as you go to aerate it. Stir in the sugar.

Add the milk to the buttermilk. Make a well in the centre of the mixing bowl and add nearly all of the milk mixture. Use a palette knife or spatula to gently work the milk into the mixture to form a soft dough. Add the rest of the milk if needed to draw in any dry bits. Don't over-work the dough or you'll end up with tough scones.

Place the dough on a lightly floured surface and press it down with the palm of your hand to a thickness of 2.5cm. Dip a 5.5cm fluted cutter into the flour and cut out the scones by pressing firmly into the dough and not twisting. Gather the leftovers, pat them out again and cut out as many scones as you can. Arrange them on the baking sheet and sift a little flour over the tops. Bake for 10–12 minutes until golden.

Allow to cool on a wire rack and serve with jam and clotted cream straight from the fridge.

Yum.

Banana and Chocolate Chip Loaf

This recipe comes from my editor – it's a tasty, sweet loaf cake that her mother has made for years and is a true family favourite. The bananas are best when very ripe, so there's no need to throw away those forgotten blackened bananas left in your fruit bowl at the end of the week: you can make this delicious treat instead! It goes perfectly with a cup of Earl Grey tea.

You will need . . .

   2 large, ripe bananas

   225g self-raising flour

   170g caster sugar

   115g margarine or butter, at room temperature

   2 eggs

   1 teaspoon baking powder

   1 tablespoon honey or golden syrup

   1 teaspoon cinnamon

   85g chocolate chips (you can usually buy them in small packets – one of these is fine)

1 tablespoon Demerara sugar, for sprinkling on top of the cake

Grease and line a 2lb loaf tin and heat the oven to 160°C (320°F/gas mark 3).

Into a large bowl, sieve the flour, baking powder and cinnamon. Add the other ingredients and mix (either with a wooden spoon or an electric hand mixer) just until smooth.

Put into the loaf tin, level the surface and sprinkle the Demerara evenly over the cake. Bake for 50–60 minutes, then test with a cake tester or fine skewer – poke the centre of the cake, it shouldn't stick to the skewer. The cake may need 5–10 minutes more; ovens can vary!

Cool in the tin for a few minutes and then on a rack. Serve with tea and be prepared for it to go quickly . . .

Chocolate Brownies

This is one of my daughter Isabel's favourite recipes: she even made it on Christmas Day as an alternative to Christmas pudding! It's supposed to make 16 pieces, but in our house, we cut it into 12 . . . They will last for days (in theory!) in an airtight container.

You will need . . .

100g lightly salted butter
150g dark chocolate
3 eggs

200g caster sugar

100g self-raising flour

Icing sugar to dust

Pre-heat the oven to 180°C (350°F/gas mark 4). Line a 20cm square cake tin or baking dish with greaseproof paper and grease lightly.

Gently melt the butter and chocolate in a bowl above a pan of simmering water.

While it's melting, beat the eggs and sugar together with an electric whisk until light and fluffy. Add the flour and mix well. Pour the melted butter and chocolate mixture into the bowl and stir until combined.

Pour into the tin and bake for 35–40 minutes. Remove from the oven when the edges are beginning to crack but the centre is still slightly squidgy. Allow to cool in the tin, sprinkle with icing sugar and cut into squares as big as you like!

Delicious served with crème fraîche or vanilla ice cream.

Lemon Drizzle Cake

My mum rarely arrives at our house without a cake, and this is one of our favourites! Some recipes melt the sugar and lemon juice to pour over the cake at the end, but the Bramleys prefer the crunchy top of this version.

You will need . . .

88g golden caster sugar

88g soft margarine

Grated zest of a lemon

1½ large eggs

88g of self-raising flour, sifted

¾ teaspoon of baking powder

A pinch of salt

For the lemon topping:

50g granulated sugar

Juice of half a lemon

Line a well-greased 1lb loaf tin with baking parchment and pre-heat the oven to 180°C (350°F/gas mark 4).

Using an electric mixer, beat the sugar, margarine and lemon zest in a mixing bowl until pale and fluffy. Gradually add the eggs a little at a time to avoid them curdling. Carefully fold in the flour, baking powder and salt.

Pour the mixture into the tin and bake for 30–35 minutes or until a skewer comes out clean and the cake is firm to the touch. Remove from the oven and leave in the tin on a cooling rack.

To make the topping, simply stir the sugar into the lemon juice and pour over the still-warm cake. Once the cake has cooled, remove it from the tin, shout 'The cake is ready!' and stand back!

Agent Fergie's Stem Ginger Cookies

I'm thrilled to include a recipe from my agent, Hannah Ferguson . . .

I can't count the number of times I've made these glorious
stem ginger cookies for friends and family. They go down
especially well with my niece and nephews, and those three
mini bakers have now mastered the art of the stem ginger
cookie for themselves. Their favourite part is scooping out
that magical golden syrup from the tin and watching it run
into the weighing scales . . . and, of course, the messy icing
at the end!

You will need . . .

115g unsalted butter

85g golden syrup

350g self-raising flour

4 teaspoons of ground ginger

1 teaspoon of bicarbonate of soda

200g caster sugar

1 egg

40g crystallized stem ginger

For the icing:

300g of icing sugar

5–6 teaspoons of water

Pre-heat the oven to 170°C (325°F/gas mark 3). Line two baking trays with greaseproof paper and then lightly grease with a small knob of butter.

Slowly melt the butter with the golden syrup in a pan over a low heat, stirring as you go. Be careful not to let it get too hot and boil! Once it is completely melted set it aside to cool.

Sift the self-raising flour, ground ginger, bicarbonate of soda and sugar into a mixing bowl. Then, once the butter and syrup mixture is barely warm, add it to all the dry ingredients in the mixing bowl.

Beat one egg and finely chop the crystallized ginger and then add both of these to the mixing bowl. Mix everything together with a wooden spoon, making sure all the ingredients are thoroughly combined. Once mixed well, divide into 24 equal-sized portions and, using your hands, roll each one into a smooth ball, about the size of a conker.

Place on to the baking tray – it's important to leave enough space between each ball as the cookies will spread when baking, so do in two batches if it is easier. Bake in the pre-heated oven for 15–20 minutes until a golden-brown colour.

Remove from the oven and transfer on to a wire cooling rack. Once completely cooled you can prepare your icing!

For the icing, weigh out 300g of icing sugar. Add 5–6 teaspoons of water a little at a time until you reach a smooth and runny consistency. Using a teaspoon, scoop up a little of the icing and run in a zigzag motion over each biscuit to create a random stripy pattern. Don't worry if it gets messy – these biscuits aren't meant to look perfect.

Leave the icing to dry – and then enjoy. Please note: these go exceptionally well with a large, hot mug of tea.

Chocolate Roulade with Fresh Cream

My friend Alison made this at her Christmas party last year and it disappeared in minutes! It looks amazing and is very light. It doesn't contain any flour, so perfect for people on a gluten-free diet!

You will need . . .

   170g dark chocolate
   4 eggs
   170g caster sugar
   300ml double cream
   Icing sugar to dust

Pre-heat the oven to 180°C (350°F/gas mark 4). Line a swiss roll tin with greaseproof paper and grease lightly. Gently melt the chocolate in a bowl above a pan of simmering water.

Separate the eggs, and mix the egg yolks with the caster sugar and melted chocolate. Whisk the egg whites until they form stiff peaks, and fold thoroughly into the chocolate mixture.

Pour into the prepared tin and bake in the pre-heated oven for 20 minutes. Remove from the oven when the sponge is springy to the touch, and allow the cake to cool completely in the tin, preferably overnight.

Turn the sponge out on to a clean piece of greaseproof paper. Whisk the double cream until thick but not solid and spread over the cake. Using the paper, roll the cake up carefully and decorate with icing sugar.

Courgette and Lime Cake

My friend Rachel is an excellent cook and we all tuck into her cakes eagerly. It was only after I'd declared this cake to be delicious that she told me what was in it. A-maz-ing.

You will need . . .

3 medium eggs
125ml vegetable oil
150g caster sugar
225g self-raising flour
½ teaspoon bicarbonate of soda
½ teaspoon baking powder
250g courgette, finely grated
For the icing:
400g cream cheese

175g icing sugar

2 tablespoons lime juice

40g pistachio nuts (finely chopped)

1 tablespoon lime zest

Pre-heat the oven to 180°C (350°F/gas mark 4). Grease and line two 21cm sandwich tins.

Beat together the eggs, oil and sugar in a large bowl until creamy. Sift in the flour, bicarbonate of soda and baking powder, and mix well. Stir in the grated courgettes until well combined. Divide the mixture into the cake tins and bake in the middle of the oven for 25–30 minutes.

Remove the cakes from the oven and carefully turn out on to a wire rack. Carefully peel off the paper lining and leave to cool.

For the icing, beat the cream cheese in a bowl until smooth. Sift in the icing sugar and stir in the lime juice.

Use a bread knife to level one of the cakes if necessary. Use ⅔ of the icing to sandwich the two cakes together (the levelled one on the bottom) and use the remaining icing to cover the top of the cake.

Sprinkle with the pistachio nuts and lime zest, and serve immediately.

Florentines

This is my grandmother, Mary's, recipe. She used to make these when she had her ladies' coffee evenings and she always seemed to have a box of them in the fridge whenever I went round to visit her. They are absolutely delicious but very rich so cut them into small squares.

You will need . . .

- 225g dark chocolate
- 125g glace cherries
- 125g sultanas (or mixed fruit if that's what you've got)
- 125g sugar
- 125g desiccated coconut
- 1 egg

Line a tin with silver foil. Melt the chocolate and pour over the foil. Place into the fridge until set.

Roughly chop the cherries and sultanas and add to a bowl with the sugar, coconut and egg. Mix well and spread over the chocolate.

Heat the oven to 190°C (375°F/gas mark 5) and bake for 20 minutes.

Allow to completely cool, pop it into to fridge to chill for half an hour and then cut into small squares. They will keep for quite a while in an airtight box in the fridge.

Helen Redfern's Pistachio Meringues

Many of you will have heard of Helen; she writes for Novelicious and has her own blog HelenRedfern.co.uk. I spent a week on a writing retreat with her recently and when I told her that I was including recipes in my book, she kindly offered to donate this one, which is perfect because something very similar appears in the Appleby Farm Vintage Tea Rooms.

You will need . . .

   4 egg whites

   200g caster sugar

   50g shelled pistachio nuts, bashed into small pieces

Pre-heat the oven to 180°C (350°F/gas mark 4). Mix the egg whites on a fast speed until stiff and able to form peaks. Slow the mixer down but keep going and slowly pour in the caster sugar. Mix on a fast speed until the mixture again can form stiff peaks.

Gently mix in the bashed up pistachios.

Lay out the baking parchment onto the baking tray – use a small blob of the meringue mixture to stick the parchment down in each corner. Draw four large circles with a pencil – I draw round a bowl measuring 12cm in diameter.

Scoop the meringue evenly onto the four circles. Use your spoon to smooth or create a swirl effect up to the pencil edges.

Place in the pre-heated oven and immediately turn it down to 150°C (300°F/gas mark 2). Bake for one hour. When the timer goes off leave to cool in the oven for at least one more hour. Remove from the oven and enjoy!

Bookcamp Biscuit Cake

Cesca Major is not only an amazing writer and organizer of Bookcamp writing retreats, she makes delicious cakes too. I'm honoured to be able to share her rather fun recipe for Biscuit Cake in her own words . . .

You will need . . .

A bar of dark chocolate

3 tablespoons of golden syrup

3 tablespoons of butter or margarine

A load of crunched-up digestive biscuits

A bar of white chocolate

A bag of Maltesers

Melt the chocolate, syrup and butter together.

Whack in a load of crunched-up digestive biscuits. Press into a pan.

When set, melt the white chocolate and spread it over the surface of the biscuit cake.

Chop up the Maltesers into halves and press them into the surface.

YUM.

Harriet Bourton's Mini Victoria Sponges

These miniature Victoria sponge cakes are actually rather like *Appleby Farm*: bite-sized, sweet and irresistibly more-ish! I find it best to cook the cakes in plain cases and then once you've halved and filled them, place them into new, clean paper cases. They are also incredibly easy to make, and I always use Bonne Maman jam – I just think it has the best flavour and you only get a dollop with these . . .

You will need . . .

170g self-raising flour
170g golden caster sugar
170g Stork margarine
3 eggs
A drop of vanilla essence
For the filling:
Double cream, whipped
1 tbsp icing sugar, plus extra for dusting
Strawberry or raspberry jam

Pre-heat your oven to 160 °C (325°F/gas mark 3). Line a fairy-cake tin with twelve cases.

Measure out all of the ingredients into a food processor or a large mixing bowl, and either blitz for 5–6 seconds or mix until everything is combined.

Spoon the mixture into the tins, then bake without opening the oven door for 16–20 minutes (depending on the fierceness of your oven).

Cool on a wire rack, and then slice evenly in half, covering one half with a teaspoon of the sweetened whipped cream and one half with a teaspoon of jam. (Spreading is easiest with a palette knife, I find.) Place together as a sandwich, and once all are done sprinkle the tops with sieved icing sugar.

Place into clean new cases and serve with a giant pot of tea!

Cathy Bramley is the author of the bestselling romantic comedies *Ivy Lane*, *Appleby Farm*, *Wickham Hall* and *Conditional Love*. She lives in a Nottinghamshire village with her husband, two daughters and a dog.

Her recent career as a full-time writer of light-hearted, romantic fiction has come as somewhat of a lovely surprise after spending the last eighteen years running her own marketing agency. However, she has always been an avid reader, hiding her book under the duvet and reading by torchlight. Luckily her husband has now bought her a Kindle with a light, so that's the end of that palaver.

Cathy loves to hear from her readers. You can get in touch via her website www.CathyBramley.co.uk, Facebook page Facebook.com/CathyBramleyAuthor or on Twitter twitter.com/CathyBramley

PAGE TURNERS

•TRANSWORLD•

Do you love talking about your favourite books?

From big tearjerkers to unforgettable love stories, to family dramas and feel-good chick lit, to something clever and thought-provoking, discover the very best **new fiction** around – and find your **next favourite read**.

See **new covers** before anyone else, and read **exclusive extracts** from the books everybody's talking about.

With plenty of **chat**, **gossip and news** about **the authors and stories you love**, you'll never be stuck for what to read next.

And with our **weekly giveaways**, you can **win** the latest laugh-out-loud romantic comedy or heart-breaking book club read before they hit the shops.

Curl up with another good book today.